The Mind Clones Trilogy

RAYMOND HAN

Little Rocket Books

Website: www.raymondhan.net
E-mail: han.raymond@hotmail.com

Little Rocket Books, Singapore
ISBN: 978-981-11-5901-5 (pbk.)

Cataloging-in-Publication Data is on file with the National
Library Board, Singapore.

DEDICATION

To my students—past, present and future.

"It is during our darkest moments that we
must focus to see the light."

Aristotle

VISIT THE AUTHOR'S WEBSITE

Find out more about Raymond Han on his
Website
at www.raymondhan.net

ALSO BY RAYMOND HAN

THE GOLDELL PRISM

SPICE OF LIFE:
SINGAPORE SHORT STORIES

ESSENTIAL GUIDE TO O-LEVEL ENGLISH
COMPOSITION

CONTENTS

WHERE THE WIND BLOWS
Page 1

THE SUN GAWKS
Page 193

DAWN BREAKS
Page 405

ACKNOWLEDGMENTS

My wife, Cindy, has been by my side offering her silent support through the Trilogy.

Where the Wind Blows

CHAPTER 1

Today was 22 May 2030. It was the last day of the examinations for year-two students at Temasek University, a sprawling campus in Yio Chu Kang. Kuan Hee had just submitted his answer booklet to the invigilator, and was on his way to the lift lobby when he felt a tap on his back. He turned. It was Lina. She was grimacing.

"Have you heard?"

"What about?"

"It's in the news. We have been taken over!"

"You're not making sense, Lina. Calm down and tell me what has happened."

"Here. Take a look at channelsingapore.com." Lina drew out her smartphone and pushed it into Kuan Hee's hand.

"Prime Minister dies. Army takes charge in Singapore," the headline screamed.

"*Alamak*. There goes our future."

"Kuan Hee. Now's not the time to jest around. It's simply horrid. We have come under martial law. You know what that is like? Remember the Philippines? The President there declared martial law back in 2017. What will happen to us here? We will lose our freedom. We will be monitored wherever we go."

"It's not that bad," said a voice from behind them.

"Tim. You are out—finally," said Kuan Hee.

"Well, it was a rather difficult paper. You know I hate Electromagnetic Fields and Waves—I'm going to fail this time. Still all's not lost. I can re-sit the paper."

"Why bother taking up EEE?"

"Nano-electronic devices. Nanotechnology—that's where the future is. That's where I'm heading," quipped Tim, spreading out both arms in front of him and looking upwards as if he was contemplating some great idea.

"For goodness's sake, stop it," stammered Lina. "The whole world's coming to an end, and here you are— carving out your sweet dreams in the air."

"Don't be s-e-r-i-o-u-s. It's the end of the exams. Time to party!"

"Look, Tim. Lina's right. Looks like we may not have jobs waiting for us when we graduate."

"Ha? What are you guys mumbling about? It's not that bad right?"

"Here! Take a look at today's headlines. Mr Chiam Toon Boon has suddenly died. And a new guy is in charge—Colonel Tee Bak Chai. Yeah, that's his name, alright."

"Gosh. Who's this chap? Never heard of him."

"We soon will hear more—and lots more, I reckon."

"It says here he's commander of the elite FF brigade. He'll be making an announcement on TV at 6:00 p.m."

"Rare surname—Tee. Like our Ah Tee."

"You mean Jordan Tee, the tall footballer."

It was getting noisy in the lift lobby. The rest of their course mates were pouring into the lobby. The resultant chatter of voices was deafening. Everyone was trying hard to be heard. Obviously, news of the takeover had spread. Everyone looked glum. Two hours ago, all were in high spirits as it was their last paper for the semester. Now, it seemed someone had dropped a huge bomb into their midst.

"Kuan Hee. Kuan Hee," said a voice from somewhere in the crowd. Navin appeared.

"Kuan Hee. You are our student leader. Tell us what we should do."

"Let's wait for Jordan. He's the senior here. But I don't see him anywhere."

"You can't miss him. He's always wearing his NY baseball cap."

"Speak of the devil—there he is. Down there in the car park. He's being fetched somewhere by some guys in tucked-out shirts."

"Looks like he's being thrown into the car."

"*Aiyah*. You really like to exaggerate things, Tim. He's merely being shown the way into the car—you are very *kaypoh*, you know."

"Hey. Look over there."

"What?"

"To the right—here come some three-tonners."

The army trucks stopped in the car park and a score of soldiers jumped off one of them. These soldiers were armed with rifles. One shouted some commands and they filed up the car park to the main building.

"They are NSmen," said Tim.

"They must have been enlisted after we ORD," said Kuan Hee.

"What's going to happen next?" asked Lina.

"I wish I knew—let's get out of here before these guys seal off the place," said Kuan Hee.

The threesome made their way to the MRT station, a stone's throw away. Even a trained eye could make out nothing out of the ordinary on the road. There were no soldiers along the way. At the station, the crowd was thicker than usual. But, most were students from the nearby polytechnic. As Kuan Hee, Lina and Tim lived in Hougang, they had each other for company till the train arrived at Hougang MRT Station.

Nobody was home at 79 Jalan Naung, a semi-detached house among a clutch of terrace houses. Kuan Hee had lived here all twenty-three years of his life. The only child of a scientist and student care teacher, he had no lack of attention at home. However, he was pretty much alone most of the time. And he had grown accustomed to growing up sans sibling fights and tussles. The blaring of an Internet screen on the wall in the bedroom interrupted his thoughts.

> We bring you the six o'clock news. Prime Minister Chiam Toon Boon passed away at 6:45 a.m. today. The government is concerned that certain elements may take advantage of the situation to launch a terrorist attack on the country. It has appointed Colonel Tee Bak Chai, Commander of the FF Brigade to take charge of the country. To facilitate detection of terrorist elements, there will be an island-wide curfew from 9:00 p.m. till 9:00 a.m. tomorrow. All residents are to remain indoors during the curfew period. Regular programming will now resume.

It was a short news segment that attempted to make normal of the situation in the country. Colonel Tee did not appear on the news programme. Everyone said—trust the Prime Minister. The Prime Minister said—trust my men. This then started the journey down the road to perdition. And it all began with trust.

Kuan Hee's mother poked her face in the doorway.
"Kuan Hee. I've bought fried rice for you," she said. "Your father won't be home tonight. He's busy at work— And, we need to talk, dear." Having said her piece, she turned back into the corridor.
"You're not making dinner tonight? Mum?—Mum?"

He did not get an answer. Perhaps, she had not heard him.

Downstairs in the dining area, as they were eating, Bertha broached the matter of the army takeover of the country.

"Kuan Hee, we must remain calm," said his mother, moving a hand to clasp his hand. Her voice was almost inaudible. There was a slight quiver in it as she continued.

"Kuan Hee—your father—your father he—the army has taken control of the defence agency where he works. He can't leave the complex for the next few days."

"Huh?"

"It seems—I mean this group that has taken control has put restrictions on entering and leaving all military installations—You know your father is doing secretive work for the defence ministry. He—he may not be coming back for a while."

"Has he called back? Have you talked to him? Did he say anything?"

"He called me at the workplace. He couldn't use his smartphone. They have banned all phones—for the time being. I can't reach him now. All calls to the agency are screened by an operator. She keeps saying he is unavailable. I just don't know what to do."

"What did Dad say?"

"We didn't get to talk long. He hinted there was someone beside him. He—he just said he was fine. He wants us to look after each other."

"Sure. No problem, Mum. Can we go visit him?"

"The curfew will come into effect in less than two hours. We have to hurry. I—I'm not sure we will get to see him—But we need to try—I'm worried sick."

"Mum—Mum, we'll be alright."

"Looks like—I think our freedom has been curtailed. Someone has grabbed power—and the government is in disarray."

Kuan Hee had no way to understand the full impact of the situation. The Singapore he lived in was like a dream country in others' eyes. All over the world, people had been flocking here to make a living, to set up home, or send their children for an education. Singapore was, in their eyes, the ideal place to be in. There was hardly any corruption. No one intentionally stopped anyone for a bribe. It was safe for women and girls to wander in the streets in the wee hours of the morning. And everything worked like clockwork—almost everything, except for the MRT system, whose frequent breakdowns continued to put a dent on people's expectations of the public transport system. Still, the MRT system was loads better than those in the neighbouring countries.

Indeed, Singapore was a haven for foreigners. Locals, however, took for granted its efficiency and cleanliness. They had been lulled into complacency by decades of pampering by the government which saw to their every need—so much so that they couldn't care less what happened in bureaucracy or who was in charge of what. It wasn't important. There was ample food on the table. Most owned their own homes, albeit HDB type—but still much bigger than the flats in Hong Kong. And life was easy and convenient. That was what counted, in their eyes anyway. The younger set—those born after 1960—had not been privy to the suffering of their parents and grandparents most of whom have since left this earth.

What a change these locals would go through in the months and years ahead—nobody knew, but anyone could hazard a guess from looking at overseas examples of military-run countries. There was no need to look far—some neighbouring countries held lessons for them.

For Kuan Hee, who had been living in the lap of luxury by foreigners' comparison, it was the same attitude. The mandatory national service he had struggled through a year ago held no meaningful lesson for him. He merely took it as a rite of passage that every Singaporean man had to pass—and then forget. That's it. Period. He had yet to be called up for reservist duties so there was no urgent reminder to him that the security of the country was something no Singaporean should take for granted. Blame this lackadaisical attitude of young Singaporeans on the previous government. On the one hand, it did a remarkable job making the island state livable and enjoyable for its people. On the other, this bred ignorance and almost total abhorrence of participation in national issues. Yes—blame it on the government. It created a good life for its people, but neglected to guard its own kitchen. It forgot that man was greedy by nature—that man was hungry for power—that with power came money and lust. Yes, money, lust and power—these three things reared their ugly heads every now and then—one or more of them had caused tumultuous changes all through man's history.

All said, no one could actually predict what secrets a face held. And Colonel Tee's was one that held many secrets. To his superiors, he was ever ready at their side, pandering to their needs. Who could resist fawning attention? He was the perfect example of a Yes man— except, he was merely acting. Ever the opportunist, he saw a chance to take power. He had soldiers. He moved around in high government. He had access to many government departments. He was trustable. The Prime Minister was pleased with his performance. And, this moment in time, he saw the right situation—The Prime Minister was alone with him in the study at Dalvey Estate. Both had been spending the wee hours of the morning poring through documents on a terrorist group that had been attacking a littoral country. According to intelligence, Singapore was soon to be the next target. The PM's minders—bodyguards by another name—were downstairs taking an early breakfast. There were no CCTV cameras in this room where the PM spent most of his time marrying personal and official matters.

It was indeed the perfect time—just before dawn. He came up behind the PM who was typing something on the screen. One jab on the neck was all it took to down the man. As the PM lay slumped in his chair, he gave some instructions over his wrist-watch phone. In minutes, the PM's minders would be coming up the stairs. He had to work fast to neutralize the communications network in the house. There was no one in the sitting room upstairs. The computer servers were in a pantry-like room next to it. He scanned a card on the screen next to the room. Once inside, he pulled out the cables behind the servers. That would shut down all communications with the outside world. He reached behind a tall cabinet and his fingers touched something cold. *Good. Nobody has noticed it*, he thought. He retrieved the gun, pulled out the magazine and snapped it back in.

Next, he had to take care of the minders—two in the pantry below, two in the servants' quarters next to the kitchen, and another two at the main gate. The house sat in the middle of a big garden—by Singapore standards—on top of a slope. It would be difficult taking out the guards from the road. The PM's wife was in the second bedroom on the other side of the sitting room. He needn't worry about her—she was a late riser. The couple had no children.

Once downstairs, he readied the Glock 19—one of the good things about a Glock was that it didn't need to be cocked, so there was no sound that would warn others—and leaned against the wall outside the pantry. He had seconds to take out these two minders—the report of the gun would send the last two minders scurrying here and raising the alarm. The next shift of minders would be here at 7:00 a.m. That's thirty minutes from now.

Two shots were all it took to take down the two minders. And they were accurate—between the eyes. Yes, he had not lost his touch, despite being out of practice for years. Once a ranger—always a ranger. He had spent his prime years as a ranger in the Special Operations Forces.

He took aim at the kitchen door—the two minders

outside would be coming through that door in seconds. He fired another two shots as the door opened, and the minders dropped onto the floor. They would have alerted the Operations Centre in Pearl's Hill. But, he didn't have to worry—the security minders had no access to the Command Room at the Ministry of Defence. They could only activate the police patrols. These were of no worry to him. The PM's wife was the least worry—She was a sound sleeper.

He stepped over their bodies and moved towards the main gate. He took down the last two minders who were running towards him. Then he whispered into his wrist-watch phone. His men were waiting at a fork in the road.

Two vans rolled up the driveway into the compound. Out jumped several men—all in tucked-out shirts. They saluted him and went about their tasks. It seemed they had been briefed exactly what they had to do. The PM's wife was awoken and dragged, together with a maid, into a servant's room. Then a huge truck lumbered into the compound. Out stepped a stout man who offered him a salute too. Colonel Tee got into the truck with the man. Inside, there were computer screens on the wall panels. There was a long counter top with telephones and foldable computers. Three other men were at the counter, typing furiously at the screens in front of them.

"Have you neutralized the Command Centre?"

"Yes Sir. Our men are in the Command Centre as of now. We are now communicating with them. Things are working as planned."

"How about the Chiefs of Army, Navy and Air Force?"

"They are in good hands, sir."

"Good. And the Deputy PM, and the Defence and Homeland Security Ministers?"

"Our men have them in custody."

"The police? We have to deal with them too."

"The police commissioner is in custody. And we should be taking over their Operations Centre in twenty minutes."

"The TV station—"

"We have control of the TV and radio stations."

"The Singapore Tribune?"

"Han is there talking to the editors of the newspapers in the News Holding Group now."

"And the border checkpoints?"

"All under control, sir."

"I want the guys at the border checkpoints to be alert. No government official must slip out of the country."

"Yes sir. What about the Minister for Foreign Affairs? He's still in China."

"No need to bother about him. The power rests with the PM. And he's—taking a long rest from politics—and this world."

"Send the order—all men in our foreign stations to be confined to barracks until further notice."

"Yes sir."

"And I want the commanders to fly back for a meeting this afternoon."

"Yes sir."

"Also, confine the Commando Unit to quarters. Place a heavy guard there—use our rangers."

"Yes sir."

"Who's in Mandai?"

"Captain Damien Tan, sir. He's now getting the tanks fuelled and ready to move out."

"Good. We can't afford to be slipshod. Our lives are at stake. We can't eliminate all obstacles in one fell swoop. But, we can try our best."

"I agree with you, sir."

"Warren,"

"Sir?"

"Use the tanks sparingly. I don't want to damage the roads. It's going to be expensive repairing them. Use more armored personnel carriers."

"Yes sir."

"It's going to be a long day."

"Yes, certainly so, sir."

"My wife? Have you got people there too?"

"We were already there just before you left for Dalvey Estate. And your son, sir, we are picking him up after school."

"Thank you. Good job, Warren."

"No worries, sir."

"The PM's guards will be here any time now with reinforcements—"

"Two armored personnel carriers are now outside—on the road. We have a squad of rangers hidden in the surrounding area. No one can get through them."

"Good. Dawn is breaking. Singapore is waking to a brand new government. I'll lead our people to greater heights."

"Of course, sir. I'm sure you will, sir."

"Warren, I need to freshen up. I need to get ready."

"The American Embassy, sir?"

"Yes. We have got to appease the American Ambassador. We must not forget—they are Goliath; we are David."

"But, the American Naval Base has long gone from Sembawang, sir."

"Yes—but they are still quite near—in Australia. Got to calm them down."

"Yes sir."

"Do we have people outside the place?"

"No, sir. I'll see to it sir."

"Assign more people there. Get Steven over there. He'll know what to do. We need to stop people going in to seek asylum."

"Yes, of course, sir."

"We have now gotten control of the most modern armed forces in SE-Asia—fighter aircraft, submarines, destroyers, tanks, and our eye in the sky, the SG17. Our neighbours won't risk offending us. It's only the

Americans and Chinese whom we need to manage carefully."

"Sir, won't the Foreign Minister give trouble?"

"Not to worry. Chiam didn't treat the Chinese well. As long as we pander to them, we'll be okay. Gosh. I plain forgot. I'll have to visit the Chinese Ambassador too, afterwards."

"Yes, sir."

"Shall I dispatch some people there too?"

"No need. Chiam's people won't go there. They know the Chinese won't welcome them—not after what Chiam did to them in 2027."

"You mean, when he commented that the Hong Kong people should be given a choice in universal suffrage?"

"Yes. And of all times, he chose to do so during the thirtieth anniversary of the former colony's handover to China. What a laugh."

"Certainly so, sir."

"Narayanan won't be able to get the Chinese to help him. Remember yesterday's news? They even gave him a cold shoulder. Fancy him—giving them expertise and guidance on developing their cities, and instead of thanks, receiving a lukewarm response during the city-handover ceremony. Hahaha."

"And the Internet, sir. Don't you want to reconsider your decision?"

"No. Not yet anyway. We need to keep business going. The last thing I need is to stir up animosity in the business community. Don't pull the plug on Internet access—yet."

"I understand. Sir, one last thing."

"Yes?"

"The bodies in the house. Should we…"

"Incinerate them at Senoko."

"Aye, aye, sir."

Shots rang out in the distance. More shots followed. Then, came the rumbling of heavy vehicles—and rapid machine gun fire. There was a succession of rapid gun fire.

Then, silence fell again.

CHAPTER 2

It was almost 8:00 p.m. Kuan Hee drove furiously through the long meandering road. His mother was next to him. There was a long silence. Neither spoke a word, but loads were spoken, albeit in their minds. They didn't need to speak to tell each other things. Their heavy hearts showed the way into each other's intimate spaces. Both were intent on seeing their beloved one.

It was 8:26 p.m. when they arrived outside the main gate of the huge Defence Agency complex in Changi East. Two soldiers were at the checkpoint; one approached the car. They were not allowed to enter the complex. Neither were they allowed to see the elder Wang. They couldn't speak to him through an intercom. Even their request to leave a note for him was turned down. Dejected, they left for home. It was a solemn mood in the car. Both said nary a word. As Kuan Hee drove on, the car's headlights pushed back the darkness of the night in front of him. But no sooner, the darkness swallowed what's left of the light behind the car. It was the same with their hearts.

At Jalan Eunos, a thoroughfare, bright spotlights flooded a section of the road, dazzling Kuan Hee's eyes. It was a roadblock. There were soldiers on both sides of the road. An armored personnel carrier was parked on the road shoulder. Sitting atop the carrier, with both hands on a machine gun, was a soldier. A soldier on the ground shone a light into the car, waving his arm to signal Kuan Hee to stop the car. He obliged immediately. He hadn't realized it—but the curfew was in effect. These soldiers were conscripts, barely nineteen years old. After giving a verbal warning, the soldier waved him on. There were hardly any vehicles on the road. Most people obeyed the curfew order; locals had been conditioned through the years to be reticent—they needed no prodding to toe the line. They were unlike Hongkongers who would challenge any order they deemed unfair. Perhaps, that was why Hong Kong thrived against the odds. Their people were resilient. The locals here were lethargic—to use a euphemism, they were untested; they had yet to find good reasons to protest—life was just too good to them, thanks to the government.

It had been a long day. Kuan Hee was dead tired. He plunked himself on the bed and fell into dreamland. His mother was awake throughout the night. Dad and Mum were very close. She couldn't sleep knowing he wasn't safe.

Army seizes power, declares curfew

This was what greeted Kuan Hee as he sat down for breakfast. He scanned the front page of the The Singapore Tribune, then flipped the front few pages, and digested the content. Prime Minister Chiam had died of a heart attack; the government ministers were said to be incompetent and corrupt. Hence, they were being detained. The President was under house arrest pending investigation of his role in colluding with corrupt ministers. Public gatherings were banned.

"Kuan Hee, it's just a pack of nonsense."

"For sure, Mum."

"Our government ministers have always been whiter

than white. I hope they are alright. I hope their families are safe."

"Mum, Dad's coming back soon. Don't worry."

"Yes, I hope so. I've always thought his job with the Defence Agency involved some risk. But, never in my imagination did I expect it to turn out this way."

"I'm not going to class today, Mum. I'll keep you company."

"Kuan Hee, I thought we should try to see your father—afterwards."

"That's my thought, exactly, Mum."

WHATSAPP:
"Meet at usual place at 11:00 a.m.?" texted Lina.
"K," texted Kuan Hee.
"Sure," texted Tim.

It was business as usual at the shops in Hougang Mall; people were streaming in. McDonald's restaurant was humming with activity, though it was not lunch time yet. People were chattering away; they were trying to make sense of the happenings the day before. Like them, Kuan Hee and company, huddling in one corner, tried to dissect the reports on news Websites. Tim unfolded the iPad and bent the screen so everyone could read the print on the screen.

"What does the New York Daily say?" asked Lina.

"Just a short paragraph under the heading 'Army takes power in Singapore'," said Kuan Hee.

"See this? The China Telegraph says: Singapore wakes up to a coup," said Tim.

"All have neutral comments. None has taken a stand in this," said Kuan Hee.

"They are simply adopting a wait-and-see attitude," said Tim.

"What about Malaysia?" asked Lina.

"Let's see: PM Wahab urges calm in Singapore," said Tim.

"Our neighbours appear to be neutral too," said Kuan Hee.

"Look. The Indonesians are asking for restraint," said Tim..

"The Internet forums are abuzz with adverse comments on the takeover. I can't see a single in support of it," said Kuan Hee.

"Any bigwigs commented?" asked Lina.

"Nope," said Tim.

"Someone has set up an online petition 'STEP DOWN COLONEL TEE'," said Kuan Hee. "And it's garnered 37,118 votes as of now."

"Here's another Website. The contributors are calling for the Police to step in and stop Colonel Tee," said Tim. "Hahaha. That's rather lame."

"STEP DOWN COLONEL TEE has hit 41,022 votes," said Kuan Hee.

"That's amazing," quipped Lina. "See this link? Click on it, Tim."

"OK. It's a call to stage a mass protest at Hong Lim Park," said Tim.

"Yes. Says here to meet at 9:00 a.m. 24 May 2030— That's tomorrow," said Lina.

"Strange," said Tim.

"What?" said Kuan Hee and Lina in unison.

"We are browsing the Internet now, right?" said Tim.

"So?" said Lina.

"So—that means the coup perpetrators have not shut down the Internet," said Tim.

"Oh yeah *hor*," said Lina.

"Maybe—maybe, they plain forgot," volunteered Kuan Hee.

"Not so, I think," said Tim. "It must be a tactical move. Sly old man."

"Please make sense of your words," pleaded Lina.

"I know what you mean, Tim," said Kuan Hee. "The old chap most probably knows that he can't shut down the Internet without shutting down communication," said Kuan Hee.

"*Hah?*" said Lina.

"Singapore needs to keep businesses running. Businesses need communication networks for their supply chains, etc.," said Kuan Hee.

"And if you shut down the Internet, that means Singapore goes out of business," said Tim. "Which means—the old man has his hands tied."

"Hurray for Singapore," said Lina.

"Hold your horses, Lina," said Tim. "Don't get so excited, for goodness's sake."

"Why?" asked Lina.

"Because—because," said Tim. "Here, Kuan Hee, you tell her."

"I really don't know," said Kuan Hee. "Sooner or later, he's going to do something about the Internet. What with all these negative comments and calls for protests."

"Yeah. It's just a matter of time, Lina," said Tim.

"Yeah. And then we'll become another North Korea," said Kuan Hee.

"Oh, really?" said Lina.

"Yeah, really, Lina," said Kuan Hee.

"Kuan Hee, I...I think that's stretching the truth a little," said Tim.

"But—it's a possibility," quipped Kuan Hee.

"Lina, just being curious," said Tim. "But—why do you like being with us?"

"Because you are both very clever," blurted Lina.

"And you are stupid?" said Tim.

"*Aw.* You are being horrid," said Lina. "Kuan Hee."

"Knock it off, Tim—Knock it off," said Kuan Hee. "She's going to cry—she's really going to cry."

"Sorry, Lina," said Tim. "Just jiving, Lina."

"You better not do it again," said Lina. Her eyes were

tearing. She was sniffling. "Or else—I'll complain to my mother about you."

"Guys, guys. Let's get serious," said Kuan Hee. "Now's not the time to fool around."

"So, guys—are we or are we not joining the protest?" asked Tim.

"Let's go for it," all three said in unison.

"I've got to go now. Got to visit my Dad, you know," said Kuan Hee.

"Can I tag along?" asked Lina.

"Yeah, can we?" said Tim.

"Sure—I don't think my mother would mind," said Kuan Hee. "In fact, I think she'll welcome the company."

"Let's make a move," said Tim.

The wind blew in noisy gusts across them, dishevelling their hair as they walked towards Jalan Naung. Hougang, whose name is *Hokkien* for 'back of the river', was known for strong winds blowing across this sleepy town. But, for the country, strong winds were heralding change.

The drive to Changi East was interrupted by several stops—there were checkpoints along the way on the main roads of the island, with conscripted soldiers manning them. When they reached the start of Changi Road, they had to turn back—the whole stretch of road leading to Changi East was now off-limits to everyone, except military personnel.

It was the second trip in vain for the Wangs, and despondency fed their growing unease.

WHATSAPP:

"Location of protest has changed," texted Lina.

"Why?" texted Kuan Hee.

"Because army has sealed off Speakers' Corner," texted Lina.

"Where now?" texted Kuan Hee.

"Orchard Road junction—where it meets Scotts Road," texted Lina.

"K," texted Kuan Hee.

"Tim?" texted Kuan Hee again.

"Think he's bathing or something. No response; will try again," texted Lina.

"OK," texted Kuan Hee.

"Meet you at MRT Station @10:00 a.m.," texted Lina.

"K," texted Kuan Hee.

When the threesome arrived at Orchard MRT Station, it was already flowing with people. They elbowed their way up the stairs onto the pavement outside Wisma Atria. People were everywhere—the crowd spilled over onto the walkway outside. There had to be at least ten thousand of them on this part of Orchard Road—the young, middle-aged and elderly. It was noisy with portable loudspeakers blaring away in the street. Some twenty-somethings were using loud-hailers, while some others were holding up cloth banners scribbled with slogans. The trio could not hear themselves above the cacophony of sounds. There were policemen in the street, on the sidewalks—everywhere, but they did nothing to stop the protesters who were out in full force today.

Some protesters had formed a train, and were snaking around the junction, then down towards Lucky Plaza. This group wore yellow headbands fashioned out of cloth. The atmosphere was chaotic. But, amidst disorder, there was some semblance of order. Most protesters had their sights trained on a figure near the bus-stop outside Tang Plaza. He was surrounded by some twenty-somethings bearing rolled-up banners and placards. From where the three were standing, on top of the escalator outside Wisma Atria, they could see as far as the Paragon building. More people were pouring into the streets from the MRT station. There was just no end to the human traffic. Indeed, it was a sea of people.

At last, the figure near the bus-stop spoke. His voice thundered through the loudspeakers. He spoke against the army takeover in the country. He asked the audience to stand up for their rights. He urged all present to join him in putting down the coup.

Suddenly, there was the rumbling of heavy vehicles in the distance. Then, the tops of armored personnel carriers could be seen emerging from Scotts Road, at the junction. The vehicles loomed into view. There were soldiers manning machine guns atop the vehicles. Soldiers were amassing near these vehicles. There were at least six armored personnel carriers and scores upon scores of soldiers bearing rifles. Some shouts were heard coming from the vehicles. Some soldiers were holding video cameras; they were filming the protesters and everyone else. The protesters were getting restless. Some leaders were cajoling them to march towards the armored personnel carriers. The crowd was getting agitated.

A soldier, probably a senior army officer—he was wearing a peaked cap whilst the others were in helmets— screamed through a loud-hailer. His voice echoed through the street. He was telling everyone to disperse. But, nobody was paying heed to him. They were chanting slogans, egged on by the protest leaders. The chanting rose in intensity. The protesters locked their arms with one another. Row after row of protesters moved slowly towards the armored personnel carriers. The trio were undecided. Should they join those in the street. Or should they remain perched on the raised walkway. They didn't have a choice. Waves of people behind them pushed them, step by step, inch by inch, down the stairs, into the street below. There was hardly any room to move. But there was no way they could fall—the whole street was full of people, packed like sardines in a humongous can.

Though tired and wary, the protesters refused to bulge

from the junction. The army did not use water cannons on them. Probably it had failed to convince the police, who had such equipment, to bring them along. Even the policemen seen here and there did nothing beyond keeping a watch on the crowd. Perhaps, they were under orders to remain neutral.

Then, a loud whistle rang out across the road. A long line of soldiers, all standing abreast of one another, raised their rifles and pointed them skywards. At a second whistle, they fired a volley of shots. Were these live rounds? No one in the crowd knew. But, it worked wonders. The crowd stepped away from the soldiers. They were still in locked arms, but it was clear—all were frightened. Everyone wanted to protest, but when it came to the crunch, their life was more important than the idea of freedom—Freedom from tyranny was a worthwhile pursuit—but not the cost of losing their lives. Only the group of twenty-somethings—the ones with their leader near the bus-stop were steadfast in confronting the armed soldiers. Were they mad? Was freedom from control of the soldiers that important? After all, life was still the same—almost. The MRT trains were running; people held on to their jobs; and there was ample food for everyone.

Soldiers moved towards the twenty-something group. They forcefully moved these protesters away from the others. It was then that someone fired a shot into the crowd—or it seemed so. Pandemonium set in. People ran helter-skelter in all directions. There was chaos in the street. Everyone was running for cover, oblivious to the aim of the protest. Some people were falling; some others were stepping onto them. Nobody cared. Nobody took heed.

"Lina—Lina," shouted Kuan Hee. "Run!—follow me."

"Here. This way, quickly," said Tim.

"I'm trying to run as fast as I can," said Lina.

"Oops! I just stepped on something—somebody," said Lina.

"Here, Lina, let me hold your hand," said Kuan Hee.

"Aaargh!" cried Lina. "My arm—it's painful."

"See the opening in front, Tim?" said Kuan Hee.

"Yeah," said Tim.

"Let's head that way," said Kuan Hee.

"Oh no." The soldiers are in front—turn back, Tim," screamed Kuan Hee.

"I can't—there're too many people here," cried Tim.

"It's too late. They have got me, Kuan Hee," said Tim. "Run. Run!"

"Lina, keep up with me," said Kuan Hee.

"I'm trying—I'm trying," said Lina.

"Gosh. We've run into a dead end," said Kuan Hee.

"Alamak!" said Lina.

"Here. Let me lift you up," said Kuan Hee. "Step onto my shoulder. Grab the pole up there."

"What about you, Kuan Hee?" Said Lina.

"Stop talking and get moving," said Kuan Hee. "On the count of three. one—two—three—up!"

"Now run, Lina," said Kuan Hee.

"I can't—I can't leave you," said Lina.

"Go! Don't look behind, Lina," said Kuan Hee. "Aargh!"

Both Kuan Hee and Tim had been captured, but Lina managed to get away. She cried all the way to the back of Paterson Road. No, the world wasn't coming to an end. It was only Lina's world in tatters. She wanted to go back for Kuan Hee. Alas, she couldn't. It was just too late. Kuan Hee was right; she had to go home now. She was of no help to them.

Kuan Hee was ushered into a large bus parked along Scotts Road. There was a score of them, lined up against the side of the road. He did not see Tim. There were too many faces around him; he did not recognise any of them. The soldiers were fresh-faced recruits—NSmen. It seemed that they had just finished basic military training. Or they could still be undergoing BMT. The buses were packed with protesters. All wore anxious expressions. It seemed they were unaccustomed to being in custody. It wasn't local culture; locals did not get hauled into buses. They crammed into buses on their way to work or school—on their own free will, that is.

The buses started their journey to an unknown destination. There were three armed soldiers to a bus. It was quiet inside the buses; everyone was in deep thought—worried about themselves, asking themselves what trouble they had gotten themselves into. Kuan Hee was different. He was worried about Tim and Lina. *Has Lina gotten home safely?* he wondered.

Half an hour into the journey, Kuan Hee realized the buses were heading to SAFTI. They were in the far end of Jurong. SAFTI was only minutes away. It was a familiar route to Kuan Hee, for he had spent the first nine months of his national service in SAFTI. It was a sprawling military installation, probably half the size of Toa Payoh Estate. But there were no detention facilities in it, he was sure. It wasn't built to house detainees; it was training grounds for recruits and officer cadets. He knew the place like the back of his hand; he could almost find his way around it blindfolded.

The buses turned into the main gate at SAFTI. Then, they moved ahead, made a left turn, and rumbled towards the Non-Commissioned Officers' training block. Some came to a stop in the parade square of the Mike Company, while others continued along the road towards Kilo Company. In the compound of Mike Company, a soldier shouted at those in the buses to alight. Everyone gathered in the middle of the parade square. And the buses left after unloading their human cargo.

There were soldiers seated at some GS tables in front of the square. The detainees were ordered to line up in single file behind each table. They were being processed for detention. Their identity cards were retained, kept in a locked metal box. All their personal belongings—smartphones, wallets, keys, etc.—were taken away from them and placed in plastic bags, with their names written on them. Then, they were herded into the different dormitories in the premises. There were twenty bunks in the dormitory which held Kuan Hee. But, there were thirty of them. *Some will have to sleep on the floor*, he thought. The layout of the place was still the same. Kuan Hee remembered the stand-by-beds he had to endure in this place. He recalled being made to do push-ups for not keeping his belongings tidy. And, yes, that bed was where some guy had poured instant glue on his hair while he was sleeping. He had complained to his trainers but they had dismissed it as a harmless prank. Till today, he did not know who had carried out the prank on him. He didn't think he was unpopular then; but, he could have offended a fellow recruit.

Kuan Hee looked out of a window. There were some soldiers smoking in the corridor opposite. Their rifles were resting against the wooden wall of a room. *Typical recruit mentality*, Kuan Hee thought to himself. He was like them till he was reprimanded by an *Enche*. He remembered the punishment—two cold nights doing guard duty at Serimbun, a deserted military training installation by a river. A jeep unloaded him there and left only to return the next morning. The place was eerily quiet and he had nobody for company.

A gunshot rang out in the distance, snapping Kuan Hee out of his thoughts. Fellow detainees in the room leaned against the windows, pressing their faces against them, eager to find out what was happening, but, at the same time, fearful of what lay in store for them.

"Did they shoot somebody?" asked a man next to him.

"Must have tried to escape," said another man.

"Don't be silly. It's Singapore, for goodness's sake," said a third. "People don't get shot by soldiers here. It only happens in Thailand or the Philippines."

"Yeah. You're right," said the first man.

"We can only guess," said Kuan Hee. "We'll know shortly."

"Maybe—some soldier's gun went off accidentally," said the third. "You read about it in the newspaper. Remember the CISCO guard at the checkpoint? Playing with his revolver?"

"Here comes a soldier. He's in a hurry," said the first.

"Look. The soldiers are gathering outside that room," said the first.

"I can't hear what they are saying," said the second man.

"They look disoriented," said the third.

"Yeah. Something bad must have happened," said Kuan Hee. "Someone must have gotten shot."

Kuan Hee looked at the other guys around him. A while ago, they were nonchalant. Now, fear showed in their faces and their tremulous voices. Yet, he wasn't fearful. He was adamant in his belief that no Singaporean would ever shoot another Singaporean in cold blood—not in his world anyway. Alas, he had subscribed to the wrong doctrine. He was part of that group of Singaporeans who had been lulled by many good years of government into thinking that evil would not find its way into government—not in Singapore anyway. He had plain forgotten about the three deadly sins of man—greed, lust and power. He wasn't a social creature; or else he could have made conversation with them to find out more about their background.

Where are the student leaders? Kuan Hee wondered. *Have they been captured? Have they also been detained in SAFTI?* His thoughts drifted back to his family. He was sure his mother was worried sick. First—his father, now he. *She doesn't know I'm here. How do I tell her? Will they let me call home? Has Lina told her what happened?* These were things that went through his mind.

"Dinner time, dinner time," shouted a soldier as he

walked past the dormitory. He and another soldier shoved takeaways in Styrofoam boxes through the window. Its occupants grabbed these and passed them around. The fragrant sesame oil smell told everyone what was inside— chicken rice, Singapore's Number One hawker food.

"Where's the water? How do we get water here?" one of them asked the soldier.

"Right behind, coming," came the reply.

Soon, a soldier wheeling cartons of mineral water came into view. With food and water in hand, the room's occupants sat down to dinner, making small conversation with one another as they ate. Army cooks went the way of the Dodo in the 1990s. That's when the armed forces realized Singaporeans weren't producing enough children to feed its national service. Gone too were the GD men— general duty soldiers who sprayed insecticide to keep the mosquitoes away, and the drivers. It was now either DIY or farmed out to contractors.

A soldier came to the window to collect the used food boxes.

"What was the commotion about," asked a man.

"What commotion?" said the soldier.

"You know, the shooting," said the man.

"Oh that," said the soldier. He looked around him. "An officer got shot."

"Protester shot him?" said another man.

"No, no—a major shot him," said the soldier.

"Why—" But before the second man could finish his sentence, the soldier had already left the window.

This was indeed news to the detainees. At once, the room woke up to an outpouring of views. Questions flew and theories were proffered. Everyone wanted to share; none remembered their fear. *Can be the officer refused to carry out an order*, thought Kuan Hee. *But, what is so serious about this defiance that warrants a shooting? Guard duty as punishment— that is plausible; certainly not a firing squad!*

Kuan Hee roused from sleep. He opened his eyes. It was dark outside. He couldn't tell the time—his iPhone was not with him. The rumbling of heavy vehicles from behind the dormitory faded away into the distance. He stretched his arm and sat against the wall. He wasn't used to the make-shift bed here—at home, the mattress was at least thirty centimetres thick. Here, bed was a blanket spread across the floor. And he was sitting between two bunks. He was too slow—others had laid claim to all available bunks in the room. He was a reticent chap—always the last to queue for a free goodie bag or go up the bus. Served him right—he deserved to sleep on the floor; in this world, it was first-come-first-served. But, if you called him a born loser, he would deny it vehemently. He would say he was merely taking his time, that there wasn't any need to hurry for such things.

It was Kuan Hee's second day in detention. He was getting restless. There were so many questions in his mind. As the minutes ticked by, more questions sprang up—*so many questions, not a single answer in sight*, he lamented. Promptly after a bare-bones breakfast, the detainees were marched to a large hall five blocks away. There they assembled with detainees from other blocks. *There has to be at least a hundred in the hall. There is no sign of Tim in the bobbing heads,* Kuan Hee thought. The detainees were subjected to some brainwashing speech. A major—close-cropped hair, brawny, and towering over the stage—delivered an impassioned oratory about toeing the line—co-operating with the army. Major David Foo—that's what he had said his name was—then flashed a sardonic grin.

The only part of his speech that all or most of the detainees paid attention to was he inviting them to enjoy the surroundings for the few days. He said he was giving them plenty of time to think about their actions the previous day. He also dispatched a warning: that if they persisted in their errant ways, they would not get to see the light of day for months, perhaps years.

That parting shot dug into the hearts of the detainees. They sat up at once, taking in the seriousness of the message. The major's facial expression showed he minced no words. *Is he the major who shot the officer yesterday?* thought Kuan Hee. He could hazard a guess; his guess would turn out right.

CHAPTER 3

It was the third day of detention. But Kuan Hee hadn't been in detention for too long to lose sight of what day it was today—Sunday. In these few days, while the others in the room had become chums, he remained aloof, sticking to mere formalities such as saying thank you when someone passed a box of food. *Drat the pesky mosquitoes,* he thought, nursing his sore arms and legs. They had feasted on him the last few days.

This morning, the barracks was a hive of activity. The detainees heard the rumbling of vehicles. Then, some buses rolled into the compound. A soldier unlocked the dormitory doors and shouted for its occupants to gather in the square. There they were told to retrieve their belongings, then they were ordered to board the buses. They packed into the buses which dispatched them to where they had picked them up and promptly unloaded them there.

Once they alighted from the buses, the former detainees quickened their paces and fanned out in different directions. Kuan Hee reached for his iPhone. They were not allowed to use the phone on the bus. Alas. Its battery had gone flat. There were no public phones in this day and age—everyone had a smartphone—even the cleaning auntie. He could not call home; neither could he phone Lina. He looked around. Tim was not in sight. He dragged himself into the Orchard MRT Station and headed home. He had not gotten a good rest the last few days. He sank into a seat, oblivious to the goings-on.

There was not a soldier in sight outside Hougang MRT Station. People were moving around doing their own things. He hurried across the field, up Jalan Naung and came to his house. The family car was in the car park— Mum was at home. He pressed the control to open the gate. As it glided sideways, the front door opened and who was standing there?—his father and mother. Both were wearing anxious looks; they rushed out to hug him. His mother kissed him all over his face. They had so many questions.

"Where did they take you to?"

"Did you eat well?"

"Why didn't you call back? Did you sleep well?"

"Lina said they manhandled you; are you alright?"

"Are you injured?"

"Why are there mosquito bite marks on your arms— and your legs too?"

"You didn't shaved. Your clothes are smelly. Did you bathe the past few days?"

"We were worried sick," said his mother.

"We looked all over for you," said his father.

"We lodged reports at the police station," said his mother.

"I asked around at the Ministry of Defence," said his father. "But, nobody knew the answer. My friends there are in the dark about the coup. Only a select few had knowledge of it."

In the living room, his mother brought a glass of Coke—his favourite drink, and sat next to him. His father was across the coffee table, taking a good long look at him.

It was now his turn to ask questions.

"Dad, when did you come back?"

"They let us go home yesterday evening. I thought everything was fine at home till your mother told me something had happened to you."

"Did they ill-treat you?"

"No, Dad. But they locked us up in the dormitory."

"Whereabouts is this place?"

"SAFTI—where I did my BMT."

"Did they torture you?"

"No, Mum—nothing like that. But, they did try to give us a pep talk—obeying the military and all that."

"Dad, Mum, I was thinking about you all the time I was in there. I was worried that with you—Dad—and me under lock and key, Mum would have a breakdown."

"Dear me—dear me."

"It's over now, Kuan Hee. All over now. Don't fret."

"Lina called me last night. She was hysterical. Said she was afraid something bad might have happened to you."

"I'll call her afterwards. I'll meet up with her later."

"Oh, I forgot—Tim called too."

"Tim? Has he been released? I couldn't find him. I thought he was still in detention."

"It seems he managed to escape when the soldiers weren't paying attention to him. He wasn't captured."

"Gosh. He's so lucky. I mean, thank God he is OK. No wonder there was no sign of him at SAFTI."

"I'm glad you're home safe and sound, Kuan Hee."

"Don't worry, Mum. I'm fine—really."

With his iPhone fully charged, Kuan Hee was ready to meet Lina and Tim. They had arranged to be at Kovan MRT Station at 2:00 p.m.

Lina practically flew into Kuan Hee's arms. He was unaccustomed to such open displays of emotions. But, it was curious. Both had known each other since primary school days. He had to have known she had a thing for him.

"Wah, Lina—Lina. There are people here." He tried to get her arms off him, but in vain. Then, he gave up trying. She was emotion-packed. *It is good for her to let her frustrations out*, he thought.

"Who cares? I misssss you so, Kuan Hee—so much."

"Okay—Okay."

"You have lost weight, Kuan Hee."

"He hasn't, Lina—he still looks the same."

"Nope. He's much thinner."

"Kuan Hee, I'm envious of you—no kidding."

"Sorry, Tim—Tim, how did you manage to escape?"

"Long story. Let's get into the MRT station first. It's bloody hot out here."

When the threesome were properly seated and hydrated in McDonald's restaurant at NEX Shopping Mall, Tim shared his story.

"After we were separated, they took me to Lucky Plaza, where a struggle broke out between some of the soldiers and the guy who was speaking over the public address system. His supporters crowded around the soldiers who threatened to shoot—but they didn't dare."

Tim paused, and, waving his arms in front of him, mimicked the soldiers pointing their rifles at the protesters. Then he continued.

"So the crowd became bolder and attacked the soldiers. There was only a handful of soldiers—all enlistees, but there were so many protesters. They overwhelmed the soldiers. That's the time I made my getaway, together with some others."

"*Wah*. So brave of you, Tim."

"So lucky."

"In the end, did the guy get caught?"

"No, Kuan Hee. Tim said he escaped too."

"Yes. Take a look at channelsingapore.com. It says here that this guy—his name is Patrick Teo—is planning another big demonstration in Dhoby Ghaut. That's where the Istana is."

"Shall we go there to give our support?"

"Kuan Hee, for goodness's sake, you just got out of a jam. It's time to lie low."

"Lina, I may be timid, but I am certainly not a coward."

"Yeah, Lina. Kuan Hee's right. Our future is at stake. If we do nothing, we are helping this Colonel Tee stay in power."

"OK. But—next time, when there's trouble, don't ask me to leave you—because I won't."

"Aw. There won't be a next time. Promise."

"Here's an update on the Website. The opposition parties are attending the demonstration too."

"What parties?"

"First People's Party, One Singapore Party and Unity Party."

"What about the Green Party?"

"There's nothing on it. Perhaps, with the party's ministers in detention, they are without a head. So, can't decide."

"Possible. Possible."

"Kuan Hee, are we going to just watch the show or participate actively?

"It's a good time to start being proactive. What you think, Tim?"

"Agree a hundred percent."

"Let's do it!" said all in unison.

CHAPTER 4

That evening, Kuan Hee's father came into his room right after dinner. He appeared troubled. He seemed to have a lot of things that he wanted to say to him. His father grabbed a chair and motioned him to be seated; then he sat on the bed. Father and son started their heart-to-heart talk.

"I have a foreboding—of worse things to come in our way."

"Why, Dad? We're both home safely."

"Son—there are some things I'm going to tell you now that I want no one else to hear of."

"Mum?"

"Not even Mum."

"Why Dad?"

"For her own safety. And—she might not agree with my idea."

"I'm all ears, Dad."

"You know I have been doing research for the government for many years."

"Yes, Dad."

"You know I specialize in nanotechnology."

"Mmm."

"But, what you don't know—is that this is top secret

work. For the past ten years, I have been experimenting with the idea of transferring memories. First—in animals. Then in human beings."

"You mean, cut open the skull, remove the brain and transplant it in another person's skull?"

"No…No—not that. You are now studying nanotechnology in electronic devices, right?" To this, Kuan Hee nodded.

"In a nutshell, it's about transferring the memories housed in electrical circuits—in this case the synapses in the human brain which are actually electrical in nature—to synapses in another brain."

"You mean—there's no need for any operation?"

"No…No. That's not it. A minor operation is needed. Just to implant electrodes on the skull, but these won't be visible as they are very small, and will be covered by the person's hair."

"I see. What you are doing is simply duplicating the brain's electromagnetic currents and copying them onto the synapses in another brain."

"Yes, Kuan Hee. Something like that—but, it's much more complicated than what you have explained."

"Have you succeeded, Dad?"

"More or less. We just need a living human specimen to use as a prototype for our experiment."

"You mean—you need a guinea pig, Dad."

"Yes—but that's a rather crude name you have used."

"Gee, Dad, It's something out of a sci-fi movie."

"Yes, but it is now a reality—not something that may be possible in ten—twenty years' time."

"Mmm."

"Another experiment—this one is a possibility, but is not feasible, as yet."

"What's that?"

"I'm looking at cloning of human beings—not human parts or organs, but entire human beings."

"Wow. That's like fantasy, Dad."

"Kuan Hee, it's not fantasy—fantasy means NEVER possible. This is science fiction—meaning technology has advanced to such a stage that it can happen—though not so soon."

"I see, Dad."

"To be specific—I'm looking at clones reproducing clones perpetually, just like us human beings giving birth and ensuring the survival of our species."

"That's real deep, Dad. I can't begin to fathom the complex electronic sequencing that needs to be coded to replicate so many different memories in one person."

"Yes, son—that's why people like me are a rare breed—that's why we are important to the government."

"Is that why you were detained?"

"No. No—son, I wasn't detained. I was only being protected."

"Protected? That's a strange way of protecting someone."

"You see—the military is afraid some people may want to get their hands on us scientists. That's why they implemented the shutdown at my workplace."

"I see."

"But—that's not why we're having this talk, son."

"Mmmm."

"I'm concerned about the near future. The new guys in charge of the military—and of course the country—may be greedy people. They may want to get their hands on this technology."

"Why? It belongs to the whole country."

"To be specific—they may want to use it for their own selfish purposes."

"You mean—they want to replicate themselves?"

"Mmm. Not quite so, but something like that."

"That's mean—real mean."

"Yes, son. For this reason, I fear—I fear they may keep me under lock and key so they can use my skills."

"Can't you resign, Dad?"

"Even if I resign, they can still get to me."

"Can't we run away?"

"We can—but where can we hide? Your mum and I are no longer young. I'm already past seventy."

"What do you want me to do, Dad?"

"Listen carefully, son. They may come to get me any time, but before they do, I want us to be able to communicate with each other any time anywhere no matter how far apart we are."

"You're not making sense, Dad."

"I mean—I want to implant a nano-electronic communication device in you and also in me—so that we can talk to each other whenever we want."

"Is that possible? I thought it's sci-fi, Dad."

"It's now reality, son. Come, follow me."

Father and son climbed down the stairs, went past the living room into the study. His father stopped in front of the floor-to-ceiling bookshelf which stood at the far end of the room.

"Go get a ladder, Kuan Hee."

"The tall one or the short one?"

"Either one will do."

Kuan Hee returned quickly with a short ladder.

"Here, give me a hand, Kuan Hee. Move the large blue and white vase aside."

Once the vase was in a new position, Kuan Hee's father placed the ladder against the bookcase, climbed a few steps and reached for the end panel of the bookcase. He pressed twice on the panel and it slid open, revealing a knob. Then, he turned the knob and the bookcase rolled sideways, exposing an opening wide enough for two persons to enter.

"Come follow me down."

He turned on a switch at the start of the stairs. Below, the cellar was not much different from those Kuan Hee had seen in the movies, only this one was under his house—and, he had no idea it existed. The cellar was slightly smaller than their living room. In it were three cupboards at one end, two chairs and a table in the centre. There were two standing fans. The room was stuffy, but the ventilation seemed to improve as the minutes wore on. Then, the room began to feel cool.

"Does Mum know about this room?"

"Of course, she does."

"Has she been down here?"

"A few times—but she doesn't like the place because of the poor ventilation. You know your mum can't stand stale air."

"Mmm."

His father took out a thin box—the size of a pencil box—and opened it. There were about a dozen tiny electronic devices—each the size of a nano SIM card—the type used in mobile phones in the early noughties.

"I just need to embed this in your arm and my arm too, and we can communicate with each other."

"How? How do we connect the earphones and the microphone?'

"We don't need these."

"Ha?"

"We communicate via brainwaves."

"Really, Dad?"

"No kidding, son. When you get a cut, you feel pain. That's because the affected tissue sends distress signals to the brain. This device uses the same route to the brain."

"Wow. So cool."

"Yes, it is—isn't it?"

"You mean, I put one of these tiny things in my body and I can talk to you? How do I know you are listening?"

"When you say 'Logon Alpha', you are connected instantly. I'll hear your voice instantly. I'll hear whatever you say."

"How do I turn it off?"

"Simply end your call with 'Ten Four Alpha'."

"What if I'm asleep, Dad?"

"If I do not hear your voice, I'll try again another time."

"You can leave a message, can't you, Dad?"

"No—it doesn't work that way—there's no inbox. Everything is done on the fly."

"Do we use the same codes?"

"Yes, it's sort of like a walkie-talkie. It can't communicate with other devices."

"Really cool, man—I mean, really cool gadget."

"Now comes the difficult part."

"What?"

"You can't tell your mother about this."

"Why not?"

"She will never accept the idea of an electronic device being implanted in you."

"Don't worry—Mum's the word."

"Hahaha, Kuan Hee. You certainly are funny."

"Dad, for the gadget to work—is there a limit to the distance between us?"

"This little thing makes use of a satellite up there. So, theoretically, there's no limit."

"Wow."

"One more question—can it penetrate thick walls?"

"Never a problem."

"That's great, Dad."

"Kuan Hee, can we put this on now?"

"Sure Dad."

"Thank you, son. It won't be very painful—just an ant's bite."

Kuan Hee's father put on surgical gloves, swabbed some alcohol onto Kuan Hee's upper arm, and applied a cream onto the area. Next, he proceeded to implant the nano device in it. As his father had said, the procedure was almost painless—just an ant's bite.

"The slit in your skin will heal in a week. You won't see any scars."

"How about you, Dad?"

"Oh, mine is already in the arm." His father rolled up a sleeve to show Kuan Hee his upper arm. It was true—there wasn't any mark on it.

His father opened a metal cabinet behind him. There were two toy soldiers and a toy tank on a shelf. Next to them was a small box. One by one, he placed them on the table.

"Kuan Hee, meet Alex and Xander, my two favourite *Kakis*."

"They are so cool, Dad."

"Yes, they are, aren't they."

"It's all AI. They have the same motor skills that you have. Plus, they can think—unlike most other robots."

"I thought it's only make-believe stuff."

"No, son. It's real, alright."

"Alex and Xander—show what you can do." The two robots did some somersaults and sparred with each other."

"Can they talk?"

"They can—but I have disabled that feature—it's not necessary, in my view."

"Where's the remote control, Dad?"

"What? Oh, there's no need for remotes. These two are not like the robots you see in the stores—you see, they can think."

"They can think? You mean, like us?"

"Yes, they are very advanced robots—the state of the art."

"Wow."

"You only need to tell them what you want to do, and they will oblige."

"Will they go against us?"

"Nope. These are kind robots—they don't do evil."

"Can I try giving commands, Dad?"

"Go ahead, son."

Kuan Hee had a smashing good time playing with Alex and Xander.

"If we are away from them, and need to communicate

with them, we phone them—They are linked to a satellite. By the way, they each have their own telephone number."

"Not using the Internet, like the appliances in the house?"

"No, that's rather archaic. The Internet of Things is an obsolete technology—in my eyes, anyway."

"How do we charge them when they run out of power?"

"No need, son. You see, they run on solar energy and they have a reserve store built into them—but, you have to bring them out once in a while to soak in the sunlight."

Next, his father opened the small box and took out two metal insect robots—a dragonfly and a large housefly.

"These little insects are your eyes in the sky. They are like the aerial drones that you see everywhere."

"They are so small, Dad."

"But—they pack a punch."

"How do we call them to give instructions?"

"We don't. Here are the remotes." His father handed him two cards—the size of credit cards. He unfolded each one to reveal a screen on one side and control buttons on the other."

"And these run on solar power, too?"

"Yes—they also have night vision capability."

"Wow. That's a nifty feature—and they are so small."

"Nano technology, son—state of the art—when you have time, take them for a spin—but, avoid places where there are people."

"I know, Dad."

"You know how to get inside this place. Come in whenever you want."

"Mum? Should I keep them a secret from Mum?"

"Hahaha. No need, son. She knows about my little toys."

"Thanks, Dad. I'll take good care of them."

"I know you will. Remember—these are powerful

tools. Don't intrude into others' privacy—unnecessarily."

"Trust me, Dad."

"I have placed the tools in your hands. The rest is up to you, son."

"Ha?"

CHAPTER 5

By the time they arrived at Dhoby Ghaut MRT Station, it was jam-packed with people, all jostling and shoving to get out of the station. Tim was in front, with Lina behind him, and Kuan Hee at the tail end, holding on to Lina's arms. Together, their little train weaved through the crowd out onto the walkway.

Every which way the looked, there were people. It was indeed a big demonstration, the likes of which the trio had not seen. It was late afternoon, and the sweltering June heat was taking its toll on the demonstrators. There were volunteers making their rounds, passing out bottles of water. Some protesters had set up small tents on the road—there were no cars or buses; apparently the burgeoning human traffic had vehicles stopped in their tracks, whether on Orchard Road itself, along Dhoby Ghaut or Bras Basah, all the way south to Victoria Street.

There was virtually no way any army could contain the protesters. It was a sea of people—young and old, wheel-chair-bound, stroller-walking, placard-holding, loud-hailer-wielding; all were chanting slogans in unison.

At the appointed time, speaker by speaker from different political parties, gathering on a small make-shift platform in front of the Cathay Building, moved up to say their piece in support of the movement to protest against the coup. They called for Colonel Tee to step down and return power to the rightful elected government. Their voices blared through speakers mounted on the roadside. Patrick Teo, leader of the protesters in Orchard Road was the last to speak. He was a firebrand. His words arouse the patriotic spirit in the audience who chanted pro-democracy slogans. It was indeed a strange sight—for Singaporeans were unaccustomed to such vocal displays of support.

Kuan Hee, Tim and Lina raised their arms in rhythm with others around them. They too chanted slogans. It was one Singapore voice reverberating across the entire city area. Then came alarm, which descended into chaos— Someone or some people had thrown Molotov cocktails onto the stage. There were screams—Patrick Teo had taken a direct hit; he was instantly set ablaze. Some on stage beat flames off their shirts and pants; some took cover behind chairs. Others jumped into the crowd below. From where they were standing, the trio could make out some protesters wrestling with two men. They pinned them to the ground. On stage, some people were carrying a darkened figure—*Is it Patrick Teo?* thought Kuan Hee— off the stage. The remaining people on stage gathered next to the microphone.

A voice over the loudspeakers urged calm. It appealed to everyone not to panic. It took some minutes before the pandemonium subsided, and order set in. Ambulance paramedics were on hand at the front of Capitol Building to attend to the injured. But, that was all they could do. There was no way their ambulance could move from its spot—there were people everywhere.

As darkness fell, the crowd grew thinner. It was past dinner time and many had yet to fill their stomachs. They were inexperienced in attending protests, so they came unprepared for the long haul. They had thought that it was just like attending a political rally speech at election time, after which they could disperse. Here, the organisers were cajoling them to stay—for the night, at the very least, or better still, till tomorrow. But, this was not Hong Kong. Here, people were still not ready to brave the elements for days for a good cause; here, people were pragmatic—bread and butter was the only important thing to them, at least for now. They would need more convincing before deciding to dig in their heels with the protest leaders.

The threesome thought the spot outside MacDonald's House they had picked was safe as it was not near the speakers' platform. But, they were in for a rude shock. A backpack that someone had left behind exploded near them. The impact threw all three to the ground. Kuan Hee quickly rolled to Lina and wrapped himself over her. Tim tried to push himself up but fell. The boys looked up. There were dust and debris around them. People were caked in dust. Some were screaming from pain; others were crying. The three of them were lucky to escape with scrapes and bruises, but the scene was ugly. There were mangled bodies; body parts were strewn on the roadside. Several people were injured by shrapnel from the bomb. Nails could be seen on the road. Apparently, the bomb was constructed to inflict maximum damage.

In the ensuing chaos, some stomped on others, while some others stumbled on the fallen. Policemen and paramedics were trying to get to the injured, but it was a painstakingly slow process—there were too many people congregating here. The explosion outside the MacDonald's House in Orchard Road put paid to the idea of staying on in the area. Kuan Hee and company decided to call it a day as it was too risky now; they could become the next victims. There was no knowing when and where the next strike would take place. It was better to be safe than sorry. The crowd apparently felt the same way, for waves of people were seen moving slowly towards the peripheral roads, away from the main protest area.

Watching the 9:00 p.m. news in the safety of his home, Kuan Hee heard the news presenter describing the demonstration in Dhoby Ghaut as a failure. She reported that terrorists had infiltrated the demonstration site. *What a laugh*, Kuan Hee thought. The presenter said they were responsible for the explosions which killed six people, including a protest leader named Patrick Teo; and injured scores of others. She urged people, for their own safety, not to attend protests.

An hour later, an army spokesman appeared on a special news bulletin. He announced the setting up of a new council named National Reconciliation Council which, he said, had authorized the dissolution of parliament. Next, he said that the NRC had vested its power in the Supreme Leader of the Council who would act as Prime Minister till elections were held. Last, he introduced the members of the NRC. Heading the list was Supreme Leader Colonel Tee, with Major Warren Tan named as Deputy Supreme Leader, and Major David Foo as Secretary-General. According to him, the President had given his assent to the appointments.

Kuan Hee, having received military training not too long ago, and, therefore, was acquainted with the military hierarchy, laughed. He scoffed at the announcements. *Fancy putting themselves above the generals in the army, navy and air forces; what a laugh,* he thought.

It was to be a long night of announcements. At 10:30 p.m., the army spokesman reappeared on national television. He said that in the interest of national security, the leaders of several political parties had been detained under the Internal Security Act. He gave no other information.

Kuan Hee heard the rattling of the gate as it rolled to the side. His father and mother were back.

"Hi Dad and Mum."

"Have you taken dinner, dear?"

"Fried rice, Mum."

"Again?"

"Yes, Mum. I needed something that would fill my stomach. I didn't eat much in the afternoon."

"Is that a special announcement on TV?"

"Yes, Dad. The army has formally dissolved parliament."

"I was wondering when they would come around to doing it."

"Dad, are we under martial law?"

"No, Kuan Hee. We are under military rule, not martial law—not yet anyway."

"Does it mean—we have lost our freedom?"

"The short answer?—Yes. And some friends of mine in government have disappeared overnight."

"Disappeared? As in—missing?"

"Yes, I'm afraid so. No one knows where they are. A likely guess would be some army camp."

"Like, in my case?"

"Yes. And the police are powerless. Some of its top brass have been transferred to project work. There's nobody running the police force presently."

"Dad, why are the coup leaders doing these things?"

"To silence dissent, of course."

"But, if you remove talented people, how do you run the country effectively?"

"They have no interest in that. What they want is to hold on to power. So, they are suspicious of everyone."

"Including the newspapers?"

"They need a tame press. So, they bully the media into compliance with their instructions."

"But—they are destroying Singapore, Dad."

"They don't care; they are obsessed with power—getting it and keeping it."

"Does it also mean there will be no elections from now on?"

"I think so, son. Elections are a no-no to dictators."

"But, just now, the presenter was saying something

about the NRC running the country till elections are held."

"Well, son. These are outright lies—said to appease people. They will come up with new excuses to delay holding elections—for sure."

"Dear, it's bedtime. You have classes tomorrow."

"OK Mum. Thanks Dad, for sharing."

"No problem, son."

"Son, remember—no one can cling on to power forever. The history books have numerous examples of fallen dictators."

"Yes, Dad. Goodnight, Mum and Dad."

CHAPTER 6

The long overpass which stretched into Temasek University was crowded with students this morning. Some soldiers manning the gate were checking students one by one as they passed through the gate. They were scanning matriculation cards into portable terminals. *Are they looking for certain students?* Kuan Hee wondered, *or are they merely taking attendance?* He and Lina were allowed in after their bags were checked.

There was a buzz on the fifth storey, outside their EEE classroom. Fellow classmates were exchanging pointers; they seemed to be discussing some important matter.

"What's up, Navin?" asked Kuan Hee.

"Kuan Hee, you are here—Mr Lee has been taken away by some soldiers," said Navin.

"S-e-r-i-o-u-s?" said Lina.

"Yeah. And for no rhyme or reason," said Navin.

"That's bad news. Are the other lecturers alright?" said Lina.

"I asked the programme officer. She said he's the only one. All his classes have been cancelled," said Navin.

"I hear Mr Lee belongs to the Unity Party. Someone

said he was one of those behind the Dhoby Ghaut demonstration," said a student.

"Look. Jordan is here—he's being escorted by two guys," said another student. The students turned their heads in the direction of the lift lobby.

"Hi. Everyone," said Jordan. His two burly escorts walked towards the opposite classroom and stood there.

"Why the fancy escorts?" asked Navin.

"Let's not talk about them," said Jordan, shaking his head. Pointing to the escorts, he continued, "There goes my freedom."

"You mean they follow you everywhere?" said Lina.

"Yeah. Even the toilets," said Jordan.

"Who are they? They look menacing," said Kuan Hee.

"Army guys," came the reply.

'Are you under detention?" asked Lina.

"Lina, how can he be under detention when he is walking around freely?" said Tim. He had just arrived and heard the conversation.

"Or is he under house arrest?" said Lina.

"Aiyoh, Lina. You are a pain—" said Tim.

"Don't be mean to her," said Kuan Hee. "Lina, they are Jordan's bodyguards."

"*Wah.* Really?" said the rest in unison.

"*Wah seh.* Is his father a millionaire?" said Navin.

"Jordan, is your father rich?" said Lina.

"Nah. These are my father's people," said Jordan. "He sent them to protect me."

"Then, your family must be rich," said Lina.

"You guys are very *kaypoh*," said Jordan. "Everything you also want to know."

"Tell us *leh*, Jordan," said Navin.

"Alright—alright," said Jordan. "My father is Tee Bak Chai."

"Who?" said Lina.

"Hah? Doesn't ring a bell," said Navin.

"Is he some tycoon?" said Tim.

"He's Colonel Tee—the Supreme Leader of NRC," said Tim.

"Gosh—the dictator," said Lina.

"Don't call my father a dictator!" said Jordan. He contorted his eyebrows and stared at Lina.

"Let's not quarrel," said Kuan Hee. "We're all friends, man."

"She started it all," said Jordan.

"Since class has been cancelled, let's go down to the cafeteria for a drink," said Kuan Hee. "My treat." He herded the group towards the lift lobby. The two bodyguards followed them.

In the cafeteria, the five of them crammed at a small table next to the clear glass panels overlooking the car park. The bodyguards sat at the next table. The air-conditioning seemed ineffective in cooling Lina and Jordan down. Kuan Hee started the ball rolling.

"Guys, give me your orders," said Kuan Hee.

"Are these guys going to tell your father what we are talking about?" said Kuan Hee when he returned with a tray of drinks.

"They won't dare," said Jordan. "I won't let them."

"Jordan, you are the deputy student leader," said Navin. "Won't you be at loggerheads with your dad?"

"He is he and I am I," came the reply.

"Kuan Hee, won't there be a conflict of interest? Father—Supreme Leader, and son—a deputy student leader?" asked Navin.

"Aiyah. We are merely student representatives—no big deal, lah," said Kuan Hee. "It's not like he's a supreme court judge and his father is Supreme Leader."

"Kuan Hee's right," said Tim. "Lina, don't you agree—Lina?"

"Don't be a spoilsport, Lina," said Kuan Hee. Lina glared at him.

"Jordan," said Kuan Hee. "Why is your father doing

this—taking over the country?"

"Yeah, why?" said Tim and Navin in unison.

"I don't know. I'm angry with him too," said Jordan. "I haven't talked to him in days—I can't understand why he is so power crazy."

"You mean, you don't agree with his actions?" said Lina. Hearing his remarks, she became her usual self again.

"I hear you guys went to the big demonstration," said Jordan. "I hear you took a hit."

"Nah. Just some minor bruises, that's all," said Kuan Hee.

"Here, look," said Tim, sticking out a leg and pointing at it.

"Sorry, so sorry," said Jordan.

"It's not your fault, Jordan," said Kuan Hee.

"Is this your father's work?" said Tim.

"I—" said Jordan, craning his neck to get a look at the next table. His bodyguards were stirring their cuppa. "I overheard my father saying something in the study."

"What is it, Jordan?" said Kuan Hee. "You can trust us. We won't tell a soul."

"We won't. We won't," the others said in unison.

The others hunched around him. His voice had softened into a whisper and they wanted to hear what he was saying.

"My father—he could be behind the explosion," said Jordan.

"What?" exclaimed Navin.

"Shhh!" said the others in unison. The bodyguards turned their heads in the direction of the students, and resumed sipping their cuppa.

"S-e-r-i-o-u-s?" said Tim.

"Your father gave the order for the explosion?" said Navin.

"Yes," said Jordan.

"And the Molotov cocktail throwers—he sent them?" said Tim.

"Yes," said Jordan.

"*Wah Lau.* People died—you know," said Lina.

"Yeah. And we were almost killed," said Tim.

"I'm sorry about it—very sorry," said Jordan. "But, I am helpless. He—just won't listen to me."

"What about your mother?" asked Lina.

"She—she's behind him all the way," said Jordan.

"Your mother, too?" said Kuan Hee.

"I asked her why—she said he worked so hard; yet he's only a colonel."

"Isn't being a colonel good enough?" said Navin. "I don't think I can even make the grade—if I try."

"My father is—an A-level holder. He didn't go to university," said Jordan. "I'm the first one to enter university."

"I see," said Kuan Hee. "I see."

"Aren't you going to try talking to him again?" said Lina.

"No use, Lina—no use," said Jordan.

"Does your father know you are a student leader?" said Kuan Hee.

"Nope," came the reply.

"Are you not going to tell him?" said Navin. Jordan was silent on this.

"Let's not push him," said Kuan Hee. "Let's drop the topic."

"Yeah. Let's talk about other things," said Lina. From the tone of his voice, she could sense Jordan's spirits sagging.

WHATSAPP:
"URGENT meeting @ open space outside EEE, 11:00 a.m. today," texted Donald Chen.

"Guys, I've got to attend a students' union meeting now," said Kuan Hee.

"Me too," said Jordan.

"Kuan Hee, I'll wait for you here," said Lina.

"Same," said Tim.

"What about your bodyguards, Jordan?" asked Kuan Hee. "We can't bring them along, you know—it's going to be about the military takeover."

"Not to worry," said Jordan. "I'll tell them to stay clear of the place."

The secretary of the Temasek University Students' Union had convened a meeting of student leaders from different faculties in the university. It was meant to discuss a soft protest along the Singapore River. The focal point of the protest was the stretch of river behind the Parliament Building. The proposal was for students from the six local universities to hold a candlelight vigil, significantly to mourn the death of democracy, and specifically to protest the dissolution of parliament and curtailment of freedom to assemble in Singapore. The NRC had announced that assemblies of six or more people were illegal and those who participated in such assemblies risked arrest.

The candlelight vigil was held to intentionally signal to the coup leaders that the students were not afraid to violate the assembly order to fight for their cause. A total of 30,000 students were expected to attend the night event which would be held on the evening of National Day itself.

Temasek University's students would occupy the stretch of river from Cavenagh Bridge to Empress Place. The organisers forecasted the event would end very late at night and said participants could leave for home on the first MRT train or bus in the area which would start running at 5:45 a.m.

CHAPTER 7

It was 9 August 2030. Today was National Day, but celebrations were far from the minds of locals. A few days ago, the military had held a rehearsal for the National Day parade at The Float, a large metal platform the size of a football field, floating next to the banks of Marina Bay. Its seating gallery had a capacity of 30,000 people. The parade was quickly put together by the army which ordered participants of the Youth Festival in June to reprise their performances for the parade.

The parade would start at 6:00 p.m. By 10:00 a.m., the entire area stretching from St Andrew's Road, Connaught Drive and Beach Road to Raffles Avenue and Raffles Boulevard had been cordoned off. Armored personnel carriers guarded the junctions of these roads. There were army soldiers scurrying around, making preparations for the parade.

The university students' candlelight vigil would stretch from the mouth of the Singapore River to Clarke Quay. As the two venues were close to each other, there was a high possibility of a clash between the soldiers and the students. Perhaps, the students had intentionally chosen the river site to stage their soft protest. Perhaps, the students would march towards the parade zone in a vehement show of force. Perhaps, the military would fire at the protesters. There was no answer to these questions—yet.

The threesome arrived early outside Raffles Place MRT Station. Kuan Hee had delegated some administrative work to his two pals. He was in charge of distributing candles and water to participants. The truck carrying cartons of the water had dropped its load at the open area next to Emplace Place. Metres away, there was a chain of soldiers blocking access to St Andrew's Road, where City Hall building was. They were backed by two armored personnel carriers. Some police vans and buses had also arrived; these were parked along St Andrew's Road. Policemen bearing shields disembarked and moved in a single file towards the protest area. The line between military coup leaders and their detractors was becoming denser.

This was Kuan Hee's first active participation in a protest. Now he wasn't a bystander; he was a bona fide student leader, with followers who would look up to him to set examples for them. Now, he was an activist, but he wasn't a firebrand like Patrick Teo. Maybe this was why Patrick Teo was in the netherworld, and he, on earth. He had yet to kindle the fire within him. It would take more than just the threat of a jobless future to wake the activist in him—In his mind, the future was still far away. Perhaps, if Lina was hurt; perhaps, if his father or mother was in danger. Perhaps, if he was staring at death in the face.

What did Kuan Hee know about being a leader? He was an only child—with no brothers or sisters to hover over him or quarrel with. His mother gave birth to him when she was forty-five years old. At that age it was too risky, so they settled for caesarean delivery. He was a mummy's boy then; he was still a mummy's boy now.

"Kuan Hee, where are the lighters for the candles?" asked Lina.

"Jordan and Navin will be bringing them here. They are

collecting them from Donald now."

News of the candlelight vigil event spread like wildfire on social media. There were numerous comments on Facebook and Twitter. Within hours, thousands swarmed into the Marina area. *"They are going the wrong way—the parade is in the opposite direction!* thought soldiers stationed at the checkpoints. These people were here to lend support to the students; they were not attending the parade. The crowds overwhelmed the soldiers. They surrounded the armored personnel carriers. In no time, the Padang was a sea of people. In the waning light, they were a large moving blob of heads. There were not enough candles to pass around to them. But, it didn't matter—they came prepared with their own. Singapore had its last major blackout back in the late 1970s and since then, people did not stock up on candles. How did these people get the candles? There probably weren't enough in the stores, if they could find them. Some others were ingenious—they used LED torches to light up the surroundings.

It was now dark everywhere; the street lamps had been turned off using IP commands. In the Internet of Things era, even street lamps had their own IPs. If the military could not stop the candlelight vigil, the least it could do without resorting to violence was to do as little as they could to help the protesters along. It soon appeared as if a swarm of fireflies had descended upon the area. Wave upon wave of flickering lights moving in an undulating manner lit up the Padang. Surveillance drones shone their lights onto the crowd.

There was blaring of music from The Float—The parade had started. Contingents of soldiers from the army, navy and the air force marched along the tarmac in front of the seating gallery. The police also had a contingent. There was a convoy of military and police vehicles in the procession. But, civilian participation was dismal. Gone were the usual contingents from the union, the telecom companies, the big MNCs and statutory boards. In their place were schoolchildren replaying their Youth Festival performances. The seating gallery was packed, but they were all uniformed staff. The military rule had gotten off to a bad start.

Over at the candlelight vigil, there were no speeches, unlike the protests in Dhoby Ghaut and Orchard Road. After the violence that marred the earlier protests, the organisers were now taking a different approach. Hopefully, tonight would pass without any incident, but it remained to be seen—for the night was still young.

Kuan Hee and company were now standing on Cavenagh Bridge; they had a good view of the river banks from this spot. So far, things had been running smoothly; except for a lost child, there wasn't anything to dampen their spirits.

A bodyguard tapped on Jordan's shoulder and whispered into his ear. Jordan followed him somewhere. He didn't tell Kuan Hee or the others. They thought he was leaving the protest. Then he returned.

"Sorry, guys. It was my father," said Jordan. "He wanted me to go home with him."

"I'm glad you didn't leave with him," said Tim.

"Yeah." The others chirped in unison.

"Jordan, the soldiers have left us alone tonight," said Kuan Hee. "Is it because you are here?"

"I doubt so," said Jordan. "My father couldn't care less about me." But his father's action contradicted this remark. After all, his father had taken the time to stop by to speak to him. And Jordan was his only child.

"Was Colonel Tee angry?" asked Lina.

"About me being here?" said Jordan.

"Nope—about people coming to our protest instead of heading to his parade," said Lina.

"Well, his face was glum," said Jordan. That remark said it all. Would Jordan's father take retaliatory action against the protesters? Nobody knew the answer, but it was plausible.

"Let's not talk about him," said Jordan.

It was almost 3:00 a.m. Many people who had joined the candlelight vigil had already left with their families. The river banks held only students and some others who wanted to enjoy one another's company in the early morning. The soldiers stood wearily on nearby St Andrew's Road. Donald then called a meeting of the student leaders. Apparently, some of them wanted to continue the protest into the morning and they had to get the others' concurrence. If only a handful of students were willing, the protest could not carry on—it would lack strength. Finally, everyone agreed to stay on. Then they mapped out what they needed to do once dawn broke. Their supplies had been depleted. They needed more water and food. Their phones and tablets were running out of juice; without a portable supply of electricity, their mission was bound to fail. And they also had to get more umbrellas; it was going to get hot come late morning.

Lina had permission to spend the night, but the next day was another thing. Her mother was asleep now; she had to wait till 5:30 a.m. when her mother would get up to go marketing. She wasn't sure she wanted to make the call. But, she also didn't want to go home alone. Kuan Hee was her world. She didn't want to leave him behind. The last time she did that—he went missing for a few days, and she couldn't sleep those few days.

As she pondered over the matter, she plain forgot time had not stood still. It was now 5:45 a.m. She had to make the call now. After some scoldings on the phone, her mother relented. She trusted Lina when she was in the company of Kuan Hee. Over the years, Kuan Hee had made frequent visits to their home, and her mother like what she saw—Here was a dependable chap, albeit on the soft side, not brawny like Lina's three brothers. He was the educated type, not like her brothers who didn't make it to polytechnic or junior college. Lina was her mother's hope—she was the only child who had made it to university. It wasn't difficult to support Lina through university as the brothers were all working. Their father had passed away when the children were young and their mother had to take on several jobs to feed the family. Hopefully, Lina could lean on Kuan Hee for company for the rest of her life.

At 7:00 a.m., two men came to take over the two who were guarding Jordan. They brought along breakfast for Jordan; it was prepared by his mother. There was enough to share with Kuan Hee and company. By now, only a tenth of the original student strength remained at the protest site. Many students who left had promised to return later in the day. They just had to report home to make their worried parents happy.

Over at the Padang, more soldiers were arriving; some to relieve the soldiers who had spent the night here; others to reinforce the numbers, in case the protest took an ugly turn. The police contingent left in their vehicles. Another two armored personnel carriers rumbled onto the Padang tarmac.

But the muted early morning was soon to turn chaotic, for the student leaders had decided to lead the students onto City Hall. It was something that the military would not turn a blind eye to. As more students poured into Empress Place, the protest leaders used loud hailers to cajole them into action. Kuan Hee and his pals were taken by surprise—they didn't expect to march to City Hall. It was a last-minute decision by some student leaders. Alas, they had no choice but to follow along. After all, they were part of the student movement. They had to be as gung-ho as the others on the heroic and praiseworthy goal of saving Singapore from the clutches of dictatorship. Yes, that was what Kuan Hee and his friends had to convince themselves.

Kuan Hee grabbed a loud hailer, so did Jordan. Together with Lina, Tim and Navin, they marched with students from the other universities to St Andrew's Road. But the soldiers were ready for them; there was a long chain of soldiers bearing rifles standing abreast in the middle of the wide road. This time, Kuan Hee's group was right in front of the procession. Their representative had drawn lots, and it was decided that Temasek University would take the lead. Donald, Jordan and Kuan Hee were in front; Lina, Tim and Navin were behind them. Tim and Navin were holding placards denouncing military rule. Jordan's bodyguards were directly behind Jordan; they were ready to pull Jordan to safety should things turn ugly. It seemed they were the only reluctant participants of the protest.

The crowd shouted slogans as they moved in step, drawing nearer to the City Hall steps, where the surrender of the Japanese forces had taken place in World War II. A voice boomed over the public address system across the Padang.

"Stop the protest and disperse immediately," the voice commanded. Soon, a jeep roared into view. The soldiers forming the chain moved aside to let it pass.

"Go home now and we will not take action against you," said the same voice. It belonged to a Captain who was standing on the jeep. He looked to be middle-aged.

The came the rumbling of heavy vehicles. Some trucks bearing water cannons appeared behind the jeep. They were police vehicles, but it was army personnel manning the trucks.

Where are the police? Kuan Hee and the others wondered.

The protesters refused to bulge and the army captain gave the order to use the water cannons against them, drenching them. The powerful jets of water fell some of them, but they got up again and relocked arms with one another. Kuan Hee and company were all wet; they were also cold, but they forced themselves to be strong. The bodyguards did not escape the drenching, but they remained in position behind Jordan. Next, some soldiers lobbed tear gas canisters into the crowd. The protesters tried hard to dodge these. As the canisters rolled on the tarmac, they emitted plumes of smoke which enveloped the protesters. People were coughing and wheezing; their eyes were tearing uncontrollably. Some vomited; others cried in pain. Some splashed water into their eyes; it made things worse. Some others covered their face with tissue paper, towel or whatever that was at hand. Kuan Hee and Jordan suffered the most as they were right in front. Poor Lina was tearing; she cried as the tear gas singed her eyes. The poor bodyguards were probably the only innocent victims in the whole affair. They covered their faces with handkerchiefs. The protesters were clearly unprepared for this latest strategy of the soldiers. For all of them, this was probably their first experience in a protest; for Singapore, it was the first time that soldiers were attacking civilians. History had been made, courtesy of the military.

There was a lull in the action as the captain had ordered his soldiers to take a break while he assessed the situation. It gave the students time to regroup and rethink strategies. Still searing from the tear gas attack, the students retreated a few metres till they were out of range of the projectiles. Some male students had now taken off their T-shirts or jerseys and were readying them to protect themselves against the tear gas canisters.

The lull was broken by a fresh volley of projectiles whizzing over the students. This time, the students were better prepared. The female students had retreated to the back of the procession, and T-shirt bearing protesters fended off the projectiles. One grabbed a canister and threw it back at the soldiers who winced in the smoke, for they too were unprepared for the tear gas attack. Another student mimicked the act. Some soldiers were seen stumbling onto the ground. Others fell onto their fellow soldiers. The captain's jeep was enveloped by tear gas. The captain coiled in despair; his eyes were smarting.

Clearly, both warring parties were incensed. The

students were petrified that the military had resorted to hardball tactics to deal with their peaceful protest. That quickly changed into anger. And the captain was indignant that the students were fighting back. Here he was trying to restore law and order in the streets; and there they were—fighting the law.

There was a flurry of action on the soldiers' side. The protesters heard the humming of engines. Then the armored personnel carriers sprang into action. They rumbled along the tarmac in front of the City Hall steps. It was to be a David versus Goliath fight—between the unarmed students and armored personnel carriers. Was it time for the students to run helter-skelter? What would the student leaders decide to do? Their lives, and those of their followers were at stake. How would the students' parents react if they knew what was happening?

It was now too late for second thoughts or decisions. The soldiers were not to be trifled with; it was either retreat or suffer defeat and injury for the protesters. Donald moved a few steps in front of the other protesters. He drew a deep breath and headed towards the armored personnel carriers. Soon he was within metres of the huge vehicles. Was he crazy, or was he fearless? What if the armored personnel carriers ran over him? He would become *roti prata*! Now the armored personnel carriers had stopped. The soldier on top of the front most armored personnel carrier was in two minds. *Should I run over the student, or should I keep still,* he thought. Undecided, he talked furiously into the headphones.

Jordan could not stand it any longer. He broke from the others and ran towards Donald. The bodyguards had no choice but to follow in pursuit. Kuan Hee did a strange thing. Timid Kuan Hee lunged after Jordan. The four of them were soon within metres of Donald. Alas. It was too late, for the armored personnel carrier lumbered along, over Donald and on towards Jordan and Kuan Hee. The two boys recoiled in horror. Their friend had been crushed under the tracks of the armored personnel carrier. They stopped in their tracks, then, recovering from the shock, they threw themselves against the front of the armored personnel carrier. The two bodyguards were talking furiously into their wireless communication devices; they were trying to get help for Jordan. The soldier atop the armored personnel carrier drew his gun and took aim at the two boys. Then he shot at them. One. Two. Three. There were three shots—one ricocheted upon hitting the front of the armored personnel carrier. Another hit Jordan's left leg. He let out a shrill cry. And a third struck Kuan Hee in his right arm. Kuan Hee grimaced in pain and fell off the armored personnel carrier onto the tarmac. He rolled in pain. A bodyguard helped him up and both hobbled away from the armored personnel carrier, towards the protesters. Another grabbed Jordan and followed them. The soldier on the armored personnel carrier trained his gun on them; he was about to shoot again. Suddenly his headphones crackled with new instructions and he put away his weapon.

Poor Lina. She saw the whole thing unfolding before her eyes. She was now wailing away. Her tears were unstoppable. It was like a well that had overflowed.

Not since the second world war had the City Hall building witnessed bloodshed. It was unprecedented in Singapore history—army soldiers firing at unarmed civilians.

CHAPTER 8

It was a two-bed ward that Kuan Hee and Jordan shared at Singapore General Hospital. Jordan's bodyguards were outside the doorway. His parents had yet to visit him. Kuan Hee's father and mother were seated by his side. Both wore anxious looks. Lina was standing next to Kuan Hee's mother. Tim was by the window.

"Mum, I'm sorry," said Kuan Hee.

"It's alright, dear," said his mother. She was grasping Kuan Hee's hand with one hand, and fingering his arm with the other.

"Is your arm still tender?" she asked. Kuan Hee nodded.

"Why didn't you tell us you were staying the night at Singapore River?" said his father.

"Sorry, Dad," said Kuan Hee, "I forgot." But, it was a lie. He didn't tell them as he was worried that they might not approve of his staying overnight at the river.

"I want you to resign as a student leader," said his father. "These army guys are not to be trifled with. This time you hurt your arm. Next time, it may cost you your life."

"Yes, Kuan Hee. Your father is right," said his mother.

"You should know your priorities. Studies come first."

"I want an answer," said his father.

Kuan Hee nodded in agreement. He had to pacify his parents now. He didn't want them to spend more sleepless nights worrying about him. He had to give a convenient, albeit untruthful answer. But, he would try to keep out of trouble for a while.

There were so many things that Lina wanted to say to Kuan Hee, but she couldn't. There were too many people in the ward. It would be awkward if she told him she almost died seeing him fall off the armored personnel carrier. She didn't care what Tim or Jordan would say. What would Kuan Hee's parents think of her? It was painful to keep her thoughts to herself, but she had no choice today.

"Don't worry, Mrs Wang," said Lina. "I'll keep an eye on him—make sure he doesn't get into trouble again."

A nurse came into the ward. Visiting hours were over and she told the visitors they could come again the next day. She waited as one by one they shuffled out of the room.

It was after visiting hours that they came. Bodyguards ushered Jordan's father and mother into the ward. Kuan Hee realized why his own father and mother, and his friends had been shooed out of the ward—VIPs were coming. It was the first time that Kuan Hee had seen Jordan's parents at close range. Colonel Tee looked no older than sixty. True to his army roots, he was tanned and had close cropped hair—albeit greying. His face was wizened. His forehead had crept into the place where his hair used to occupy. At first look, you were attracted to his bushy disheveled eyebrows. He spoke in a husky voice.

Jordan's mother looked like any auntie you met at the market. She was not the polished type you would see in high society. It was clear Jordan was her son—he took after her features. You could see her long face and bony cheeks in him; but, he had his father's small eyes. She, too, spoke in a soft tone.

Both Mr and Mrs Tee were thrifty with words in the ward. But, their long silence spoke volumes. Perhaps, they were not comfortable speaking their mind with a stranger in the room. To them, Kuan Hee was an unknown. But, they were polite enough to ask after Kuan Hee and wish him a quick recovery.

Colonel Tee and his wife were busy people. They didn't stay long. Once Mrs Tee was convinced that her son's injury were not life threatening, they left. His mother promised to come the next day.

It was the second day of Kuan Hee's stay in hospital when the twenty-somethings could talk freely. Kuan Hee's parents had left early; they had to attend a wedding.

"So, what's the buzz?" asked Jordan.

"There's nothing in the news on what happened at City Hall," said Tim. "The newspapers and TV only reported on the candlelight vigil in a terse statement."

"What?" said Jordan. "These army guys fired on us and nothing gets reported?"

"Yeah, that's true," said Lina. "The newspaper and TV stations have been gagged, I believe."

"But, it's all over the Facebook and Twitter," said Tim.

"Yeah, photos of the shooting have been uploaded onto Facebook," said Lina. "And, it's gone viral."

"Here, take a look," said Tim, thrusting his smartphone into Jordan's hand.

"Come, Kuan Hee, see mine," said Lina.

Both patients swiped, pinched and jabbed the screens as they perused news articles and social media posts on the smartphones.

"Look. You and Jordan are famous now," said Lina.

"Yeah, they are saying how brave both of you were," said Tim. "Fancy running headlong into an armored personnel carrier."

"Donald died a martyr," said Kuan Hee.

"Donald's actually the real brave one," said Jordan.

"He gave his life for freedom."

"Agree," said the others in unison.

"Where's the wake for Donald?" asked Kuan Hee.

"It seems they still have not released his body to his parents," said Tim.

"I still can't believe the army moved in on us," said Jordan.

"I still can't accept the newspapers keeping mum about it," said Lina.

"It's so surreal," said Kuan Hee. "Are we living in a vacuum under military rule?"

"See, people are ranting like crazy on Facebook," said Tim.

"You can stop some of the people some of the time, but you can't stop all of the people all of the time," said Kuan Hee.

"Wow. That's deep," said Lina, impressed.

"I seem to have heard that before," said Tim. "Some American saying, right? You changed the words right?"

"Yes, *lah*," said Kuan Hee.

"Why use 'stop', why not use 'fool' instead?" asked Jordan. "It's a more accurate word."

"I'm glad we have Websites like Facebook. They help broadcast our plight," said Lina.

"I agree. The military can tame the local media—but they can't control the foreign media," said Kuan Hee.

"I hope they won't get the ISPs to shut down access to Facebook," said Tim.

"I think it's only a matter of time," said Jordan.

CHAPTER 9

It was near the end of September. Kuan Hee's parents had been awaiting, albeit in vain, news of Kuan Hee's fate in the aftermath of the City Hall confrontation. They had received neither letters nor e-mails from the police or the military government. They were getting anxious. *Will he be charged for his role in the protest?* they wondered.

When Kuan Hee came down from his bedroom, his parents were in a pensive mood in the living room.

"We can't be calling the police to find out whether you will be charged," said his father.

"But, we can't keeping waiting," said his mother. "The suspense is killing me."

"I'm sorry for giving you guys so much trouble," said Kuan Hee.

"It's not you," said his mother. "You did nothing wrong."

"Yes, son. Your mother is right," said his father. "You did the right thing, fighting for our freedom."

"We are proud of you, dear," said his mother. "So proud."

"We thought you were getting too soft," said his father. "We were regretting we didn't give you the opportunity to voice your views—to speak your mind."

"What your father means to say is—we have been overprotective parents," said his mother. "Isn't that right, dear?"

"Of course, dear," said his father.

"It isn't that we didn't want brothers or sisters for you," said his mother. "We tried very hard—but—"

"It's not your mother's fault," said his father. "Nature hasn't been generous with us."

"Aw. It's OK, Mum and Dad," said Kuan Hee. "Serious. I am very happy. I have Mum and Dad; I have my friends, Lina and Tim. I'm satisfied."

"I'm sure you are, dear," said his mother.

"Can—can I remain in the union?" asked Kuan Hee.

"Dear, if you stay in the union, you are courting trouble," said his mother. "These are different times. We are under military rule."

"But, Mum and Dad, just now you were saying how good it was for me to be more vocal—more proactive," said Kuan Hee.

"Yes, I know," said his father. "Still—I feel uncomfortable about it."

"I'll be careful—I promise." said Kuan Hee. "Please, please."

"Let me think…" said his father.

"Dad, I want to be able to do something good—useful for the country," said Kuan Hee. "I promise I won't be rash."

"Alright—alright," said his father. "But—be careful OK?"

"Thanks Dad, and Mum," said Kuan Hee. "Thanks a million."

WHATSAPP:

"Meet at ToastBox 11:00 a.m.," texted Lina.

"Will be slightly late," texted Tim.

"K," texted Kuan Hee.
"Bring AleXander," texted Lina.
"K," texted Kuan Hee.

ToastBox on basement one of Hougang Mall was their other go-to watering hole. There was a smattering of customers at this modern-day take of the traditional coffee shop; it was not yet lunch time. Hunched over a table at a corner, Kuan Hee and Lina engaged in small talk while waiting for Tim.

"Is your mother still fuming over the incident?"

"She has forgotten about it—thank God for that."

"Will I be welcome at your place?"

"Of course you will. My mum doesn't keep grudges. Anyway, it's not you she's mad with; it's me."

"When—when I was shot, were you shocked?"

"You know the answer."

"I'm sorry." Kuan Hee put his hand over hers, and tightened its grip. Then he massaged it.

"It's OK. It's already over so long ago."

"I heard you wouldn't stop crying."

"Did you? Who told you?" Lina's voice was getting croaky.

"Someone—I heard you were trembling."

"In that situation, anyone would, you know."

"Thanks."

"For what?"

"For caring about me."

"Mmm."

"Can I hop over later?"

"If you want to."

"Your Mum?"

"I already told you she's alright now."

"*Wah*. Sitting side by side already," said Tim. "Hope I'm not disturbing you guys."

"Tim," said Kuan Hee. "Have you heard?"

"What?" said Tim.

"Jordan's the new man in charge of the union," said Kuan Hee.

"Won't that make his old man angry?" asked Tim.

"Tim says he doesn't care," said Kuan Hee.

"He doesn't mean it, Kuan Hee," said Tim. "He's his parents' pet, you know. I'm sure he's not that cruel."

"I have taken Jordan's place," said Kuan Hee.

"I expected it," said Tim. "But, I thought your parents are against the idea."

"They finally caved in to my request," said Kuan Hee.

"Great," said Tim. "I think they know the military won't be hard on us."

"Why do you say that?" asked Lina.

"I've been thinking," said Tim. "With Jordan by our side, his father will think twice before he does anything to hurt us. It's tantamount to hurting his own son."

"Yeah, Tim's right," said Lina.

"I don't quite agree," said Kuan Hee.

"Why?" said Tim.

"Well, Jordan was with us at City Hall, right?" said Kuan Hee. "And we suffered much damage."

"*Aiyoh*. Kuan Hee's right," said Lina.

"Just whose side are you on, Lina?" said Tim.

"Both arguments make sense," said Lina. "But—Kuan Hee's makes more sense."

"*Alamak*. Lina," said Tim. "You guys are one voice."

"We are not only one voice," retorted Lina. "We're also one couple."

"*Alamak*," said Tim. "I give up talking to you."

Kuan Hee took his two friends to a large field in Changi. What they saw in front of them was a bare flat piece of grassy land with no trees for as far as the eye could see. They put down their backpacks and sat on the grass.

"I didn't know that Singapore has got such a big field," said Lina.

"There are a few more—if we bother to look for them," said Kuan Hee. "These are all state land."

"What?" said Lina. "And we keep hearing people complain we are short of land in Singapore."

"Kuan Hee, take out the robots," said Tim. "Let's have a look at them."

"I only brought Alex," said Kuan Hee. "My father says not to bring out both at the same time."

"One or two, doesn't make any difference," said Tim.

"Alex. Alex, come out," said Kuan Hee.

"He can understand commands?" said Tim.

"Of course, he can," said Kuan Hee. The robot peeked out of the backpack. Then it lifted itself out of the bag and somersaulted onto the grass. It got to its feet and stood at attention. Alex was a handsome robot. It stood about thirty centimetres tall. It sported black hair and had glassy eyes. Its entire body was metallic silver in colour. You could see the joints on its arms, hips and knees. It was wearing a pair of boots. Lina and Tim were captivated by it, unable to utter a single word.

"Alex," said Kuan Hee. "Say hallo to Lina and Tim."

"Hi Lina. Hi Tim. Glad to meet you," said Alex the robot.

"Wah. I must say I'm impressed," said Tim. "It—I mean he is unlike any robot I have ever seen. He's agile."

"Yes, and fast too," said Lina.

"What's in this?" said Tim, pointing to a rectangular outline on the torso of the robot.

"Don't know," said Kuan Hee. "I asked my father. He said he would let me in on the secret compartment soon."

"Wow. A secret compartment," said Tim. "Bet you it conceals some weapons."

"Don't be silly, Tim. It's so small," said Lina.

"Lina, aren't you also studying nano-technology?" said Tim. Lina blushed.

"What is the robot made of?" said Lina.

"My father says it's gold-titanium alloy—four times

stronger than titanium," said Kuan Hee.

"It must be expensive. It's gold you know," said Lina.

"Is it indestructible?" said Tim.

"It's been coated with a special liquid chemical—state of the art material. It's like armor," said Kuan Hee. "My father says the liquid looks like custard. But, it's strong stuff."

"Custard?" said Lina. "But, it's—it's so squishy."

"Can I test it?" said Tim.

"How?" said Kuan Hee.

"By throwing it a distance," said Tim.

"Aw. Don't be naughty," said Lina.

"Go ahead, Tim," said Kuan Hee. "I'm sure Alex won't mind."

"Of course, he won't, Kuan Hee," said Lina. "He's a robot, for goodness's sake. Robots have got no feelings. They also can't think."

"Not this one, Lina—not this one," said Kuan Hee.

"You mean, Alex can decide if he wants us to throw him?" said Lina,

"Alex," said Kuan Hee. "Can I throw you over a distance?"

"If you wish to, yes, of course," said Alex the robot.

"*Wah*. He sure is intelligent," said Lina. She was impressed.

"May I, Alex?" said Tim.

"Yes, please," said Alex the robot. Gripping the robot, Tim placed it under his jawbone and flung the robot as if he was throwing a shot put. The robot flew in a trajectory over the open space and landed on the grass about thirty feet away.

As quickly as it landed, the robot jumped to its feet and strode across the field back to where the three were. Then it stood at attention.

"Gosh. There's no dent on it," said Tim. It looks brand new."

"Don't believe me right?" said Kuan Hee.

"Alex runs pretty fast," said Lina. "When does its battery run out?"

"He runs on solar power," said Kuan Hee. "The whole surface of the robot is embedded with tiny solar panels."

"Wah. I didn't know they could make solar panels so small that I can't even see them," said Tim. "Unbelievable. I sure have a lot to learn about nano technology."

"Does it sleep?" said Lina.

"No, it doesn't, Lina," said Kuan Hee. "But, it does need to recharge—every week," said Kuan Hee. "That's why Alex is here—He's taking in sunlight energy."

"How do you know it's fully recharged?" said Lina.

"Boy, you sure do have a lot of questions," said Kuan Hee. "I don't have all the answers, though. Let me ask my father when I get home."

The foursome had a pretty good time together that day. Little Alex entertained the others with his little antics, while the three pals marveled at his ability to engage them in conversation.

CHAPTER 10

It was a wet Christmas; it was pouring with rain every other day. Kuan Hee and the two robots were getting along nicely. The past few months of friendship between them had endeared the robots to Kuan Hee. He wasn't lonely at home anymore; they had become his pals. In his bedroom, the robots stood side by side, eyes wide open, and hands clasped, on a desk next to the window. They could now compete with Lina for his attention. She wasn't pleased when Kuan Hee refused to meet her a couple of times on the pretext of having loads of homework to complete. He was actually playing with Alex and Xander, getting to know them and their capabilities better.

Kuan Hee's father had revealed the secret behind the square panel on the front of the robots. Alex and Xander had lethal weapons hidden in them. His father had held Alex in one hand and pressed a protruding button on the back of the robot. The front panel had swung open exposing what looked like a mishmash of tiny gear mechanisms and armatures. In its centre was a round plate with shafts fanning out of a protruding lens. His father had said this little contraption was a laser weapon system capable of producing fifty thousand watts of energy. It could burn through virtually anything within thirty metres.

Xander's front panel, when open, revealed three small rockets on launchers standing parallel to the robot's body. At the elder Wang's command, the rockets leaned at an angle to the panel. His father had said this was a miniature version of rocket artillery used by the army. There was no recoil, unlike gun artillery, so little Xander would not be knocked onto the ground each time a rocket was fired. A single rocket could blast through an army tank—it was that deadly.

Kuan Hee was mesmerized by the gadgetry. His father was indeed a genius. He remembered his father had also warned him against playing with the deadly weapons. He could only use them when facing a life-or-death situation.

The robots' weapons, his father had explained, could only be activated if the front panel was open. When shut, the robots could not fire the weapons on their own. It was a safety measure, according to his father. While he felt Alex and Xander were kind robots who could be counted on to do good only, he was also worried they might make a wrong decision on their own. So, he had included a manually operated door in the otherwise futuristic robot. It was a precaution he had to incorporate in the robot's design.

It was at this time that Lina was getting jealous of—of all things—Alex and Xander. To her, the Christmas season was a time to be spent with loved ones, doing window shopping sprees and huddling together in the cold wet weather. But, it was not to be, for Kuan Hee was instead spending more time with his two 'toys'. However, to Kuan Hee, these were not mere toys; these were intelligent robots with a propensity to think. Why, he had even put aside his favourite online games to make more time to play with his robots.

Thus began a spate of petty quarrels between Lina and Kuan Hee over the strange three-sided relationship: Lina, Kuan Hee and his robots. When they finally met, Lina would scowl at him and give him the cold shoulder on a cold day when they should have been cuddling each other instead.

It was a difficult time for Kuan Hee with Lina blowing hot and cold every other day. Now, they couldn't decide on simple matters such as where to meet or what place to eat at. It was getting frustrating. Kuan Hee would sometimes ask her whether her *ta yi ma* had arrived for a visit. It was a euphemism for her having her period. Indeed, she would admit to having her period but pour cold water over the connection between her behaviour and the menstruation period. Altogether, it wasn't a merry Christmas for the couple.

Things got to a boil one afternoon when Kuan Hee missed their appointment at NEX Shopping Mall. They had agreed to meet outside a bank in the atrium of the mall. He had stood her up. He had plain forgotten. And in their WhatsApp conversation, she had vowed not to leave the spot until Kuan Hee appeared. He had to put away his two robots and scrambled off to meet her.

In her home, everyone—her mother and her three brothers—gave in to her. She was the youngest, and the only girl in the family, so they would pander to her whimsical needs. It was, therefore, conceivable that she would expect the same of Kuan Hee.

"Sorry, sorry—I'm late," said Kuan Hee. "A thousand apologies."

"You're not late," said Lina. "You are very late."

"I was busy doing my homework," said Kuan Hee. "I forgot the time."

"Even my brothers don't dare do this to me," said Lina.

"Sorry," said Kuan Hee. "I promise I won't do it again." He was used to her princess-like behavior and knew it was futile to talk back to her when she was in one of these 'strange' moods. Meek obedience was the only thing that would assuage her anger. To him, being late was a small matter; she was making a mountain out of a molehill. But, that was her trademark. And early in their friendship she had registered this trademark with him. So he knew she would not fail to use it.

"I'll tell my mother what you did to me," said Lina. Tears were welling in her eyes. She was sniffling. But, they were in the middle of crowd. He could not have her crying in front of so many eyes. It would be embarrassing.

Kuan Hee brought her to watch a movie. He whispered sweet nothings into her ears in the cinema. He took her to eat her favourite Hazelnuts and Chocolate ice cream at Anderson's. *Oh, the things I have to do to pacify her*, he lamented.

"Kuan Hee," said Lina. "I want…I want."

They had come out of Hougang MRT Station and were walking towards her block of flats. Of course he knew what she wanted. How could he not know? She had been dropping a hint here and there the past few weeks. First, little ones, then direct hints. Any fool could not mistake the message she was sending him.

Being of reticent character, he was slow to react to her moves. It wasn't that he did not love her. There wasn't any other girl in his life, for God's sake. It was simply he was reluctant to make the first move—and for no rhyme or reason. They were both of marriageable age. There wasn't anything standing in their way—except for Alex and Xander the robots, of course.

Is today to be a moment of great love for us? he wondered.

"Kuan Hee," said Lina. "Are you listening? Are you paying attention?" She was getting cross. Was she about to exercise her trademark again? Then she leaned against Kuan Hee. Their pace was getting slower. Her weight on him was making their walk tedious.

Kuan Hee didn't realize it then, but, he had made a right turn towards Jalan Naung, instead of treading a straight path on to her home.

The couple found themselves in Kuan Hee's bedroom.

His parents were not home; he had just found out. They had the whole house to themselves.

Is she getting a little horny? he wondered. *Am I getting excited*, he wondered again. His heart was pounding in his thumb. He could feel its reverberation in the twitching of his thumb.

Then came that moment—their moment of great love.

"The condom—I don't have it."

"I don't want—no sensation."

"You want me on top?"

"Yes."

"My hands—can touch?"

"Yes."

"Can bite?"

"Nibble, *lah*—bite—painful *lah*."

"Your hips, so big; I didn't realize."

"My mother says…big hips—more children."

"Mmmm."

"So strong, yours."

"Then?"

"Ouch!"

"Oh."

"Painful, you know."

"Sorry."

"That's better."

"Can go in?"

"Wait a while. We girls need more sensation, you know."

"Can go in now?"

"A little longer."

"Suckle me."

"Mmm."

"More—more."

"Mmmm."

"Can go in now?"

"Yessss—"

"Cannot go in leh. Hole too small. So tight, painful."

"Me painful too."

"Feel anything?"

"A tingling sensation. Faster—faster—"

"Still a little tight. I'm using all my strength."

"Faster. Use more force."

"I am going as fast as I can."

"Deeper—deeper–"

"I'm trying—really—"

"What's the smell? What's that liquid?"

"Lubrication—natural lubrication."

"So much? It's gooey—like nail polish remover."

"Aw…Faster."

"Coming out!"

"What?"

"Don't touch…wait…wait. It's sensitive."

"OK."

"Not sensitive now. Going in again."

"You know I've been waiting for you, don't you."

"Mmm."

"Faster, please."

"Mmm."

"Coming out—I can't stop it. Oops!—it's all over your belly button. And—"

"It's all over me—my breasts too. So much sperm. You're so strong—Gee! It's warm and sticky—squishy like raw egg white."

"Let me clean it up. I'll get some tissue paper."

"Ouch. My leg. You just pressed your leg on my leg."

"Sorry."

"I'll wipe your big brother—no, it's little brother now. It's getting spongy. And droopy."

"Mmm."

"It's alive again. It's pushing against my fingers; it's growing in my hand…I—I want more."

"But I'm tired."

"More—more—"

"Next time, can? No more strength…need a break."

"Aw. You're bad. I hate you."

Lina snuggled up against Kuan Hee's warm chest, planting small little kisses on it. *Tomorrow, perhaps,* she thought. He ruffled her long hair and gave it little pecks.

"I love you, Kuan Hee—I really do."

"Me too. Love you…lots."

"Why didn't you…why didn't we…"

"I—I."

"Ouch!" Lina had given him a love bite on his neck.

"That's to remember today."

"Mmm."

"I—I don't want to get pregnant…I'm only twenty-one."

"I know."

"I'm a little afraid…getting pregnant."

"I know."

It was the first time for both of them. It was awkward for both. But, it was pleasurable for both. Lina wrapped her arms around Kuan Hee and closed her eyes. Her head was now resting on his arm. It was awkward for Kuan Hee; his arm was getting numb, but he couldn't move it; he didn't want to wake her. She stirred in her sleep. Both had become intimate. Before, they were bosom friends; now they were a couple. He didn't want to interrupt her sweet dreams. Soon it was morning.

"You forgot to call home," said Kuan Hee.

"Nope, I did not," said Lina. "I told my mum I was spending the night with a girlfriend, mugging for a test."

"What if Tim finds out—about us?" asked Kuan Hee.

"Mmm?" said Lina.

CHAPTER 11

It was a year after the military takeover. The citizenry was cowed by the relentless efforts of the National Reconciliation Council to control dissent in the country. Singapore had become a police state. The press and the broadcast stations had become a parrot for the military government's propaganda. Social media were being monitored around the clock by the army's Cyber Watch Group, whose original function was to prevent cyber attacks by foreign elements. Its actions were pervasive. The Group had a few thousand personnel working round the clock, filtering posts and comments on local and foreign social media.

Local media were served with shutdown notices whenever anti-government articles or comments were found on their Websites. It was more difficult to control foreign social media such as Facebook so the government blocked locals' access to these Websites. However, it was easy to circumvent the orders. People flocked to foreign Websites providing Virtual Private Networks.

Telecom companies too had a hard time, for the army stationed personnel at their exchanges to listen in to the telephone conversations of individuals deemed to be subversives. All data routed through the telecom networks were routinely filtered by the army's CWG.

The government was trying to create an atmosphere of mistrust among its citizens. People were enticed with privileges and benefits each time they reported misdeeds of their friends, acquaintances or neighbours who were arrested on trumped-up charges.

In spite of the concerted efforts of the government, residents' camaraderie remained high. People found ways to work around the inconveniences brought about by the government. The presence of foreign social media on the Internet, no doubt, spurred their never-say-die spirits. Netizens from all over the world continued to type messages of support for the people of Singapore. Some composed inspirational songs cajoling Singaporeans to stand up for their country.

Thus, the circumstances gave birth to a new underground movement named SAVE SG. People from all walks of life embraced SAVE SG's noble aims. They used social media to get their messages across to fellow residents. It was easy as frequenting these Websites had become second nature to locals here. People had become helpless without social media, for a way of life had been woven around such media.

University students led by Temasek University's student union hosted a commemoration of the first anniversary of the army's brutal crackdown on protesters outside City Hall. Jordan was to take the stage to deliver a belated eulogy to honour the late Donald Chen and lament the death of democracy in Singapore. But he went missing on the day of the event. So Kuan Hee had to hastily prepare a speech for the occasion.

The plan was to march as a peaceful procession from Cavenagh Bridge to St Andrew's Road, retracing the route of student protesters on the day of the army crackdown at City Hall. But the army had got wind of the event. Metal barricades had been put up to block both sides of St

Andrew's Road, and armored personnel carriers stood at the entrances to the road.

Kuan Hee and fellow student leaders from the other local universities then decided to stage a protest march along Orchard Road—where tourists flocked. Groups from several civic organisations had indicated their wish to participate in the event. So, SAVE SG PROTEST MARCH was born. It now had a critical mass.

Thousands of protesters, from the universities and their alumni associations to professional and civic groups, moved through Orchard Road, watched by thousands from all walks of life, including curious tourists.

The military government had stationed several companies of soldiers along both sides of the route. There were armored personnel carriers and water cannons at the junctions. It had failed to stop the protest, but it was determined not to let the protesters run riot in the streets, not in Singapore.

It was Kuan Hee's first major test as a leader of men; he had been a squad leader in his national service days, but that didn't count. He performed admirably well, and received praises from others. The one most impressed, of course, was his other half—Lina.

Today, the army was restrained in its behavior. It could be due to the presence of picture-snapping tourists or the watching eyes of the foreign press who were reporting on the event for their country's consumption. So, the event went without a hitch. After today, SAVE SG became internationally known.

Jordan remained unreachable for the next few days. Kuan Hee's calls to his smartphone went unanswered. Jordan's friends could not contact him too. They were unable to visit his residence as the street where his house stood had been cordoned off. Soldiers guarded both ends of the street. No one could enter it without an invitation from the army. His house was now the official residence of the Supreme Leader of the NRC.

One evening, as Kuan Hee was watching television in his bedroom, he heard a noise at the balcony. Someone or some creature was making a noise there. He grabbed the nearest thing he could use as a weapon and pushed aside the glass door. It was Jordan! He had scaled the pipes on the outside wall of the house. Jordan was wearing his trademark cap. He looked tense and Kuan Hee could hear his heavy breathing in the quiet of the surroundings.

"Where have you been?"

"Can we go inside?"

"Here—take a seat."

"Kuan Hee, come away from the window. Do you have something to eat?"

"I can rustle up something. How about Maggie mee?"

"That will be great."

"Come downstairs with me."

"Are your parents home?"

"Nope. They are out attending a dinner function."

"OIC."

"Some vegetables for you?"

"Sure. Let me help with the bowls." Soon they were seated in the dining room. Jordan slurped up the noodles. It was as if he had not eaten in days. Kuan Hee resisted the urge to ask more questions. He didn't want Jordan to choke on the food.

They were not close friends and, as far as he knew, Jordan did not know where he was living. Kuan Hee found it strange that Jordan had turned up at his place.

Kuan Hee repeated his question. "Where have you been?"

"My father kept me locked up in the house. He wouldn't let me go out, no matter what I said."

"He didn't want you to attend the protest?"

"It's not just that. Do you have a drink?" Kuan Hee opened the fridge and retrieved a Coke for Jordan.

Jordan placed his NY cap on the table. Kuan Hee could now have a better look at his face. His eyes sported dark rings. He didn't appear to have slept well.

"Can you put me up here?"

Ordinarily, if it was Tim, Kuan Hee would not have spared a second thought. But, this was Jordan. His father was the military ruler of Singapore. There would be repercussions if he let him stay over, especially since he had left home without his father's knowledge.

"It would be difficult, you know—your Dad is a bigshot. He might not like the idea."

"Kuan Hee, help me, please." Jordan was now pleading with him. He still hadn't disclosed the real reason. *Should I let him stay, or shouldn't I?* thought Kuan Hee. He was in two minds. Lina was not here, otherwise he would have asked her for her opinion. Finally, he relented.

His parents came home past midnight and retired to their bedroom promptly. His mother did not pop into his bedroom. The two men shared Kuan Hee's bed. It was king-sized and both weren't big-sized. On the bed, Kuan Hee recounted the happenings during the protest in Orchard Road. Jordan steadfastly refused to divulge his reasons for leaving home; and Kuan Hee, ever the good host, did not press on with his questioning.

However, Jordan did talk about his father. He rambled about his father's unhappiness with the previous government. They had overlooked him for promotion to General. A young President's scholar in the elite administrative service had the honour of becoming the first Brigadier-General to lead the FF Brigade. Colonel Tee was relegated to second in command when the young upstart took over the reins. Then he nursed his grievances with the administration. They didn't recognise talent, he had said to his son. They would rather promote untested individuals who lacked experience. The only thing they had was an honours degree in some ivy-league university in the United States. What did they know about running an army?, he would complain to his son. These were mere boy scouts, wet behind their ears—he would blare into his son's ears.

Then he would boast about how he got into the good books of the deceased Prime Minister, doing everything that he hated so that the PM would trust him and let him run important departments in government. It was a godsend, he would tell his son. He managed to wrestle control of essential services in the armed forces, though he was, in his own words, 'a mere colonel'. That's when he hatched the plot to take over the government. He felt he had to put things right—make sure deserving people in the service would be promoted, regardless of their education level. That was why his trusted lieutenants were now running the country with him. To him, they were extraordinarily talented; to him they deserved the positions that he had given them now—heading the various important departments in the military government.

Kuan Hee was all ears—Jordan was telling him things that no one else in government or Singapore had privy knowledge of.

The plainclothes came looking for Jordan the next day. They admitted they had no search warrant, but they didn't need them, in this day and age, to run their dirty fingers over every nook and crevice in the house.

Earlier, hearing vehicles stopping outside the gate, Kuan Hee had hidden Jordan in the secret cellar. He had hesitated before doing so, fearing his father's secret might be leaked out. But, the exigency of the situation demanded urgent action—he made the urgent decision alone.

Kuan Hee didn't have time to hide Alex and Xander. The men had come too suddenly; he didn't have time to think. The two robots stood cheery-eyed throughout the search. The plainclothes apparently were too busy looking for a person to cast their eyes on things in the house. They left after a fruitless hunt.

WHATSAPP:
"Meet at Kovan MRT @ 11:00 a.m.,"
texted Kuan Hee.
"Why?" texted Lina.
"Bringing J out," texted Kuan Hee.
"Jordan?" texted Lina.
"Yeah," texted Kuan Hee.
"How about Tim?" texted Lina.
"Not this time," texted Kuan Hee.

Kuan Hee wanted to keep Jordan's name out of the chat; he was afraid the government would be monitoring online conversations. But, it was too late. Lina had blurted out his name. Anyway, it was just possible they would miss this conversation; after all there were many thousands of conversations being carried out every minute in Singapore. How could the government keep track of everything? But, he was wrong, of course. The government had access to supercomputers that could crunch big data to make sense of the information in no time.

The trio were careful not to let Jordan use his bank cards or MRT cards for the day's transactions. They were afraid such transactions would pinpoint Jordan's location. Jordan had left home prepared with some money from his piggy bank.

From Orchard MRT Station, they walked to Wisma Atria and Takashimaya, enjoying the strong air-conditioning—a proper respite from the hot weather outside. At 313 Orchard, the guys browsed the New Era store where Jordan eagerly fingered the latest caps on display on the wall. He chose a black NY cap and paid for it with cash. All three had a jolly good time that afternoon.

They were in Somerset MRT Station when Jordan spotted some men milling around the 7-Eleven Store. His face turned pale. He tapped on Kuan Hee's shoulder, gesturing that they reverse tracks and leave the station. Alas, it was too late. The eagle-eyed men had seen him.

They made quick steps towards the three. Kuan Hee grabbed Lina's hand and together, they made a dash for 313 Orchard with the men in hot pursuit.

They ran through 313 Orchard, passed Orchard Gateway and were about to cross the underground passageway to CentrePoint Shopping Centre when they stopped in their tracks. In front of them, at the other end of the passageway, were some burly plainclothes. They were trapped. The plainclothes approached them. They caught hold of Jordan and hurried him off, leaving Kuan Hee and Lina bewildered. Clearly, these guys were not interested in them.

"How did the plainclothes manage to find us?" Kuan Hee said to Lina. She did not know the answer either.

"Was it the WhatsApp chat that led them to us?"

"If it was so, then they would have caught us at Kovan."

"Yeah—just how did they do it?"

The duo were momentarily lost. The men had taken the group by surprise, and they had yet to recover from the shock. They walked in CentrePoint Shopping Centre directionless.

Then they decided to head home. As they walked through the gate into Somerset MRT Station, Kuan Hee looked at the monitor screens overhead. It showed a live video of them moving through the gate. It dawned on him that the cameras in the MRT stations had captured them going in and out of the stations. *Our movements are being recorded,* he said to himself.

"It's the cameras—they gave our position away."

"How can they? There must be more than a hundred stations on the island with a few thousand cameras altogether. How can they monitor all the cameras? They will need many, many men."

"Nope, you are wrong, Lina—they use facial recognition software. They use supercomputers which can process tremendous amounts of data received from the cameras—makes sense, alright."

"That's bad, real bad—there's no way we can hide from these cameras—unless we don't use the MRT or the bus."

"Yeah. It's bad news alright."

CHAPTER 12

Lina followed Kuan Hee back to Jalan Naung. Both were spending an inordinate amount of time alone at his house. They were now intimate, having moved on to more lovemaking trysts since their very first experience in his bedroom. Kuan Hee's mother was waiting in the living room. Her lips were pursed; she was a bundle of nerves. Apparently, something had upset her.

"Kuan Hee. Kuan Hee—your father's missing," she said.

"Not again, Mum," said Kuan Hee. "He didn't call you the whole day?"

"Not since this morning," said his mother. "He never misses the lunch time call."

His mother was right. In their forty-two years of marriage, he had never missed a single lunch time call, except the time when the army shut down his workplace when they usurped power.

"Mum, you know Dad—he could have forgotten the time. You know when he's at work, nothing else matters," said Kuan Hee.

"But, he's never like this, not in a million years."

Kuan Hee and Lina retreated into their private space,

leaving his mother to her thoughts. *Come morning, he will be home,* thought Kuan Hee as he snuggled into bed with his beloved.

But, morning came and went. There was still no sign of Kuan Hee's father. By nightfall, his mother was expecting the worst. *He had to be in detention,* she thought. But, there was no way to get hold of him. Her calls to his office-cum-laboratory went unanswered. The receptionist said he hadn't come in the last two days. *She is lying,* thought his mother. *Lying through her teeth! That's what it is.*

Kuan Hee could call his father with the implanted mobile device, but he had forgotten about it. Then the moment came. There was a voice in his brain. It was calling out to him. *Am I dreaming?* he wondered. There went the voice again. It sounded like his father; in fact, it was his father. He was sure this time.

Son, son, can you hear me? the voice in his mind said.

Was his father talking to him in his dreams? But, he wasn't dreaming. It was broad daylight and he was alone in his bedroom. Then it hit him. He realized his father had been calling him on the implanted phone in his arm. He had plain forgotten about the device.

"Kuan Hee, please answer me," said his father's voice.

"Now, how do I talk to Father?" Kuan Hee asked aloud. He remembered the notes he had written about his father's strange contraptions. He retrieved the note from a drawer in his desk. He flipped the pages. *Here it is,* he told himself.

> To call, say **LOGON ALPHA** aloud.
> To talk to the other party, speak aloud.
> To end call, say **TEN FOUR ALPHA**

"LOGON ALPHA."

"Kuan Hee, It's me, Dad. Can you hear me?"

"Dad, I can hear you. Are you alright? Mum's worried sick about you. You didn't call home the past few days." It was information overload. Kuan Hee had rattled the string of sentences without a pause. It was too much for his father's brain to process. The electrical impulses took time to convert to signals that his brain would understand.

"Kuan Hee—slow down, slow down, please."

"S-o-r-r-y D-a-D."

"No need to be that slow, son."

"Sorry."

"I was saying—Mum misses you."

"I miss her too, please tell her that for me."

"Dad, where are you?"

"I have been held against my will, son."

"Who? Why?"

"Colonel Tee's men, son."

"Why, Dad?"

"They want me to carry out a secret operation for them. I refused, so they are keeping me hostage till I agree."

"What? Secret operation? What's that, Dad?"

"It's a long story, son. In a nutshell, they want me to transfer someone's memories into another person's."

"Who's this person, Dad?"

"Colonel Tee, son."

"The dictator?"

"Yes, son."

"Will they harm you, Dad, if you go against their wishes?"

"I don't think so—not for now anyway. They need me. I'm important to them. But, they may harm people dear to me—to make me do what they want."

"They want to harm Mum?"

"Yes, son—and you, too."

"Can't we run away?"

"I can't, but you and your mother can. I want you two to get out of the country—this instant."

"Dad, Mum won't do it. She'll never leave you, you know that."

"Son, you must try to persuade her. Talk to her now. Pack the essentials and leave immediately. Go out of harm's way. If they can't find you, they can't change my mind. But they know you are my Achilles' heel."

"I will, Dad. How do I get in touch with you? Where are they holding you?"

"Use the implant, son. You can call me using the implanted phone. If I don't answer—just keep trying. And, I'm in a lab somewhere—not sure where. It's not at my workplace definitely."

"OK. Dad."

"Don't use the SIM card in your iPhone. Use the Polaris SIM—it's in the cellar—top shelf—in a box. It's linked to a satellite."

The connection was broken. His father had terminated the call.

"Dad? Hallo Dad. Dad?" *He's gone offline,* Kuan Hee told himself. *Got to tell Mum.*

Try as he might, he could not persuade his mother to leave the country—not without his father. When she had cooled down from knocking down the idea, she took to chiding him for implanting the mobile device in his arm. Then she stopped her racket. It was the mobile device that had come to their aid during these difficult times. Without it, the family would have been hopelessly pining for his father. The device was indeed a good idea. It had taken a brilliant chap to come up with such a magical piece of work, his mother told him. It took someone with foresight to have seen this situation coming, his mother added. Then she cried again. His mother was missing his father again. He went bleary eyed whenever he saw her crying.

I have got to change the SIM card, he told himself.

Kuan Hee retrieved the Polaris SIM card from the cellar and replaced the one in his iPhone with it. He turned on the iPhone. It was working. On the top left of the screen appeared the carrier's name: POLARIS.

The next day, Kuan Hee's mother went missing. She had gone marketing as she usually did at 6:00 a.m. It was already 9:45 a.m. And she was not home yet.

Kuan Hee went looking for her at the neighbourhood market where she usually shopped. Then Lina joined him. They walked around the neighbourhood, but there was no sign of his mother. She had vanished into thin air. He called his mother's friends, but they too had not seen her. Kuan Hee suddenly had a dreadful thought—she had been captured by Colonel Tee's men. *It has to be so,* he reasoned to himself. He had to call his father.

Back at Jalan Naung, with Lina seated beside him, he phoned his father. There was no reply. He tried again. Still no answer. *Is Father asleep?* Kuan Hee wondered. *It's almost lunch time; he couldn't be sleeping in the middle of the day. Is someone with him? That's a possibility.* He decided to try again in half an hour. Soon, the suspense was getting to his nerves. He paced up and down his bedroom. He didn't notice—Lina's eyes were welling.

"LOGON ALPHA."

"Dad, are you there?" There was silence in his mind.

"Hallo Dad. Hallo." He couldn't hear anything in his mind.

Lina was choking back her tears. She too was anxious. "Can you leave a message?"

"It doesn't have an Inbox. Everything is done on the fly."

"Keep trying."

"Dad. Calling Dad. Answer me, Dad."

"Son, I am here. I'm listening."

"Dad. They have taken Mum."

"I know son. Colonel Tee was here just now."

"Dad, what should I do?"

"Keep safe, son. Go into hiding. They may come looking for you."

"But, where can I hide?"

"Go stay with a friend—stay with Tim. And bring AleXander and the flies with you."

"Is Mum alright?"

"They have not let me see your Mum yet. Maybe—today they will."

"I'm sorry, Dad. I should have watched Mum carefully."

"Isn't your fault, son. Isn't your fault." Then there was a hollow sound in his mind; his father had gone offline.

"My father wants me to hide at Tim's place."

"Can't you hide in the secret cellar?"

"They will be watching the gate."

"You can climb the—"

"I can't take the risk. I'm the only one left—Dad and Mum have been caught. I can't let them catch me."

"How about staying with me?"

"Your house? But, it's too crowded. There are five of you in there."

"You and I can occupy one room, my mother and oldest brother one, and my two other brothers one—just nice." Lina's face lit up. She wasn't teary anymore.

"Does your mother mind? Will your brothers mind?"

"Don't worry. I call the shots in the house."

"I may get them into trouble, you know."

"But—we are one big family—you, me and my family."

CHAPTER 13

Lina and her family lived in a four-roomed HDB flat in Hougang Avenue Five. It was lively in her home; there wasn't a moment of silence in the flat, not with three grown-up brothers and her mother all bumping into one another as they went about doing their things in the small space. Kuan Hee was unaccustomed to living in small spaces. His semi-detached home—all two floors of it— housed his father, mother and him. There were three bedrooms upstairs and one downstairs—more than enough for them.

At 79 Jalan Naung, Kuan Hee had the whole bathroom to himself. Here, he had to queue up to use the bathroom. But Lina tried her best to make him feel at home. She told her mother to share the second bedroom with her eldest brother. She herself would occupy the master bedroom with Kuan Hee. It had its own adjoining bathroom, but no water heater though—that was in the common bathroom in the kitchen. *Kuan Hee will be pleased—no need to use the common bathroom*, she thought.

Lina's mother never asked why she was living together with a man. She didn't have to explain to her brother that the couple were merely sharing the room—not cohabiting.

99

They had seen Lina and Kuan Hee going out with each other since she was in primary school. It was only natural that they would eventually marry each other—so there wasn't any need to bother about the requirement to get married first before they could *tong fang*. It was already the 2030s—no need to follow traditional Chinese values to the letter. And her eldest brother had told Kuan Hee to take good care of his little sister.

Theirs was a typical *Hokkien* family, where the household revolved around the matriarch—her mother; only that in Lina's home, the matriarch's authority had been supplanted by little *Huang Ah Ma*—Lina! Like all other arrangements in the household, the Goh family was accepting of this one. After all, Lina ruled the house.

At dinner time, her brothers would gesture to Kuan Hee, and ask him to eat, to eat more. Her mother would keep the chicken drumstick for him. That was their way of making him feel welcome. Soon he settled down at Block 308.

But the police cameras in the void deck—keeping watch of the two lift lobbies and staircases in the block bothered Kuan Hee. He was sure these cameras were connected to some central monitoring authority—the military government could track his movements easily. Using facial recognition technology, they could find him effortlessly. He should not continue staying here; he would be putting the Goh family in trouble if the plainclothes came for him. In the meantime, whenever he went out of the flat, he would wear a baseball cap and cover his face with a flyer.

But now, I have to find out more about Colonel Tee, Kuan Hee thought. *Yes, I've got to spy on his house.*

Jordan had told Kuan Hee where he lived. In fact, Jordan had said many more things about his parents. The Tee family lived in Belmont Road, off Holland Road, in the upscale Holland area. The house had belonged to

Jordan's maternal grandfather. Upon his grandfather's death, his mother had inherited the property. Colonel Tee had an inferiority complex. He thought his wife was too good for him. He had felt insecure when he was dating her, and her father didn't make things easier on him. Her father was always harping on his inability to provide a good life for her—his only child. When they married, Colonel Tee was only a lowly Lieutenant in the Rangers. Instead of getting their own house, they lived with her father in the Belmont Road bungalow. He had to put up with his father-in-law's idiosyncrasies. Colonel Tee vowed to make good one day. Indeed, he had done so, albeit in an evil way.

It had become standard practice for Kuan Hee to take AleXander and the two flies with him wherever he went. They sat comfortably in his spacious Crumpler backpack. Kuan Hee and Lina alighted from a taxi on busy Holland Road, next to a condominium. They made their way up a small road which forked into Belmont Road and Cornwall Gardens. Belmont Road had been cordoned off, but not Cornwall Gardens. The Tee bungalow nestled between the two roads.

Kuan Hee and Lina took up position on Cornwall Gardens. They brought out drawing blocks and some pencils. They were pretending to be young artists penciling the houses and trees there. She was wearing a straw hat and he a baseball cap—as disguise. Squatting on one side of the road, they didn't seem to blend into the area, try as they might. But they were a young couple whom nobody might take notice of. Ahead of the pair, up the slope on their side of the small road was a tennis court in the Tee residence. *This house is ultra big,* Lina thought. *Yes, opulent.*

Hardly any vehicles passed them this morning. Kuan Hee set the titanium housefly on his lap and let it take off into the air above them. In the silent surroundings, the housefly did not make any buzzing sound. Its wings took it over the tennis court into the swimming pool area where it danced and darted in rhythmic waves. The pair watched the small screen on the remote-control card intently.

"Moving nearer to the house. Looks like a two-storey bungalow."

"Fly into that window on the right, Kuan Hee."

"It's a sitting room. Nobody here. Let's turn right."

"It's got one, two, three—three bedrooms upstairs, like yours."

"Yeah, but slightly bigger. No one in here too. Not here also. The last one—the door's closed. Mmm. How about under the door? No good either. There are bristles on the bottom of the door—to keep cool air in."

"Can't see inside?"

"Let me use the infra-red scanner on its nose. Nope, the room's empty too."

"Mr Fly can sense heat?"

"Mr Fly can also smell—then it feeds the data into a decoder which identifies the smell."

"Wow!"

"Shush!"

"Kuan Hee, they can't hear us."

"Oh, I forgot, sorry."

"Don't go knocking into the furniture."

"Don't worry." He had had many dry runs with the two flies at home in the past few months. He had become proficient. *I've earned my flying licence,* he told himself.

Lina tapped his knee. "Wait." They took their eyes off the screen and pretended to be taking a perspective of the house across the road. A car was droning past them.

"Let's go downstairs."

The housefly flitted down the winding staircase with its elaborate balustrades. The pair admired the timber floorboards and columns which supported the bedrooms above. There seemed to be no one at home. Outside the house were some guards idling around in the compound.

Having been brought up in an HDB environment her whole life, Lina was not privy to how the rich in Singapore lived. Today was indeed an eye-opener for her. She had marveled at the size of Kuan Hee's semi-detached. But, this house was far bigger. *I didn't know Singapore has such big houses and gardens,* she told herself. *There must be at least a dozen big trees in the garden.*

"Let's call it a day. Let's come back another time."

"OK." The visit had not yielded any fruit. "We'll come back in the evening."

"Ha? So soon?"

"Jiving, just jiving. Tomorrow *lah.*"

"We've been busy today. By the way, have you named these drones yet?"

"Lina, these aren't drones—they're nano-robots."

"What shall we call them?"

"You just gave me an idea—your remark—'busy'. Shall we name them Busy and Tizzy?"

"Great. But who's who?"

"You say *lor.*"

"Housefly—Busy, and dragonfly—Tizzy."

"OK. Set."

"Let's go home, Busy and Tizzy."

CHAPTER 14

In the car park behind Block 308, there was an unmarked government car. Kuan Hee had learnt to recognize them by their QX prefix. He had seen such cars zip into SAFTI when he was doing guard duty during NS. *Are G men looking for me?* he wondered. He gestured to Lina for her to wait in the void deck of the opposite block, behind a pillar.

About half an hour later, they saw two men approaching the car. They had come out of Lina's block. Lina recognized one of them.

"It's a neighbour from upstairs. He has lived here for many years."

"OIC. Just being careful, Lina. Just being careful."

"You're being paranoic. That's what you are."

"You never know. We can all get into deep trouble—if they are Colonel Tee's men."

In Lina's bedroom, Kuan Hee let out his desire to move back into his house.

"But, they are looking for you. They'll be watching your house."

"There's this popular saying—the most dangerous place is the safest place."

"Please, *lah*. It's only a saying. What if they caught

you?"

"They won't. I'll be careful—very careful."

"Then I want to come along."

"But, it won't be convenient. And it's dangerous."

"I don't care. Either I tag along OR no deal."

Poor Kuan Hee, Lina was acting up again—like a princess. "Alright. Alright. But, does your mother mind?"

"She already knows we are together. She knows we go everywhere together. Besides, I am already twenty-one."

"OK. I get it. Pack some things and let's get going when darkness falls."

79 Jalan Nuang stood back to back with 85 Jalan Payoh Lai. The pair stole into the narrow passageway between the two semi-detached houses. Then Kuan Hee lifted Lina over the wall and soon they were tiptoeing along the cobbled backyard. It was dark, for the spotlights, usually controlled by a timer, were unlit.

Kuan Hee unlocked the kitchen door and both used their hands to guide them along the wall and up into his bedroom. The curtains overlooking the balcony were drawn. Kuan Hee peeked through a slit at the edge of the curtains. Street lamps illuminated the lane in front of the house. There wasn't a soul out there. No cars too. *They can't be watching my house twenty-four seven*, he thought. *Maybe they installed a camera outside.* He surveyed the lamp posts and the street sign. *Nothing*, he told himself.

"Are we sleeping here or in the cellar?"

The light from the street lamps helped illuminate the part of the bedroom next to the curtains.

"We can't use the air-conditioning."

"I know. So here or down in the cellar?"

"We'll go down when the situation get bad."

"OK. I'll jump in first."

"Kuan Hee."

"Yes?"

"When are we having children?"

"You don't make sense, you know. My parents are in trouble and we are hiding here. Is that all you can think about?"

"Aw, don't be mean. I was merely asking—for fun."

"It's not my idea of fun."

"Kuan Hee."

"What?"

"I don't want children."

"You just said you wanted children and now you are saying the opposite—make up your mind, please."

"When did I say I want children?"

"Just now—a minute ago."

"No *lah*. I was only wondering whether we will have children. It doesn't mean I want children."

"OIC. You mean we aren't going to have children?"

"I want to wait. I have seen these girls in my block. They are slim and pretty. But after they get married and have children—their bellies swell. Can't wear body-hugging jeans any more. And the cellulite on the back of their hips—eek!" There was no response from Kuan Hee.

She elbowed him. "Kuan Hee."

"Mmm."

"Weren't you listening?"

"I—I was. But, I was also thinking about my parents."

"Things will turn out well."

"Hope so."

Lina flashed him a cheeky look. Her eyes told it all. She wanted—.

"It's warm inside. Come right in."

"You are heavy."

"I'm not. You're bony, that's why. Can't even take my weight. Fancy a little thing on top of you—and you go complaining."

"I'm only afraid—it will break."

"So strong, how to break. See?"

"Aw. Don't grab so hard, can or not."

"Serve you right. If you don't know what to say—shut

up."

"Sorry, dear."

"Don't grip my breasts so hard, lah."

"Like that can?"

"Kiss me. Kiss me."

"Your hair's all over my face. Very ticklish. Need to breathe; don't press my lips so hard. My ears—don't use too much force."

"Kuan Hee, I love you."

"I know."

"Say you love me."

"I love you."

"Again."

"I love you. It's coming out. Quick. Get off—I need to pull it ou—"

"It's all over your body and my thighs."

"Too late—couldn't stop it."

"Kuan Hee, I want you to sleep naked tonight."

"Mmm."

CHAPTER 15

A popular saying goes like this:

After the rain comes sunshine.

It had been raining cats and dogs for the past two days. *When will sunshine come back into my life,* wondered Kuan Hee. He didn't say it aloud, for he was afraid Lina would misunderstand him. Of course, Lina was his sunshine; so were his parents. He wasn't thinking about her; he was thinking about his parents. *What if they use torture? Can my parents survive the ordeal?* he wondered.

His father once told him that worms came to the surface during heavy rain. He had explained that the water made the worms moist so they could easily move to a new location to escape predators. *Can we…will we get a chance to escape to a new place…a new life?* he wondered. Then he remembered Lina. *With Lina, of course, all four of them,* he thought.

Were his thoughts sending out cryptic messages to him? He could not decide. A voice in his head was speaking to him now. It interrupted his train of thought. It was his father. He wanted Kuan Hee to meet him somewhere—now. There was great urgency in his voice. His father had terse instructions for him; he told Kuan Hee to shut up and listen when Kuan Hee kept asking questions.

Kuan Hee grabbed his Crumpler bag. "We need to move now. Grab your backpack."

"Where to?"

He reached for Lina's hand. "Just follow me." They descended the stairs and made for the front gate.

"That's the front gate."

"Never mind. No time to use the back. Hurry."

Reluctantly, Lina tagged along. On Upper Serangoon Road, Kuan Hee hailed a taxi and they got in.

"Bukit Timah Plaza," he said to the taxi driver.

Upon arrival, Kuan Hee asked the driver to let them alight along Jalan Anak Bukit. Then he paid the driver and they got off. He waited a few minutes, till the taxi had disappeared from view. Then he grabbed Lina's hand and ran across the road with her. He was careful to avoid the road junction—there were cameras overhead. All this while he did not say a single word. When Lina protested, he merely put flicked a finger onto his mouth. She understood immediately.

The pair walked down Dunearn Road and turned into Rifle Range Road. They moved along the perimeter of a firing range. After a fifteen-minute walk, they found themselves near a building. A sign read:

Temasek Officers' Mess

The place was deserted. The building was dilapidated. It seemed nobody had taken care of the premises for some time. Grass was creeping onto the front porch. It had populated every nook and crevice in the area. The windows were nailed shut with timber planks. The paintwork was peeling off from the walls; there were pockets of air bubbles in it. Whatever grandeur the building might have had in the past, it showed no trace of it now.

Kuan Hee led the way along the edge of the building. Soon they came to a narrow passageway—it separated the main building from the narrow one behind. He opened a door at the far end of the narrow building—it creaked as it swung open. They stepped into a narrow corridor and came to an enfilade of rooms.

"Dad. Mum."

"Uncle. Auntie."

There was a noise in one room. Then the elder Wang appeared in its doorway. He waved them into the room. There they were—his father and mother—standing in front of him. He hugged them one by one. They hugged him. Then they hugged each other. Lina was in tears. The moment was too much for her.

"Come sit down and talk," said his father. He motioned for the pair to sit on a pile of wooden pallets. His parents sat on wooden crates. Their buttocks pressed on the rough grainy surface of the makeshift chairs.

"Kuan Hee, listen carefully," said his father. "We need to get out of the island as quickly as we can."

"How did you guys escape?" said Kuan Hee.

"It's a long story. In a nutshell, we scooted off when the people guarding us were distracted," said his father.

"Yes, it was like a miracle," said his mother. "Almost a miracle."

"How did you get out of the building?"

"Well, it wasn't the same building that they put us in at first," said his father. "I had complained that I did not have my tools and instruments. They relented and moved us to my workplace."

"Yes, it was easy for your father there," said his mother.

"Yes. I know the place like the back of my hand. I have access to all parts of the complex," said his father.

"How did you get here?" asked Kuan Hee.

"Let your father speak his piece," said his mother.

"We came in a taxi. As a young man, I used to frequent this place. In this room, I spent many hours reading my research notes and chatting with friends," said his father. "That's why I came here. I am relaxed here. I feel at home here. I think better here." His father paused to collect his thoughts.

"I have contacted a good friend. He's willing to help," said his father. "He has arranged for a boat near Coney Island tonight. It will take us to Pasir Gudam in Johor Bahru."

His father paused again. Then he continued. "I have spoken to the Americans. They are happy to have me working for them. We will take a taxi from Pasir Gudam to Kuala Lumpur. Airport. From there, we will board a USAF plane which will take us to Geraldton in Western Australia. That's where the American spy base is located."

"Dad, why can't we simply go into the American Embassy? Like in the movies," said Kuan Hee.

"They may take us down before we even step foot in the embassy," said his father. "There are G men stationed outside the embassy twenty-four seven. I can't take the risk—not with your mother around."

"Can you trust this friend of yours?" asked his mother.

"We have been friends since schooldays. He's my schoolmate at Victoria School."

"But Dad, people have been telling on one another, ever since the regime took power," said Kuan Hee.

"I have no choice," said his father. "It's a risk we have to take. Anyway, it's set. We need to get ready for the journey."

"Lina, you can't come with us," said Kuan Hee

"Yes, Lina, Kuan Hee is right," said his mother. "We can't take you along."

"I understand, Auntie," said Lina. She was also sure her mother would never let her leave Singapore with Kuan Hee.

Lina was glad they had had their little tryst two days ago. She didn't know when they could be together again. Australia was nine hours of plane ride away. She would miss Kuan Hee dearly. The pair retreated to a corner in the room and cuddled each other. Who knew when they could feel each other's warm embrace again? They were resigned to their fate.

CHAPTER 16

The moon looked big and round tonight. It was smiling down at the four dark figures treading along sparsely illuminated Rifle Range Road towards Dunearn Road. Was it telling them everything would go as smoothly as its surface? Kuan Hee, his parents, and Lina were busy thinking about what lay ahead for them the next few weeks—and months too. They did not have the time to take in the view.

A taxi took them to Edgefield Plains in Punggol. They alighted on the side of the road, careful not to be in view of the cameras in the HDB blocks. Then they walked along Punggol Nature Walk towards the west entrance of Coney Island. The promenade was deserted; occasionally, two or three joggers would pass them. They could see the entire south side of Coney Island from where they were. There was a police post at the head of the Nature Walk, a ten-minute walk away. They had to keep away from the post.

Soon they came to a sheltered rest-stop. It was where they would meet the boat. There was no sign of it in the distance. Above them, the moon seemed to be watching them; it was illuminating their surroundings. It was quiet out here.

The chugging of an engine punctured the silence. First, faint sounds, then loud droning sounds. Then it appeared in the distance. The boat slowed as power to its engine was cut off. It drifted close to the edge of the promenade and a man in it jumped onshore. Using a rope, he pulled it against the embankment, then beckoned the passengers to board. The elder Wang boarded the boat first, then he helped his wife into the boat. It was Kuan Hee's turn. He was heavy-hearted; Lina was emotional. She was on the verge of crying. But she held back the tears. She wanted to look strong in front of Kuan Hee today.

"Kuan Hee, Say your goodbyes; the boat is leaving," said his father.

"I'll miss you, bye," said Kuan Hee.

"Don't forget me. Don't ever forget me," said Lina.

The boat's engine roared into life and the boat moved away from the embankment. The Wang family waved at Lina. She waved back.

Suddenly, a voice boomed over a loudspeaker.

"Stop! Stop! Coastguard," said the voice.

A patrol boat came into view. There were soldiers—not policemen—in it. They looked menacing.

"Kuan Hee, quick, jump into the water," said his father.

"No Dad, no. I can't leave you and Mum," said Kuan Hee.

"Jump now, or it will be too late," screamed his father. It was the first time his father was screaming at him. His father had to be real mad this time.

"But—" It was too late for words; his father had pushed Kuan Hee overboard.

"Swim. Swim quickly," said his father.

"Kuan Hee, take care of yourself," said his mother.

Recovering from the initial shock, Kuan Hee swam towards the shore—to where Lina was standing. He wanted to stop and take a look at his parents, but he couldn't. The patrol boat was faster than his little body. He could fall into their hands. And his parents would be sorely disappointed with him. He fought back the tears in the water and swam with all his might.

On the embankment, Lina helped Kuan Hee up. They took a long look at the silhouette of the two boats. It was to have been a happy day for the Wang family. *How did it end up this way?* Kuan Hee wondered. Lina pulled him away from the shore. It was dangerous for them to remain in the area. The G men could come for him any moment.

CHAPTER 17

Kuan Hee was now determined. He had to find out where the G men had taken his parents. He had to get them out. The person who had knowledge of their whereabouts was Colonel Tee. The place to get information from him was Belmont Road.

Kuan Hee and Lina sat on the grassy verge on the side of the road. They had come prepared with folding stools this time. It was a brooding Kuan Hee who stabbed at the drawing block with his pencil. His parents' capture by the G men was still fresh in his mind.

Lina touched his wrist. And his thoughts returned to the present. He released Busy the housefly into the air and flipped open a remote-control card.

The titanium housefly flitted over the plainclothes in the garden, into the living room. They were in luck— Colonel Tee was seated in a big armchair next to the coffee table. Mrs Tee was walking into the room. She was carrying a tray of pastries and coffee or tea.

Busy the housefly landed on a picture frame next to the verandah doorway.

There was nothing interesting—they were having small talk. The minutes wore on. Evidently, Colonel Tee did not discuss work with his wife. Inside the house, the Tee couple were having coffee. On the roadside, Kuan Hee and Lina were watching for mosquitoes. The pests had taken some bites out of the pair.

It is another fruitless day, the pair thought. Lina suggested they fly little Busy up into the bedrooms to see if Jordan was in. Busy the housefly was flitting through the living room when the pair saw Colonel Tee rising from his seat. Mrs Tee passed him an attaché case and he left the house. Kuan Hee had a change of mind. He commanded little Busy to fly after him. Colonel Tee got into a Mercedes and the car moved down the driveway. Little Busy had perched itself on an antenna at the back of the car. The car was now moving out of Belmont Road.

"It's going out of range, Kuan Hee."

Kuan Hee pointed at the sky. "No, it won't—see? Satellite. That's what the fly relies on. It'll never go out of range. That's what Dad says."

It was a short journey. The Mercedes cruised down Holland Road with bodyguards in two Volvos—one behind and one in front, moving under the flyover to the lower part of the thoroughfare. The convoy continued down the road and turned into—Gleneagles Hospital! Colonel Tee wasn't going to work.

Is he visiting someone, Jordan, perhaps? wondered the pair.

Colonel Tee and his bodyguards entered a suite on the third level. There were more plainclothes waiting for them there.

In an office, stood three men in clinical white.

"They must be doctors," Kuan Hee.

Colonel Tee wore a grave look. He listened intently as the doctors, one by one, delivered their prognosis.

Who are they talking about? Is it Jordan? the pair wondered.

The doctors told Colonel Tee his prospects of recovering from advanced leukemia was poor. He learnt he had at most six months to live.

It is not Jordan, after all, but the dictator himself, the pair thought.

After the doctors had sworn to keep the prognosis a secret, Colonel Tee and his minders left with Busy the housefly hovering above them.

The convoy moved on the opposite side of Holland Road and turned left into Minden Road and then Sherwood Road. The passengers disembarked at the front of a large building. A large sign read:

Prime Minister's Office

But, the PMO was at the back of the Istana. *Has it moved here?* wondered the pair. *When?*

A small sign on a pillar of the building read:

Tanglin Complex

The Tanglin Complex had housed the Ministry of Defence back in the 1970s and 1980s. It was now supposed to be the address of the Ministry of Foreign Affairs. Kuan Hee and Lina sat bewildered. They were oblivious to the lady walking her three dogs on the other side of the road. The dogs' barking woke them from their thoughts. They had to get out of the place, for the barks were drawing the attention of men in the garden above them. The pair ran towards the main road, with hands clutching drawing boards and pencils.

Tanglin Complex was within walking distance. The pair had been sitting on the grass for ages and it was good exercise for them to walk to the building. Also, boarding a bus might mean they would be monitored by cameras on the bus.

As they made their way down the lower part of Holland Road, they kept their eyes on the small remote-control screen. In their haste to get out of Cornwall Gardens, they had no time to monitor Colonel Tee.

Apparently, Colonel Tee was in a bad mood today. In

his office, he kept reprimanding his subordinates. His minders were careful to keep some distance between him and them.

By this time, Kuan Hee and Lina had reached the beginning of Minden Road. There were sentries at a guard post thirty metres ahead of them. A metal barrier gate floated a metre above the tarmac. Tanglin Complex was visible from the main road. It was sitting on top of the slope.

The pair decided to take up position on the roadside. They reprised their routine, pretending to draw Tanglin Complex.

Busy the housefly was atop an air-conditioning unit in Colonel Tee's office. The room was longish, spanning the entire width of the building. Colonel Tee sat hunched behind a huge wooden desk, against a window with its curtains drawn. He was alone. The room was dim, with only the light from a table lamp on the table to illuminate it. But, it was bright daylight outside.

It was apparent Colonel Tee did not like bright places. The door opened and a female soldier walked in. She held it open and some men came in. There was a disheveled man between two burly plain clothes.

"It—it's Father," Kuan Hee.

The pair glued their eyes to the screen. They had stopped pretending to draw.

"Professor Wang, what is your answer?" said Colonel Tee.

The voice came crisp and clear through the small speakers of the remote.

"I refuse to do your bidding," said Kuan Hee's father. "You can't force me to do things against my will. This is a democracy."

"Professor Wang. This is indeed a democracy. It's my kind of democracy—my kind of rule," said Colonel Tee. "Don't you want your wife to go free?"

"You are worse than an animal," said Kuan Hee's

father. "You're a beast."

"Call me what you want. Any names also can," said Colonel Tee. "I don't care—as long as you agree."

Just what does he want Dad to agree to? wondered Kuan Hee.

"Soon your family will be complete," said Colonel Tee. "I have men looking for your son—Kuan Hee. Is that his name?"

"Don't you dare lay your filthy hands on my son," said Kuan Hee's father. "Don't you dare."

"You care about your son, right?" said Colonel Tee. "I have a son, too." He paused.

"I'll give you another day to think over," said Colonel Tee. "Just one more day—but, don't test my patience."

He flicked a finger and his men removed Kuan Hee's father from his room.

"You are a beast! You don't give a damn about your son," screamed Kuan Hee's father.

"Dad, Dad," said Kuan Hee.

But his father could not hear him. Colonel Tee couldn't hear him either. Lina leaned her head against Huan Hee's shoulder. Then he remembered where he was—on the roadside.

Kuan Hee's eyes were red. He was tearful. The moment had been heartrending. He could see his father on the screen, but he was helpless to him. Lina consoled him.

"Things will get better, don't worry." Then she stiffened. "Quick. Follow your father."

Kuan Hee dispatched Busy the housefly after the men. They were nowhere to be seen. Alas! He had been distracted. He blamed himself. Little Busy flitted through the corridors of the building and then out into the compound.

They couldn't have disappeared so quickly, Kuan Hee thought. *I had taken my eyes off them for only a few seconds.*

Then the pair saw his father and his guards. They had come out of a doorway at the far end. They bundled him into a minibus. Kuan Hee sent Busy the housefly after them. The metallic housefly attached itself to the top of the minibus as it was moving out of the compound.

"Are we going to follow them?"

"No need. Little Busy has got GPS capability."

Today, the pair had learnt some new things. Chief was that his father was alright. He appeared unharmed. Next was that Colonel Tee was dying soon—in a matter of months.

His dictatorship is to be short-lived, they thought. *Soon, Singapore will be free again.*

The pair still did not know what Colonel Tee wanted Kuan Hee's father to do for him. And they were soon going to find out where the G men were holding his parents.

"Let's pack up."

"Aren't we going to find out more?"

"No need. He can't run away. We know he's here. We can always come back."

"Where are we going?"

"To find my parents, but first, let's quench our thirst."

CHAPTER 18

The red dot was flashing on the remote-control screen. But, it was no longer moving. Busy the housefly had arrived at the place where the G men had taken Kuan Hee's father.

The map showed Maju Camp next to the red dot. It was situated on a grassy patch of land just behind Ngee Ann Polytechnic in Clementi.

Kuan Hee and Lina were enjoying a cold drink at nearby Tanglin Mall. They had spent hours in the sun today. They ordered some food to go.

"It's quite near Temasek Officers' Mess. About eight hundred metres away. I need to go there right away."

"I know. I want to tag along."

A taxi took the pair to Maju Drive. They alighted about fifty metres from the camp and trudged up the road, at times peering into the camp through the perimeter fencing. Cables running along the middle of the fence told Kuan Hee the fence was electrified. Ahead, the perimeter fencing parted at a road opening which was guarded by armed soldiers—not a single fresh face, all regulars. A metal barrier gate cordoned off the road, which led to two large single-storey buildings standing parallel to each other about a hundred metres away.

The flashing dot on the screen showed little Busy was between the two buildings. The buildings were longish with casement windows and a sloping tiled roof. The bottom quarter of the walls consisted of red bricks. The upper portion was whitewashed. Cameras were mounted on the corners of the building. No doors were seen on the side facing the road. Soon it would be nightfall and cold air would envelop the surrounding area. The pair had not come prepared for an overnight stay.

"Can you get little Busy to give us a view of the surroundings?"

"Let me get to the live screen."

"Doesn't little Busy run out of juice? It's been ages since we activated it."

"It's got tiny solar panels wrapped over its body."

"You mean—so many? Tinier than tiny little Busy?"

"Yes. That's what Dad said."

"Where is little Busy now?"

"It's still on the minibus. Shall we get it to start work?"

Little Busy flitted into life. It flew along the open space between the two identical buildings. There were four sets of double-louvered doors along each building. The doors sat between casement windows. Two armed soldiers—regulars—stood guard at the doorway in the middle of the first building.

Could Dad be in the first building? wondered Kuan Hee.

Kuan Hee piloted little Busy through the louvres into the building. There were men in white lab coats shuffling along the corridor. On one side of the corridor were doors.

Which one should I try first? wondered Kuan Hee.

Little Busy turned right and flitted to the farthest door. There was no opening either under the door or above it. It went from door to door—there were no openings anywhere.

How is little Busy going to look into the rooms? wondered

Kuan Hee.

"Look, someone is coming out of a room."

"I'll get little Busy to follow him."

Little Busy flitted into a room with a man in white lab coat. It seemed to be a laboratory of some kind. There were cupboards lining the walls and sophisticated equipment on a large counter top in the centre of the room. Two men were at work in the room. One was peering through a microscope.

"Negative here. We'll have to wait till someone enters or leaves."

It was a good hour's wait. It was cold out in the open, and the pair were famished. They chomped on the Big Macs they had bought at Tanglin Mall.

"Are we really going to barge into the place to rescue your parents?"

"If they are in there, of course, I am."

"But, we—we are alone. We don't have support. We are unarmed."

"Don't forget these two—he opened his backpack and AleXander's heads popped out."

Lina looked amused. She still didn't believe these two toy robots could be that lethal.

"Look! The door is opening."

Little Busy flitted through the door into the corridor. Two armed soldiers were making their rounds. They did not enter any of the rooms.

Then a soldier came in from the front door. He was carrying some food boxes. Little Busy flew above him as he made a turn and knocked a door. The door opened and both went in. The room was about the size of a four-roomed HDB flat. There were at least a dozen servers in cabinets along the walls. There were computer monitors on a big table on the left and in the middle sat a circular glass enclosure—something like the capsule lift in Wisma Atria, only bigger. An armchair was in the capsule. Overhead was what looked like an oversized coat hanger on a metal stand. It had thick cables fanning out of it, and dangling in the air.

There was no sign of Kuan Hee's father or mother. Only a lone soldier who was now chatting with his comrade. He took a food box to what seemed to be a pantry while the other sat at the table eating his dinner. Then he returned to join the soldier. Both were now partaking of their food.

"Kuan Hee, get little Busy to go into the side room. There's someone in there. The soldier came out without the food box."

Little Busy's wings flapped busily as it flew into the pantry. It wasn't a pantry—it was a small office. There it hovered over the cabinet and—someone in a chair.

"It's Dad."

"Go nearer. Go nearer."

The elder Wang looked sullen. He was unshaved and his eyes had dark circles under them. He was slouched over an office chair. His arms were on the armrests—but they were not restrained. The food box lay unopened on a desk next to him.

Little Busy swooped down to his ears.

Kuan Hee spoke into the microphone on the remote. "Dad, Dad."

His father roused. He looked dazed. Then he saw little Busy. "Son."

"Dad, are you alright?"

"Yes son. How did you know I'm here?"

"We followed you from Colonel Tee's office."

"You did? Where are you now?"

"Outside—down the road. Where's Mum."

"I don't know—she's not with me, son. I don't know where they have taken her."

There was an awkward silence, for they had heard the shuffling of feet. A soldier appeared at the doorway. He had thought he heard something. *Must be talking to himself,* the soldier thought. Seeing nothing was amiss, he returned to his partner.

"Dad, I'm going to get you out."

"How? You are alone and these are professionals—rangers, not NSmen."

"I've brought AleXander with me."

"No, wait, son. You can't—not now. If they find me gone, there's no telling what they will do to your mum. You can't."

There was silence on Kuan Hee's side. He was stupefied—he did not know what to say to his father.

"Son, I want you to do something for me."

"Yes, Dad."

"Listen carefully, go to the American Embassy—don't visit them. Don't call them. Don't e-mail them. Use the chat on their Website. It's encrypted and safe. Ask for Brigadier Walmsley of Special Forces, Department of Defence. His name is James Walmsley. J-a-m-e-s. W-a-l-m-s-l-e-y. You got that?"

"Lina has scribbled down the name."

"She's with you?"

"Yes."

"Good. When he contacts you, tell him what has happened to me. Tell him everything. Ask him to get your mum and me out."

"Do they know where Mum is?"

"They have the means. They are Delta Force."

"Tell him—Colonel Tee is dying. He won't live past this year. Tel—"

"I know that news, Dad."

"You do? How—never mind. Listen, don't interrupt. Tell him Colonel Tee wants me to let him live in another person's body. Tell him he wants me to do it these few days. Tell him to act fast. You got all that down, son?"

"Lina, all jotted down?"

"Yes."

"Yes, Dad."

"Good. Now get out of here. You can't do anything for

me here. Go find Brigadier Walmsley. Go find your mother."

"Yes, Dad—take care of yourself, Dad."

"Uncle, please eat something. You need to be strong."

"I will. I will. Now go. Kuan Hee, leave the housefly with me. Go to the remote's main menu. Set it to 'Others', then 'Voice Command'."

"All done, Dad."

CHAPTER 19

In Hougang Bus Interchange, Kuan Hee and Lina loitered, keeping an eye out for a bearded old Caucasian wearing a hunting hat. That was how Brigadier Walmsley had described himself.

There he was, standing next to the Buzz Convenient Store. He was much taller than Kuan Hee. They greeted each other and strolled across the road towards Hougang Mall. Along the way, the Brigadier fanned himself with his hat, complaining about the hot weather in Singapore.

At ToastBox in basement one, Kuan Hee and Lina sat next to each other, with the Brigadier facing Kuan Hee.

The Brigadier had both arms on the table. He asked for *kopi oh kosong*. He seemed to know some *Singlish*.

"I am curious—why did you guys move out of Sembawang?"

"Your previous government didn't want to anger the Chinese," said Brigadier Walmsley. "It wanted to show to the world it was neutral. So—we had to get out—move to Australia."

As the Brigadier sat twiddling his thumbs, he recounted the times he had spent in Singapore—in his youth mostly. He had also worked at the American airbase in

Sembawang.

Kuan Hee felt the Brigadier was just making small talk; he was actually sizing up the surroundings—to see if there were spies in their midst. He was ever so careful in his casual ways.

"I'm sorry to hear about your Dad."

"Thank you, Mr Walmsley, for your concern."

"Call me James. Everyone calls me that."

"Yes, Mr Walmsley."

"Your father is a rare breed. Talented—immensely talented."

Kuan Hee blushed. It was the first time he had heard someone heaping praises upon his father.

"Here, come closer." He hunched over the table and Kuan Hee did the same. Then Kuan Hee felt something touch his knee.

"Take this." The Brigadier passed something to Kuan Hee under the table. It felt like paper—folded paper and a candy-bar shaped thing, with a protruding rod, probably metal—it was cold to the touch. Kuan Hee quickly pocketed them.

"This is how we get in touch from now on."

Kuan Hee nodded, though he didn't quite understand how they would get in touch. He inferred it had something to do with the things in his pocket. *Perhaps, the Brigadier doesn't want others to hear, just in case someone is eavesdropping,* Kuan Hee thought.

Near Hougang MRT Station, the pair bade farewell to the Brigadier. He had come in a taxi, but wanted to take a ride back to the embassy on the MRT.

"Don't worry, your father will be OK. And your Mum too."

"Thank you, Mr Walmsley."

In his bedroom, Kuan Hee emptied his pocket. The candle-bar thing was a walkie-talkie. It was slightly bigger than the palm of his hands. The other thing was a folded note. He opened the paper. The typed text read:

> **This walkie-talkie has a range of one hundred kilometres. It works anywhere in Singapore. Use it to talk to me. It is linked to a satellite. Everything is encrypted. Set to Channel three. Keep it safe.**

"The Brigadier didn't say much."

"He's being careful. He's an old hand at such things. But he said enough."

"What's next, Kuan Hee?"

"Get something to eat. Come. Let's go down to the kitchen."

The pair clambered down the dark stairs. Having had plenty of practice the past weeks, they were sure-footed— they could almost move around the dark house blindfolded. It was plain Maggie mee for the pair again, for they had run out of eggs.

"Little Busy is no longer with us. Poor big Tizzy is going to be lonely."

"Yeah. I guess so. But Dad needs little Busy more than we need it."

"Are we going to find your mother?"

"Why do you ask?"

"The Brigadier said he would help us, didn't he?"

"Isn't it better if both sides try?"

"How are we going to find your mother?"

"Guess it is by spying on Colonel Tee again."

"Are we going to Tanglin Complex again?"

"Looks like it."

CHAPTER 20

A famous saying goes:

All men think all men mortal, but themselves.

Colonel Tee believed in power—seizing it and holding on to it by force. He knew man was mortal, but he had forgotten he was mortal too. Perhaps, he thought he could live forever, but through human existence on earth, what man had succeeded in cheating death? History held numerous examples. Emperor Shih Huang Ti sought the elixir of immortality, but failed to escape death. Colonel Tee, likewise, wanted a long life to enjoy the power he had amassed. Alas, he had forgotten the adage:

What man proposes, God disposes.

Colonel Tee was dying. To remain powerful, he had to live. Was there such a Holy Grail? If there were, then Kuan Hee's father held the key to it. Colonel Tee knew Professor Wang was the one man who could let him carry on living—albeit in another person's body. He was willing to pay any price to satisfy his ego. He would even sacrifice his own son.

Professor Wang had been ordered to carry out an operation to transfer Colonel Tee's memories to another person's brain. Colonel Tee's son, Jordan made a good specimen. Colonel Tee would live in his son's body. It was akin to the Hermit Crab which salvages an empty snail shell to use as its home.

Jordan is my own flesh and blood, so power would still lie in the Tee family, Colonel Tee had reasoned to himself. *My son and I would become one soon.*

Colonel Tee had grand plans for the professor to execute for him. Moving forward, Colonel Tee wanted Professor Wang to speed up his nanotechnology research on reproductive cloning of human beings. Though it was ten to twenty years before this would become feasible, he was sure Professor Wang could do it in double time. That was why Professor Wang was so important to Colonel Tee.

The Tee Dynasty should not end with me and my son, Colonel Tee thought. *It should go on perpetually.*

Professor Wang was a brilliant scientist. *He could replicate my son's body and my memories repeatedly,* Colonel Tee thought. *This way, we would live forever, and hold power indefinitely—Father and son.*

Colonel Tee had forgotten Professor Wang was a mortal. Professor Wang would certainly not be by his side for eternity.

"He hasn't bated an eyelid in ages. Is he dead?"

"I think he's in deep thought."

"Why are things going so slowly today?"

"Don't be impatient."

Kuan Hee and Lina had stationed themselves at the road junction where a lane of traffic filtered into Holland Road. This time they took on the role of survey staff. They sat on the grass clicking on counters as the cars moved past them.

"Kuan Hee, the sky is getting dark. It's going to rain

soon."

"Shush."

Colonel Tee had stirred in his armchair. Someone had entered his room. He was waiting for Colonel Tee to wake.

"Sir, Sir," said the man in a low tone. Tizzy the dragonfly flitted over the man. In the dim light, Kuan Hee could make out the emblems on his epaulettes. One crest. He was a major.

"Sir," said the major. The volume was louder now.

"Whaaat?" The Colonel had wakened.

"Sir, it is ready."

"Oh. So he's finally agreed, hasn't he."

"Yes, sir."

"Thursday then."

"This Thursday, sir?"

"Yes. Let's do it first thing in the morning. 8:00 a.m."

"Yes, sir."

"What's that thing?"

"What, sir?"

"On the wall behind you."

"I—I think it's a dragonfly, sir."

"Drat. These pesky insects. Ask my secretary to get someone to get rid of it."

"Yes, sir."

Before the major could speak to the colonel's secretary, little Dragonfly had scooted out of the room. It was now flying back to the pair.

"I told you, big Tizzy is too big for a spy job."

"Never mind. Let's close shop for today."

With big Tizzy safely in their hands, the pair walked towards Tanglin Mall.

"I think he is talking about my father."

"I think so too."

"So—the operation will take place in three days' time. I've got to tell the Brigadier."

"What if we are wrong?"

"It's got to be it. We can't be wrong."

The pair were now in an open space outside Tanglin Mall. Bringing out the walkie-talkie, Kuan Hee pressed the push-to-talk button.

"Calling Mr Walmsley. Calling Mr Walmsley. Over."

"Yes, Kuan Hee. This is James. Over."

"Mr Walmsley. Colonel Tee's operation will take place on Thursday at 8:00 a.m. Over."

"How did you know, Kuan Hee? Over."

"I overheard him telling a major. Over."

"I see. You were with the colonel? Over."

"No, Mr Walmsley. But Tizzy was in the room with him. Over."

"Tizzy? Over."

"Yes. Mr Walmsley. Tizzy the dragonfly—I mean the titanium dragonfly my father invented. Eh. Over."

"Yes. I see what you mean. Tizzy is a drone robot. Over."

"Yes, Mr Walmsley. Using a remote-control device, I can see and hear what it sees and hears. Over."

"So Colonel Tee said Thursday 8:00 a.m. Is that it? Over."

"Yes, that's correct. Mr Walmsley. Over."

"OK. I got it. Thanks very much, Kuan Hee. I appreciate it. I will get things going. Not to worry. By the way, we've found your mother. Over."

"Really? That's great. How's my mum? Over."

"My guys say she is well. Not harmed. Over."

"Thank you very much. Mr Walmsley. Over."

"We'll take her to safety soon, Kuan Hee. Over."

"Thank you, Mr Walmsley. Over."

"That's it then, Kuan Hee. Bye for now. Over."

Such a polite young man, thought the Brigadier as he put away the walkie-talkie. *Takes after his father.*

"Bye bye, Mr Walmsley. Over."

"It's good news, Kuan Hee."

"Yes, it is." Kuan Hee was beaming. "It's been a long time coming. I've been waiting too long for this moment."

CHAPTER 21

It was late evening. The air over Maju Camp was cold and a blustery wind was sweeping the open field where Kuan Hee and Lina sat huddled. They had come because Kuan Hee wanted to tell his father the good news about his mother. He could have used the embedded device in his arm, but he also wanted to take a look at his father—to see if he was doing fine. Maju Camp was the place to be.

The pair had come prepared to spend the night there. *We and your father are near each other tonight—that's what's important,* Lina thought as she leaned against Kuan Hee.

Kuan Hee had awakened little Busy. It wriggled out of the elder Wang's pocket and darted into the air. His father was taking a nap in the room. His eyes were shut, and he didn't stir when little Busy was buzzing in his pocket.

"Let's not wake your father. Let him sleep."

"Yes. He hasn't had a good rest for some time. Dad seldom sleeps like this. He must be dead tired."

"Look around the room, Kuan Hee."

Little Busy flew out into the main room and took in the view of the surroundings. The same two guards were sitting at the table, playing a card game. Their rifles were resting on the wall next to them. The room was crowded with equipment now. There were two motorized gurneys at one of the walls.

"Looks like they are getting the place ready for some big thing. Probably going to hold the operation here."

"You mean the one on Colonel Tee—tomorrow morning?"

"Yes. If the Brigadier's men do not take action by tonight, then Colonel Tee will live in a new body—Jordan's."

"It's so quiet here. I doubt anything will happen tonight."

"Commandoes like to do their thing just before dawn—when people are bound to be asleep or falling asleep."

"How do you know?"

"The movies, my dear. The movies."

Suddenly, the sky above them roared. A large dark object was hovering over the building.

"It looks like an Apache!"

"Quick. Let's take a closer look."

Some dark figures were rappelling down ropes dangling from the attack helicopter. There were only a handful of them—eight, perhaps. No. There were six. As they descended, they fired their sub-machine guns from their hips. Some soldiers on the ground were firing back. The firefight was deafening in the silence of the night. Soldiers were shouting and the sound of running boots was heard. An armored personnel carrier roared into life in the distance. A soldier atop the carrier fired at the intruders.

Within the room, the elder Wang had awakened. His minders were ushering him out into the corridor, rifles slung. Little Busy flitted after them. There were soldiers running in the corridor. Many were holding their rifles in their hands. Someone was shouting orders. As the soldiers ran out into the compound, some were gunned down by the intruders. Others retreated behind the door. In the corridor, above the soldiers, an intruder fired into the soldiers, knocking them down with precision. This commando took two shots at the soldiers with the elder Wang. They fell to the ground; they didn't even have time to unsling their rifles. They were not rangers after all—just plain clumsy regulars.

The remaining soldiers in the corridor fell one after another as other commandoes entered the building. Two commandoes grabbed the elder Wang and they scurried out of the building. Another two were in the compound watching the area. Two were engaged in a firefight with the armored personnel carrier. It was commandoes against armor. The rumbling of a heavy vehicle could be heard from behind the armored personnel carrier. A Leopard tank was lumbering towards the commandoes. There were a score of soldiers at its side. They fanned out across the two buildings.

The whole area was noisy and chaotic. The Apache was now hovering almost a metre above ground some thirty metres away in the open field.

The two commandoes and the elder Wang ran into the field, with another two close behind, covering their back. The last two commandoes lobbed some grenades at the armored personnel carrier and the tank. They too ran in the direction of the Apache.

It was almost like in the movies. Except this was for real. The cranking of the tank's cannon could be heard. Then a loud boom echoed through the air. The tank was firing at the Apache. It was like a sitting duck!

By now the armored personnel carrier had rolled into the open field. Its machine gun fired furiously at the commandoes. A commando dropped onto the ground. Another grabbed him and together they hobbled towards the Apache. The elder Wang was hit. So was the commando next to him. Two commandoes helped them into the Apache. The last two commandoes to board stood on a metal bar outside the helicopter which fanned the ground as it rose into the air.

Now the Apache was ready to take on the armored personnel carrier. It shot a rocket at the carrier, disabling it. The soldier atop the carrier was nowhere to be seen. Plumes of smoke were billowing from the top of the carrier.

The tank appeared at the side of the carrier. It cranked its cannon skywards taking aim at the Apache. But the Apache was now in its element. It promptly dispatched two anti-tank missiles at the tank, sending it up in balls of flames and plumes of smoke. It shot another two rockets at the first building, opening big gaping holes in its side. Apparently, it was targeting the laboratory where the elder Wang had been held.

All the while little Busy was perched on a louvred door, taking in the happenings and sending them to Kuan Hee and Lina.

"Dad's injured. Dad's injured."

Lina was wailing. "What shall we do? What shall we do?"

Kuan Hee wiped off his tears with a hand. He was emotional. He had to breathe hard and deeply. He had to calm down and collect his rampant thoughts.

Turning to Lina, he clutched her arm.

"We've got to get out of here. It will be crawling with soldiers soon."

"What?" Lina had yet to compose herself. She looked bewildered.

"Busy—got to get Busy back." He tapped furiously on the remote.

Then they ran into the darkness, with the buildings, the tank and the armored personnel carrier burning behind them.

CHAPTER 22

The walkie-talkie crackled into life. The Brigadier was calling Kuan Hee. Kuan Hee and Lina were now in the dimly lit open space outside Bukit Timah Plaza. The flyover towered overhead. They had run all the way from Maju Camp and were now taking a breather. They thought they were safe here.

"Kuan Hee, your father's safely with us. Over."

"Mr Walmsley. Is he badly injured? Over."

"How did you know? I was about to tell you. Over."

"I was there—in the field, watching the whole thing unfold. Over."

"I see. Your father is being fetched to a hospital on board our ship. I am told he was shot in the chest. But, not to worry, it's not near the heart. Over."

"Is he conscious? Can he talk? Does he respond? Over."

"He is unconscious now. But don't worry. We have the best medical equipment on board. He'll be fine. Over."

"Thank you very much, Mr Walmsley. Over."

"Another thing—your mum is also safe in our hands. Over."

"Is she? That's good news. That's great news. Where is she? Can I talk to her? Can I see her? Over."

"Hold your horses, Kuan Hee. Calm down. She's fine and shipshape. She's been taken to the same ship. Your parents will be together shortly. Over."

"It's a miracle. A real miracle. Mr Walmsley. Over."

"Yes, it is. We try to create miracles in the name of freedom. I'll contact you soon when I get status reports on your father's condition. Over."

"Thank you. Mr Walmsley. Over."

"In the meantime, Kuan Hee. Keep safe. Go into hiding. Do not do anything rash. You understand? Over."

"I understand, sir. I understand. Over."

"Mr Walmsley says I have to hide. We have to hide."

"Can we go back to Jalan Naung?"

"Yes, of course. Let's do it now."

Kuan Hee and Lina took an Uber ride back to Hougang. They alighted along Upper Serangoon Road, just before the start of Jalan Nuang. Then they trod towards his house. It was almost 5:00 a.m. In the silence of the night, they could hear their own footsteps. They were careful not to speak, for in the night, their conversation would appear crystal clear in the bedrooms of their sleeping neighbours. Who knew—one of them could snitch on them!

At the turn into the row of terrace houses next to his house, they paused. There was a car parked outside 79 Jalan Naung. It had a QX licence plate prefix. They could see two heads in the front seat of the car. The G men were looking for them.

"We can't go home right now."

"Where then? My house?"

"Alright. For tonight only."

"It's already morning, dear."

"Mmm."

By the time the pair made it into Lina's bedroom, it was already 5:20 a.m. Lina's mother had woken and left to do her marketing at the shops opposite the road.

The pair slept till late evening. They had been too tired the previous night. They had missed lunch. It was now dinner time. Lina's mother had cooked her favourite dishes today. They tucked into the food ravenously.

In the living room, the television was playing her mother's favourite Korean drama. Suddenly, the programme switched to a news studio and a news presenter appeared on the TV screen. The news bulletin was being broadcast live in English on a Chinese channel.

> This is a special news bulletin. Supreme Leader Tee Bak Chai passed away peacefully at 11:04 a.m. The National Reconciliation Council has appointed his son, Jordan Tee, as the new Supreme Leader. The armed forces have pledged allegiance to the new Supreme Leader whose appointment starts today.
>
> Supreme Leader Tee died of a heart attack. His body will lie in state at Parliament House from tomorrow at 9:00 a.m. till Sunday. A state funeral will be held on Sunday at 2:00 p.m.
>
> All flags will fly at half mast from today till the day of the funeral. The public is advised to wear black or non-bright colours till Sunday. All entertainment programmes are hereby cancelled.
> This concludes the special news bulletin.

The Korean programme was abruptly cancelled and instead sombre music was played the rest of the evening. It was the same on other channels in Singapore.

Kuan Hee and Lina stood glued to the television. They were shocked beyond words.

Is it true that Colonel Tee the dictator has died? they

wondered.

But Jordan had taken over as the Supreme Leader. That meant Colonel Tee had undergone the operation. But the operation was supposed to be this morning and Kuan Hee's father had been rescued early this morning.

"It only means one thing."

"What?"

"Colonel Tee had his operation, not this morning, but most probably yesterday morning. We were too late to prevent him from going ahead with it."

"So Colonel Tee is now Jordan?"

"Yes, dear, I'm afraid so."

"How can this happen? We overheard him saying Thursday."

"Yes, you and I heard it right. He must have got wind of something. He must have gotten suspicious. It could be big Tizzy. He must have realized it was a spying device and changed his schedule."

"So he is going to live! He's not dying after all."

"Yes, I'm afraid so. I'm afraid that's the unfortunate truth."

"We've got to do something or our whole life will be messed up. We won't have our freedom back. We won't be able to get on with our normal lives."

"We've got to meet up with Tim. And Navin. We've got to get their help to deal with this dictator."

"Yes. Yes."

"Lina, why is my Korean programme not showing?" asked Lina's mother. Lina explained to her mother what had happened.

WHATSAPP:

"Meet at usual place. 8:00 p.m. today," texted Lina.

"OK. *Long time no see.* Where have you guys been?" texted Tim.

"It's a long story," texted Lina.

> "Where the hell is Kuan Hee?" texted Tim.
> "With me," texted Lina.
> "Has he changed his phone number?" texted Tim.
> "Tell you everything when we meet," texted Lina.
> "OK," texted Tim.

"Tim must be pretty angry. He's never used 'hell' on me."

"Can't blame him. We practically disappeared, you know."

The usual place meant ToastBox café in Hougang Mall. The pair got their bags and, after saying goodbye to Lina's mother, went towards the lift.

"Look, there are police cars downstairs."

"Two of them. And there are plainclothes in the car park."

"And over there in the void deck at the opposite block."

"I have a sneaky feeling that they are looking for us. After Dad's escape, they must want me pretty bad. They need me to get Dad back."

"How did they know you are here?"

"Remember the police cameras in the lift lobby? I've always been suspicious of them. Looks like I'm right. The cameras are connected to a central monitoring station." Kuan Hee paused. He was in deep thought.

"They must have used supercomputers to do face recognition scans on all the camera footages in the lifts in Singapore. That's how they found me. They used algorithms. That must be it."

"They haven't come up for us yet."

"They still do not know which unit we are in—unless they do a house-to-house search. Gosh! I think that's what they are going to do soon. We've got to get out of here."

"How? They are downstairs."

"You can see that they have just arrived. We've still got time to make a getaway. Quick! Let's use that staircase."

The pair scrambled down sixteen flights of stairs—Lina lived on the eighth storey. There was a camera monitoring the bottom of this staircase but they had no time to bother about it. They snuck into the car park at the far end, away from the two police cars, and ran towards Upper Serangoon Road. It was a close shave.

"Lina, quick. Call your mother. Tell her to tell these people she has not seen me."

"OK. OK. I will."

"Phew. What a lucky escape."

CHAPTER 23

Tim was getting impatient. He had been sipping his cuppa waiting for Kuan Hee and Lina to turn up, and he had just finished the coffee. There was no sign of the pair. They finally did turn up, after sizing up the surroundings. Boy, did they had an earful from him.

"You guys are some bunch of friends," said Tim as the pair sat down beside him.

"Sorry. Sorry. A thousand apologies," said Kuan Hee.

"We're really sorry, Tim," said Lina.

"First, you disappeared for ages without so much as a word. Now you make me wait for you," said Tim. "What the hell is up with you guys anyway?"

It is the second time he is using this cuss word, thought Lina.

"You two guys, spending many weeks by yourselves, ignoring your best friend, worming into each other's hearts," said Tim.

"Wait a minute. Hold your horses," said Kuan Hee.

Then his voice dropped to a whisper. "Tim, we have got some serious stuff to discuss," he said. "But we can't do it here. Let's drink up and move somewhere else quieter."

The ToastBox cafe in Hougang Mall was only meant to

be a meeting point.

Hougang MRT Station was not a quiet station today. There were strange looking men, either standing or sitting on the benches next to the station, poring over the faces of people who entered the station. They had to be looking for Kuan Hee.

The three friends abandoned their plan to travel on the MRT. Instead, they took an Uber ride to Punggol Park, on the outskirts of Hougang town. They sat next to some swings on the playground. It was deserted.

Kuan Hee proceeded to tell Tim what had happened to him and his family the past few weeks. He ended with a blow-by-blow account of the commandoes' rescue mission in Maju Camp.

"Fancy going on an adventure of a lifetime without me," said Tim.

"No, it wasn't an adventure. It was dangerous. It was nerve-racking, you know," said Lina.

"Funny. There's nothing in the news about the attack on Maju Camp," said Tim.

"Yes, strange that it wasn't reported on," said Kuan Hee. "An attack by unknown military force not getting into the news is indeed strange."

"And it is true—Jordan is no longer the Jordan we know. He's become his father," said Tim.

"Yes. And my Dad was held in detention because Colonel Tee wanted him to do the operation for him and his son."

"So that's why Jordan went missing the day he was supposed to lead the protest in Orchard Road," said Tim.

"That's right. I had asked Jordan when he came to my house one night to seek shelter," said Kuan Hee. "He was in fear, but he wouldn't reveal what was happening—no matter how hard I tried to pry it out of him."

"Now he's become his father—the new dictator of Singapore," said Lina.

"Is that why you are on the run now?" said Tim.

"I have no choice. Colonel Tee or Jordan—whoever's in charge now wants to get my Dad through me," said Kuan Hee.

"What can we do?" asked Tim.

"That's the reason we are here—to discuss how to deal with Colonel Tee or Jordan," said Kuan Hee.

"We need weapons," said Tim, "if we are going against him or them."

"Yes. We need a plan too," said Kuan Hee. "I have a proposal."

"Out with it man," said Tim.

"I want to try to take him out on the day of the funeral," said Kuan Hee.

"How?" said Lina.

"As he—I mean Jordan follows the coffin, I intend to take a shot at him," said Kuan Hee.

"You want to kill Jordan?" said Lina.

"For goodness's sake, Lina. It's not Jordan now. Jordan's dead. It's Colonel Tee in Jordan's body. He's evil all over. If we don't kill him, he will continue to harm people. Singapore will not be safe from his clutches."

"I've got friends in the army. They are in national service but they work in the armory," said Tim.

"Good. We need some SAR21s," said Kuan Hee. "Also, try to get me a Steyr SSG 69."

"We've also got artillery. AleXander are our artillery," said Lina.

"But, they are too small to be of any use," said Tim.

"No. They are not. Alex has got laser weapons and Xander can launch rockets," said Lina.

"Calling Kuan Hee. Calling Kuan Hee. Over."

"It's the Brigadier," said Kuan Hee. He pulled out the walkie-talkie from his backpack.

"This is Kuan Hee. Over."

"Kuan Hee. I see they haven't caught you yet. Over."

"Mr Walmsley. You seem to be hinting they should catch me. Over."

"Kuan Hee. Just joking. Over."

"Me too, Mr Walmsley. I was just joking. Over."

"I am calling because I need to wrap up our operations. Over."

"What do you mean, Mr Walmsley? Over."

"It means—I need to get you out of the country—to safety. Over."

"Be with my parents? Over."

"Yes, Kuan Hee. Let you reunite with your parents. Isn't that great? Over."

"I'd love to join my parents. But I also need to tie up some loose ends here. Over."

"What exactly are you talking about? Over."

"I want to kill the dictator. Over."

"Don't be rash. Kuan Hee. You can't possibly do it alone. Just come with us to safety. Don't let your parents worry about you. Over."

"Are you going to join your parents?" asked Lina.

"You heard me right? I told him I am staying put. I'm going to kill Jordan Tee if it is the last thing I get to do," said Kuan Hee. "Don't try to dissuade me. I've made up my mind."

"Where are you staying now?" asked Tim.

"That is what I want to talk to you about," said Kuan Hee. "I can't put up at Lina's place anymore. The plainclothes are swarming over her place, looking for me there."

"So you want me to put you up. Is that it?" said Tim.

"Yeah. We're good friends, right? Buddies right?" said Kuan Hee.

"Yeah, but—" said Tim.

"No buts. Just do it," said Kuan Hee.

"I can't take you to my house. That's for sure," said Tim. "But—you can hide in the storeroom above my grandfather's shop."

"The one in Upper Serangoon Road—Ah Kong Reflexology Centre?" said Kuan Hee.

"That's the one," said Tim.

"That's a good idea," said Lina approvingly.

"So when can I move in?" asked Kuan Hee.

"You mean—we," said Lina.

"Both of you are staying?" said Tim.

"Appears so, Tim," said Kuan Hee.

"Let me ask my grandfather first," said Tim. "Give me a minute." Tim drew out his smartphone and tapped a button on it. Then he rattled off in *Hock Chew*. Being not conversant with the dialect, Kuan Hee and Lina didn't understand a single word.

"OK. Set. My grandfather's agreed," said Tim. "Shall we go there now?"

"Yes, let's," echoed the pair.

CHAPTER 24

Ah Kong Reflexology Centre was a foot massage shop in the middle of a row of three-storey shop houses along Upper Serangoon Road. Access to the upper floors was via a concrete staircase that ran the entire width of the shop. The staircase was situated outside the shop—on one side. As the three friends approached the shop, the pungent smell of liniments and Chinese herbs permeated the air.

"*Ah Kong*," all greeted in unison.

Tim's grandfather waved to them, said something to Tim and the threesome climbed the stairs. Tim had gotten a key to the second-storey premises from him. They found themselves in a wide corridor with two rooms on both ends and an open area in the centre. The toilet was in the rear. Tim opened the door on their right. The room was about the size of a HDB master-bedroom. He opened the glass-paneled windows to reveal the road below. Downstairs, on the roadside, were parked vehicles. Some cars were double-parked. It was a popular waiting area for vehicles, for a dozen food shops straddled the road. It was almost a dining paradise.

"Here's where you will be staying. No air-conditioning, I'm afraid. Only this table fan," said Tim. "The other room is a storeroom."

"It's a super place. No need for air-conditioning. The fan's great," said Kuan Hee. He placed his backpack on the small table at one wall.

"There's no bed," said Lina.

"No need for a bed. We can get a mat and some blankets from the shops later," said Kuan Hee.

"Sorry. This place isn't meant to be a bedroom," said Tim. "It is actually a spare storeroom."

"It's alright. We should be the ones saying sorry—for putting you out like this," said Kuan Hee.

"Let's get cracking," said Tim.

Tim got down to contacting his army mates while Kuan Hee phoned his friends in the students' union.

The spare storeroom above the shop was also the group's meeting venue. It took them two days to put together a workable plan to take down Supreme Leader Jordan Tee. In the meantime, Tim's army buddies had handed him the weapons he needed. These were laid out on the table in front of them.

"SAR21s," said Kuan Hee.

"Check. Three SAR21s," said Tim, "with a hundred cartridges."

"Steyr SSG 69," said Kuan Hee.

"Check. One Steyr SSG 69," said Tim, "with two magazines—each with five cartridges."

"Wah. It's so easy to get these weapons," said Lina.

"These are not from the active armories, so they won't be missed. These come from a five-year reserve stock," said Tim.

"What's that?" asked Lina.

"This is stuff kept in deep freeze—opened only in times of war," said Tim. "Too many of them stacked together in the warehouse. Nobody will miss a thing."

"I didn't know the Singapore army keeps such a large supply of weapons," said Lina. "These weapons must surely need many warehouses."

"The Singapore army not only has reserve weapons; it also has reserve tanks, armored personnel carriers, three-tonners and so on and so forth," said Tim.

"By George, where do they keep them?" asked Lina.

"Oh. That's a trade secret," said Tim, amused.

"We have to find bags long enough to fit these weapons," said Lina.

"No need, Lina. They can be taken apart and reassembled," said Tim. "They will fit in a backpack."

"Gosh. You guys are really cool," said Lina. "Fancy knowing how to handle these rifles."

"We didn't spend two years doing national service in the army for fun, you know," said Navin, chuckling as he ran his fingers over the SAR21 in his hands.

"Did you manage to get some grenades?" said Kuan Hee.

"Eh. That one—quite difficult to get our hands on," said Tim. "No luck."

"Never mind. What we have are good enough," said Kuan Hee. "We also have AeXander's rockets and laser weapon system."

"Did you manage to rope in Navin?" said Lina.

"Yeah. He's in on the plan," said Kuan Hee. He will join us tonight. We're all sleeping here tonight. Just in case."

"Don't you need to practice using the Steyr SSG 69?" said Lina.

"Lina, he doesn't. He went to sniper school during NS. He's unlike the rest of us army guys—he's a sharpshooter through and through," said Tim.

"I'm not that good," said Kuan Hee, blushing.

"He is—the best of the crop, Lina," said Tim.

"I believe you, Tim. I believe you," said Lina. Kuan Hee was always modest with his achievements.

"We'll wait for Navin to come before we go through tomorrow's mission," said Kuan Hee.

It was 9:00 p.m. when Kuan Hee, Lina and Tim finished their dinner. Navin had just arrived and they were now seated on the floor in the room. There was a long silence. Then Navin tuned in to an Internet radio station on his smartphone and pop music flooded the room.

"So everyone understands the high risks in tomorrow's operation," said Kuan Hee. All nodded.

"You can choose to back out now, if you wish to," said Kuan Hee. No one said a word.

"Navin, OK?" said Kuan Hee. "Your girlfriend?"

"OK. I didn't tell her a thing," said Navin.

"Tim? OK?" said Kuan Hee. Tim didn't have a girlfriend.

"Lina. You stay in the background—at this spot," said Kuan Hee, pointing to a spot on the map in front of them. "If anything goes awry, run and then hide. Do not turn back. Do not come to us—even if we are injured or— dead."

Lina was hesitant. Her lips were quivering. A moment ago she was nonchalant about the danger they were getting themselves into.

"Lina, do you understand?" said Kuan Hee.

"Eh. Yes," said Lina.

Kuan Hee went through their mission, detailing the positions each would take the next day. He got the rest to repeat what he had said. His national service stint was coming into good use.

"No one leaves this place from now on," said Kuan Hee. All nodded. "Tomorrow, we will take down the dictator." All nodded again.

"Our rendezvous is at Punggol Park after the mission, whether sunshine or rain," said Kuan Hee. Sunshine and rain were codes for success and failure respectively.

There were three guys and four rifles so one SAR21 was a spare which they would take with them—just in case. Then Kuan Hee, Navin and Tim cleaned their weapons. They let Lina try cleaning the spare SAR21.

The hours ticked away. Dawn was breaking but the mission members had not slept a wink. They lay resting against the wall, staring into space. No doubt, everyone was tense and uneasy.

What will tomorrow bring? they were wondering.

Navin was fingering a cigarette. He was the only smoker among the four friends.

"When Jordan falls—will another dictator take his place?" said Navin.

"I don't know. I really don't know," said Kuan Hee. He was right. The politics of a country was unpredictable. Just when you thought everything was going fine, someone might drop a bomb in your midst.

"We'll take one step at a time," said Tim.

"Yeah. Cross the bridge when we come to it," said Lina.

CHAPTER 25

The area around Parliament Building in North Bridge Road had been cordoned off. Armored personnel carriers guarded the junctions of High Street and Parliament Place. Soldiers formed a chain across these roads. There were spectators behind them, and along both sides of North Bridge Road. These people had come to bade farewell to the late Supreme Leader Colonel Tee, albeit involuntarily for most of them.

The mission members were across Elgin Bridge, in the crowd lining South Bridge Road. Security was not tight in this area; they could slip in unnoticed with their weapons. Navin and Tim's role was to fire at the soldiers and plainclothes after Kuan Hee had done his work. This would give some precious minutes for Kuan Hee to make his getaway. Lina was with the two men. Her job was to keep the spare SAR21 in her backpack. It was needed in case a rifle jammed. She had also been taught how to fire the SAR21 should the need arise.

Kuan Hee had taken up position on a staircase landing in an apartment building across the river. His target was within the effective range of the Steyr SSG 69 which was eight hundred metres. He had a clear line of sight of this part of North Bridge Road where the funeral procession would be moving through. There were army snipers at some buildings; the glint of light on their scopes gave away their positions. He made sure he was out of their sight.

The cortege of mourners was coming out of the front gate of Parliament House. As the procession turned into the main road, a convoy of vehicles—two Mercedes limousines and four Volvos joined the group of people surrounding the new Supreme Leader. Men were standing on both sides of the first two Volvos, holding on to opened doors. There had to be scores of these plainclothes mingling with the procession. The Supreme Leader, with his mother next to him, was flanked by his bodyguards.

Kuan Hee loaded the magazine and readied the rifle. The magazine held five rounds. He could take five shots without having to reload. His sweaty hands slid slightly on the smooth molded fiberglass. He grabbed the frame firmly. Then he cocked the Steyr SSG 69 and pressed his eye against the scope. The new Supreme Leader had come into its cross-hairs. He took a deep breath and held it. Then he squeezed the trigger. A shot rang out and, in the distance, there was a cry. Then pandemonium set in. Bodyguards were clambering over the new Supreme Leader and bundling him into the nearby Mercedes.

Have I hit him? wondered Kuan Hee.

He wasn't sure. He didn't get to make a second shot, for some army snipers were now targeting his position. A few bullets whizzed through the air. Some hit the wall, two ricocheted off the wall, with one landing in his left shoulder. It was piercing pain that hit him. Kuan Hee knew he had to leave fast. He slung the rifle on one shoulder and clambered down the stairs to the ground floor. It was now his team members' job to keep the soldiers and plainclothes busy so that he could make his getaway safely.

Lina was at the bottom of the stairs waiting for him. She had been worried and, despite his order, had run to the apartment building to look for him. She was in a frenzy when she spotted him. But she recovered from shock in time to help stop the bleeding from his wound with a packet of tissue paper. Both swaggered towards New Bridge Road. They stopped along the way for a few seconds so he could dismantle the rifle and put it in his backpack.

At the chaotic scene, Navin and Tim fired at the soldiers and plainclothes. People were running in all directions. The duo were careful not to shoot into the crowd. Then they ran into a row of shop houses and turned into the streets of Chinatown. Hovering in the air were two drones. Navin shot them down easily, for he was a marksman in his NS days. Then they dismantled their rifles and mingled with the crowd. As planned, Navin and Tim separated in Hong Kong Street. They would meet at Punggol Park.

Lina and Kuan Hee had not counted on him being injured. With his injury, there was no way he could move through crowded Singapore without being spotted. Lina phoned her eldest brother for help. The pair took cover in the staircase of an old shop house.

Her brother arrived in his van within fifteen minutes— he had been on an errand for his company—buying cartons of toilet paper. He hid the pair under bags of toilet paper and drove off. He drove along Merchant Road towards Clemenceau Avenue. There was a road block being prepared at the junction ahead. Soldiers were hastily getting metal barricades off a three-tonner. A soldier raised his hand to signal to Lina's brother to stop the vehicle. The soldier was disarmed by her brother's co-operative gesture—he had volunteered to unload the cargo onto the road for the soldier to inspect the van. He waved the van off.

The van raced through the city area and entered the suburban districts. Then it cruised into Hougang. Lina's brother stopped the van in the car park of Punggol Park.

Then he opened the door and jumped in.

"The coast is clear," said Lina's brother. "You can come out now."

Lina and Kuan Hee pushed aside the bags of toilet paper. Her hands were coated with blood, so were her blouse and shorts. Luckily, she managed to stop the bleeding. Kuan Hee was feeling faint. He was in pain.

There was no sign of Tim or Navin. Hopefully they had managed to escape. She couldn't phone them. They had agreed not to use their smartphones for fear their calls were being monitored.

"He needs medical attention urgently. We can't wait for your friends," said Lina's brother.

"Where shall we go? said Lina. "Kuan Hee, what shall I do?" But Kuan Hee was delirious and could not hear her.

"Let's take him to Dr Koh. He won't tell on us," said Lina's brother. Dr Koh had been the Goh family's go-to doctor for many years. He ran a clinic in Hougang Avenue Five.

"OK. Let's move, then," said Lina.

Her brother drove them to Hougang Avenue Five. He left them in the van and strode to the clinic to speak to the doctor. Then he returned to take the pair into the clinic through the back door. The clinic had already closed for business but the doctor was still in. The doctor had shooed off his clinic assistant before opening the back door for the sudden visitors.

"The bullet is lodged in the flesh. Luckily, it's not pierced any organs. Landed away from the heart and missed the clavicle—the collar bone—by almost a centimetre. Lucky chap," said Dr Koh. "I'll have to pry it out."

He took a pair of forceps and some gauze to clean the wound. Then he injected an anesthetic into the skin around the wound. He waited for a minute for the anesthetic to take effect and proceeded to remove the bullet from the shoulder with another pair of forceps.

Kuan Hee was feverish and incoherent.

"He'll be fine. No major damage done," said Dr Koh. "I'll give him some antibiotics to kill the germs."

"Doctor, he is still running a fever. What shall I do?" said Lina.

"I've given him an antipyretic injection. The fever will subside within hours. In the meantime, you'll need to monitor his condition. Let him take the paracetamol as prescribed. If his condition worsens, you can call me."

"Thank you, doctor," said Lina.

"Here's the bullet. It seems different from bullets I have seen," said Dr Koh. "Dispose of it where no one can find—he's a brave lad, fighting the dictatorship. Not many fine youngsters like him nowadays."

"Thank you for saving his life, doctor," said Lina.

"No problem. It's my duty to save people," said Dr Koh. "Just be careful with him for the next few days. Remember—no seafood for a week."

"I'll. I'll. Bye Dr Koh," said Lina.

Dr Koh switched off the lights in the clinic. He did not want to draw attention. He opened the back door, glanced around and then waved them to the door. He watched them getting into the van before closing the door.

"Where to now?" asked Lina's brother. She directed him to Ah Kong's shop in Upper Serangoon. It was late evening and darkness was setting in. Her brother waited till the walkway was clear of people before carrying Kuan Hee up into the second-storey premises. Then he left.

Lina did not switch on the lights; there was ambient light from the road outside filtering into the room through the windows. There they were—Kuan Hee lying motionless on a mat and she sitting next to him, fingering his hair. She would look at the bundle of bloodied clothes in the supermarket bag across from them. Then she would look at Kuan Hee. Occasionally, she would wipe off her tears and then with the same wet fingers, she would pat his hair. When she undertook to join the mission, Kuan Hee had told her that injury was a foreseeable result, but she had not counted on it actually happening—not to her beloved Kuan Hee. She was in a bind. Not knowing what to do next, she thought the best thing was to do nothing but wait—wait for Kuan Hee to wake up, wait for Tim and Navin to return. She hoped they were alright.

It was 1:00 a.m. Lina heard some sounds coming from the corridor. First, it was a door creaking open. Then, it was the patter of footsteps. She froze. She held Kuan Hee close to her.

What am I to do now? she wondered.

The door opened and who did she see standing there?—Navin and Tim!

"I'm so glad to see both of you," said Lina. She was now tearing.

"How's he?" asked Navin.

"His fever is going down. The doctor has given him some fever medicine." Then she told the two men what had happened in their absence.

"He's indeed lucky. He escaped death," said Navin. He related how Tim and he made their escape. When they reached the rendezvous place, there was no sign of the pair. They waited in vain for hours. They thought something bad had happened to the pair. Then they decided to return to the shop, hoping against hope that the pair would be there.

"It's good both of you are safe," said Navin.

"We need to hide the weapons," said Tim. "It's too dangerous to keep them here. There are workers coming up and down regularly for the goods on the second level."

"Let's bury them," said Navin.

"It's a good idea," said Tim. "I'll think of a place."

"Aren't you going to return them to your army friends?" asked Lina.

"We may need them later," said Tim. "Besides, the weapons won't be missed for months. And if we can end the dictatorship, my army friends won't get into trouble."

"Any news on the Supreme Leader?" asked Lina. "I've been too busy taking care of Kuan Hee to do anything else."

"It appears he wasn't injured. Someone behind him took the bullet for him," said Navin. "That's what the news said."

"I don't trust the news. It's all propaganda," said Tim. "The only way to be sure he is unharmed is to see him on live television."

"We went to so much trouble," said Lina, "and Kuan Hee got hurt badly as a result—and this guy—nothing has happened to this guy?"

There was silence in the dark room.

"Lina, look. There are pictures of you and Kuan Hee on channelsingapore.com. You are wanted by the military government," said Navin.

"These shots were taken yesterday," said Tim. "The cameras must have caught you leaving the apartment building."

Lina looked at the news article, then at her two friends. She was sullen.

"They are bound to identify me. What if they go after my mother—and my brothers?" said Lina in despair.

Navin and Tim had no answer.

Kuan Hee, Kuan Hee, if you could only wake up and tell me what to do, she thought. But Kuan Hee had not heard her thoughts. He was asleep.

CHAPTER 26

Early next morning, Navin and Tim left in a car that Navin had borrowed from his brother. They had taken the weapons and ammunition with them. Kuan Hee was still asleep. There were many thoughts running through Lina's mind; she had not slept the whole night.

"Calling Kuan Hee. Calling Kuan Hee. Over."

It was the Brigadier on the walkie-talkie. Lina got out the walkie talkie from the backpack. She pressed the PTT button.

"Yes, Brigadier Walmsley. This is Lina. Eh. Over."

"Oh it's you, Lina. Where is Kuan Hee? I need to talk to him. Over."

"Kuan Hee—he's—he's unconscious. He was shot in his shoulder. Over."

There was a moment of silence.

"I see. Is he the one who attempted to assassinate the Supreme Leader? Over."

"Yes. He, me, and some friends of ours. But he's the only one injured. Over."

"Is his condition serious? Have you sought medical attention? Over."

"His fever has subsided, but he hasn't woken yet. A

doctor removed the bullet from his shoulder. He said he'll be fine—only a flesh wound. Over."

There was silence over the airwaves again.

"I see. Lina, when he wakes up, can you tell him his father's in stable condition. He is now conscious. He wants to talk to Kuan Hee. Over."

"He's conscious now? That's great news. I'll tell Kuan Hee. I'll ask him to call you. Over." Lina was beaming. She had forgotten her woes—for the moment.

"And, Lina. If his condition becomes worse—call me. Over."

"I'll, Brigadier Walmsley. Over."

"Keep safe. Don't do rash things. Bye for now. Over."

"Bye bye, Brigadier Walmsley. Over."

Lina put down the transceiver. She flashed a weak smile.

Kuan Hee will be so happy to learn his father is awake and in stable condition, Lina thought.

"Kuan Hee, when are you going to wake up? I'm all alone. I'm afraid." He did not answer her.

Navin had told her to turn off her smartphone. The G men could be tracking signals from her smartphone. She remembered Kuan Hee's iPhone was powered by the Polaris satellite. She used his iPhone to surf the Websites. She was looking for news of the assassination and their wanted status.

On the Ministry of Homeland Security's Website, there were grainy pictures of her and Kuan Hee. There were no names mentioned—only pictures. Perhaps, the G had not been able to identify them positively. Perhaps, it was hoping people would recognize them and feed information to the G.

There were no reports on Navin and Tim. The G had not got wind of them yet.

At least, things are not that bad, Lina told herself.

It was midmorning when Kuan Hee stirred. Lina

opened her eyes. She had felt him touch her arm. Kuan Hee had woken.

"Where am I?" He had opened his eyes and was now looking around the room. Then he remembered where he was. "Lina, your eyes are red."

"Thank God you are awake. I was so worried."

Kuan Hee by now was conscious of his surroundings and of the situation they were in.

He pressed two fingers on his eyebrows. "Have Navin and Tim got away safely?"

"Yes, dear. They are safe and well. They've gone to hide the weapons."

"You look thin. Have you eaten?" He looked around again. There were some buns on the table.

"Tim bought some buns from a bakery. But I wasn't hungry. Kuan Hee, we are now fugitives. Our pictures are everywhere on the news Websites."

"It's alright, Lina. We can handle it. Just need to be more careful."

"And Kuan Hee, the Brigadier called this morning. Your father—he's conscious and in stable condition."

Kuan Hee's pale face lit up.

"He is? What else did Mr Walmsley say?"

"He wants you to call him."

"Quick, pass me the walkie-talkie."

Lina handed him the walkie-talkie.

"Calling Mr Walmsley. This is Kuan Hee. Calling Mr Walmsley. Over."

"Hi. Kuan Hee. You are awake. Over."

"Mr Walmsley. My father—he's OK? Really OK? Over."

"Yes, Kuan Hee. Alive and kicking. Do you want to talk to him? Over."

"Yes, Mr Walmsley, Of course. When? How? Over."

"In fact, he's right here now—next to me. I'm on the ship with him. Let me pass the walkie-talkie to him. Eh. Professor Wang, your son. Kuan Hee wants to speak with you … Kuan Hee, Kuan Hee. It's Dad. Are you alright, son? Over."

"Yes, Dad. Great to hear your voice again. How are you and Mum? Over."

"We're fine, son. Say hallo to your mum. Over."

"Hi. Mum. Miss you guys. Over."

"Hi. Kuan Hee. Your Dad is fine. He can walk now. I'm worried about you. Is your shoulder better? Over."

"Mum and Dad. I am OK. Really miss you guys. Over." Kuan Hee was at a loss for words. The Wang family was reunited again—albeit over the airwaves.

Soon we'll be together, soon, thought Kuan Hee.

"Son, I have an important thing to tell you. Listen carefully. Over."

"Yes Dad. I'm all ears. Go ahead. Over."

"Kuan Hee. You know I operated on Colonel Tee's mind. Colonel Tee's memories are now embedded in his son, Jordan's mind. Over."

"Yes, Dad. I know. Over."

"Now, here's the important part. I deliberately created a schizophrenic condition during the memory transfer process. So now, Colonel Tee does not control Jordan's mind completely. At times, Jordan's memories will overlap with his memories. I did not erase Jordan's memories completely. Do you understand me so far, son? Eh. Over."

"Yes, Dad. You mean Colonel Tee is now like Dr Jekyll and Mr Hyde in Robert Louis Stevenson's novel? Over."

"Correct, son. I purposely created a Jekyll and Hyde condition in their memories. Over."

"Dad, what can Jordan do? He's powerless. Over."

"But, you see, son. His men do not know he's Jordan. You and I know. That's the difference. Over."

"I understand. Dad. How do I wake up Jordan? How do I know when Jordan is in control? Over."

"Now that's a problem. Actually, I couldn't find a way to activate Jordan's memories. Otherwise, it would have been plain sailing—just switch over to Jordan permanently and everything is OK again in the country. The only way is to observe them. See when they are Jordan and when they are Colonel Tee. Use the housefly and the dragonfly. Over."

"OK, Dad. I understand. Over."

"Son, now we have a way to deal with Colonel Tee. Listen. When Colonel Tee acts like Jordan—when he talks like Jordan, persuade him to undo the harm his father has done to the country. Over."

"How? Dad. Over."

"Son. Difficult as it is—You are going to have to ask Jordan to kill himself. Save the country by killing himself. Over."

There was silence. Kuan Hee was shocked by his father's words.

"Kuan Hee. Listen. You have to do it. That's the only way to rid Singapore of this menace. Over."

There was no response from Kuan Hee again.

"Kuan Hee. Listen again. If this is difficult to do. Find another way. Use their Jekyll and Hyde condition to deal with Colonel Tee. Over."

"OK, Dad. I will think over what you have said. Over."

"You heard what my Dad said, right?" said Kuan Hee. "What shall I do?" Kuan Hee had indeed forgotten he had told himself Jordan was now no longer the Jordan they knew.

Minutes later, Kuan Hee spoke again.

"Another way—my Dad mentioned, another way. I need to think over this other way." Lina left him to his thoughts. When Kuan Hee behaved like this, it would be hours before he spoke to her—or any one else. It was typical Kuan Hee syndrome. He was having a recurring attack now. Suddenly, she felt hungry. She devoured the buns on the table.

"Lina, I'm famished. Let's get something to eat." It was

2:30 p.m. and Kuan Hee had finished with his thoughts and his stomach was growling. But Lina had cleaned the table of the buns.

"We can't go out yet. It's not safe. Let's wait a little longer. Navin and Tim should be back soon."

"Let's not wait. I'm really hungry; I could eat a horse."

"But you haven't fully recovered. You still look pale."

There was just no dissuading Kuan Hee when he had made up his mind.

CHAPTER 27

Kuan Hee and Lina were now fugitives. There were pictures of them, albeit grainy ones, flashed across five-metre tall screens mounted at vantage points on buildings and at traffic light junctions. These screens, a common fixture across the island, served advertisements and government notices.

The pair were just across the road from Kovan Heartland Mall when they saw their faces on the large screens. The G notice accompanying their pictures had this statement:

Wanted!
Reward offered for information leading to the identification and arrest of the following persons:

The pair instantly recognized themselves. But it would take a discerning eye to pick them out from the throng of people in the streets. And both were now wearing baseball caps. They would have worn face masks if they could but in this day and age, face masks were banned. It had been banned in many countries around the world since the early

2020s.

Soon the pair were at McDonald's, located at the other end of the Kovan Neighbourhood Centre.

"I didn't get your favourite Quarter Pounder for you. I thought Filet-O-Fish would be better—till you fully recover."

They were indeed hungry. Both wolfed down their food. Their next stop was to be NEX Shopping Mall. They wanted to buy some clothes to replace the ones which were soiled with blood. It was crazy; these two were travelling around when the military government was looking for them. Weren't they afraid? In fact, Kuan Hee was trying to lift Lina's spirits. She had been cooped up for ages, and it would do her a world of good to move around—do the things they usually did together. She would feel better, he had hoped. She sorely needed the change.

The pair had come out of the train at Serangoon MRT Station and were moving up the escalator, heading for the exit point. It was then that some police officers of the Transport Command on the lower platform took notice of them and started climbing the same escalator. They were going after them.

Kuan Hee saw them behind the pair and motioned to Lina to run up the final few steps of the escalator. Instead of heading for the exit point, they turned into the passageway leading to the Circle Line. They ran onto a long travelator, brushed past other commuters and strode towards the other end of the travelator. The policemen were hot on their heels.

They ran down another escalator to the lower platform of the Circle Line's Serangoon Station. The train was unloading passengers at this station and the pair dashed in just in time, for the doors were closing onto Kuan Hee's backpack. The first few of the policemen were too late. They could only watch the train with the pair inside ramble off. Kuan Hee took a deep breath and held his injured shoulder. The pain had returned. He had overexerted himself, but he told Lina he was all right.

At the next station, the pair got off and waited for the next train moving in the opposite direction. They were heading back to Serangoon. Kuan Hee had said other policemen could be lying in wait for them at the next few stations. The train came in two minutes and the pair went in. They were careful to keep their faces away from the overhead cameras on the train. This train stopped at Serangoon Station, where minutes earlier they had boarded another train. They got off at this station and walked back to the North-East Line's Serangoon Station. This time they blended with the crowd of passengers heading in the same direction.

On the platform of North-East Line's Serangoon Station, the pair boarded a train heading towards Harbourfront. They thought they had shaken off their pursuers. But they were wrong. At Dhoby Ghaut Interchange, there were policemen piling onto the platform. Evidently they had got wind of the pair's movement. They were waiting for the train to come to a stop. Their eyes were on the passengers on the train. Kuan Hee and Lina were trapped. It would be difficult for them to escape. Luckily, the train cars were teeming with passengers for Dhoby Ghaut Interchange was a busy station. The pair squeezed through the packed platform, hunching their backs and making sure they were in the thick of the crowd of passengers.

But lady luck was against them this time. They thought they were clever, but they had forgotten their caps were a giveaway. An eagle-eyed policeman had spotted their caps and signaled to the others the pair's position. Then all hell broke loose as the policemen congregated near the escalator which the pair were about to board. The crowd was terrified for policemen were running into them. Two policemen elbowed their way into the crowd and grabbed hold of Kuan Hee. They couldn't reach Lina, for she had followed the other passengers up the long escalator to the ground level. It was too late for Kuan Hee. He had been caught. Lina made a getaway when she reached the entrance of the station. Soon she was out of sight of the station. She sat sobbing at a corner of a building, oblivious to the curious stares of passers-by.

Kuan Hee was bundled into a van and taken to the Police Cantonment Complex in New Bridge Road. His personal belongings and belt were taken from him and placed in a big envelope which had his name written on it. Then he was taken to a holding cell of the Warrant Enforcement Unit. It was slightly bigger than an HDB living room. The floor was concrete screed. At the opposite end of the cell door was a squat pan with a low concrete wall next to it, presumably to afford some privacy to the squat pan user. Except for this, the room was bare. There were three other male occupants in the cell.

No one said a word to him in the first two hours he spent in the cell. He was not told why they were holding him. Nor was he charged with a crime.

Then a policeman came for him. He was handcuffed and taken upstairs to a room on the third level. It seemed to be an interview room. There was a video camera standing on one side of the room. A table and two chairs were the only other furniture in the room. The policeman handcuffed him to a chair and left the room.

It was cold in the room. It was to be another half hour before the door opened and two policemen walked in. One had three pips on his epaulette—a Senior Inspector. The other had a crest and two pips—a Superintendent.

The Superintendent sat opposite Kuan Hee. He took out an Identification Card from an envelope and placed it on the table.

"You must be Wang Kuan Hee."

"Yes. I am him, sir."

"Do you know why you are here?"

"No, sir."

"Let me tell you."

The Superintendent took out a large photograph from the envelope and placed it in front of Kuan Hee. It was a grainy picture of Kuan Hee in a lift lobby.

"Does this face ring a bell?"

"Yes, sir. He looks like me."

"Yes, indeed. Do you know who he is?"

"No, sir."

"Let me tell you then. He is a suspected killer."

"Killer, sir? Whom did he kill?"

"Oh. My mistake. He did not kill anyone. He attempted to kill the Supreme Leader of the NRC."

"He is that brave? Fancy having the guts to kill the Prime Minister of the country."

"Yes. He sure is brave. He had the guts, as you have said, to kill a VIP of the country. An ordinary person would not dare to do such a thing. In fact, many brave souls in this country also do not have the courage to carry out an assassination on this VIP."

"I am not him, sir."

"You do not look like a brave chap, I must say."

"Of course, sir. I am timid. I am *kiasi*. I will never be able to summon the courage to kill a person."

"Assuming you were this guy—why would you want to risk your life doing such a dangerous thing?"

"For life, liberty and the pursuit of happiness, of course."

"Well said. Very well said."

The Superintendent clenched his fists and paused for some minutes.

"Kumar."

"Yes, sir."

"Take him away. Return his things. Set him free."

"Sir? This man is a highly wanted criminal."

"Wanted by whom, Kumar?"

"Wanted by the military government, of course."

"So are we the military, Kumar?"

"No, sir, but we report to them, sir."

"We don't report to them. We report to the Commissioner of Police. And he is in their custody. So we report to no one now. Do you understand?"

"Yes, sir. I understand, sir."

"Kumar—do as you are told."

"Yes, sir."

"And Kumar—don't tell a soul."

"Sir, how do I report this?"

"Do you need me to tell you exactly what you need to do?"

"Yes, sir. I mean, no, sir."

"Kumar, report this as a case of mistaken identity."

"Yes, sir. I will do as ordered, sir."

Turning to Kuan Hee, the Superintendent nodded and left the room.

CHAPTER 28

It was a tired Kuan Hee who climbed the stairs to the storeroom above Ah Kong Reflexology Centre. He had no way to contact Lina, for she could not use her smartphone. He thought she had to be here—there was nowhere else for her to go. She could not go home.

As he opened the door, he saw, in the dark room, a figure curled up in a corner, sobbing away. Outside, the traffic droned and the buses rumbled.

He reached for the figure, grasped it with his arms and sobbed in unison with it.

"Kuan Hee. I am scared."

"Me too. Me too."

"Don't leave me. Don't ever leave me, Kuan Hee."

"I won't. I won't."

"Promise me, promise me."

That said, she held him in her bosom. In the darkness, the pair felt their emptiness spread thin and vanish. In its place now was the warmth of their hearts. In each other, they had found home.

"Kuan Hee, I—I want."

She needn't wait long this time. He had glided out of his clothes and was helping her take off hers.

She pushed him into her warm home.

"In there, you're safe. With you, I am safe."

"Mmm."

"Kuan Hee."

"What?"

"I don't want to get pregnant."

"I'll use a condom."

"I don't want a condom. No feeling."

"*Alamak!* What do you want?"

"I want you."

"Alright. I know what to do. Trust me."

The next morning, Navin and Tim finally turned up at the storeroom.

"Where have you been?" asked Kuan Hee.

"You guys went missing for days," said Lina.

"It's a long story," said Tim.

"We kept waiting for you guys," said Lina. "We thought you would be back by noon that day."

"The situation was getting dire. There were road blocks everywhere. Instead of coming here, we went home," said Tim. "We thought if we stayed together, everyone would be caught together. If we were in different places, there is still a chance of survival for some of us."

"The army and the police are swarming the island looking for the people behind the assassination attempt," said Navin. "Every which way we went, there were soldiers and roadblocks."

"I know," said Kuan Hee. "I got caught in the MRT station."

"You did?" said Navin. "You are damned lucky then. You are still here—safe and sound."

"How did you get free?" said Tim. "Did you escape?"

"No, *lah*," said Kuan Hee. "They let me go."

"They let you go?" said Navin. "Just like that? Did they follow you here? Perhaps, it's just a ruse—they want to catch us all in one fell swoop."

"Yeah, I agree," said Tim. He was suddenly a bundle of nerves. "What if they are waiting for us outside? Oh God. My grandfather—they will shut this place for good."

"Calm down, everyone," said Kuan Hee. "Sit down. All of you. Keep away from the window."

It took some minutes before the group of friends collected themselves and the uneasiness subsided.

"My guess—is that the police are not keen on catching us," said Kuan Hee. "The Superintendent who interviewed me said something about the Police Commissioner being held in detention by the army. When he came to this part, he sounded defiant. It was as if he was sore about the matter. And he gave me a strange look when he left the room."

"What strange look is that?" asked Navin.

"I can't put my finger on it," said Kuan Hee. "He nodded to me—as if approving my actions. But he didn't say a word—not a single word."

"That's really strange," said Navin.

"Calling Kuan Hee. This is James Walmsley. Over."

Kuan Hee reached for the walkie-talkie in his backpack.

"Yes, Mr Walmsley. This is Kuan Hee speaking. Over."

"Kuan Hee, I am calling to tell you the military regime is facing a backlash from the police soon. It seems the police top brass are indignant that their Commissioner has been held incommunicado for a long time. Tension between the police and the army is simmering. Now is a good time for you to act. Get Jordan to do work for you. Over."

"Does it mean the police will help us rid Singapore of the dictator? Over."

"Yes. And it's going to be messy with the police and the army at loggerheads. Over."

"What shall I do with Jordan? Over."

"Get him to release the Police Commissioner. Over."

"How about the army generals? Over."

"He won't be able to release them. The moment he gives the order, his men will smell a rat. That won't be good for us. Over."

"Mr Walmsley, I'll try my best. Mr Walmsley, tell my Mum and Dad I miss them. Over."

"Thank you, Kuan Hee. And don't worry, I'll send your regards to your parents. Over."

"You guys heard what the Brigadier said. We've got to get to Jordan," said Kuan Hee.

"There are too many of us," said Kuan Hee. "The G men will be suspicious."

"What do you suggest then?" said Navin.

"I think—let's do it this way. Lina and I will approach Jordan. You and Tim will be the backup. You two will create a ruckus outside so that we can have some time alone with Jordan."

"One question, Kuan Hee. How will you know when he is Jordan and when he is Colonel Tee?" asked Navin.

"Yeah, how?" echoed Lina.

"Eh. That one—I have no answer," said Kuan Hee, tapping his fingers on his lap. "We'll watch them till Jordan's side appears."

"That'll be forever," said Tim. "We can't wait forever."

Kuan Hee paused in thought. "OK. We'll do this— Lina and I will watch them," said Kuan Hee. "You two will not be involved at this stage. Wait till we have had a chance to talk to Jordan. Then we will get you into the picture. OK?"

"That's fine by me," said Navin.

"Me too," said Tim.

Kuan Hee and Lina were again on Holland Road. This time, they reprised their artist routine. Both pretended to take perspectives of the Tanglin Complex and its surroundings. Then they sat down to work, drawing their creation. In the meantime, little Busy was flitting up towards the Supreme Leader's office on the second level of Tanglin Complex. Soon the robot drone was hovering over the Supreme Leader's desk. He was reading something on his large screen. It was a news Website—Channel Singapore. There was no one in the room. This time, the ceiling lights were switched on, flooding the room with brightness it had not been accustomed to seeing in a long time. The window behind the Supreme Leader's desk showed a clear view of the lush garden behind.

"It's strange—not like before."

"I thought Colonel Tee liked dark places."

"I thought so, too. This is unlike the Colonel."

"There's only one explanation—Jordan is in charge of his own mind now. It means—we've got to act, and fast."

"What if we are wrong?"

"We have no choice. Time is against us. Besides, we are out here. He's in there. It's safe. Nothing ventured, nothing gained, they say."

"I'll try using the microphone to talk to him."

Kuan Hee manoeuvred little Busy towards Jordan. Now it was just above his ears.

"Not too loud, or else someone outside will hear us."

"Here goes nothing."

"Jordan, Jordan."

Jordan tilted his head. He had heard something. He turned to his side. There it was—little Busy was hovering in front of him. Jordan looked perplexed.

"Who's that?"

"Jordan, it's me—Kuan Hee."

"Kuan Hee? Where are you?"

"I'm outside. I'm speaking through the drone's speaker."

"Is that really you, Kuan Hee?"

"It's my voice, for goodness's sake. Can't you recognise it?"

"Alright. Alright."

"How have you been, Jordan?"

"Well, sometimes I know where I am and at times I seem to be asleep. I can't put my finger on it."

"Jordan. Do you know you are your father right now? Oh gosh. I said wrongly. I mean, do you know your father's in you—in your mind, with you?"

"I kinda guess so, Kuan Hee. I see my father's men bowing to me and asking me for instructions. And sometimes I just lose consciousness and I don't know a thing. Then I wake up—like right now, and see myself again."

Jordan, your father is using your body. He's dead but his mind's alive and kicking. It's living in your brain with you."

"I thought so, too Kuan Hee. You must want something from me, Kuan Hee. What is it?"

Kuan Hee knew Jordan was smart. He was not only smart. His mind was quick too. He always got to be top student in polytechnic. And in university, he topped the examinations again. Maybe, that was why he was chosen as Student Leader at Temasek University.

"Jordan, I need your help. The Police Commissioner has been detained for ages on trumped-up charges. He is innocent. The police force needs him. Can you release him?"

"The Police Commissioner? Why did my father jail him? He's a good man. He's incorruptible. I remember during our polytechnic days we invited him to speak at a forum on law and order. He was humble but intensely knowledgable."

"Yes, I remember."

"I think you already know—your father has thrown into jail all who oppose his rule. The Police Commissioner is different from your father."

"Let me think—how to go about doing it. You know, these few days—I've been slipping in and out of consciousness. In my conscious times, I've been reading up, keeping myself abreast of happenings," said Jordan. "I read—you tried to kill me. Why? Kuan Hee? We are good friends."

"Jordan. Eh. I—it was a difficult decision for me," said Kuan Hee. "You were Colonel Tee—your father. At that time, I didn't know you could be yourself again. Honest. I didn't know. Otherwise—"

"But we are good friends—buddies, Kuan Hee," said Jordan. "How—aargh, my head, it hurts…"

"Men," called Colonel Tee. A minder came into the room. "I seem to hear some voices in the room."

"Sir, there's no one in the room."

"Are you saying I'm lying?"

"No, sir. Not that. I'll check the room again, sir."

"Why is my room so bright? Who switched on the lights? And who drew back the curtains?"

It was time for little Busy to fly back to the pair.

"Lina, we've got to get the hell out of here—the G men are turning the corner on the main road."

"They are making their rounds again? So fast?"

"Quick! Lina!"

CHAPTER 29

It was splashed on the front page of the local newspapers.

Army releases Police Commissioner

"Eh. Kuan Hee. Good news!" said Tim. "Here, take a look at the headlines."

Kuan Hee and Lina huddled over the newspaper.

"He's really done it," said Kuan Hee. "It's been a week. I thought he didn't want to help us. After all I tried to kill him."

"Could be—Jordan didn't get a chance to occupy his own mind. Maybe, the last few days, Colonel Tee was in control of Jordan's mind," said Tim.

"Yes, that could be it," said Kuan Hee.

"Good job, Kuan Hee," said Tim.

"Calling Kuan Hee. This is James Walmsley. Over."

It was the Brigadier again on the walkie-talkie.

"Mr Walmsley, I'm here. Over."

"Kuan Hee. Marvellous work. Simply marvellous. You have helped a great cause. Over."

"It's not only me, Mr Walmsley. It's also Lina, Navin

and Tim. They all chipped in. Over."

"Well done, all of you. My friends in the police force say they are preparing for a confrontation with the army. Now that the Police Commissioner is back safely, they see no reason to let the military destroy the country. Are you listening, Kuan Hee? Over."

"Yes, Mr Walmsley. I'm all ears."

"Sorry I'm being long-winded, boy. It's old age, you know. You just want to ramble on and on. Now, back to important things—listen carefully, my boy. The police are planning a pre-emptive strike on the Supreme Leader in two days' time. That's Friday. Do you copy? Over."

"Yes. I copy you. Pre-emptive strike on Friday, right? Over."

"Correct, Kuan Hee. The police commandoes plan to take over the Ministry of Defence and attack the Supreme Leader's office in Tanglin. ETA 5:00 a.m. Friday. Do you copy? Over."

"I copy, Mr Walmsley. Over."

"Now, what I need you to do is—get Jordan to release the army generals. Over."

"But, Mr Walmsley. The Colonel's men may not obey Jordan's orders. Over."

"That's where you come in, Kuan Hee. Your father has proposed something. Your father wants you to use AleXanders' rockets and laser systems to create a diversion at Tanglin Complex. Make it appear as if some people are attacking the premises. His minders will be kept busy. Then, get Jordan to run off with you. Are you following me so far, Kuan Hee? Over."

"Yes. Mr Walmsley. Where do I take him to? Over."

"Yes. I'm coming to that now. You go with Jordan to Dieppe Barracks in Yishun. Get him to personally escort the generals out of jail. You can do it, Kuan Hee. Over."

"It may be difficult, Mr Walmsley. If the soldiers see him alone, they may think something is wrong. Over."

"Not to worry, Kuan Hee. That part—the police will

help. The police will arrange for cars and men to go with you and Jordan. Over."

"I understand, Mr Walmsley. You want me to enter Jordan's office and get him to follow me to Dieppe Barracks to release the detained generals. Am I right? Over."

"Yes, that is correct, Kuan Hee. Do it on Thursday evening—before the police raids on the army. Over."

"I'll, Mr Walmsley. Over."

"And Kuan Hee, one last thing. Be careful. Colonel Tee is a treacherous chap and he was an army commando. He can kill you in the wink of an eye. Over."

"I'll be extra careful this time, Mr Walmsley. Over."

"Guys, you heard the Brigadier. Tomorrow's the day. We've got to get Jordan to come with us tomorrow evening."

"What's the plan?" asked Tim.

Kuan Hee, Lina and Tim pored over a map of Tanglin Complex. As he was describing their plan of action, Kuan Hee drew lines and 'X' marks on the map.

"Do we need the weapons?" said Tim.

"Nope, Tim. Not this time," said Kuan Hee. "I'll be using AleXander. Their arsenal will be enough."

"I don't think Navin can come. His father's funeral won't be over till late in the day," said Tim.

"Let him mourn his father first—it's more important," said Kuan Hee. "We'll make do."

"What time are we taking action?" said Lina.

"We will hop over around noon and we'll wait for an opportunity. We don't know for sure when Jordan will wake. We'll just have to watch them the whole day—from noon till the next morning," said Kuan Hee. "Tim, you take charge of Alex, and I'll handle Xander."

"OK," said Tim. "What's his phone number? I'll need to practise with him."

The sky over Tanglin Complex was threatening to open up on Thursday afternoon. Dark clouds were gathering over the horizon. Kuan Hee, Lina and Tim pretended to be survey assistants, clicking on number counters in their hands. They were huddled on the grass verge next to the busy road junction. Alex was sitting in Tim's backpack and Xander was lying in Kuan Hee's backpack.

"Remember to open the front panel on Alex," said Kuan Hee.

"I won't forget," said Tim.

The trio took turns to monitor the Colonel's activities in the office. They were sure the Colonel was in charge of Jordan's body, for the room was dimly lit and the curtains were drawn. They had to wait for Jordan to reappear. There just was no other way. The minutes dragged by, then the hours. It was still dark in the office.

"It's going to pour soon. The dark clouds are looming overhead now."

"We've got to work fast. There's no shelter from the elements for us here."

"Pray hard, pray hard that Jordan will awaken," said Lina.

"It's the only thing we can do," lamented Tim.

"Is that lightning I see up there?" asked Lina.

"Yes. I'm afraid so. Here comes the thunder," said Kuan Hee. The skies were rumbling.

"Kuan Hee. Look! On the screen. The room is bright!" said Lina.

"You sure are right, Lina. We must thank our lucky stars tonight," said Kuan Hee.

"But, there aren't any stars tonight," said Lina.

Kuan Hee flashed her a glare. "Joking, just joking," said Lina.

"Let's get going, guys," said Tim.

The men let Alex and Xander out of the backpacks. The two robots clambered up the slope towards the building. They adopted a prone position on the edge of the slope, ready to spring into action.

"I'll be with the robots; pass me your phone too. I'll take care of Xander too," said Tim. There had been a change of plan. Tim would control the two robots and the pair would go into the Supreme Leader's office.

Tim crawled up the slope and the pair separated from him. They took another path up to the building.

Just then, a figure came up behind Tim. It was Navin. He had come.

"Navin, you are just in time. I thought you won't finish with the funeral till very late," said Tim.

"My father would have wanted me to come here tonight," said Navin. "I'm sure he won't mind."

Here—take this phone. You control Xander with this phone and I'll control Alex with mine," said Tim. "Don't worry, I'll guide you."

"Kuan Hee, call Jordan. Tell him we're on the way," said Lina.

"Jordan, we're coming in. Please draw your bodyguards away," said Kuan Hee into little Busy's remote.

The pair climbed up a low wall into a long corridor. There was no one around. The cameras were pointing the other way. It was safe for them to move into the Supreme Leader's office.

The door to the office opened. Jordan was standing at the doorway.

"Come, quick," Jordan beckoned to them.

In the room, the pair were quick to strike a conversation with Jordan. They didn't know when his father would suddenly decide to pop in; they couldn't take any risks.

"Why are you here again?" asked Jordan. "It's dangerous here."

"We need your help again, Jordan. The army generals—we need you to release them," said Kuan Hee.

"But, I already told you it would be difficult. These men won't obey my orders. My father has told them if he gives them strange instructions, they need not act on them immediately," said Jordan.

"We have a solution, Jordan," said Kuan Hee. "Your men here won't listen to you, but the men in Dieppe Barracks will—your father hasn't got to them yet."

Jordan stood in deep thought for a moment.

"Alright. But, how do we get there? We are alone; the men in Dieppe Barracks will be suspicious," said Jordan.

"The police will help us. They will dress up as your bodyguards. They have got cars too," said Kuan Hee.

"I see, OK, alright," said Jordan. "Let's do it."

Just then a bolt of lightning struck the building, and its walls and pillars reverberated.

"Argh! My head—my head, it's painf—"

"What are you two doing in my office?" Colonel Tee boomed.

"Men!" he shouted.

But, his men had not heard him, for just then, a loud blast rocked the building. It was not thunder this time. It was Xander's rocket, blasting a wall of the building. Then there was another explosion. This time, Xander had fired his rocket at some plainclothes who were charging at him.

A third rocket from Xander hit an armored personnel carrier which had roared into the compound.

In the room, Colonel Tee retrieved a thirty-centimetre-long knife from a drawer in his desk, drew it from its scabbard and approached Kuan Hee and Lina. Lina was shocked stiff. Kuan Hee pushed her behind him. They backed away from the Colonel. But there wasn't much space left for them to retreat—the wall was only a metre behind them.

"You are the cause of this rift between my son and me," said Colonel Tee. "You shall pay dearly for this."

Colonel Tee was now lunging at Kuan Hee with the knife.

"No! No! Jordan! No! Jordan! He's your friend. He's not your enemy," screamed Lina.

Suddenly, Jordan woke. Seeing his father using his hand to attack Kuan Hee with the knife, he was in despair. Everything seemed clear to him now. The revelation came pouring into his mind.

> And shall come forth; they that have done good, unto the resurrection of life; and they that have done evil, unto the resurrection of damnation.

He knew what he had to do now.

He turned the knife into his own chest—plunged it deep into his torso and carved a path up towards his heart.

"No! Jordan! No!"

Then father and son collapsed onto the floor.

It was all over. The Tee Dynasty was over and done with. Singapore was free of the dictator's grip finally.

As Kuan Hee, Lina, Navin and Tim retreated from Tanglin Complex with AleXander safely tucked into Kuan Hee's backpack, Lina pointed to the sky.

"Look! Up there! The dark clouds are clearing. The wind is blowing them away," she said.

CHAPTER 30

In the ensuing days, the army tanks and armored personnel carriers rolled back into the army camps. Soldiers returned to their barracks and were placed under house arrest. Their coup leaders were arrested and put in prison to await court martial. Political party leaders detained during the army crackdown were promptly released and new elections were slated to take place in the coming months.

The Police Commissioner took charge of returning law and order to the country. He also presided over the repeal of the laws that the Tee military regime had passed in its short time in power.

It was also time for Kuan Hee's parents to return to Singapore. Kuan Hee and Lina were at Seletar Airport to welcome them. A military transport plane had flown them in from a United States Air Base in Australia where Kuan Hee's father, Professor Wang, had been recuperating under the watchful eye of his mother.

"Mum, Dad!" shouted Kuan Hee as the Wang parents stepped into the arrival hall.

"Uncle, Auntie," screamed Lina in sheer delight.

The Wang family were reunited finally. And Singapore was free again.

It was thanks to these twenty-something Singaporeans that Singapore could breathe easily again—but, for how long?—this was anybody's guess. Hopefully, perhaps, at least as long as the pair lived.

* * * * *

The Sun Gawks

CHAPTER 1

Kuan Hee paced the corridor outside the delivery ward on level two of Kandang Kerbau Hospital. He was in a pensive mood and thoughts were running wild in his mind. He had elected not to witness the birth of his first child with Lina—he was afraid of blood, and seeing blood would send him into a squeamish state—so he could not fault others. How he regretted this decision. If only he had mustered the courage to face up to his Achilles' heel.

But, it was too late. Lina had been in the delivery suite for ages. No one had come out since. Kuan Hee was getting frantic, but he suppressed the urge to barge into the room.

Then the door swung open and a gaggle of nurses and attendants waded out.

Kuan Hee wanted to push past them, but stopped. Someone had come out, cradling a baby in her arms—his daughter!

"Mr Wang, congratulations," said a nurse. "The baby is beautiful."

"She sure is," Kuan Hee exclaimed. "She sure is. Can I hold her?"

"Not yet, Mr Wang," said the nurse. "She needs to go

to the observation ward first. You can take a look from the corridor window later." Having said her piece, the nurse strode off, not giving Kuan Hee a chance to reply.

Next to come out of the delivery suite was Lina, looking pale on a gurney. He grabbed her nearest hand and squeezed it. He searched for words in his mind, but none came. She understood his thoughts and flashed a weak smile.

In Ward thirty-two on level three, the pair found themselves alone in the four-bedded room.

"Sorry, dear. Sorry."

"It's alright. I'm fine. Really. Did you see the baby?"

"Yes, beautiful—very beautiful."

"Yeah, I thought so too. Looks exactly like you."

"No, *lah*. More like you. She's got your big eyes and small nose."

"Too bad, Mum and Dad aren't here. They'd be thrilled to bits."

"Kuan Hee. It's been ages since we last spoke to them. Why haven't they contacted us?"

"You know my Dad's doing top-secret work for the US government. He would disappear for months at a stretch. Sometimes Mum would get all upset with him. But, they are together now. She would take good care of him. They should be OK, I guess."

"I'd love for them to see our baby."

"Soon, dear. Soon."

"So are we set on Huei Huei for her name? Or should we continue waiting for your father and mother?"

"Let's wait a little longer, dear. I'll try to contact them again."

The door to the ward flew open and two uniformed women stood in the doorway. One had a clipboard in her hand and the other was holding the handles of a wheelchair.

"Lina Goh. Ms Lina Goh, is it?" asked one.

"Yes," said Lina.

"You have to come with us, Ms Goh," said the woman.

"Why, where to?" asked Kuan Hee.

"Are you the husband?" said the woman.

"Yes, she's my wife," said Kuan Hee.

The woman tore off a sheet of paper from the clipboard and thrust it into Kuan Hee's hand.

"Here. Take this. Your wife needs to follow us. We are taking her to the Transition Centre in Tampines."

In Kuan Hee's hand was a Ministry of Social Affairs notice ordering Lina to report to the Transition Centre for follow-up. These two women were working for the Ministry. The Transition Centre was a euphemism for detention centre. They were going to take her there for compulsory tubal ligation.

"But, my wife is a university undergraduate," said Kuan Hee.

"Not here—in this form. It says 'Highest Standard Passed: Polytechnic'," said the woman.

"She's merely on a hiatus. She's going to rejoin the university after the delivery," said Kuan Hee.

"That's not for me to decide. You can file an appeal," said the woman. Much to Lina's chagrin, the woman grabbed her and sat her in the wheelchair.

"Sorry, but we have to hurry along," said the woman. Ignoring the pair's protests, they marched Lina off in the corridor towards the lift.

"Kuan Hee, my smartphone—my smartphone," said Lina.

"You don't need that where you are going," snapped the woman.

"I'll lodge a complaint," shouted Kuan Hee.

"Go ahead. Be my guest," said the woman. "Everyone says the same thing to me. But nothing happens to me. By the way, my name's Sanita."

These Singaporeans, she muttered under her breath. *They never tire of complaining.*

Kuan Hee stood helpless, clenching the slip of paper.

Having collected his thoughts, he whipped out his iPhone and googled the address given on the paper. The Centre stood between Tampines Industrial Street sixty-one and Tampines Place. *It's behind the row of temples in Old Tampines Road,* thought Kuan Hee. *Why, that's the old foreign workers' dormitory. They must have converted it into a holding centre for non-graduates.*

Kuan Hee and Lina had passed the building many times on their way to the Tampines hub of shopping centres where they would spend many a weekend browsing the shops and taking their lunch.

This is a piece of shit, Kuan Hee thought. *Holding people against their will and forcing them to undergo sterilisation. What government would do such a thing! This is not the twentieth century, for God's sake.*

But this was the reality in Singapore. In 2035, a new government under the Green Party had been elected into power, sweeping all but eight constituencies. The party could enact any law it deemed fit, for it had a two-third majority in Parliament. And enact a slate of new laws it did. The Green Party government thought well of graduates and feted them with benefits and status. It scorned non-graduate mothers. These mothers were separated from their spouses and their babies, and housed in a detention centre to await compulsory sterilization. The freedom of the individual was sacrificed in favour of the collective wellbeing of the state.

At the helm of the Green Party was Ong Chwee Seng, a political veteran who had been detained along with other political leaders under the Tee regime in 2030. The Tee regime's departure had been greeted with glee. Nobody expected the regime's excesses to be reprised in the new Green Party government—until it was too late. The Green Party government had four more years to do more damage to the country. And nobody could do a thing about it. After all, the party was elected in a democratic process. The people reaped what they sowed.

Kuan Hee slid into his father's Honda Accord, chose a cruising speed and put the car into autopilot. He needed to think, and weaving in and out of traffic would distract his thoughts. The car moved out of the hospital grounds and entered the main road.

The last five years had seen a quantum leap in the adoption of technology. After a lengthy fifteen-year trial run, buses and cars were finally allowed to ply the roads on autopilot. Heavy vehicles had to endure a longer wait. But autopilot wasn't for anyone in a hurry. At cruising speeds of less than fifty kilometres an hour, journeys on it were a tad slow for impatient Singaporeans. However, it fitted Kuan Hee's present need. He had to figure out a way to get Lina released from the detention centre—and quickly. She would be scared stiff in such a cold unfriendly environment. And to make things worse, she had just delivered! She was in no state to endure shock.

Oh yes, the Ministry of Social Affairs, thought Kuan Hee. *That's where I should be going now.*

He tapped the autopilot screen on the dashboard and selected the ministry on the map. Then he leaned back in the driver's seat.

The visit to the Ministry of Social Affairs was a futile exercise. He received the merry-go-round treatment. The staff pointed him to the Ministry of Family and Children, which in turn redirected him to the Prime Minister's Office. He learnt the Prime Minister's Office had issued the directive to the Ministry.

Gosh! I've forgotten to see Huei Huei, thought Kuan Hee. *But it's too late to go back. Visiting hours would be in the evening.*

The iPhone beeped. A notification had just come in from the Ministry of Defence's app. It was a mobilization exercise. Kuan Hee had to report to camp immediately.

"Drat!" said Kuan Hee under his breath. "What a day!"

Kuan Hee stared in disbelief at the iPhone screen.

Should I or shouldn't I? he thought. He was in two minds. He could make a quick detour to the reporting centre—an army camp in Portsdown Road—and then get out of the place in no time. He needn't bring along his army wear for they were stored in his camp, ready for him whenever he reported to camp. It was a paid service he had subscribed to, for the sake of convenience.

It's settled then, Kuan Hee told himself. He switched off the car's autopilot and drove at top speed to Portsdown Road.

CHAPTER 2

Portsdown Road meandered on an undulating terrain. Sitting atop was a row of two-storey buildings, which had seen active service during the colonial years. The roofs of the buildings stuck out like the jagged edge of a serrated knife against the clear blue sky, ready to slice into the hearts and minds of its unsuspecting visitors today.

There was a long line of cars waiting to get through the main gate. Reservists on foot streamed past the cars. *There must be at least a brigade of men gathering here today,* thought Kuan Hee. He had not seen such a large congregation of soldiers since Exercise Surprise two years ago. He parked the Honda some distance from the main building and took in the view.

At one end of the parade square were rows of three-tonners. The louvred doors of the building in front of the square were folded back, revealing counters and shelves of army gear. It seemed to be a warehouse. Instead of soldiers, there were khaki-uniformed men manning these counters. From their accent, Kuan Hee could tell they were foreigners. The Green Party government had begun hiring foreigners for non-essential services in the army. With a local resident population of five million and a nonresident strength of three million, this new government policy seemed plausible. There were more khaki-uniformed men sitting at a line of GS tables perpendicular to the building. They were registering the attendance of reservists who had arrived earlier.

Kuan Hee kept an eye out for familiar faces but saw none. *This doesn't seem like a mobilization exercise for my battalion,* Kuan Hee thought. Then he frowned. As the reservists cleared the registration process, they were ushered into the building where soldiers at check-out counters handed out back-packs, uniforms, socks, underwear, foot powder and boots to them. These were brand new issue. Not since their recruit days had these reservists seen such stuff dispensed to them in an assembly line.

It's not a routine reporting exercise this time, Kuan Hee thought. *I've made a wrong decision.* He was right. The queue of reservists snaked into the warehouse and then out the other end into—more three-tonners waiting for them behind the building. With their human cargo safely aboard, the three-tonners rumbled out of the camp through the back gate. The reservists had tried in vain to find out where they were being ferried. There had been no briefing at the camp. It was merely a check-in and check-out process.

As Kuan Hee sat on the packed three-tonner with other strangers, he tried to make sense of the route the truck was taking, oblivious to the chatterings of those around him. A three-tonner behind the truck blocked much of the view of the road. Buildings, trees and open spaces fleeted past him. As the truck rumbled through kilometre upon kilometre of road, he realized it was heading either to Khatib Camp or Nee Soon Camp.

"For sure, it's going to Nee Soon Camp," said a reservist. "Khatib Camp is too small to hold so many of us."

"How long are they going to keep us there?" grumbled

another. "I've a business to run. I'm a one-man show."

"Why no advance notice?" complained a third man.

Kuan Hee had come unprepared too. He hadn't gotten a chance to see his Huei Huei. He was supposed to try to get Lina out of the detention centre. It was a bad day set to become worse. What was the intention of the military, calling up so many reservists at one go? Was war imminent? Or was a big-scale exercise in the works? No one on the three-tonner had the answer.

Yes, Germaine. Why didn't I think of her? Kuan Hee thought. He took out his iPhone, sought out her name and tapped furiously on its screen. Germaine Goh was Lina's paternal cousin. She had spent several years in the United Kingdom, first for her degree in business administration, then for her post-graduate studies. She had recently returned to Singapore. Being three years older than Lina, she was like an elder sister, for Lina had none.

Done! Kuan Hee told himself. *Now just have to wait for news from Germaine.* He pocketed his iPhone.

Kuan Hee regretted not taking along little Busy the robot housefly. It could have given him a first-hand view of Lina. He would have been able to talk to her through little Busy. *Aiyah! It's my work,* he thought. *I've always been immersed in my work. Too engrossed to think clearly.* Kuan Hee was now a research assistant at Temasek University where he graduated last year. He was attached to the Cyborg Intelligence Unit, hoping to hone his skills at nanotechnology—his father's speciality.

The three-tonner rocked as it climbed a slope. Then it slowed down. The shops lining the side of the road came into view. Then the arched gates of Nee Soon Camp loomed overhead. The three-tonner had reached its destination.

Jumping down the three-tonner, Kuan Hee surveyed the surroundings. Nee Soon Camp was an unfamiliar place. He had spent most of his national service days in SAFTI in Jurong. Although he had occasion to visit the nearby Dieppe Barracks, it was only a brief stay for training.

"Third Sergeant Wang Kuan Hee," shouted a voice. Kuan Hee woke from his thoughts. "Third Sergeant Wang Kuan Hee," went the voice again.

Kuan Hee snapped to attention and raised his arm.

"Third storey, Block C, Room B," said the voice. It belonged to a senior NCO.

The third storey was where ghosts were reported to have caused fear to fellow soldiers over the past forty years. Kuan Hee had heard stories of ghosts appearing in the middle of the night, turning on water taps in the toilets. Online forums also told of recruits jumping off the third storey of the building. *Is this building one of those mentioned? Are these recruits still haunting the place?* Kuan Hee wondered. Goose pimples appeared on his arms, unhinging his thoughts momentarily.

Along with other reservists occupying the room on the third storey, Kuan Hee inspected the metal cupboard and the bunk. He was to sleep on the lower of two bunks. He dumped his belongings into the cupboard and, like the other occupants, returned to fiddling with his smartphone. It was the one ubiquitous preoccupation of people these days.

So far, there had been no flurry of activity consistent with the urgency of the call-up exercise. Then the order came for a briefing in the parade square at 2:00 p.m. When everyone had assembled, an officer mounted the concrete platform in front of the flagpoles. His voice boomed through the speakers in the big parade square.

"Gentlemen, you must all be wondering why you have been called up this time," said the officer. "I am here to provide the answers—clear your doubts, so to speak."

Instead of clearing the doubts of the audience, he rambled on about the virtues of performing reservist duties at a time when the country was at peace. As he droned on, he lost the attention of everyone in the square.

Then he came to the part about extending the reservists' stay in the camp. That was when the reservists were all ears.

The officer said the brigade was embarking on Exercise Panther, which would take two weeks to complete. All reservists present would be served with in-camp orders immediately. As part of a pilot programme, they would be issued with wrist tags to monitor their health in real-time.

"Must have taken the idea from Changi Prison," murmured a reservist next to Kuan Hee. "A friend of mine was wearing something like that when I visited him in prison."

"Maybe he worked in Changi Prison before he became a soldier," quipped another reservist.

"But the wrist tag is not for monitoring the health of the wearer," said the first reservist. "It is meant to track our movements. There is a GPS device embedded."

"Really?" said the second reservist.

"Seems like it," said Kuan Hee.

Kuan Hee cocked his head to get a better look at the figure on the dais. There was row upon row of reservists in front of Kuan Hee, some of whom were a head taller than him. It was difficult to see the platform clearly. But something in the figure triggered Kuan Hee's memory. He had seen this man before—somewhere. He stretched his neck. This guy had close-cropped hair and a brawny frame. And the way he ran his fingers over his ear. There was no mistaking it. It was—horror of horrors—Major David Foo in person! Kuan Hee blinked; for a moment he couldn't believe what his eyes were telling him. But, it was Major David Foo in the flesh all right. Nope. This time, Major Foo was wearing a lone star on his epaulette. The Major was now a Brigadier General! Kuan Hee stared in disbelief. *How did he become a Brigadier General?* he wondered. *This guy had been arrested after the downfall of Colonel Tee. Shouldn't he have been court-martialled?* But Kuan Hee had no ready answers to his questions. Instead of receiving punishment,

Major Foo had been promoted and now he was cockier. *Must have bootlicked his way up the ranks,* Kuan Hee consoled himself.

Two weeks—the reservists had to contend themselves with restricted movements for that long. The brigadier general told them the military had served the relevant notices on their employers. There was no need for them to contact their employers. Though it was a disruption that their employers' businesses could ill afford, in the eyes of BG David Foo, it was a necessary distraction. Moral values that the Green Party government wanted to promote were far more important than mere inconvenience to commercial enterprises. To the Green Party, it was moral values, but to those on the receiving end, it was an indoctrination programme. The Green Party, through the military, was trying to pass off the indoctrination of reservists as a routine military exercise. The reservists were not training to prepare for war. Instead, they were to learn how to become better citizens under the Green Party government.

2035 was to be a year when citizens' right to self-determination would be stomped upon. With the implementation of these wrist tags, their privacy rights were also being trampled upon. Their privacy had to be sacrificed for the good of the State. But, there wasn't any need for such a step, for terrorism fears of the 2020s had been quelled with the extermination of radical elements around the world. Since then governments had put into service specialized units, which targeted cells fomenting radical ideas. These units nipped radical cells before they had a chance to take root.

What was to lay ahead for Kuan Hee and his fellow reservists in the coming days? They did not know.

What they did know was—their smartphones were being confiscated. The camp administrators had said they were keeping the smartphones in safe custody for the reservists. But this was an outright lie. Apparently, the administrators did not want the reservists to get word out about the indoctrination programme these reservists would be undergoing. In the age of social media, was this going to be possible? Kuan Hee, like the rest of his campmates, surrendered his smartphone. He wasn't a bit worried, for he still had Lina's smartphone with him. In her hurried exit from the maternity ward, she had left behind her smartphone which was now safely in his possession. He knew he had to hide it somewhere safe from prying eyes. The camp administrators might conduct a spot check of their sleeping quarters.

Kuan Hee was not one for making conversation with others. He tended to keep to himself and spoke little, except to close friends such as Tim and Navin. But this time, he engaged in animated conversation with those who shared the room with him. He had to find out more about this call-up exercise.

Though his roommates came from different reservist units, there was one common denominator. Whether old or young, all were sniper-trained. They were from different batches ORDing in different years. That was why he did not recognize any of them. Kuan Hee learnt from one of them that the reservists occupying the adjoining rooms were signallers. *There is some semblance of order in the selection of this big heap of reservists, after all,* thought Kuan Hee. *What could be the intention of the military?* he wondered. *What is their plot?*

That night, Kuan Hee pulled the blanket over him and pretended to be asleep. He waited till his roommates were in bed. He wasn't on familiar terms with them and didn't want any of them to squeal on him. He snuck out to the corridor overlooking the parade square. He had a clear view of the surroundings, including the two staircases on both ends of the third storey. He hid in a recessed portion of the wall. Taking out Lina's smartphone, he tapped on the WhatsApp app.

WHATSAPP:

"Germaine. This is Kuan Hee. I'm using Lina's phone. Did you get to see her? How is she?" texted Kuan Hee.

There was no activity on the screen for the next few minutes. Kuan Hee was getting anxious. He could not stay out too long. There might be camp administrators making their rounds soon.

"Germaine, are you there? Please reply asap," texted Kuan Hee.

"Sorry, KH. Was in bathroom," texted Germaine. "Tried to message you pm, but there was no reply."

"My iPhone has been confiscated. I'm in reservist training now," texted Kuan Hee. "Can't talk long. How's Lina? How's the baby?"

"*IDK*," texted Germaine. "I couldn't get to see her. But the counter staff said she would undergo a surgical operation—tubal ligation—on Aug 3. We must get her out before then."

"K," texted Kuan Hee. "Little Huei Huei?"

"Huei Huei. This is the baby's name?" texted Germaine. "Don't worry. Lina's mum is taking care of her now."

"*GTG*," texted Kuan Hee.

Kuan Hee sidled into the bunk quarters. His roommates were stirring in bed; they were tired after a long day in camp.

August 3! I must get her out before August 3, thought Kuan Hee as he slid Lina's smartphone into a hidden compartment in his Crumpler backpack. Lina's smartphone was safe in it.

The next day saw khaki-uniformed men slapping wrist tags on the reservists. These were made of a flexible titanium alloy and when snapped closed, needed a detacher to open. Some electronic monitoring device had been embedded. With this wrist tag, the reservists' every move was being monitored.

Then the reservist snipers were herded up a three-tonner to the nearby Nee Soon Firing Range where they were issued with Steyr SSG 69s and live cartridges.

What would the military want with snipers this time? Kuan Hee wondered. He was to get the answer to his question today.

"For some of you, it will be the last time you get to fire a Steyr SSG 69," said a Major. He was the conducting officer for the live firing practice. The reservists who were standing in a line next to the firing points smiled. *Good, then. We can go packing up and head for home,* thought one. Then they realized another row of shooters had formed up right behind them. These men were armed with SAR25s.

"You have five seconds to run to your firing point ahead, and five seconds to shoot your target," said the Major. "Fail to do so, and you could end up dead."

He must be kidding, Kuan Hee thought. This was a reservist training practice. But the line of shooters taking aim at him and the other five snipers looked menacingly serious. At once he could hear his heart thump. *These guys mean business. I can't take chances,* thought Kuan Hee. *I've Lina to live for—and to save.*

The reservist snipers ran for their lives towards their respective firing points. A hail of gunfire echoed through the range. These were real bullets whizzing through the air behind them—not mere blanks. Kuan Hee made the spot in good time. Two others were not so lucky. When he turned, he saw them lying limp on the ground. There was blood on them. The Major's warning was for real! He wasn't mincing his words. Kuan Hee steadied his breath and fired in succession at his target, five hundred metres away. Then he put down the SSG 69. The flag above his target told him he had hit pay dirt.

Back in the bunk quarters, Kuan Hee learnt that the two fallen comrades were the ones sleeping across from him. They did not make it back alive. The room was abuzz with animated chatter. All were shaken and fearful for their lives.

"This is cold-blooded murder," said a roommate. "These guys are crazy."

"Yeah. It's madness—killing our own people instead of the enemy," said another.

"Someone should report this incident," said a third.

"We can't let them get away with murder," said the first.

"We are lucky to have made it back here alive," said Kuan Hee. "But, what about tomorrow? Will there be a repeat of today's incident?"

"*Wah piang*," said the first. "It might be my turn to die tomorrow."

"We must do something—and fast," said the second.

"We must make a getaway," said Kuan Hee. "Or we will be dead meat these few days."

"Yeah. Agree," said everyone in unison.

"Anyone familiar with this camp?" asked the first. None replied. Nee Soon Camp was home to a mishmash of military units—combat engineers, band, infantry brigade and medical corps—but not snipers.

"Too bad we don't have our smartphones with us, or we can use Google Maps' real-time terrain to guide us," said the third.

"OK. We can make do. Let's plan now," said Kuan Hee. The roommates huddled together at one of the bunks, careful not to speak above a whisper.

It was an hour after dinner that night when armed soldiers barged into the bunk quarters of Kuan Hee and his roommates. Apparently, the camp administrators had got wind of the roommates' plan to escape.

BG David Foo appeared at the doorway. He walked past the reservists and turned around. Then he scrutinized them one by one.

"Just because you are reservists—you think you can forget about discipline, is it?" said BG David Foo. "Dereliction of duty is a serious offence."

He paced the room and eyed the reservists.

"Don't know how serious it is?" said BG David Foo. "Let me show you just how serious it is." He drew his SIG Sauer P226 and shot the reservist next to him in the head. The lifeless body fell onto the floor. Kuan Hee, who was standing next to the fallen reservist, felt the blood splatter onto his temple. He stood frozen in fear. The roommate next to him wetted his pants. The liquid pooled at his feet. Another roommate cowered in a corner. These reservists had never seen death in national service. Today, they saw three in a row. It was an earth-shattering experience for them.

"Try again if you dare," said BG David Foo. "Go ahead. Make my day."

That said, BG David Foo left the room. It seemed like a page from the movies. It couldn't be real. Here was a Singaporean army officer killing one of his men at point-blank range.

Three soldiers came in with a body bag and dragged out the body. Another two soldiers stood watch outside the room. The seven remaining roommates stared at one another for a long while. They were shell-shocked.

Someone must have told on us, thought Kuan Hee. *Otherwise, the room must be bugged.*

The shooting had put paid to their plan to escape.

Nobody had the guts to bring up the proposal again—at least, not for a while. Kuan Hee decided he had to do it alone. He could not take the chance of trusting any of his roommates—not after what had happened today. By hook or by crook, he had to make his getaway—for Lina's and his sake. Time was ticking away. Today was July 24. Lina's surgical procedure would take place in ten days' time. He had no time to waste. Who could he turn to for help? Kuan Hee searched his memories for a clue. He had tried in vain to reach Tim and Navin. *Oh yes, why didn't I think of him?* Kuan Hee thought. *Brigadier General Walmsley, the American operative.*

CHAPTER 3

There was no way for Kuan Hee to contact Brigadier General Walmsley. The walkie-talkie the Brigadier had given him was lying somewhere in 79 Jalan Naung. It was impossible for Kuan Hee to lay his hands on it, for there were twelve days left in his in-camp stint. Alas, it was back to the drawing block for Kuan Hee.

There were ten of them sharing the bunk quarters when Kuan Hee arrived at Nee Soon Camp. Now there were seven. These seven snipers were confined to quarters. They were expecting punishment, for AWOL or attempting to AWOL was a serious offence in the army. Three days had passed but nothing had happened to them. It was strange the camp administrators did not send them to the Court-martial Centre in Kranji Camp.

The next morning, after breakfast, the snipers were escorted to an office three blocks away. *They are finally taking action,* Kuan Hee thought. But there wasn't the usual *hentak-kaki* march that they had expected to do before disciplinary proceedings. Instead, they were being ushered into a conference room. Standing in front of a large screen was BG David Foo.

The Brigadier General greeted the snipers warmly this

time. He gestured for all to be seated.

"I'm sending you on a secret mission," said the BG. "Do it well, and you will be rewarded. I'll also forget about the AWOL matter."

"But, bungle it, and you will face dire consequences," he continued.

The BG raised his arm and his staff placed a manila envelope and a watch in front of each sniper.

"Your individual target and destination are detailed in the sealed envelope before you," BG Foo said. "It's marked 'top secret'. Do not open the envelope now. Do it when you are alone. Remember—do not discuss your target or destination with anyone. Do you understand?"

"Yes, sir," the snipers chorused in unison.

"ETA for your destination is 19:00 today," BG Foo said. "Synchronise your watches now." With that done, he dismissed the snipers.

One by one, the snipers were led into different holding rooms, with a guard stationed outside each room.

Kuan Hee surveyed his new surroundings. The room, slightly bigger than a pantry, was furnished with a chair and a small desk placed beside a lourved window. A fan whirling on the wall provided ventilation in the room. He tried to open the window. It seemed to be nailed shut from the outside. He peered through the louvres. He saw grassy sloping ground. There was the stench of urine and faeces in the air. *I must be near a toilet or sewage system,* Kuan Hee thought. The door opened, and a soldier placed a Steyr SSG 69 and a cleaning kit on the desk. Then without a word, he left.

Kuan Hee ran his fingers along the cold barrel of the rifle and let his fingers slide on the smooth fiberglass stock. *This is new issue,* he told himself. It was rare to see new Steyr SSG 69s. The sniper rifle had gone out of production in the 2010s. There was only a limited stock of about 3,000 new units left at the time. But the SSG 69 was a fine dependable weapon. It was loads better than the ones in use in armies around the world. *How did the army get their hands on new stuff?* Kuan Hee wondered. *Did they manage to find a new factory?* Then he remembered the envelope in his hand. He tore open the flap and emptied the contents on the desk. There was a large photograph of—the President. *The BG wants me to kill the President,* Kuan Hee told himself. *Why, that low-down son of a bi—* He managed to stop himself from uttering the cuss word. Even in his thoughts Kuan Hee would not swear. *This is treason. I can't do it. I just can't do it—not in a million years,* he told himself. Yet, Kuan Hee knew he had to, for his life depended on it, unless, of course, he aborted the task right at the last moment. He had to keep his plan close to his heart, for if anyone found out, he would be killed immediately.

Next to the photograph was a map. Kuan Hee pored over it. A triangle marked the firing point he was to station himself at. It was a staircase in an HDB block in King George's Avenue. It was about five hundred metres from his target's position—the porch of the Ministry of Family and Children's main building in Tyrwhitt Road. An 'X' marked the spot his target—the President—would be standing.

Kuan Hee stood in deep thought for many minutes, oblivious to the droning of the fan. Then he opened his eyes. He knew what he had to do now. He plotted his moves for that evening in his mind. That done, he went back to reminiscing the times he spent with Lina. It was the only way he knew to remain sane in difficult times.

A guard came into the room with his Crumpler backpack. It contained his civilian clothes. He said Kuan Hee was to change into civilian attire and keep the disassembled rifle in the backpack. A magazine with five cartridges would be given to him when he left for his destination.

When the guard had left, Kuan Hee reached inside the secret compartment of the backpack. He fingered the edges of the iPhone. *Good,* he told himself. *They haven't found it.*

He resisted the urge to take it out. *There might be a hidden camera somewhere in this room,* he told himself. *Can't take the risk—not now, not yet.*

The ambient heat from the windows seemed to be subsiding. Kuan Hee glanced at his watch. It showed 5:25 p.m. Shortly he would be on his way to King George's Avenue. A guard came in with a bottle of mineral water and his dinner—a box of steamed rice with some slivers of pork and julienned cabbage. He picked at the food and took swigs of the bottled water.

Then two men entered the room. They were in civilian clothes. They took him to a van whose driver was waiting in the compound. There were several of these vehicles, and as he passed them, he inhaled the fumes from the humming engines. *These other vans must be waiting for my roommates,* Kuan Hee told himself.

The van unloaded him along King George's Avenue. The magazine was now in his trouser pocket. He looked up at the HDB block façade and then at the Ministry of Family and Children's main building in the distance. Slinging his backpack, he walked past the shops on the ground floor, keeping an eye out for overhead cameras. Then he turned the corner of the block. A staircase stood in front of him. There was a police camera perching on a pillar opposite the staircase. He walked to the back of the building. *Yes, the staircase landing is only two metres high,* Kuan Hee told himself. Seeing nobody was around, he grabbed the water pipe next to the staircase and lifted himself up to the landing. *I'll use this way to get out of the building,* he told himself. He climbed the stairs up to the seventh storey and surveyed the view. *Still too low,* he thought. He walked up to the eighth storey. Here he had a clear line of sight to the target building's porch. A wooden platform had been erected in the driveway and there were people scurrying around like ants in the distance.

Kuan Hee was sure the BG's men were keeping watch

on him from somewhere in the buildings around him. He had to act the part, pretending to be studious in his task. *They will be reporting my every move to BG Foo,* he thought. Then he smiled. *I sure can act,* he told himself. He sat down behind the parapet, out of view of everyone. His watch told him it was now 6:35 p.m. He had twenty-five minutes of idle time before his target appeared. He retrieved his iPhone from the backpack and powered on the device. *Good, there's still eighty percent battery left,* he told himself.

Kuan Hee browsed channelsingapore.com but found no reports of the deaths of NSmen. *It's as if nothing happened,* he told himself. *What a cover-up.* But online posts on social media alluding to these deaths had gone viral. The forums were alive with discussions on the matter. Everyone who commented was aghast at the horrific tactics of the military. There were pictures of the dead snipers—alone, with loved ones, and beside daughters and sons. Kuan Hee fingered the screen. These men were living and breathing just days ago. *How can a government be so cruel and bloodthirsty?* he wondered. *I should alert everyone.* He hesitated. *This is Lina's smartphone. What if she gets into trouble?* he asked himself.

Hey, facebook is foreign media, he convinced himself. *The G can't access its servers.* Then he joined in the online tirade, adding little mussels of information about the army's excesses.

"Drat this wrist tag!" Kuan Hee fumed as the wrist tag brushed against his iPhone. He had forgotten about it. It could track his every move. With it on him, he was in perpetual danger. *I will need a diamond cutter or some similar tool to cut it open,* he told himself. *Ah! Lina's elder brother should have such a tool.* Her brother worked in a company specializing in heavy machinery.

Kuan Hee stood up and peered over the parapet. The Ministry of Family and Children's grounds were crowded with people. Many were milling in the driveway. Then they were waving little flags. A limousine, and behind it, a

Volvo, entered the driveway, with two outriders in front of them. *The President is here,* Kuan Hee told himself. He snapped the magazine into place on the SSG 69. Then he steadied the rifle, taking aim at the figure in a navy blue suit. It was evening, but the ambient light was good enough for him to see his target in the crosshairs of the rifle. He took a deep breath and squeezed the trigger. A shot rang out. Then there was pandemonium in the Ministry's grounds. There were screams and shouts as people pushed and shoved to get out of harm's way. Bodyguards threw themselves around the fallen President. They bundled him into the limousine. It sped off with the Volvo trailing, and siren wailing.

Kuan Hee disassembled the rife and placed it in his Crumpler backpack. Then he recoiled in pain. He had been shot. He was bleeding in his left chest. He grabbed a packet of tissue from his backpocket and pressed it on the open wound. He grimaced and disappeared behind the parapet. Someone had taken a shot at him from a nearby building. The size of the open wound told him it was a sniper's 51mm that had lodged in his chest. *One of my roommates must have done it,* Kuan Hee surmised. *The guy's mission is to kill me off after my job is done. Thank God, he spared my life. He's a good chap, after all.*

Kuan Hee slung his backpack over his right arm and staggered down the stairs to the second storey landing. He climbed the railing and jumped onto the floor below. He could not stop, for he knew the G operatives would be coming after him any moment.

The two men who came with him in the van were a streetlamp behind him. They had seen him. He dashed across Horne Road and entered Penhas Road. He strode through the dimly lit five-foot-way of the shophouses and weaved through a line of black hearses parked behind a large building. Lavender Street was home to a cluster of funeral parlours. At the back of these buildings was a coterie of busy men and women in black. He hid behind them. His pursuers hurried past the group, eyeing every moving thing fleetingly. Then they moved into the next street.

Kuan Hee turned into Lavender Road. At the junction, a van stopped abruptly. It jolted him. Then he saw Lina's elder brother at the wheel. Kuan Hee pulled aside a sliding door and threw himself onto the floor of the van. He landed on top of his backpack and he grimaced in pain—his chest hurt. The van disappeared into the busy evening traffic, leaving Kuan Hee's pursuers perplexed.

It was the second time Lina's elder brother had come to his rescue. Earlier, on the eighth storey staircase landing Kuan Hee had texted her brother for help. He had asked him to pick him up along Lavender Street. But there was no reply from her brother. Lina had always boasted to him about how her brother had never let her down. He was just like how she had described him. Kuan Hee couldn't see where the van was heading. He didn't want to risk being seen so he kept out of sight on the floor of the van. The van cruised for many minutes. Finally, it came to a stop and the side door opened.

Lina's brother climbed into the back of the van and examined Kuan Hee's wound.

"It looks bad," he said. "It needs immediate attention, otherwise—"

"The wrist tag—it must come off. They can track us using it," said Kuan Hee.

"Not to worry," said Lina's brother. He rummaged through a large toolbox in the back of the van and retrieved a pair of cutters with long handles.

"This thing can cut through steel and titanium," he said. With a quick snap, the wrist tag broke into two pieces.

"We must hurry along," said Lina's brother. He grabbed the broken pieces and exited the back of the van. He took the wheel of the vehicle and drove furiously.

Along the way, he flung the broken pieces into a bush. "There—they can't find us now," he shouted into the back of the van.

Minutes later, the van pulled into an HDB car park.

"Come, Dr Koh is waiting for us," said Lina's brother. "Leave the backpack in the van." He helped Kuan Hee to the back of Dr Koh's clinic. It was situated in an HDB block in Hougang Avenue five. Only the doctor was in the clinic as it had closed. Lina's brother lifted Kuan Hee onto the exam table in the consultation room. Then he excused himself from the room.

"Kuan Hee, what have you gotten yourself into this time?" said Dr Koh.

"Sorry, Doctor. Have to trouble you again," said Kuan Hee.

The doctor got to work cleaning the wound and then injecting Kuan Hee with an anaesthetic.

"My, my. This is a fine piece of work. Clean shot— landed near the manubrium," said Dr Koh. "51mm— rarely seen. Must be a sniper's bullet."

Kuan Hee tried to hold back his tears as the doctor dug the forceps into his chest. The doctor twisted the instrument a few times. With the other hand, he dabbed clean gauze pads generously on the blood oozing out. Then he pulled out the forceps. He was now holding a bullet with the forceps.

"You are either very lucky, or this chap intentionally missed your vital organs," said the doctor.

Turning to Kuan Hee, Dr Koh said, "It will heal in two weeks. Lie low and don't do anything but rest."

Lina's brother returned with a clean set of clothes for Kuan Hee. "It's yours," he said. "You left it behind the last time you stayed over at the house." He helped Kuan Hee change and bundled the soiled clothes together with the bloodied gauze pads into a polystyrene bag.

Dr Koh rinsed the bullet and handed it to Lina's brother. "Here, get rid of it at once."

CHAPTER 4

The President was not the only one targeted. The local newspapers reported the deaths of the Chief Justice and the Police Commissioner. They had been shot as they arrived home. The newspapers blamed foreign elements seeking to undermine the country's interests. What stood out to Kuan Hee was the President's health. He pinched the smartphone screen to enlarge the page. The news article reported that the President had escaped life-threatening injuries and was now recuperating in hospital.

Kuan Hee smiled. He was glad he had not hurt any innocent party. Just like the sniper roommate who shot him, he had shot the President in the shoulder. He had done what BG David Foo wanted him to do—only he missed killing the President. *It isn't my fault that the shot wasn't deadly,* Kuan Hee told himself. *After all, I was standing five hundred metres away from my target.* So he reckoned the BG shouldn't be too angry with him. Hopefully, the BG would cut some slack for him and let him off, for he needed to save his Lina.

It had been two days since his assassination attempt on the President. Kuan Hee was now recovering from his wound. Lina's brother had put him up on the second level of an old shophouse unit squeezed between several units in Realty Park in Hougang. It was a mere six hundred metres from 79 Jalan Nuang. Kuan Hee could walk home in five minutes! The shophouse belonged to Lina's paternal uncle. The ground floor was rented out as a hairdressing salon. The upper floor was vacant. Kuan Hee was now in the room facing the front, from where he had a clear view of a large field, and, beyond it, Hougang Avenue two.

It is dangerous to keep using Lina's SIM card, Kuan Hee told himself. *I've got to get the Polaris SIM card from the cellar— yes, AleXander too, and not forgetting little Busy and Tizzy.*

The Polaris SIM card was named after its carrier Polaris, an orbiting satellite. It belonged to his father, Professor Wang. He had used it previously when he had a run in with the now-deceased dictator Colonel Tee.

There was the sound of footsteps outside the room. Someone was coming up the stairs. Kuan Hee kept still. He heard three taps on the door. It was Xaden—Lina's brother's teenage son. He was here to deliver his lunch.

"I need to go over to my house to get a few things," said Kuan Hee. "I can't do it alone. Can you come with me?"

"Sure. When?" Xaden asked.

"Tonight, after dinner," said Kuan Hee.

"Do I bring along anything?" said Xaden.

"Just yourself," said Kuan Hee.

Xaden left after Kuan Hee had finished eating. He had to return the tiffin carrier to his grandmother—Lina's mother. Lina's mother was the one who took care of Kuan Hee's meals. She also cooked for the extended Goh family, which included all her children and grandchildren. They would come to the flat every evening for dinner, though they lived in different places in Hougang and Sengkang HDB estates.

It was 7:15 p.m. when Kuan Hee and Xaden made their

way across the road to Jalan Naung. Kuan Hee had expected his house to be under surveillance by the G operatives so they took a longer route, moving through the terrace houses behind Jalan Naung and then entering the narrow walkway between the backs of Kuan Hee's semi-detached house and the terrace houses. The smell of *sambal belacan* permeated the air. Some household was having *belacan* for dinner. He whiffed the fragrant air and recalled his favourite *Kangkong Belacan* dish, which his mum used to prepare for him. *Gosh, I miss her cooking,* he told himself.

Kuan Hee's shoulder still hurt and Xaden had to help him up the wall. Then they jumped into the rear of 79 Jalan Nuang. The inside of the house was dark, but outside, spotlights, turned on by an automatic timer, illuminated the garden. Kuan Hee took a key from underneath a potted plant and opened the back door. The duo felt their way through the kitchen into the storeroom where Kuan Hee retrieved a ladder and carried it into the study. There, he placed it next to the floor-to-ceiling bookshelf and climbed it. He pushed twice on the end panel. It moved sideways, revealing a knob. Then, he turned the knob and the bookshelf glided to one side, revealing a hidden doorway wide enough for two men to enter.

Kuan Hee switched on the lights and motioned for Xaden to follow him down the steps. The cellar was small but there was enough space to hold three cabinets, two chairs and a table. The musty air gradually made way for cooled air as a concealed air-conditioning unit kicked in. Kuan Hee opened a cabinet and AleXander, the two robots shone in the illumination. It was as if they were delighted to see him again. He placed them on the table. Next, he retrieved little Busy the housefly and Tizzy the dragonfly. He placed their remote controls on the table. He bent down and took a metal box from the bottom shelf.

"What's in the box?" asked Xaden. Kuan Hee opened

the box. There were six little rockets lined up neatly in it.

"These look like toy rockets," said Xaden. "They must be fun to play with."

"They may be small, but they are deadly—definitely not playthings," said Kuan Hee. "Each rocket can blow a hole in an army tank."

"Wow! Really? And these are neat stuff," said Xaden, fingering the two robots. "How do we switch them on? Are these the remote controls for them?"

"Meet Alex and Xander the intelligent robots," said Kuan Hee. "Together, they are called AleXander. There aren't any switches. They respond to oral instructions."

"But, they are not moving or responding to us," said Xaden.

"That's because they run on solar power," said Kuan Hee. "And they have been holed up in this cellar for a few months, so their energy level is near zero. That's why they are still."

"Is that so?" said Xaden. He was clearly mesmerized. He had never laid eyes on such handsome robots. They were different from the ones he had seen in shops and on television. "What are these?" said Xaden, pointing to the metal insects.

"This is little Busy the housefly, and that is Tizzy the dragonfly," said Kuan Hee. "They are intelligent drones, capable of eavesdropping on conversations."

"You mean they have microphones on them? But they are so small!" said Xaden.

"It's the wonder of technology—state of the art stuff— my Dad's invention," said Kuan Hee. "They also have night vision capability."

"Can I try them out?" asked Xaden.

"You'll get plenty of chances to play with them," said Kuan Hee. "But, not now. We have to hurry." He took the Crumpler backpack from Xaden and placed AleXander, the two flies and the remotes in it. Then he looked around for the Polaris SIM card. He remembered leaving it on the table, but it was nowhere to be seen.

"Is this what you are looking for?" asked Xaden, holding a SIM card in his hand. "I found this on the floor."

"Thanks, Xaden," said Kuan Hee. He took out Lina's smartphone and replaced the SIM card with the Polaris SIM card. He handed the backpack to Xaden. They were about to leave the cellar when Kuan Hee stopped.

"I plain forgot about BG Walmsley's walkie-talkie," Kuan Hee muttered. "Now, where did I leave it? It's not here."

"Let's go up to my bedroom," said Kuan Hee. "I need to get something."

In his bedroom, Kuan Hee opened a drawer and took out a thick wad of hundred-dollar bills. *These will come in handy,* Kuan Hee thought. He passed these to Xaden who placed them in the backpack. The ambient illumination filtering through the curtains across the balcony let him see his way around the room. He searched his cupboard, then his other Crumpler bags. The walkie-talkie was in one of the bags. He grabbed the walkie-talkie. Then he moved to the balcony and peeped through the curtains. The road in front of the gate was deserted. But he didn't want to take a chance. He gestured for Xaden to follow him out through the kitchen.

Instead of heading back to Realty Park, the duo walked past some HDB blocks and crossed Hougang Central. Then they doubled back to Hougang Avenue five where Lina lived. They had to use this circuitous route—just in case there were G operatives loitering in the vicinity looking for Kuan Hee.

There was a twelve-year difference in the duo's ages, but they seemed to get along well.

"Do you want me to take over carrying the backpack?" asked Kuan Hee.

"It isn't heavy," said Xaden. "I can manage."

As they approached the junction, Kuan Hee lowered

his head. There were cameras perched on top of metal posts next to the junction and he didn't want these to recognize him. At Lina's block, instead of using the lift, they climbed sixteen flights of stairs to Lina's flat. It was a four-roomed HDB flat, two doors away from the staircase.

"Auntie," greeted Kuan Hee. Though he and Lina had registered their marriage, they had yet to go through the customary wedding ceremony, so he would address Lina's mum this way.

"*Ah Ma*," greeted Xaden. He lived with his parents in a four-roomed HDB flat in Sengkang but his family would gather at *Ah Ma's* house for dinner every evening.

Lina's mother led Kuan Hee to the master bedroom. This was Lina's room. She was the apple of her mother's eye and it was natural she would have the best that the family could afford—this included the master bedroom.

There she was, lying on a cotton mat laid in the middle of the queen-sized bed. Little Huei Huei was wrapped in a plain towel. She peered at him with her little eyes. It was not clear whether she recognized him.

"She can't hold things yet. She's only a week old," said Lina's mum. "You will have to put her hand in yours."

The baby made little noises as he placed her little hand in his.

"That's all she can do at the moment," said Lina's mum. "Make grunting sounds."

Kuan Hee wanted to cuddle her in his arms, but Little Huei Huei was drifting into sleep. *Another time, perhaps* Kuan Hee consoled himself. He watched her as she slept, not letting her little hand out of his. *You are so pretty; prettier than your mother,* Kuan Hee thought. Then he reminisced the times Lina and he spent together. *She'll be alright,* Kuan Hee told himself. *I'll get her out before Friday.* Friday was the day Lina had to undergo the sterlisation procedure.

Lina's mum was worried about her daughter, but she tried to hide her feelings. Kuan Hee already had a load on his mind. She didn't want to add to his worries.

Kuan Hee took out his wallet and retrieved a few pieces of hundred-dollar notes. He placed them in Lina's mother's hand.

"It's our share of the monthly expenses," he said. "I forgot, sorry."

She pocketed the money and nodded. Her eyes were getting teary. It would be good for Kuan Hee to make his exit now. Kuan Hee stood up, took a long look at little Huei Huei and bade goodbye to Lina's mum.

"Auntie," said Kuan Hee. "I'll get Lina out before Friday. I promise."

At the shophouse in Realty Park, Xaden put down the Crumpler backpack and gestured he was leaving. It was Monday the next day and he would return with Kuan Hee's lunch after school.

"It must be inconvenient for you, coming here after school," said Kuan Hee.

"No, not at all," said Xaden. "My school is just across the road from here." He pointed in the direction of Holy Innocents' High School.

"But, you live in Sengkang," said Kuan Hee.

"We lived with *Ah Ma* before we moved to Sengkang," said Xaden. "So I'm used to this place."

CHAPTER 5

Kuan Hee powered on the walkie-talkie. The battery level indicator was at the quarter mark. He would have to buy six AA batteries soon. But he was able to make a call to Brigadier Walmsley now. He hoped the Brigadier was available. He picked up the walkie-talkie. Then he stopped. There were footsteps in the staircase. Someone was here. Kuan Hee grabbed a metal rod and stood behind the door. He readied the weapon. There were three taps on the door, then silence. It couldn't be, but it was—Xaden had returned. This time he was slinging a backpack and carrying a duffel bag in his hand.

"I told my father I would keep you company for the next few days," said Xaden, "and he agreed."

"Won't it be troublesome for you?" asked Kuan Hee.

"This place is actually nearer to school," Xaden explained. He went to work laying some blankets on the floor. It would be his bed for the next couple of days. The duffel bag would be his pillow.

Kuan Hee sat the walkie-talkie on the table and pushed the PTT button.

"Mr Walmsley, this is Kuan Hee calling. Over."

There was no response. Kuan Hee tried again. *Perhaps, the Brigadier is away from the walkie-talkie,* Kuan Hee told himself. After some minutes, the walkie-talkie crackled with activity.

"Actually, Kuan Hee, I've been trying to get you on the walkie-talkie, but you didn't respond. Over."

"Sorry. I left the walkie-talkie in the cellar. I've gotten into a bit of trouble, Brigadier Walmsley. Over."

"What have you gotten yourself into now, Kuan Hee? Over."

Kuan Hee told the Brigadier how Lina landed in a detention centre and how he came to be a wanted man.

"I'm at my wit's end, Mr Walmsley. Please tell me what to do. Over."

"That's really quite a knot you've gotten yourself into, Kuan Hee. Let me think for a moment. Over."

There was silence over the airwaves. The minutes ticked away. Then, the Brigadier broke the silence.

"So, Kuan Hee, what do you intend to do? I want to hear what you have to say first. Over."

"I have been thinking. Perhaps, I should attempt a rescue. Over."

"How? Kuan Hee. Over."

"Storm the detention centre using AleXander the robots. Over."

"That doesn't sound like a good solution, Kuan Hee. Over."

"I thought so, too. Brigadier Walmsley. Over."

"Mmm. I suggest—I suggest. I mean, let's do it this way. Get Lina to feign illness so they will take her out of the detention centre. Rescuing her will be easier—and less messy if she is out of the place. They will take her to a hospital. Follow them or find out which hospital they take their patients to. Attempt a rescue there. Over."

"The detention centre is in Tampines. The nearest hospital is Changi General Hospital. I think they will likely take her there. Over."

"Kuan Hee, you must be sure, otherwise, it will be a waste of time—and you don't have time to waste. I suggest that you position yourself at Changi General Hospital and get someone to follow her at the detention centre. If there is a change in destination, you will know straightaway. Over."

"I understand, Brigadier Walmsley. I'll do as you say. Over."

"One more thing, Kuan Hee. I have been meaning to talk to you about your parents. Over."

"Yes, Brigadier Walmsley. I'm listening. Over."

"Listen carefully to what I have to say, Kuan Hee. Over."

"Yes. Brigadier Walmsley. Over."

"Kuan Hee. I'm afraid I have bad news to tell you. Over."

"Brigadier Walmsley. Are they hurt? Over." Though he did not say it out, Kuan Hee was preparing himself to hear the worst news. He clenched his fists.

"In a nutshell, your parents are missing. They have vanished into thin air. Over."

"How—how did it happen? Over."

"The entire research team based in Western Australia has vanished. We suspect some foreign government has abducted them. Over."

"You mean the research team my Dad is in charge of? Over."

"Yes, Kuan Hee. I'm afraid so. The team is based in Airlie Beach, on the Whitsundays Coast. We found out they have been missing for more than a year. Over."

"More than a year? You mean, Mum and Dad went missing in 2034? When did you find out, Brigadier Walmsley? Over."

"Only a week ago, Kuan Hee. I'm very sorry. Indeed very sorry that this has happened. The research unit is top secret and our contact with it has been through an agent. He had been feeding us with false information for over a year. Apparently, he had been bribed. He has gone missing too. Over."

Kuan Hee didn't know what to say. He blamed himself for not checking up on his parents regularly. He had been complacent, figuring they knew how to take care of themselves. If he had tried to contact them, he would have gotten wind of the kidnapping earlier. Now, a whole year had gone past. Any clues would have gone cold a long time ago.

"Kuan Hee, are you there? Over."

"Yes. Brigadier Walmsley. I'm here. Over."

"Don't fret, Kuan Hee. The US government is resourceful. We have people all over the world. I've agents working twenty-four seven. We'll get to the bottom of this very quickly. I promise you. Over."

"Yes, I understand. Brigadier Walmsley. Over."

"In the meantime, if you need help with Lina, let me know. Over."

"I will, Brigadier Walmsley. Good night. Over."

Xaden left Kuan Hee to his thoughts. He went to bed; he had to wake up early for school the next morning.

It was 2:30 a.m. when Kuan Hee drifted into sleep. He had let his thoughts wander—from his parents to Lina and the predicaments all of them were in now.

CHAPTER 6

Kuan Hee knew he could not act alone. He needed his pals' help. But, Tim and Navin were not responding to his WhatsApp messages. Like him, they could have been called up for reservist training. Their smartphones could also have been confiscated.

Kuan Hee had four days left to carry out his plan to rescue Lina. After he and Xaden had had lunch, they set off for the bus stop along Upper Serangoon Road. They were heading to the detention centre in Tampines. Kuan Hee had brought AleXander and the two robot flies with him. Little Busy would help him get in touch with Lina.

On board bus number 72, Kuan Hee was careful to keep his head down. The baseball cap he was wearing hid his face from the cameras aboard the bus. It was a twenty-minute ride to Tampines and the only passengers on the upper deck of the bus were far from where they were seated. Kuan Hee used the time to brief Xaden on what he had to do on Wednesday afternoon. Kuan Hee had decided that Xaden would keep watch outside the detention centre while he and his pals took up position at Changi General Hospital.

Kuan Hee and Xaden alighted fifty metres away from

the main gate of the detention centre. They walked along the perimeter of the premises to seek out the best position from which they could observe the place undetected.

The duo settled on an open spot on the edge of a large field across the road from the detention centre. *Nobody will take any notice of us here,* Kuan Hee thought. *Only little Busy will have to fly a longer distance.*

Kuan Hee had come prepared with some *layangs* he had bought from a provision shop. Fortunately, he had some experience flying *layangs* so he could teach Xaden the ropes. It was better that they busied themselves with an activity so they would not attract any unnecessary attention.

Xaden took AleXander out of the backpack and stood them on the grass. The two robots were happy to soak in the sun's energy; they had spent too long a time in the cellar. Kuan Hee released little Busy into the air. He guided Xaden who was holding the remote. Little Busy zigzagged over the road and flitted up the slope towards the dormitories. *Xaden needs more practice with the remote,* Kuan Hee thought. As they did not know where Lina had been held, they could only instruct little Busy to search the dormitory rooms one by one.

"Why did you choose Wednesday instead of Thursday or Friday?"

"As a precaution. Just in case they should change their mind and hold the sterilization procedure earlier."

"Shall I get little Busy to go up one floor?"

"Yes. Look inside the rooms via the exterior windows. It is safer for little Busy; she won't be easily noticed."

The sun was high in the sky and the August heat was sweltering. There was not a single tree in the sprawling field. Xaden was beginning to feel the effects of the heat but they had yet to find Lina. Kuan Hee almost wanted to call it a day, but Xaden insisted on continuing with the search.

"You understand I won't be with you on Wednesday,

don't you?" said Kuan Hee.

"Yes," said Xaden.

"So if you have any doubts, let me know now so I can clear them for you," said Kuan Hee. "We simply can't afford to have anything go wrong on Wednesday. Lina's safety depends on us."

"I'll try my best," said Xaden.

"Look! It's Aunt Lina," said Xaden. Little Busy was hovering over a room on the third level. Kuan Hee looked at the screen and then up at the building beyond. He pointed to a part of the building.

"That's where she is held," Kuan Hee exclaimed. "Fly little Busy up there on Wednesday. Xaden looked at where he was pointing; he nodded.

Little Busy flew through the window grilles into the room. It hovered above Lina; she was sitting on the floor in a corner of the room. She took no notice of the robot housefly.

"Lina, Lina," Kuan Hee's voice amplified through little Busy's tiny speakers. She had not heard him; she was in deep thought.

"Lina, it's me."

Lina looked around the room, then at little Busy. She beamed.

"Kuan Hee, you are here at last." She got up and peered through the small opening in the metal door. *The corridor is deserted,* she told herself. Then she sat in the corner.

"Dear, Xaden is with me. We are across the road. You look pale."

"I'm alright. It's just that I'm not used to this place. It's cold and unfriendly. What took you so long? I've been waiting for ages."

Kuan Hee recounted the happenings of the past few days.

"It's not an adventure. It's danger. How horrid of the army to treat you this way. It's the second time you have been shot in the shoulder. Does it still hurt? I wish I could see you." She rattled off in succession. She desperately wanted to see her other half, but technology had yet to reach the stage where little Busy could project a live image of Kuan Hee into the air in front of her—not just yet anyway. In the meantime, she had to contend with merely hearing his voice.

"Soon, dear, soon." Kuan Hee understood her feelings.

"Xaden, say hello to your aunt."

"Hi. Aunt Lina."

"Xaden. You're helping your uncle now."

"Yes. Aunt. He's teaching me how to use the remote. I'm to watch you on Wednesday while he waits for you at Changi General Hospital."

"Changi General Hospital?"

"I meant to tell you just now. I've a plan to get you out of this place. Report sick on Wednesday morning. Pretend you have post-natal abdominal pain. They will take you to Changi General Hospital. I'll be waiting there to rescue you."

"Kuan Hee, Xaden's only fifteen years old. You've got to be careful; don't put him in danger."

"I know, dear. He'll do the safe things. I won't put him in harm's way."

"Aunt, I'll be careful."

"Huei Huei—have you seen her? How's she?"

"Huei Huei is fine. Your mum is looking after her. She sleeps most of the time. Her fingers are so little that I had to be very gentle holding them."

"I'm looking forward to seeing her soon. This has been an exasperating time for us."

"Don't worry, we'll be together shortly."

"How's my Mu—" Lina broke off abruptly. She had heard footsteps in the corridor. There was creaking of hinges as the metal doors clanked open. "Someone is coming. It's row call again. You'd better go now."

"Remember—Wednesday morning. Wait for Xaden to

come with little Busy."

"I will. I will."

"Bye, dear." Kuan Hee caressed Lina's image on the screen

Little Busy flitted out of the sparsely furnished room into the open air and back to the duo.

"You have to monitor your aunt's every step on Wednesday," said Kuan Hee. "This means you'll be here from early morning—you can't go to school that day."

"Don't worry, I'll *ponteng* school," said Xaden.

"Good. I'm sure your father won't mind," said Kuan Hee.

Despite his attempts, Kuan Hee could not reach his pals, Tim and Navin. *If they were called up for reservist duties on the same day as me, it means they will only be released on August 6,* Kuan Hee told himself. *It will be too late. Lina's sterilization procedure is on August 3.*

If I can't get hold of Tim and Navin, I'll have to go it alone, Kuan Hee told himself. He hoped it wouldn't come to that state.

What shall I do? Kuan Hee asked himself. He realised he had to cobble up a team to do the rescue. He went to work, penning a list of trusted individuals who could help: Lina's elder brother, Germaine and Ella. Ella was Germaine's sworn sister. They had been friends since childhood days. They were inseparable. He needed one more. *Yeow Xi—why didn't I think of him?* Kuan Hee asked himself. Yeow Xi was Kuan Hee's and Lina's classmate at Holy Innocents' Primary School and his schoolmate at Victoria School. In their primary school years, the two boys had spent most of their time together at a student care centre in Hougang Avenue five, where Kuan Hee's mother was working as a teacher. Yeow Xi left for Australia after his O-levels as his father had been posted there as a country manager. After his parents returned to Singapore, he stayed back for further studies. He only came back to Singapore a month ago, after graduating from Monash University with a Master's degree. Their mothers knew each other well as Yeow Xi's mother would fetch him at the student care centre after work, and the two mothers would engage in animated conversation about their sons.

I have his phone number somewhere, Kuan Hee told himself. *It's been ages. But I'm sure he will lend a hand.*

But, Yeow Xi was unreachable. It suddenly dawned on Kuan Hee that Yeow Xi too had been called up for reservist training. It appeared that this call up exercise was a major one. All his good friends had been called up. Kuan Hee had to make do with just four helpers.

That evening, Kuan gathered Lina's brother, Xaden, Germaine and Ella for a powwow at Realty Park. He laid a map of Changi General Hospital on the table and they huddled over it. He briefed the team members on their duties for Wednesday August 1. Xaden was to keep an eye on Lina's movements at the detention centre and enroute to the hospital. He could track her location using the GPS embedded in little Busy. He had to text Lina's position on the road every few minutes. They might have to change their plan if the ambulance took her to another hospital instead of Changi General Hospital.

Meanwhile, Kuan Hee, Germaine and Ella would be in Lina's brother's van. Germaine and Ella would enter the A&E Department together and Kuan Hee would station himself near the registration counter. Xaden was to text Kuan Hee the moment the ambulance arrived at the hospital. Germaine and Ella were to distract Lina's escorts so that Kuan Hee could rescue her. He and Lina would leave the A&E Department through the rear exit. They would go to Tampines Avenue five where Lina's brother would station his van. Germaine and Ella would leave the premises together once Kuan Hee and Lina had made their getaway.

"It looks easy on paper," said Kuan Hee. "But, anything can go wrong that morning. That's when you have to act accordingly. Remember—your safety is important."

"Are the escorts armed?" asked Germaine.

"I can't tell for sure," said Kuan Hee. "Just distract their attention. Ask for directions or something like that. The guards can't pull out their gun for no rhyme or reason."

"Won't it be risky for you?" asked Ella.

"They might shoot when Lina and I make a run for it. But, I don't think they will, especially when there are so many people in the A&E Department. They may not want to take a risk."

"I can't park along Tampines Avenue five. It's a busy road," said Lina's brother. "If a traffic policeman sees me, I will have to make a big round to come back to the hospital. So I'll wait on a service road. Once I see you and Lina, I will drive onto the main road."

"OK then. Any questions?" asked Kuan Hee. "Xaden, can you manage on your own?"

"Yes, I can," said Xaden.

"Remember to tell your aunt to act as if she's in terrible pain," said Kuan Hee.

"I will, don't' worry," said Xaden.

"And, remember to get little Busy to fly to the van once your aunt arrives at the hospital," said Kuan Hee. "We can't afford to lose little Busy."

"Yes, Uncle Kuan Hee," said Xaden.

CHAPTER 7

The day of the rescue came. It was a blustery morning. Dark clouds threatened to pour rain over Singapore, but these cleared quickly. The sun remained in hiding behind the clouds most of the time.

Xaden had stationed himself on the open field across the road from the detention centre in Tampines. It was a good day for flying a *layang* here, for the winds were howling away and dishevelling his hair. Xaden ran his fingers through his hair, trying to comb it into place. But it was an impossible task. The next gust sent it into an untidy mob again. He lay prone on the grass near the road; Kuan Hee had told him to be on the alert for lightning strikes, for he was an easy target on the flat open ground. Little Busy flitted unsteadily through the turbulent air towards its destination—the third level of the detention centre. Soon it was hovering over Lina in her holding room.

"Aunt Lina, Uncle Kuan Hee says he will take action at the A&E Department," said Xaden through little Busy's speakers.

"Righto," said Lina. She was in high spirits today; then she remembered the roleplay she had been entrusted to carry out. She furrowed her brows, clutched her stomach as if some tormenting animal was inside it, ready to wreck hell in it. She curled into a ball and sat in a corner, wailing at the top of her voice. She screamed as if she had never screamed before. Her voice echoed through the quiet corridor outside her room.

In seconds, there were heavy footsteps approaching her room. Then the door creaked open, and two female guards appeared. They took turns to try to calm her down, for she was disturbing the otherwise tranquil peace on the level. Clearly exasperated, one suggested taking her to seek medical attention. She was afraid Lina would die under her care; she would have a lot of explaining to do to her superiors. They grabbed Lina's arms and shuffled out of the room with little Busy flying discreetly behind them.

On the open field, Xaden busied himself giving updates of Lina's movements to Kuan Hee who had reached Changi General Hospital in Lina's brother's van together with Germaine and Ella. Lina's brother parked his van in a street behind Changi General Hospital. The street opened into Tampines Avenue five where he would be picking Lina and Kuan Hee. As arranged, Germaine and Ella would leave separately. The team waited in the van; they would attract unnecessary attention if they loitered in the hospital premises.

Little Busy flitted into an ambulance together with Lina and her escorts. It perched itself on a shelf on the side of the ambulance, from where Xaden had a good view of the occupants and the back window of the vehicle. Xaden could monitor the housefly's position using the map on the screen. He reported the ambulance's route to Kuan Hee via his smartphone.

It was some minutes before Kuan Hee could ascertain the destination of the ambulance. It did not leave Tampines. Instead it turned into Tampines Avenue five and was now passing Tampines Swimming Complex. Kuan Hee knew the ambulance was heading for Changi General Hospital. It was now four junctions away from the hospital. Lina's brother gave them the all clear to leave the van. Germaine and Ella left together, followed by Kuan Hee seconds later. The two groups took different routes to the A&E Department on the ground floor. It was difficult for Kuan Hee to avoid the eyes of the two CCTV cameras perched on the walls of the A&E Department. Between them, they covered the entire hall. The cameras could see Germaine and Ella too. It was a risk they had to take. There was no way for them to neutralize the cameras; there were too many eyes in the hall.

Kuan Hee sat among the patients in the corner, near the rear exit. Germaine and Ella had just entered the place. They walked around the hall, pretending to be curious visitors. Suddenly, Kuan Hee sat up; Xaden had texted Lina's arrival at the hospital. He kept his eyes peeled for Lina. The front door rolled back and Lina entered the hall in a wheelchair with a paramedic and two female escorts. *Good. They are not armed,* Kuan Hee told himself. Germaine and Ella had seen them too, and were walking towards them. The paramedic stopped the wheelchair next to a curtained consultation area and gestured one of the escorts to follow him to a counter. Now, Lina was alone with the other escort. At once, Germaine and Ella reprised their act. They pretended to be lost and asked the excort for direction. Kuan Hee took the chance to come behind the three. He grabbed hold of Lina's hand. Together, they sprinted towards the back exit, leaving the three still in conversation. Suddenly, the escort at the counter shouted. She had seen the pair moving towards the exit. The other escort turned and ran towards the pair. Meanwhile, Germaine and Ella quickly made their exit via the front door.

By now, Kuan Hee and Lina were running along the service road behind the hospital. Lina did not dare to look back. The two escorts were no match for the youngsters and the pair was soon on Tampines Avenue five where the van was waiting for them. The side door was open. They jumped into the back of the van and shut the door. The van screeched off. There was no sign of their pursuers.

Lina hugged Kuan Hee tightly. They had not seen each other for nine days; to Lina, it was an eternity. She planted little kisses on Kuan Hee's face.

"Kuan Hee," she cooed. "I'm so glad to see you. Aren't you glad to see me, Kuan Hee?"

"Yes, dear. Of course, I am, dear." Pressing Lina against his side, he continued, "You are much thinner."

"Is that supposed to be good or bad?"

"Why, dear, it's both good and bad—good that you are getting slimmer, and bad that you have not been eating well."

"You are so bad."

"Seriously, I miss you. Huei Huei misses you. So too your mum and family."

"I forgive you, Kuan Hee." She snuggled against him. She had missed the warmth of his body the past week. "You know, I almost became sterile."

"Yes, dear."

"Just imagine. No more children for the rest of our lives."

"I know, dear."

"Where's little Busy?"

"Don't worry. It's perched safely on top of the mirror in the driver's section. Xaden piloted it back here once you entered the hospital."

"Xaden's a good help, isn't he?"

"Yes dear. So too your cousin Germaine and her friend Ella."

"Yes, *hor*. We have good friends."

"Yes, dear."

"Where are we going?"

"Realty Park, dear."

"My uncle's shop?"

"Yes, dear. I've been hiding there the past few days."

"Can I see Huei Huei now? Can we go see her first?"

"Not yet, dear. We need lie low for a while first. Perhaps, later."

"But, I haven't seen my baby, Kuan Hee."

"All in good time, dear."

The smartphone beeped. Xaden had texted Kuan Hee. He was on his way back to Hougang on bus number 72. Then Germaine texted to say both she and Ella were taking an Uber ride home.

Good. Everyone's safe, thought Kuan Hee. After nine days of pouring rain, some sunlight had come into the pair's lives.

But, they were not home free yet. The G operatives were looking for them. They had to be on the run from now on, but for how long? It was a question neither had an answer to.

The van came to a stop behind the shophouse in Realty Park. After unloading its human cargo, the van drove off. Lina's brother was not of many words. In his silence, he showed his concern for his little sister. He knew the pair wanted to be alone; after their ordeal, they surely had a million things to tell each other.

Xaden texted Kuan Hee using his smartphone again. His father was fetching him home so he would not be coming to Realty Park. Kuan Hee knew it wasn't a coincidence; they all meant well.

Kuan Hee and Lina sat huddled on the floor of the small room above the hairdressing salon in Realty Park. They felt the warmth of sunlight coming through the uncurtained glass panels of the window above them. The opposite wall glared in the sun's reflection.

"We are fugitives now, dear."

"We've got to be in hiding always?"

"I'm afraid so. As long as this government is in power."

"I can't go home?"

"It would be dangerous, dear."

"Our Huei Huei? We can't see her?"

"Certainly not, dear. When the situation improves, we will take her back, but in the meantime she needs your mum to take care of her. Perhaps, in a month or two."

"But, it's too long a wait."

"We can video call your mum and watch Huei Huei on the screen."

"We will be staying here forever?"

"Not forever, dear. Maybe, for a few months."

"Kuan Hee, what's wrong with us?"

"Why do you say that, dear?"

"Because we seem to be getting into trouble quite often."

"It's not us. We are OK. It's the country—it's in bad shape. With the wrong leaders, it's going into a tailspin, and there's probably nothing we can do about it."

Then there was a long silence. Kuan Hee was thinking deeply again. Kuan Hee cuddled Lina as she curled up against his body.

"Kuan Hee, shall we…"

"Of course, dear." He knew what she wanted; she didn't have to say it out. The pair spent an intimate afternoon caressing each other and saying sweet nothings. It was a necessary respite from the shocking experiences of the past few days.

That evening, Xaden brought dinner and a message from Lina's mum. Some people from the Ministry of Social Affairs had come to the house. They asked her whether she had seen Lina. They told her Lina had absconded from the transition centre and it was an offence to harbour her.

"That settles it. We can't visit your mum for the time being; they might be watching the flat."

"Can we video call my mum now? I miss Huei Huei. I want to see her."

"Sure, dear. Let me launch the Skype app."

So, though Lina and Kuan Hee were unable to see their little daughter in person, they could watch her live on the screen. It was pure entertainment for the pair, seeing little Huei Huei wriggle on Lina's bed and make grunting sounds. It wasn't a perfect arrangement, but in these difficult times, it was second best.

CHAPTER 8

Brigadier Walmsley was on the walkie-talkie again to update Kuan Hee on the search for his parents.

"Where are the AA batteries we bought yesterday?" asked Kuan Hee.

He replaced the weak batteries with the new ones that Lina handed him.

"Kuan Hee, in a nutshell, we believe your parents are being held in Singapore. Over."

"So it's not the Russians after all? Over."

"We have reason to believe your parents were abducted by elements of the Singapore army. Over."

"Brigadier Walmsley. Why would the Singapore army want to kidnap my parents? They are citizens here. Over."

"Kuan Hee, that's what I want to know too. But our operatives have confirmed that the mole in the research unit led a special unit of the Singapore army to the secret base in Airlie Beach. Our investigations indicate these soldiers were Singapore commandoes in civilian clothes. They took the research staff to the Singapore army camp in Timbuktoo, North-east Australia. From there, your parents and other research staff were bundled on a

Singapore airforce transport plane and flown to Singapore. It all happened more than a year ago. Over."

"Brigadier Walmsley, whereabouts are my parents now? Over."

"I have no news presently. But, we learnt the mole is still in Australia. We are confident of ensnaring him soon. Once we have him in custody, we will be able to get to the bottom of the matter. Over."

"Thanks very much for your help, Brigadier Walmsley. Over."

"Now that we are done with the big thing, let's deal with the others. Did you manage to get Lina out of the detention centre? Over."

"Yes, Brigadier Walmsley. In fact, she's here with me now. We rescued her at the A&E Department in Changi General Hospital. Thank goodness, she's in good shape. Over."

"Why, that's good news indeed, Kuan Hee. But, this means both of you are fugitives from the law. It's bad news. Can you two take care of yourselves? Over."

"It will be difficult, but we sure will try hard, Brigadier Walmsley. Over."

"Good. Good. Kuan Hee. I have got to go now. Will get in touch with you again soon. In the meanwhile, keep safe. Over."

"Yes, Brigadier Walmsley. We will. Over."

Turning to Lina, Kuan Hee said, "If the Brigadier says so, then it must be true—Mum and Dad are in Singapore. They have been living here the past year and we didn't even know it."

"What's with the Singapore government? Why are they doing evil things nowadays?"

"I don't know, Lina. I really don't know. Ever since the last election, the Green Party government has been trampling on us ordinary folks. Looks like these people are hungry for something. I can't put my finger on it—not just yet, anyway."

Then Kuan Hee remembered the communication device embedded in his arm. His father had inserted the device in both their arms five years ago so they could communicate using their brainwaves. They didn't need smartphones!

"Why didn't I think of it? I plain forgot. I can communicate with Dad."

But Kuan Hee had forgotten how to activate the device. He paused. He gestured Lina not to interrupt him; he was now deep in thought. He was trying to recall the passcode. After a long while, his face lit up.

"I remember now." He leaned towards Lina and placed a finger over his lips.

"LOGON ALPA."

"Dad, can you hear me? It's me, Kuan Hee."

There was no one speaking in his mind. Try as he could, he could not hear any voices in his mind. His father was not responding. *Is he sleeping?* Kuan Hee thought. *But, it is mid-morning now.*

"Any luck, Kuan Hee?"

"Nope. Let me try again." He was getting exasperated.

"LOGON ALPA."

"Dad. Dad. Answer me, Dad."

Despite several attempts, he could not get through to his father. Then he sat up.

"Oops! I forgot. This thing has a life span of three years. Dad said the internal mechanism would drain its tiny power cell, even though it's in idle state." Kuan Hee sank in the chair. He placed the back of his hand over his forehead.

"What am I to do now?" he lamented.

Lina comforted Kuan Hee. She shared his helplessness.

Only a few days had passed, yet the room above the hairdressing salon was getting to look like home now. It had the little comforts of home. There was now a television set and a portable refrigerator, brought over by Lina's brother. He had also bought a Samsung smartphone for his sister, with a SIM card in his name. Kuan Hee and Lina had bought two foam mattresses, some blankets and pillows from the neighbourhood shops. There was a coffee maker with which they could make their favourite blend of coffee and a small kettle to boil water to drink. Outside there were two pairs of slippers for them to wear when they visited the toilet at the rear of the premises.

CHAPTER 9

It was August 6. Kuan Hee's smartphone was flooded with calls from Tim, Navin and Yeow Xi. They had been released from reservist training and their smartphones were back in their possession. Tim and Navin knew of the Polaris mobile number, but Yeow Xi was clueless. He merely called back to find out who was trying to reach him.

That evening, Tim and Navin visited Kuan Hee at his new home in Realty Park.

"Why have you moved here?" asked Tim. "Fancy giving up living in a semi-detached and downgrading to a one-room accommodation."

"What happened to your iPhone?" asked Navin. "Why are you using the Polaris line?"

"Hey you guys," said Kuan Hee. "One question at a time please. I can't handle so many."

"Tim, please don't tease Kuan Hee," said Lina. "He's in bad shape already. Don't rub salt into his wounds."

"Jiving. Just jiving, Kuan Hee," said Tim. "No hard feelings."

"Not at all," said Kuan Hee. He was used to getting doses of ribbing from his pals.

"Let's toast to our friendship," said Navin.

"Yeah!" they all said in unison.

"I see you guys aren't wearing the wrist tags," said Kuan Hee.

"They removed it when I went to collect my identity card," said Tim. "I was afraid they might leave it on me."

"Luckily for us, they didn't," said Navin.

"What is this about you being on the run?" asked Tim.

"This guy BG David Foo wanted me to assassinate the President," said Kuan Hee. "Instead, I aimed for his shoulder. He escaped death."

"What? So you are the one who tried to take his life. I thought a foreign government was involved," said Tim.

"Yes. After that, I had no choice but to disappear," said Kuan Hee. "I think they are after me now."

"Why would anyone want to kill the President?" asked Navin.

"I can only guess. Perhaps, the President is in someone's way," said Kuan Hee. "So this someone acted to get rid of the thorn in his flesh."

"I thought with Colonel Tee's death, dirty politics had ended," said Tim. "Looks like it's round two happening."

"When will this clamour for power end?" asked Navin.

"One power hungry party goes out and another even more vicious one comes in," said Tim.

"I thought Singapore would be back on the right track with the Green Party in charge," said Kuan Hee. "But, it seems to be descending into dictatorship again. We can't trust the Green Party government."

"Why do you say that?" asked Navin.

"First, they forced non-graduate mothers to go for sterilisation. Then they killed the Police Commissioner and the Chief Justice. Now, they have retired the high court judges and removed all the remaining judges. Just imagine, they are letting computers act as judges."

"Are you sure it's the Green Party government who ordered the killings?" said Navin.

"The Green Party government is definitely behind this. They used us reservist snipers to do their dirty work for them. They want to get rid of me too—to remove the evidence," said Kuan Hee. "These people are merciless. Do you know they killed three of my fellow snipers just like that?" He snapped his fingers in demonstration.

"Who exactly is this 'they' you are talking about?" asked Tim.

"Brigadier General David Foo and his gang," said Kuan Hee. "He drew his gun and shot dead a fellow sniper in front of me for no rhyme or reason."

"That's surreal, Kuan Hee," said Tim.

"But true, I swear," said Kuan Hee. "Never in my life have I seen such disregard for human life. This David Foo is a murderer."

"No one reported him?" said Navin.

"It's all covered up, including the murders of two other reservist snipers. They killed these two snipers simply because they couldn't run to their designated spot in five seconds."

"The devil!" said Tim. "That's cold-blooded murder."

"So that's why you were frantically trying to reach us the past few days," said Tim. "You want us to think of a way to expose this killer."

"Not so *lah*," said Kuan Hee. "I wanted you guys to help rescue Lina." He proceeded to describe how Lina was detained at Kandang Kerbau Hospital and held in detention. He ended with a blow-by-blow account of the rescue at Changi General Hospital.

"Fancy going on an adventure without us two," said Navin.

"I didn't mean to," said Kuan Hee. "I had no choice."

"By the way, congrats!" said Navin. "Boy or girl?"

"It's a girl," said Lina.

"A real pretty princess," said Kuan Hee.

"*Wah*, you two work so fast," said Tim.

"No, *lah*," said Kuan Hee. "It was an accident." He

grinned from ear to ear.

"Kuan Hee, you talk too much," said Lina. "You are drunk."

"Lina, he's not," said Navin. "Look! He's only had two beers. And his face is not flushed."

"No more beers for you," said Lina. She pushed the beer cans towards Navin and Tim.

"There's another thing that I wish to share with you," said Kuan Hee.

"Don't keep us in suspense, *leh*," said Navin. "Out with it, man."

"My mum and dad have been kidnapped," said Kuan Hee.

"What? Not again!" said Tim. "Kuan Hee, your parents are a magnet for kidnappers."

"Be serious, Tim," said Lina.

"Sorry, *lah*," said Tim. "Just jiving again."

"How did it happen?" said Navin. "I thought they are in Australia."

"Brigadier Walmsley, whose organisation my dad works for, told me my parents were kidnapped by Singapore commandoes in Airlie Beach," said Kuan Hee.

"Singapore commandoes?" said Navin. "Are you kidding?"

"Do I look like I'm kidding?" said Kuan Hee.

"Sorry," said Navin. "Why would they do such a thing?"

"My dad is doing top-secret work for the US government," said Kuan Hee. "I reckon the Green Party government wants to get its hands on this top-secret technology."

"I guess they have taken your parents back to Singapore," said Tim.

"That's exactly what I think too," said Kuan Hee. "Brigadier Walmsley is investigating the disappearance. He says he will be getting back to me soon. I forgot to add— the entire research team has been kidnapped."

"If I didn't hear this from you, I mean, if someone else had told me this," said Tim, "I wouldn't believe him. The very idea that our government can be so despicable."

"It took me some time to accept this idea too," said Kuan Hee. "Like I said earlier, I am pretty sure this Green Party government is evil. We have elected the wrong guys into government."

"Count me in," said Tim. He knew what was on Kuan Hee's mind.

"Me too," said Navin.

"Here we go again," exclaimed Tim. *My life is never dull, not with Kuan Hee as my friend,* he told himself.

CHAPTER 10

Brigadier Walmsley had contacted Kuan Hee on the walkie-talkie and told him he wanted to meet up with him. This time, their venue would be ToastBox Café at Plaza Singapura.

"I think the Brigadier has found my parents," said Kuan Hee.

"How do you know?" asked Lina.

"The urgency in his voice," said Kuan Hee.

The Brigadier had not said much, beyond suggesting the meeting place. The pair was seated in the alfresco part of the café, facing the taxi stand. They had arrived early to grab some seats. ToastBox Café outlets were popular with the locals.

The Brigadier waved to them as he walked from the taxi stand. As usual, he was wearing a hunting hat.

"Sorry to keep you waiting," said the Brigadier.

Aside from sporting more wrinkles across his temple, the Brigadier was much the same man that the pair had met five years ago in Hougang Bus Interchange.

"I've grown to like the *kopi oh kosong* at ToastBox," said Brigadier Walmsley, as he stroked his straggly beard. "I must remember to buy some when we leave afterwards."

Even as he was talking, Lina was already on her feet. She went to queue at the counter and returned with two bags of coffee powder. Kuan Hee and the Brigadier were engaging in small talk.

"You know, Kuan Hee," said the Brigadier. "In the late 1970s, Plaza Singapura was a favourite venue for families during the weekends."

"It still is," said Lina.

"Is it?" said the Brigadier. "If my memories serve me right, there was a department store by the name of Yaohan here. It occupied the ground and basement floors. People flocked here to buy groceries and shop for clothes."

"Yes. My dad told me he spent his Saturdays here with his schoolmates," said Kuan Hee. "They would meet at Medo Restaurant, opposite the road, for a Western lunch before hopping over to Plaza Singapura to while away the afternoon."

"Is that so, Kuan Hee?" said the Brigadier. "I used to come here nearly every weekend too. Let me see now. I was based in Sembawang at the time."

It took a while before the Brigadier got down to business. It was his habit to seize up the surroundings first.

"Kuan Hee," said the Brigadier. "In a nutshell, your parents are in Singapore right now."

Kuan Hee and Lina sat at the edge of their seats. They were now listening intently to the Brigadier whose voice had dropped to a whisper.

"Your parents and the other researchers are being held at the Battle Box in Fort Canning Hill," said the Brigadier.

The pair gasped. Fort Canning Hill was a tourist attraction. The Battle Box was where the British military commanders sited their Command Centre in Singapore during the Second World War.

"The Battle Box is merely a stone's throw away from here," said Kuan Hee. "It's—it's—" He was about to point in the direction of the Battle Box when the Brigadier caught his hand and gently placed it on the small table.

"There's no need to draw attention to us," said the Brigadier as a matter-of-factly.

"Sorry, Mr Walmsley," said Kuan Hee. "I got too excited, I guess." By now he had realized the reason for the Brigadier choosing to meet at Plaza Singapura.

"Our sources in Singapore tell us your parents have been held there for the past year," said the Brigadier. "It's now a restricted area, guarded by soldiers around the clock. It would be difficult to mount a rescue."

"Will you help us, Mr Walmsley?" said Kuan Hee.

"You know, Kuan Hee. The last time, we were dealing with a dictator who usurped power in a coup. So we could mobilise the Delta Force. This time it is a democratically elected government in office. My government would think very hard before agreeing to move against a legally installed government. Remember—the United States stand for Life, Liberty and the Pursuit of Happiness. We fought hard for these ideals. We try our best to protect these ideals too. Anywhere in the world."

"But the soldiers kidnapped my parents and the others from your research centre in Australia," said Kuan Hee. "That should be enough reason for the US government to take action."

"Kuan Hee, even though we know this, we can't send our rangers into Fort Canning to rescue them. It's a politically sensitive matter. My hands are tied," said the Brigadier. "You see, after the downfall of the military regime in your country, there were discussions on moving our logistics support group back to Sembawang Naval Base. But this has been put on the backburner by the Green Party government. We need to be careful how we move in this situation."

The Brigadier twiddled his thumbs as he sat in thought. Then he took a sip of coffee and looked in Kuan Hee's eyes.

"I can't carry out a rescue. But, I can provide you with support—equipment, information and backup," said the

Brigadier. He took out a paper bag from his jacket pocket and handed it to Kuan Hee.

"This will be useful to you," said the Brigadier. "Go ahead, open it."

Kuan Hee unfolded the bag and peered inside. It looked like two pairs of glasses. He took them out and held them in his hands. With the coffee cups and cake plates, there was hardly any free space left on the small table. He passed a pair to Lina.

"State-of-the-art technology," said the Brigadier. "Put them on."

"They look like Google Glass eyeglasses," said Lina. "How do I use them? What do I use them for? How do I activate them?"

"Slowly, dear girl," said the Brigadier. "So many questions. How do I answer them all?"

"Sorry, Mr Walmsley," said Kuan Hee. "She just can't contain her excitement."

"These are manufactured by a project at Google Glass. They are in the experimental stage," said the Brigadier. "You can hide your identity by wearing them."

"Hide my identity?" said Kuan Hee.

"Yes. What I mean is—cameras can't identify you. CCTV cameras will see a different you. Try scrolling the different figures you can use. Simply say 'menu', then 'identity choices', then 'OK'."

Kuan Hee and Lina did as instructed and they were treated to a variety of faces, of different races and cultures. They chose one.

"Kuan Hee, you still look the same," quipped Lina.

"You too, Lina," said Kuan Hee.

"My dear children," said the Brigadier. "Only digital devices cannot recognize you. You will still look the same to anyone you meet. Anyway, the good thing is—you can move around unencumbered."

"How does it do that?" asked Lina.

"It projects a chosen face that hugs your face, so digital

devices see only the chosen face. They can only scan that face," said the Brigadier.

"Thank you very much," said the pair in unison.

"It will take a while for you to get used to the features. It's voice activated, you know, like other Google Glass devices. You can google information on Google Glass. These glasses can do all other Google Glass devices can do, and more," said the Brigadier. "You can also use it to contact me, to talk to me. No need to use the walkie-talkie."

"How do I change the battery?" asked Lina.

"These run on solar energy," said the Brigadier. "It's impregnated with solar cells. Also, it uses the Polaris satellite, so no one can track you."

"That's the same carrier that Dad uses," said Kuan Hee.

"I know," said the Brigadier. "I gave him access to Polaris. You know, Polaris is a secret US government spy satellite."

"Is that so?" said Lina. "No wonder, I can't google information on it."

"How do I use it to talk to you?" asked Kuan Hee.

"All the instructions are in the guide in your glasses," said the Brigadier. "Call up the menu and scroll through the options. My number is already listed in the Contacts section. Remember, when I talk to you, only you can hear me, others can't. The device uses bone conduction."

"Bone what?" said Lina.

"Just google 'bone conduction'. You will find all the information you need," said the Brigadier. "This part is not classified information."

CHAPTER 11

It was the second time in a week that the four friends had gathered in the small room above the shophouse in Realty Park. They were here to discuss the rescue of Kuan Hee's parents and the other researchers. Their focus point was the Battle Box, a relic from the Second World War.

"I visited the Battle Box during my secondary school days. It was a museum then," said Kuan Hee.

"I can still recall the layout of the place," said Kuan Hee. He took a piece of blank paper and proceeded to sketch a plan of the underground bunker. He paused now and then, erased some lines and drew new ones. In minutes, the plan was complete. Everyone leaned forward to take a look.

"It's big," said Tim. He counted the number of rooms. "There must be at least twenty rooms."

"There should be more. I can't recall the locations of the other rooms," said Kuan Hee. "So I have not drawn them in."

"Where does this stairwell lead to?" asked Navin.

"The park above the bunker. There is a concrete block protruding above the ground and a metal door on it. Let me google the place," said Kuan Hee. He took out his smartphone and searched for 'battle box' on google.com. Then he clicked on the images tab. Columns of pictures appeared on the screen and he scrolled down the thumbnails of the pictures till he found what he was looking for.

"Here it is," said Kuan Hee. He pointed to the protruding structure in the middle of an open grassy space. He visited thebattlebox.com. It hosted the picture they were viewing.

"Wow! It has everything about the Battle Box," said Lina. "There are many more pictures on this Website."

"Yes, it is a goldmine of information," said Navin. "The museum has been closed for a long time, and yet this Website is still online."

"We are indeed lucky," said Kuan Hee.

"See whether it has a map of the place," said Tim.

"Click on the side menu, Kuan Hee, where it says 'Inside'," said Lina.

The Inside section listed all the different rooms: Fort Commander's Office; Commander, Fixed Defences Room; Orderlies Room; Gun Operations Room; and Escape Route. There was no map of the place.

"Click on Escape Route, Kuan Hee," said Navin.

"According to this Website, the escape route was a closely guarded secret," said Tim. "Here are pictures of the corridor leading to the stairwell. And here is the staircase in the stairwell." He pinched the screen and spread two fingers to enlarge the pictures.

"Kuan Hee, go to Exit," said Lina, pointing to the last item on the sidebar.

On the Exit page were photographs of a pair of metal doors, which fitted snugly against a fern-laced backdrop protruding from a steep slope. On top of this slope was a continuous metre-tall granite wall running parallel to the slope.

"I remember we came out this way after the tour, and sat here eating our lunch," said Kuan Hee, pointing to the wide granite walkway in front of the Battle Box's exit.

"How about the Entrance?" said Tim. "Let's take a look."

The entrance was similar to the exit. Both the entrance and exit were built flush against the two sides of a hill, with a wide walkway running parallel southwards and ending at a roundabout.

"I didn't know there are roundabouts in Singapore," said Lina. "I thought they went the way of the Dodo."

"This one is steeped in history," said Navin. "It's been around since the Second World War, so they won't destroy it."

"What's beyond the roundabout?" asked Lina.

"It's a steep slope with a staircase running down to the road below," said Kuan Hee. "My classmates and I climbed up Fort Canning using it."

"I thought the coach took you there," said Lina.

"Nope. The coach dropped us at the National Museum, a stone's throw away," said Kuan Hee. "After visiting the National Museum, we walked to Fort Canning Park for the Battle Box visit."

"I see," said Lina. "What's this?" Lina was pointing at the Interesting Things tab on the sidebar.

Kuan Hee clicked on the tab. There were pictures of different things which could be found in the Battle Box: old oil drums, oil lamps, jerrycans, helmets, signalling sets—all from the war era.

"What's this?" said Navin, fingering a flat metal plate on the screen.

"It's a manhole cover," said Kuan Hee. There is an underground drainage system running throughout the bunker."

"Mmm. Water goes into the bunker. To prevent flooding of the bunker, they arranged for water to be disposed of using this drainage system," said Tim. "Ingenious. Simply ingenious, the British."

"Hey! That's it. The water goes out of the bunker," said

Navin. "There's another way out of the bunker."

"Yeah. But where?" asked Lina. "It doesn't say anything on the Website."

"Yes, I wonder where," said Kuan Hee. He was now fingering the stubble on his chin. He had forgotten to shave today.

"Who's the owner of the Website?" asked Navin. "Perhaps, we can find out more from him or her."

"Considering the amount of information contained on this Website," said Tim. "This fella must be fond of the Battle Box."

"I agree," said Lina.

"There's no contact information," said Kuan Hee. "It doesn't have a contact form either."

"Go to the About page," said Tim.

"It says 'online since 2010,'" said Kuan Hee. "It's twenty-five years ago."

"I suggest we do a whois search," said Navin.

"Just a moment," said Kuan Hee. He typed the domain name on the whois search engine.

"The contact number looks fictitious," said Navin. "But the address seems real."

"Block 227A Yishun Street twenty-one, #02-711," said Kuan Hee.

"Now that's a lead," said Navin. "Who's going there?"

"I will," said Kuan Hee.

"Me too," said Lina.

"That's settled then," said Tim. "Give us an update when you are done."

"Let's google the plan of Fort Canning Park," said Navin.

Kuan Hee typed Fort Canning Park in the search box on google.com.

The map that came up in the search results detailed the different landmarks on the hill. But it was difficult for them to view it on the small smartphone screen. They had to squint.

"Here. Click on this link," said Navin.

"*Wah*, it's a heritage site," said Lina. "Look at the nine-pound cannons, the old gates and the memorials."

"What's this large coloured patch?" asked Tim. "Zoom in on the writing, Kuan Hee."

"It says 'Fort Canning Service Reservoir," said Kuan Hee.

"Gee, I didn't know there's a reservoir on this small hill," said Lina.

"The reservoir is so close to the Battle Box," said Navin. "I wonder—maybe the drainage system in the bunker empties into the reservoir."

"Possible," said Tim.

"Shall we go recce the place?" asked Navin. "We need some perspective on the hill."

"Let's wait for Kuan Hee to talk to the Website's owner first," said Tim. "At least, we'll have some direction, instead of feeling around in the dark."

"I agree," said Kuan Hee. "The owner may have intimate knowledge of the bunker that we can put to good use."

CHAPTER 12

"This driverless bus is too slow," said Kuan Hee. "It's almost like crawling from one stop to another."

"It isn't slow," said Lina. "Look! The car alongside it is moving about the same pace. You are just too anxious." She was right. Kuan Hee was eager to get his parents out of the Battle Box; he was getting impatient.

Kuan Hee and Lina were on their way to check out the address given in the domain ownership

The pair alighted at the bus stop in front of the neighbourhood centre. Block 227A was opposite the bus stop. It was a new block towering 25 storeys above the ground. They climbed the stairs to a second-storey unit at the corner of the block.

A fortyish fair-complexioned woman opened the door. The pair learnt she was the daughter of the Website owner.

"My father is not living here," said the lady. Kuan Hee's lips pressed against each other. He had been hoping for positive news.

She scribbled an address on a piece of paper and handed it to Kuan Hee. "He lives alone in a studio apartment. He's frightfully independent for a seventy-seven-year-old man."

"He's that old?" said Lina. She couldn't contain her astonishment. She had been imagining a middle-aged man." Kuan Hee glared at her. They were there to fish for information and such words didn't help.

"Yes, he worked at the Battle Box as a guide in the 1990s," said the lady matter-of-factly. "It's been forty years since."

"Thank you very much," said the pair in unison. Kuan Hee was glad the lady saw no offence in Lina's remark.

"Look for him in the evening," said the lady. "In the day, he likes to move around. You see—my father can't keep still."

"Thanks for the tip," said Kuan Hee. "How shall I address your father?"

"You can call him Mr Hon," said the lady.

The pair bade goodbye to the lady and made their way to the bus stop.

"Where's he living?"

"Surprise! It's Hougang Meadows. It's right opposite Holy Innocents' High School. We can walk there from Realty Park."

"It's so near us and we didn't have an inkling. Are we going there now?"

"Yes, dear." Kuan Hee was one who couldn't wait. Once he had set his mind on doing something, he wouldn't rest till it got done.

On the way back by bus, Kuan Hee kept complaining about the slowness of the bus.

"These driverless buses are a pain in the neck." Kuan Hee was leaning forward again for the return journey. It was a different bus. This was a double-decker and they were seated on the upper deck as usual.

"What to do? There aren't enough workers. It's all because our people are not reproducing themselves in sufficient numbers. Besides, this bus isn't slow. It's just your imagination, Kuan Hee."

Kuan Hee wanted to look up Mr Hon immediately, but

Lina was having hunger pangs. He had no choice; they had to adjourn for lunch first.

After a hurried meal at ToastBox café in the basement of Hougang Mall, the pair walked over to Hougang Meadows. Mr Hon lived on the eighth storey of a twenty-storey HDB apartment block. No one opened the door at his unit. They stood there for a while before Kuan Hee realised Mr Hon was not home. Then he remembered what the lady had told him earlier. They had made the trip in vain.

All was not lost. Mr Hon lived within walking distance of Realty Park. They would return to his flat later in the evening.

It was 6:30 p.m. In the dwindling daylight, Kuan Hee and Lina parked themselves in the void deck of the block of flats opposite Mr Hon's apartment. From there, they had an unhindered view of his flat. It was dark inside. He wasn't home yet.

They saw windows in the block light up one by one. Soon, most of the windows were lit, but Mr Hon's remained in darkness. The pair was getting tired, for they had been craning their necks all evening.

Then they saw his unit light up. Mr Hon was finally home. The pair ran to the lift.

A sprightly, wizened old man opened the door. He welcomed them into his flat. He was not surprised to see them; his daughter had told him of their visit to her place. It was a studio apartment, with a small living room and an adjoining bedroom. The kitchen was slightly bigger than Kuan Hee's pantry at 79 Jalan Naung. A statue of the God of Wealth stood atop a tall thin wooden cabinet facing the front door. There were Coca-Cola paraphernalia displayed in it. A sofa sat adjacent to two armchairs in the living room. A MacBook computer and some books sat on a desk set against one wall.

The pair sat on the sofa while Mr Hon leaned forward

in an armchair next to them.

"What is it about the Battle Box that you two youngsters are keen on knowing?" asked Mr Hon.

"Mr Hon, we are interested in the history of the Battle Box," said Kuan Hee.

"So you must have visited my Website," said Mr Hon.

"Yes, and we learnt quite a bit about the Battle Box," said Kuan Hee. "But, there's no map of the bunker. We don't know the exact layout of the place."

"Forgive me for being brunt, but why are you interested in the Battle Box?" said Mr Hon. "It's an old bunker and is of no use to anyone except historians and tourist guides. You two don't strike me as belonging to either group."

"Mr Hon. The truth is—my parents are being held hostage in the Battle Box. My friends and I want to get them out. We need to know the area well so we can plan a rescue," said Kuan Hee.

"Are these people kidnappers?" asked Mr Hon. "Or do your parents belong to some underworld group?"

"Neither," said Kuan Hee. "My dad is a scientist. He works for the American government. He was kidnapped with my mum and other research staff from Australia. They were flown here and kept in the bunker."

Mr Hon was now stroking his sideburn. He leaned on one arm of the chair and gazed into Kuan Hee's eyes. He seemed to be sizing up Kuan Hee. There was a long silence.

"Kuan Hee, that's your name right?" said Mr Hon.

"Yes, Mr Hon," said Kuan Hee. "And she is my wife, Lina."

"Right," said Mr Hon. He was now running a finger across his chin. "To tell you the truth, your story seems far-fetched. It's not that I don't believe you. It's just that this is our first meeting and I do not know you well."

"Mr Hon, I have no reason to be lying to you," said Kuan Hee.

"Kuan Hee, you said your father was kidnapped in Australia and flown to Singapore," said Mr Hon. "Who kidnapped him?"

"The Singapore government—I mean, the Green Party government," said Kuan Hee. "Dad is working on some top secret project for the American government and our government wants in on it."

"Now, why would our government do something like this? And if they really did, the American government would be able to get your father and the other researchers back," said Mr Hon. "So why involve you and your friends?"

Lina was finding it difficult to keep to her seat. She was now sitting at the edge of the chair. Kuan Hee placed a hand on her lap. He was telling her not to crash his efforts.

"Mr Hon, I am in contact with an American operative who works with my dad. He says that the Green Party government is legally elected so his people can't step in to help," said Kuan Hee.

"But, these researchers are working for them," said Mr Hon. "There's no reason for the Americans to turn a blind eye."

"That's what I thought so," Mr Hon. "But the American operative says the American government doesn't want to antagonize the Singapore government, unless there is proof."

"Proof? Proof of what?" said Mr Hon.

"Proof that the researchers are being held here," said Kuan Hee.

"I thought the Americans have got state-of-the-art equipment. Getting proof is a simple affair for them," said Mr Hon.

"I guess they don't want to be embarrassed—in case the rescue fails, or it turns out the researchers are not in the bunker," said Kuan Hee.

"Then how do you know for sure they are there?" said Mr Hon.

"I don't," said Kuan Hee. "That's why I have come here to see you. I thought you might know a way for us—my friends and I—to get inside the bunker so that we can confirm my parents are in it. The American operative has promised to help us after we have got my parents out."

"Is that so?" said Mr Hon. He pursed his lips in thought. "Let me think."

It was getting late and the pair was getting nowhere with Mr Hon. Instead of giving them the information they so badly needed, he took them on a circuitous path that brought them back to square one.

"Who is this American operative?" asked Mr Hon. "And where in Australia are your father and the other researchers based?"

Kuan Hee paused. He could not decide whether to divulge the Brigadier's name. After all, Mr Hon was a stranger. He wasn't sure he could be trusted. Then he realized both Mr Hon and he had something in common. They were dealing with total strangers, and neither could decide whether to trust the other. He reasoned he had to make the first move to break the barrier.

"Brigadier James Walmsley is his name. He is with the Special Forces. Dad's research unit is based in Airlie Beach, on the Whitsundays Coast in Northern Australia," said Kuan Hee.

Mr Hon jotted down what Kuan Hee had told him. He leaned forward again.

"Tell you what," said Mr Hon. "I'll study this and get back to you. Let me have your phone number."

Kuan Hee had prepared himself for this moment. Unlike Lina, he wasn't at all surprised. He told Mr Hon his mobile number.

"This isn't a local number," said Mr Hon.

"It's a satellite carrier number," said Kuan Hee. "It belongs to my dad."

"Really?" said Mr Hon.

"Yes," said Kuan Hee. "What I have told you is the

truth. My dad is really a scientist. Let me demonstrate one of his inventions." Kuan Hee took out little Busy and opened its remote control panel. At once, little Busy rose and flitted into the air. It flew around Kuan Hee, Lina and Mr Hon.

Kuan Hee showed Mr Hon the screen. It had a live video of the view of the room from the cameras in little Busy's eyes.

It was clear Mr Hon was mesmerized. He had never seen anything so fascinating as little Busy.

"Is this for real?" Mr Hon exclaimed.

Kuan Hee let little Busy land on Mr Hon's arm.

"It's so tiny," said Mr Hon, "and futuristic. I've not seen anything like this before. The technology for miniaturizing this robot is way ahead of the times. It must be top-secret."

With its mission accomplished, little Busy flew back into Kuan Hee's backpack.

"Let me sleep on it," said Mr Hon. "I'll contact you again."

The pair thanked Mr Hon for his time and left his flat. Downstairs, Lina fumed.

"We spent two whole hours for nothing."

"No, *lah*. I think Mr Hon has been convinced. He'll help us."

"Will he? I got the feeling he was merely giving us a merry-go-round."

"I think little Busy worked wonders on him. I think he believes what I said. Like he said, give him some time to think over."

Though Kuan Hee was trying to convince Lina with his words, he himself harboured some doubts.

CHAPTER 13

The four friends met at an open space outside Dhoby Ghaut MRT Station. They had come prepared for an afternoon of fieldwork. Fort Canning Park was atop a small hill and there was plenty of walking and standing under the glare of the hot sun. All adorned caps to shade their faces.

"What's with the glasses?" asked Navin. Kuan Hee and Lina were sporting eyeglasses.

"These aren't eyeglasses," said Kuan Hee. "These are Google Glass devices. They help disguise us."

"You guys still look the same to me," quipped Tim.

"They hide our real faces from the CCTV cameras," said Lina.

"*Wah!* Is that for real?" said Navin. "I didn't know Google Glass eyeglasses have got this capability."

"The eyeglasses work. They really do," said Lina. "Brigadier Walmsley gave these to us. He knows the G operatives are after us."

"Let's move off," said Kuan Hee. "We are drawing curious looks here."

Tim and Navin were tasked to explore the hill on the

reservoir side. So they separated from Kuan Hee and Lina who were to check out the Battle Box. The four friends would rendezvous at the old gate near the Registry of Marriages.

Kuan Hee and Lina walked across Penang Lane, climbed up the steps next to the Park Mall Dragon Fountain, crossed a small road and clambered the long concrete stairs leading to the roundabout on Fort Canning Hill. As they ascended the last step on the slope, they panted. Lina bent over, pressing her hands on her knees. She looked back down the steep slope.

"We must have climbed more than a hundred steps," she groaned.

"It's actually ninety-three steps," said Kuan Hee, bending down. "I counted them as we moved up the stairs."

"I'm definitely not going down this way afterwards," said Lina.

The pair saw soldiers about fifty metres ahead, in front of a white single-storey rectangular building with a gable roof. The cobbled lanes on both sides of the building were cordoned off with metal barriers. The building had doors facing the roundabout and the left lane. A soldier, armed with a rifle, guarded each of the lanes. It appeared the building was being used as a guardhouse.

"We can't go any further without attracting the sentries' attention. They have got a clear line of sight all the way to the roundabout. This was a tourist area previously; now the area is sealed off."

"Where's the Battle Box?"

"Both lanes lead to the Battle Box. It is about fifty steps from the entrance to the lane. In fact, the bunker is situated underground between the two lanes."

"And the reservoir?"

"The reservoir lies beyond the Battle Box. The Battle Box and reservoir are all in a straight line from here."

Kuan Hee raised his hand directly in front of him and pointed ahead of them.

"We can't even get close to the Battle Box. How are we going to mount a rescue when we can't even see the Battle Box from here?"

"Lina, things don't look too bad. Don't forget—we've got little Busy with us."

"How could I have forgotten about it?"

"Now, we've got to find a cosy place to hide."

The pair made a left turn before the roundabout and followed the winding road. Kuan Hee spied a small open space on the grass behind a clump of bushes. He signalled for Lina to follow him. This spot was in front of a tall Tembusu tree so it provided shade from the hot afternoon sun. They could not see the guardhouse from here, but they had an unobstructed view of the surroundings. It would be easy to make an escape if soldiers chanced upon them. Kuan Hee checked to see the ground was clear of ant routes before the pair settled down on the grass. He didn't want a colony of ants to startle Lina. Kuan Hee placed the remote control for little Busy on his backpack. Little Busy flitted out of the backpack and hovered over them.

Meanwhile Navin had texted Kuan Hee to tell him they had to abort the recce; Fort Canning Park was crawling with soldiers. There was no way for them to observe the area unnoticed. It was too risky. Kuan Hee communicated the pair's location to Navin.

The pair heard the rustling of leaves on grass. It was Tim and Navin. Kuan Hee raised a hand above the bush and the two men joined them behind the bush.

"Did you have better luck here?" asked Tim.

"We couldn't even get near the Battle Box. The old building in front of the roundabout has been turned into a guardhouse. Anyone there can see all the way to the roundabout. There's no way to get past the soldiers undetected," said Kuan Hee.

"We walked around the hill towards the reservoir, but there is a chain-link fence running around the perimeter. There are soldiers patrolling behind the fence. It seems Fort Canning Hill has become a military installation," said Navin.

"How can a tourist attraction become a military camp?" said Lina.

"It's difficult to move around without being spotted by people on the hill. It's an attacker's nightmare."

"Don't forget Fort Canning Hill was originally an army camp hosting the British armed forces. It was purpose-built, with the bunker as a top-secret command centre for the British commanders," said Kuan Hee.

"How are we going to rescue your parents?" asked Tim. "It looks like an impossible task."

"Let's see what little Busy can tell us about this place," said Kuan Hee. He instructed the robot housefly to fly towards the guardhouse.

"Who's taking notes of our findings?" asked Tim.

"Let me do it," said Lina.

As little Busy flew over the guardhouse and up the cobbled lane, the four friends were treated to an aerial view of Fort Canning Park. There was a lone guard outside the entrance to the bunker. Aside from this, there was no one in the open space between the bunker's entrance and the building opposite it.

Little Busy flew over the bunker's entrance, up the slope to a large open park. There was not a soul in sight. The old historical gates and arches adorning the park, accustomed to the fawning attention of photograph snapping tourists, looked out of place in the deserted landscape.

Little Busy flew down the other side of the park onto the exit of the bunker. There was another guard stationed here. The metal doors were shut too. There was no gap through which the robot housefly would use to sneak into the bunker.

At the edge of the granite walkway was a chain-link fence running parallel to it. Beyond it, on the bottom of a steep slope, stood another historical building, now a hotel.

"This slope is the shortest route to the Battle Box," said Tim. "Only the fence stands in the way."

"The galvanized steel mesh is clean of rust. It could not be more than a year old," said Navin.

"Seems this is the easiest and fastest way to get to the bunker," said Kuan Hee.

"So we use this way to escape from the bunker too?" said Navin.

"Anyone disagrees?" asked Kuan Hee. There was silence.

"Now, we have to wait for someone to come out or go inside the bunker," said Navin. He took a puff on a cigarette he had lit. He was an occasional smoker. "It may be a long wait."

"No choice," said Kuan Hee.

"Can we move somewhere else to keep watch?" asked Lina. She was scratching her arms and legs. Then she slapped her face and looked at her hand. "The mosquitoes here are pesky." Kuan Hee had been careful to choose a spot free from ants, but it did not occur to him that Fort Canning Hill was a magnet for mosquitoes. None of the four friends were spared.

"I don't think there is a better place than here. Any nearer and we could be found out," said Kuan Hee. "Besides, the whole hill seems to be infested with mosquitoes. Even if we change to another spot, there is no guarantee it will be mosquito free."

"I agree with Kuan Hee," said Navin. "Anyway, we can always rub some oil over the bites."

"Next time, I will remember to bring some mosquito repellent patches," said Lina.

"Nobody is coming in or out of the bunker," said Navin. "We can't continue waiting like this."

"I saw some round things protruding out of the ground in the park," said Tim. "Can we get little Busy to check them out? Perhaps, it is a way in."

"Where?" asked Kuan Hee. He directed little Busy to fly over the open ground on top of the slope.

"See the metre-long circular tops coming out of the ground?" said Tim. "Get little Busy to fly closer."

"Look like air vents," said Navin. "It's logical for them to be here. The bunker needs ventilation."

"I'll fly little Busy into the—the air vent," said Kuan Hee.

The four pressed their heads closer to the remote control screen. It was dark in the air vent but little Busy's eyes had thermal and infrared imaging sensors. It made short work of moving around in the dark. It was simply amazing how little Busy managed to avoid hitting the walls of the duct. The housefly flitted through a long winding duct, which made several ninety-degree turns before finally ending in a rectangular contraption with louvred openings on one side.

Finally, little Busy peeped through the lourved opening and darted out into the open space. The room, the size of a HDB kitchen, was brightly lit. It had a high ceiling. The contraption occupied nearly half the room. The doorless room opened into a long corridor. LED tubes installed at regular intervals on the ceiling provided illumination for the bunker.

Little Busy hovered in the corridor. It could not decide which direction to explore.

"Turn left, Kuan Hee," said Lina.

Kuan Hee laid the map he had drawn next to the remote control.

"See—the bunker is a rectangular labyrinth of rooms, with the entrance located on one breadth of the rectangle and the exit on one length of the rectangle," said Kuan Hee.

"Where is little Busy now?" asked Lina.

"Here," said Kuan Hee, pointing to a corridor on the map.

Little Busy turned left and flew through the corridor; Kuan Hee moved his finger in unison. There was a fork in the corridor now.

"A left turn will take little Busy past these few rooms and then to the exit," said Kuan Hee. "And a right turn will bring it to the first few rooms at the entrance, which is here."

"Let's see the entrance area first," said Navin. "Find out how they guard the bunker."

Kuan Hee manoeuvred through the passageway towards the entrance.

"There doesn't seem to be anyone around," said Lina.

"They could be in the rooms," said Kuan Hee.

Little Busy was now at the end of the corridor. A metal door stood in front of it. On both sides of little Busy were rooms.

"This door leads to the entrance of the bunker," said Kuan Hee. He remembered being treated to the screams of a loud wailing siren as he and his schoolmates entered the bunker for a visit.

"The left room was the Orderlies Room," said Kuan Hee.

Little Busy flitted into the doorless Orderlies Room. There were two bunk beds, one on each side of the room, and a desk and chair between them. A rifle rack stood next to the doorway. There was hardly any space left for more furniture. No one was in the room.

"Four beds equals four guards," said Tim.

"How do you know they are for guards?" asked Lina.

"See the rifle rack?" said Tim.

"These are for rifles?" said Lina.

Tim nodded.

"Why don't we see people in the bunker?" asked Lina. "Where have they all gone?"

"The place seems deserted," said Tim.

"But the thermal sensors on little Busy show the air temperature is twenty-two degrees Centigrade. The air-conditioning is switched on," said Kuan Hee.

"Where could your parents be?" said Navin.

Little Busy flew back through the passageway and turned right this time. It passed room after room but there was no way to enter them—there were no gaps between the metal doors and the floor. It made a left turn and another right turn and the four friends found themselves looking at a metal door at the end of a long corridor.

"It's the exit," said Kuan Hee, pointing to its location on the top of the map.

"Let little Busy go into the room on the left," said Tim.

"Looks like another room for the guards," said Navin.

"There are three bunk beds here," said Lina. "This room is bigger and longer than the other one."

"Six plus four equals ten guards," said Tim.

"This number doesn't include those at the guardhouse and patrolling the grounds," said Navin.

"Must be a platoon of men," said Kuan Hee.

"How many is that?" asked Lina.

"Around forty to fifty men," said Kuan Hee. "Makes sense. This is a sprawling park that the bunker sits under."

"That many?" said Lina.

A metal door cranked open somewhere in the bunker. Then came the shuffling of boots. The sounds echoed through the passageways into little Busy's microphones.

"Someone or some people are here," said Tim. "There's no way to tell how many from the echoes."

"Let little Busy fly towards the entrance," said Navin.

Little Busy made two turns and the four friends saw at least ten people walking through the passageway. There were two soldiers in front and another two at the back of the group. In between them were civilians.

The four friends were now glued to the screen, trying to make out the faces of the civilians.

"That's Dad," said Kuan Hee. He was now pointing at a head on the screen.

"Yes, it sure is Uncle," said Lina. She was used to calling Professor Wang Uncle though the pair was now married.

"I don't see Mum," said Kuan Hee. "She's not in the group."

Kuan Hee did not recognize the other civilians. They could be members of his father's research team.

"There are six civilians here, not counting your dad," said Lina as she jotted down the information in a little notebook in her hand.

Kuan Hee piloted little Busy over the civilians towards his father. The high ceiling was a boon for little Busy; they would not notice it, unless they craned their necks upwards.

Two soldiers led the civilians into the room at the intersection of two passageways, whilst another stationed himself outside the door. The last soldier was now standing at the entrance.

"These soldiers look like regulars," said Kuan Hee.

"Quick! Follow them into the room, Kuan Hee," said Tim.

It was the first, and smaller, of two adjoining rooms. It served as a changing room. The civilians put on a white gown and wrapped a mesh over their heads. Then they wore masks and visors over their faces.

"It used to be the Fortress Commander's Office," said Kuan Hee. "The adjoining room was the Gun Operations Room."

The civilians walked through a doorway into the larger room. As little Busy flitted through the doorway, it flipped and wobbled. Then it stabilized itself.

"There seems to be turbulence in the air. There is an invisible curtain of some kind of air particles bombarding the doorway continuously," said Tim.

"I think there is a decontamination zone at the doorway," said Kuan Hee. "The larger room must be a clean room."

There was equipment everywhere in the larger room. It was bigger than a classroom. Computer monitors sat on metal racks positioned against one wall. On the other walls, several server cabinets housed a multitude of servers with cables running behind them and trailing across the length of the room. It looked like a mainframe computer room, except there wasn't a platform for cables to run under.

"This must be the brain centre of the bunker," said Navin.

In one section, there were robotic assemblers and next to them, a big piece of equipment, the size of a dining table. On one side was a label: DNA Molecular Assembly. Alongside was a big rectangular box on a stand. It had a pair of rubberized openings through which one could insert one's hands. Inside the box was an array of tubes and capsules on a rack. At the far end of the room was a floor-to-ceiling glass partition. Behind the door on the partition was what seemed to be a small operating theatre.

"Looks like a cloning laboratory," said Tim. Like Kuan Hee, he had majored in nano-technology at Temasek University and was familiar with some of the equipment.

"Yes, indeed," said Kuan Hee. "The walls between the Gun Operations Room and the two rooms beyond have been torn down. So this room is now triple its original length."

A lone soldier was watching over the civilians in the room. The other was resting in the changing room. They were taking turns to keep watch over the civilians.

"The only way in and out is through the changing room," said Navin. "The other doors have been sealed shut."

Professor Wang was now seated at a desk with two assistants flanking him. He was pointing at the computer monitor in front of him and talking to his assistants. He had not noticed little Busy perched on the wall in front of him.

"Looks like the whole bunker has been stripped bare of the museum props," said Kuan Hee. "The mannequins, old telephone exchange, surrender chamber furniture and the large platform on which stood a map of Malaya and Singapore are all gone."

"The bunker is now a bona fide research centre," said Tim. He pointed at the screen. Professor Wang was moving towards the computer servers. He was alone. Little Busy launched itself into the air and flitted towards the professor. It was now hovering over his left ear.

Kuan Hee tapped the microphone icon on the remote control. He slid the volume lever to low.

"Dad. Dad, it's me Kuan Hee," said Kuan Hee.

Professor Wang turned his head. Although the visor and mask hid his face, the corners of his mouth had turned upwards, and his cheeks peaked. He was beaming. He looked behind him. The other researchers were engrossed in their work and the guard was staring blankly into space.

Using a finger, Professor Wang scribbled 'Hi' on the flap of the server rack in front of him.

"Where's Mum?" asked Kuan Hee.

The professor drew a rectangle and a smaller rectangle on its upper right. Then he scribbled an arrow and 'Exit'.

Lina pointed to the rooms next to the exit. "Uncle means Auntie is in one of these rooms," she said.

"It's good Mum and Dad are safe," said Kuan Hee.

Kuan Hee didn't have time to ask more questions, for the professor's assistants were now approaching him.

"Shall we leave little Busy with Uncle?" asked Lina.

"Yes, of course," said Kuan Hee. He directed little Busy to fly under his father's lab coat. It attached itself to his trouser pocket.

"Time to leave the hill," said Kuan Hee. "Our work's done for today."

The other friends were glad to leave Fort Canning Hill. The mosquitoes had been feasting on their blood the whole afternoon.

CHAPTER 14

Sitting at a table next to the glass windows of the food court on the third level of Marina Square, the four friends had a panoramic view of the Marina Bay area. The spiky edges of the 'durians', the nickname for the Esplanade Theatre, cut a stark contrast with the clear blue sky.

"Hey, Kuan Hee," said Navin. "You can remove these glasses now. They look funny on you."

"I simply dread these CCTV cameras," said Kuan Hee, taking off the Google Glass.

"These cameras have been around for ages," said Navin. "But I didn't hear you complain about them before."

"That's because I wasn't being targeted then," said Kuan Hee. "Now, that the G operatives are looking for me, these cameras have become a nuisance. I had to keep avoiding them all the time."

"Not anymore, right?" said Tim. "You have the Google Glass."

"Yes, thank goodness for it," said Kuan Hee.

"The network of connected CCTV cameras in public areas came about because of the terrorist threat in the 2010s. Remember the terrorist attacks in Europe?" said Tim.

"It was good for the purpose then. The world was on edge. We were continually looking over our shoulders, dreading an attack in the streets," said Kuan Hee. "But that's the past. Now this network is letting the G keep watch over us ordinary citizens. It's a double-edged sword. Under a good government, this network was put to good use. But, now under the Green Party government, it's being exploited. That's bad. We have no privacy anymore. Just imagine—they are all over the place. At the MRT stations, bus stops, on the trains and buses, in taxis, along roads, outside shopping malls, walkways, HDB void decks and lift lobbies. They seem to be everywhere."

"Now that you mention them," said Tim. "I agree, they are a pain in the neck." He looked around the food court. "There are CCTV cameras on the pillars here too."

"But these aren't linked to some central monitoring station," said Kuan Hee. "Unlike those in public areas and HDB estates."

"The whole Marina area is swarming with people. There are many soldiers and policemen everywhere we go," said Lina.

"It's the NDP parade, Lina," said Tim.

"Oh, gosh! Today's National Day," said Lina.

"You mean, you didn't know?" said Tim.

"Tim, stop teasing her," said Kuan Hee. "I too forgot today's the big day. Too many things on our minds, you know."

"Sorry," said Tim. "I forgot. It's your parents you are worried about."

"So can we discuss the rescue now?" said Navin. "We've had our fill. Now's a good time to get down to business."

"Remember to keep our voices down," said Tim. "This is a public place."

Kuan Hee unfolded the map that he had sketched and an online map of Fort Canning Hill he had printed. He laid them alongside each other on the large round table. The four friends leaned forward to take a closer look.

"This is where Navin and I explored," said Tim. He fingered a rectangular patch on the map. "That's the reservoir—it sits on Fort Canning Hill. We can't get near the area. There's a chain link fence running around the hill, just after the slope. There are cables on the fence. I believe the fence is electrified."

"The area we recced is farther away from the Battle Box. The shortest route to the Battle Box seems to be where the exit to the bunker is," said Navin.

"I agree," said Kuan Hee. With a finger, he drew a line from the bunker's exit to the hotel down the slope from the hill. "This is the shortest way to the Battle Box."

"Problem is—how to get your parents and the other researchers to go down the slope safely," said Tim. "It's quite steep, you know. And there are only three of us."

"Four," snapped Lina. "You forgot to count me in."

"Sorry," said Tim. "I was talking about muscle power, Lina."

"Let's look at other options," said Kuan Hee. "There are three ways out of the bunker—entrance, exit and the opening on top of the bunker in the open space."

"Are there any secret openings?" asked Lina. "I'm sure they have some means of escape, just in case an enemy attacks."

"According to Mr Hon's Website, the opening on top of the bunker is the secret means of escape. It said only the top brass knew of this escape route," said Kuan Hee.

"How can it be?" said Navin. "The door is in plain sight of everyone in the open space in the park."

"Beats me," said Kuan Hee. "But it was in the past. Perhaps, the open space was a restricted area too. It's difficult to tell now."

"Perhaps, we can ask Mr Hon," said Lina.

"If he agrees to meet us again," said Kuan Hee.

"Hasn't he got back to you yet?" asked Tim. Kuan Hee shook his head.

"These options," said Navin, "aren't good ones. All are equally difficult to use to mount a rescue. I mean, if there are snipers around, we'd be dead meat when we run out of the bunker."

"We still have to choose one," said Tim. "I reckon the exit is the best choice. We can do a diversion, to give time for your parents and the others to escape."

"It seems to be the only option," said Navin.

"Agree," said Kuan Hee. "What about firepower?"

Tim looked around the food court. "We still have the SAR21s and the SSG69 that I have hidden," said Tim in a low voice. "Three SAR21s with one hundred cartridges, and one Steyr SSG 69 with two magazines of five rounds each."

"The last time, I fired one round at Colonel Tee," said Kuan Hee. "So there should be nine cartridges left."

"Tim, I thought you were supposed to return the weapons to the reserve store," said Lina.

"Well, my friends didn't ask for them," said Tim, "and I sort of dragged my feet."

"In a way, it's fortuitous," said Kuan Hee. "We don't have to hunt for weapons."

"These rifles may not be enough to stave off a platoon of soldiers," said Navin.

"Don't forget we have AleXander the robots," said Kuan Hee. "Together, they have enough firepower to take down the bunker."

"You must be joking," said Navin. "The bunker was built to withstand bombs dropped from airplanes, you know."

"Alright," said Kuan Hee. "But the two robots can do big-time damage to a tank."

"I agree," said Navin.

"A surprise rescue just below dawn, when everyone is still in dreamland—that will be the best bet," said Kuan Hee.

"But how will we know where your parents are being held at night?" said Lina.

"Don't forget, I left little Busy behind," said Kuan Hee. "So we have to be on the hill again to monitor your parents," said Lina.

"Yes," said Kuan Hee. "We need more information on Mum and Dad—when they sleep, where they sleep, also where the guards keep watch, when the guards change shift."

"Have we forgotten anything?" asked Navin.

Just then there was a commotion in the food court near the entrance. Someone was shouting something. He was pointing to where the four friends were seated. They could not make out what the man was saying; they were too far away. But, it was clear the patrons of the food court were affected. Some left the place hastily.

Tim stood up to look outside the glass windows. The balcony next to the windows blocked his view of the road.

"Something must be happening outside," said Tim. "Shall we go take a look?"

They got up and left the food court. As they passed the cashier's counter, they heard the staff talking about people being killed.

"Let's quicken our paces," said Navin. "I'm curious."

There was hurried activity in Marina Square Shopping Mall. Shoppers were making a beeway for the exits. The four friends followed the crowd and found themselves at the outdoor piazza along Raffles Avenue. It was jampacked with people. Many were taking videos of the happenings in front of them. The crowd spilled into the street.

It was mayhem in the street. There was an unruly mob attacking stalled buses at the bus stop in front of the Esplanade Theatre. There were more than a hundred of them. Soldiers were pouring in from the nearby grandstand where The Float@Marina stood. They had their rifles readied for action. On the road, placards, banners and wooden poles were strewn. Five people were sprawled on the ground. There was blood on them. Some people were helping their fallen friends. Puddles of blood were seen on the tarmac.

Then there was an explosion. The empty buses were being set on fire. The raging fire spread to the bus shelter and soon the bus shelter was but a charred skeleton of itself.

There was a standoff between the mob and the soldiers who had formed a human chain across Raffles Avenue. The soldiers were determined not to let the mob move near the grandstand where the Prime Minister and his ministers were watching the National Day Parade.

But the mob was not made up of burly drunken men. Instead, these were ordinary men and women—office workers, students and passers-by. They were all locals. Some of them were carrying placards reading 'Dump the Green Party', 'No justice, no peace' and 'Return democracy to the people'. Some held caricatures of the Prime Minister showing him with the devil's horns growing out of his head. Others were waving their arms in the air. Some were clapping. They were all chanting 'No one likes the Green Party; remove dictator Ong Chwee Seng' in unison. These were protesters who had turned unruly. Their fellow protesters had been shot and they were now emboldened by anger.

The protesters charged at the soldiers. Then some of them fell in the volley of shots that rang out. The soldiers meant business. They had not qualms about using their rifles. These were regulars, not NSmen. There were screams in the air. The protesters helped their injured comrades and made a retreat. They were sitting ducks against the might of bullets.

Lina pressed her face onto Kuan Hee's chest. He wrapped his arm around her. She was squeamish. She could not take bloodshed. This was Singapore. It could not be happening again—the ruthlessness of the Colonel Tee regime was repeating itself here, five years after the downfall of the regime. For the four friends, it was a nightmare revisited. For Singapore, it was a return to dark times.

"This is insane," said Kuan Hee. "We're killing our own people again." The other friends could not hear him above the cacophony of noises in their surroundings.

Some in the crowd on the outdoor piazza moved into the street. They were disgusted with the soldiers' behavior and were lending their support to the protesters.

By now, the soldiers had erected barricades next to the grandstand. Two soldiers in white ceremonial uniforms were giving orders to some soldiers.

"Must be generals," said Tim. "These two are wearing peak caps with golden embellishments on them. They are too far away for me to make out their ranks."

The cranking of metal wheels on rolling tracks could be heard in the distance. The rumbling became louder as the tops of armored personnel carriers came into view behind the chain of soldiers. The military commanders had summoned help. These heavy vehicles were all spiffed up for ceremonial use. There was not a grain of sand in their tracks. They were diverted to deal with the protesters.

Meanwhile, policemen on duty along the road kept a safe distance from both protesters and soldiers. They were supposed to keep law and order but appeared undecided whose law to uphold—military or civil.

There was a strong stench of irony in the air above the four friends. On the side of the grandstand facing Raffles Avenue, bystanders were treated to a horrific display of the army's ruthlessness. On the other side facing placid Marina Bay, the audience was in a rapturous mood, clapping away and cheering the military parade marking Singapore's National Day. Such was the stark contrast on a supposedly joyous occasion.

Were the invited guests at the grandstand oblivious to the killings taking place in the street behind them? In this day and age of social media, with video postings of the soldiers' ruthlessness going viral, it was unlikely the audience was in the dark. If the guests turned a blind eye to the morbid happenings, it was because they had hidden their conscience behind their fear.

Online forums and editorials condemned the Green Party for its ruthlessness. Articles poured scorn on Prime Minister Ong Chwee Seng for his hypocrisy. He had rooted for the masses during the Tee regime. They thought he was one of them. Now that he had amassed power, he had discarded his Mr Good Guy disguises and shown his true colours finally.

At a command from one of the white-uniformed officers, the armored personnel carriers roared into action. The line of soldiers disintegrated behind the armored personnel carriers, which moved into the path of the protesters. It was a standoff. Either the protesters ran helter-skelter or they would be crushed into smithereens. Just who would blink first? There were just seconds to decide. The armored carriers were menacingly close to the protesters.

In the end, the protesters caved in. They did not have the mettle to stare the raw strength of heavy metal in the face. They screamed their lungs out. They ran as if they had never run before. The armored personnel carriers cleared the road of protesters in no time.

It was now time for the ambulances to do their work. Paramedics attended to the injured and sent them to hospital. The crowd of protesters and spectators disappeared into the surrounding roads and shopping complexes. What were left were soldiers and armored personnel carriers.

The four friends saw firsthand the army's callous disregard for human life.

"Today's happenings show clearly the need for civilian control over the armed forces," said Tim.

"But we have a civilian Prime Minister and

government," said Navin.

"They are only civilian in looks. Definitely military in behavour," said Kuan Hee. "This PM brooks no dissent."

"It's surreal," said Navin. Images of the burning buses and fallen protesters were fresh in his mind. "I thought such things only happen in movies."

"But it happened once—in Little India in the 2010s," said Navin.

Tim browsed through reports on online news media. "It says on one Website it started as a peaceful protest," Tim said. "Tan Eng Chai got his supporters together to hijack the National Day celebrations at The Float@Marina. The protesters couldn't get past the soldiers so they picked Raffles Avenue to stage their protest."

"Tan Eng Chai, isn't he the secretary general of the Unity Party?" asked Lina.

"Right, Lina. Anything happened to him?" asked Kuan Hee.

"He isn't among those injured," said Tim.

"This editorial on a blog I am reading says we should unite to put the tyrannical government out of business," said Navin.

"Singaporehappenings.com castigates Members of Parliament for turning a blind eye to injustice and murder," said Kuan Hee.

"Wait! Here's breaking news on channelsingapore.com. Minister for Transport Ngoh Shi Ping has resigned. He has pulled out of the Green Party together with a group of MPs," said Navin.

"Did it say how many?" asked Kuan Hee.

"Let me see—twenty-three Green Party MPs," said Navin.

"That means by-elections for the parliamentary seats they vacated," said Kuan Hee. "There is hope, yet. Maybe the Green Party won't have a two-third majority after all. Then they won't be able to pass laws at their whim and fancy after all."

"Ngoh Shi Ping—the veteran politician?" said Tim. "Good *lah*. He's a respected guy. He's popular too."

"So was Ong Chwee Seng, his comrade at the Green Party," said Kuan Hee. "Look what has happened. He did an about-turn after he became PM."

"At least Ngoh Shi Ping is doing the right thing now," said Tim.

"Any other news?" asked Lina.

"The Website of local newspaper The Singapore Tribune reports 'Army crushes demonstration, arrests protest leaders'," said Kuan Hee.

"Is Tan Eng Chai among them?" asked Tim.

"Nope, but some Unity Party members are," said Kuan Hee.

"Where are the other political parties?" asked Navin.

"Search me," said Tim. "Perhaps they can't work together."

"With a common enemy," said Kuan Hee, "they should bury their differences."

"For the good of the country, they should," said Lina.

"It's early days yet," said Tim. "Give them some time to work things out."

"Shouldn't we join in the protests?" asked Navin.

"We should, shouldn't we?" said Lina.

"Of course, we should," said Kuan Hee, "but not yet. Let's get my parents out first."

"Kuan Hee, Are you going back to work at Temasek University?" asked Navin.

"Pretty soon," said Kuan Hee.

"Won't it be dangerous?" said Tim. "The army might be looking for you. You went AWOL, you know."

"Correction. They wanted me to commit treason. I merely tagged along with them," said Kuan Hee. "So if they dare look for me, I will blare out everything."

"You mean you are confident they won't do a thing to

you?" said Navin.

"Er. I think so, *lah*," said Kuan Hee. "Let me try going back to work first. If I smell something wrong, I will scram."

"They may send people to silence you," said Tim. "You know, like this." He slid his hand across his throat in demonstration.

"Aw, Tim. You are horrid," said Lina. She folded her arm over Kuan Hee's and leaned against him.

"Don't frighten the little girl," said Navin.

"Yeah, Tim. You sure are brunt," said Kuan Hee. "But it's possible they will come after me. Just have to be careful."

"Then don't go back to work," said Lina. "I'm afraid, Kuan Hee."

"I am too," said Kuan Hee. "I can't foretell the future. In the meantime, I have applied for a week's leave to cover my absence this week, but I don't have much leave left. So we must get my parents out pretty soon."

CHAPTER 15

Kuan Hee and Lina were watching little Huei Huei on the Samsung smartphone. It was strange that these two newly minted parents had yet to see their daughter in person. Only Lina had held little Huei Huei in her arms, but that was only for a minute or so after she was delivered in the maternity ward.

"Kuan Hee," said Lina. "I miss Huei Huei. I miss her so."

"Me too, dear," said Kuan Hee.

"Shall I ask my mum to bring her here?" said Lina.

"Not a good idea," said Kuan Hee. "She can't be exposed to airborne germs in the open air yet. Her immune system isn't stable yet. It will be bad for her health."

"You mean we have to wait two whole months?" said Lina.

"That's what your mum said, remember?" said Kuan Hee. "Wait at least one more month, dear, OK?"

Kuan Hee's smartphone rang. It was Mr Hon. He wanted to see Kuan Hee.

"He's changed his mind," said Lina.

"I think so," said Kuan Hee. "I hope so." The chat

over the telephone was brief; it was just long enough to set an appointment.

"Mr Hon, what made you change your mind?" asked Kuan Hee. He was in Mr Hon's living room with Lina, Tim and Navin. They wanted to tag along and Mr Hon agreed with the idea. The room was uncomfortably small, but the four friends didn't mind. They were eager to learn everything about the Battle Box from an old hand like Mr Hon.

"I was born in difficult times in Singapore. I lived through riots and curfews, strikes and strife," said Mr Hon. "Then a new government came in and I saw progress and prosperity. Now this fragile thing called peace that I have been accustomed to for most of my life is under threat. Not from a foreign source, but from within Singapore."

Mr Hon paused. With a finger, he stroked his eyebrow.

"What the soldiers did to the protesters in Marina Bay is incomprehensible," said Mr Hon. "This Green Party government is indeed ruthless."

He looked Kuan Hee in the eyes. "I'm sorry I doubted you," he said.

"It's all right," said Kuan Hee.

"Enough digression. Let's talk about the Battle Box," said Mr Hon. "I worked there as a guide for many years. Though it was an old place, it held fond memories for many, many people—from all over the world. The British and Australians visited the bunker the most, for they had fathers or grandfathers who fought the war here in Singapore. They came to honour these people."

Mr Hon paused to take a sip of tea. The four friends flashed awkward smiles at one another. They wondered when he would get around to telling them what they wanted to know. They knew it was pointless to hurry him. Then Mr Hon flipped open a large album yellowed by age and pointed to some photographs.

"These tourists brought not only their memories of

their loved ones, they also gave me some keepsakes left behind by their fathers or grandfathers. They wanted me to share these with other visitors to the bunker. I received letters, ration cards, photographs, etc."

By now, Kuan Hee and Tim were getting fidgety. Navin and Lina were not as impatient as the other two. *Could it be Mr Hon is trying to test them?* Lina wondered. *But why would he want to do such a thing?*

"I'm sorry I am digressing again," said Mr Hon. "It's old age, I guess. Memories are all the more important in our twilight years. But the last point I made earlier is important. A visitor from the United Kingdom passed me something her father had left behind. She came to see the place her father had worked in during the war years."

"You mean her father worked in the Battle Box?" said Kuan Hee.

"Incredulous that this sounds," said Mr Hon, "it is indeed true. She handed me a map of the bunker."

The visitors sat up. They were now all ears. It was the moment they had been waiting for.

Mr Hon turned the pages of the album and stopped at one. He pushed the album nearer to the visitors. They leaned forward. It was a map of the Battle Box drawn in ink on parchment paper. Evidently the map had been folded and then stored for a long time, for the parts of the map along the folds were unreadable. The ravages of time and the tropical weather had taken its toll on the paper. Still, it was possible to make out pertinent information on the map.

Mr Hon tapped his finger on a spot on the map. "See this dotted line running from here to the reservoir?" said Mr Hon. They nodded in agreement.

"It's a secret escape route from the Battle Box," said Mr Hon.

"But I thought the secret escape route was this stairwell leading up to the door on top—where the park is," said Kuan Hee, pointing to the passageway next to the stairwell on the map.

"That's a cock-and-bull story. The real escape route is this tunnel that goes under the bunker," said Mr Hon.

At this point, his visitors were gawking at him. *A secret escape route Mr Hon described on his Website is not a real secret escape route,* they thought in unison. *Why on earth would he want to mislead people?*

"But we got the information from your Website, Mr Hon," said Kuan Hee.

"Why did you mislead people, Mr Hon?" asked Lina. Immediately, Kuan Hee nudged her knee.

"Don't mind Lina, Mr Hon." said Kuan Hee. "She likes to say the wrong things at the wrong time." He didn't want Mr Hon to throw them out of his flat—not when they were so close to finding a secret way into the bunker. Lina pouted her lips. She stared at Kuan Hee but said nothing.

Mr Hon's bushy eyebrows almost met as he glared at Lina. He was not pleased with the way Lina had phrased the question.

"Young girl, I did put the information on my Website," said Mr Hon. "But I didn't mislead people. I told them exactly what the British were telling everyone in their time. I couldn't very well state the truth right? It's a secret tunnel after all."

"Tell us about the secret tunnel, Mr Hon," said Navin. He was anxious to move the conversation away from a confrontation.

"Yes, Mr Hon," said Tim. "Where does it open into the bunker?"

"Oh yes, I was about to get to that when I was rudely interrupted," said Mr Hon. "You see this spot marked 'X' on the map? The tunnel stops here, in the passageway outside the Fort Commander's Office. Here, there is a manhole reaching into the drainage system for the bunker. Open the drain cover and jump inside. The tunnel is three feet wide and two feet deep from here all the way to here."

"Who's taking notes?" asked Tim.

Lina raised her hand. She started scribbling on a small notepad. *Good, this will keep her occupied,* Kuan Hee thought. *She won't have time to think of awkward questions for Mr Hon to answer.*

"The tunnel at this point is wide enough for one person to move through. But it is not deep enough so you have to crawl your way in it," said Mr Hon.

"Mr Hon, how do we get into the tunnel from outside the bunker?" asked Kuan Hee.

Mr Hon fingered a spot marked with a cannon symbol on the map. "Let's see, this nine-pound cannon about a hundred feet away from the bunker is where you enter the tunnel," said Mr Hon. Then he looked through another album and pointed to a picture of an old cannon.

"See this low wall next to the cannon?" said Mr Hon. "Right under the barrel of the cannon, about six feet away, is a hatch opening. You can't see it. You have to dig apart the soil, but it's there all right. It's big enough for one person to jump in, but you have to bend a little for a couple of feet. It opens into a small room just below the cannon. You guys follow me?"

"Yes, Mr Hon," the four friends collectively answered.

"Good. It looks like a dead end, but actually isn't," said Mr Hon. "On the wall, you will see a metal wheel with eight spokes."

"Do we turn the wheel?" asked Navin.

"No, no," said Mr Hon. "Listen carefully. At the end of each spoke you will see an emblem. There are eight different emblems. Look for the golden fish and the parasol. Use your strength. Press them hard simultaneously and kept them depressed until a door opens on the wall next to the wheel."

"Lina, are you taking everything down?" asked Tim.

"Yes, of course," said Lina. "Mr Hon, what are the other emblems?"

"Let me see now, there is a lotus flower, an endless knot, treasure vase, banner, conch, and—what have I missed now—oh yes, a wheel. Gosh, how did I forget the wheel?" said Mr Hon. He opened his fingers one by one as he counted the eight emblems aloud.

"Can all the emblems be depressed?" asked Navin.

"Yes, they can," said Mr Hon. "But they don't do anything for you."

"Mr Hon, how did you know about the emblems?" asked Tim.

"It took me many months," said Mr Hon. "I was working there and, after work, I would try my luck. It needed a lot of brainwork, but it was worth it."

The four friends didn't know Mr Hon was so clever. They were impressed. He was indeed some investigator.

"I was younger then. I thought there was treasure in the secret tunnel—the Yamashita treasure, you know. The thought of finding treasure kept me going," said Mr Hon. "Alas, it was not to be. It was all an illusion. But, all was not lost. I found the secret of the Battle Box. It was a great achievement."

"Yes, Mr Hon, indeed you have," the four friends chorused in unison. He had digressed again, but they didn't mind this time.

"Where did I stop? Yes. Go down the steps into a bigger tunnel. It's a passageway. It's about six feet wide and tall enough for you to walk without having to bend," said Mr Hon. It actually goes on for about a hundred feet until you reach this place." Mr Hon pointed to the manhole marked 'X' on the map.

"There you have it, the secret tunnel," said Mr Hon. He was beaming. He seemed pleased with himself.

"Mr Hon, it was clever of you to find a way in from the cannon," said Lina. She was saying something right this time. Mr Hon's eyes were gleaming; he had forgotten her earlier snide remark.

"Any questions?" said Mr Hon.

"Mr Hon, isn't it dangerous having a tunnel in a hill?" asked Lina. "I mean, won't it collapse if the soil erodes?"

"Dear girl," said Mr Hon. "I was waiting for someone to ask this question. The whole hill sits on a limestone boulder bed. The foundation is, as they say, 'as solid as a rock'. The tunnel will never collapse."

"Mr Hon, you mean the secret passageway goes straight to the manhole at this spot?" asked Tim.

"Oops! I must have forgotten to tell you guys about the contraption near the manhole," said Mr Hon.

"Is there another secret contraption to access to get into the bunker?" asked Kuan Hee.

"Yes. It is another wheel, similar to the one at the cannon," said Mr Hon. "It's at the end of the tunnel; you will see it on the wall. Press hard on the same two emblems. The door on the wall will slide open. Go through it and you will find yourself in the drainage tunnel, about six feet away from the manhole."

"Will the door shut automatically?" asked Kuan Hee.

"It remains open until you shut it," said Mr Hon.

"What if it is shut and I am in the drainage tunnel? How do I get into the tunnel?" asked Kuan Hee.

"On the other side, that is, in the drainage tunnel, there is a similar wheel. Press on the same emblems," said Mr Hon.

"So, Mr Hon, you are saying that at both ends of the tunnel, on both sides of the wall, there is a wheel that controls the door," said Kuan Hee. "And all the wheels operate using the same emblems—golden fish and parasol."

"Correct, Kuan Hee," said Mr Hon. "You catch on quite fast, young man," said Mr Hon.

"Mr Hon, what if the drainage tunnel has got water in it? Doesn't it mean that when we open the door, the water will come rushing in, and the tunnel will be flooded?" said Navin.

"So you finally opened your mouth," said Mr Hon. Navin flashed a grin.

"As far as I know, the drainage tunnel has never been

flooded with water. The water level in the drainage tunnel rises till it is flush with the small drain—about a foot wide and six inches deep. So if you are in the drainage tunnel, you won't get your feet wet. Unless, of course, you happen to step into the small drain, which won't happen unless you are clumsy, of course."

"Thanks, Mr Hon," said Navin.

"So you thought you might be drowned if you went into the tunnel, right, dear boy?" said Mr Hon. Navin grinned sheepishly.

"The tunnel's actually quite safe," said Mr Hon. "I worked at the Battle Box for a little over twenty five years. I had never seen the drainage tunnel flooded."

"Guys, any more questions for Mr Hon?" said Kuan Hee. There was silence in the room. "Mr Hon, I guess that's all the questions we have right now. Can I call you if we should need more information?"

"Sure, you can, Kuan Hee," said Mr Hon. "Always glad to help. But it is very dangerous what you want to do. Do be careful. These army chaps aren't to be trifled with. You may lose your lives."

"Mr Hon, we'll be very careful," said Kuan Hee. "Don't worry, we'll take good care of ourselves, won't we?"

The other three nodded in agreement.

CHAPTER 16

The four friends were at the bottom of Fort Canning Hill, standing next to the Gothic Gate on Canning Rise. They were here to recce the place and plan their moves for the rescue of Kuan Hee's parents.

"These steps lead up the slope to the nine-pound cannon," said Tim. "It's about three minutes' climb from here."

"We can park the getaway vehicle here," said Navin. "There aren't any cameras in the area, except at the Registry of Marriages over on the left. It's a hundred metres away so any cameras there can't see us here."

"The chain link fencing runs parallel to the road on top, all the way from the reservoir on the left to the Fort Canning Centre on the right," said Navin.

"The fence starts right after the cannon, along the low wall," said Tim. "Where did Mr Hon say the hatch is?"

Lina glanced through her notes. "On the ground, about five feet away from the low wall. The cannon barrel points the way," she said.

"Let's go up the slope," said Kuan Hee. "Be on the lookout for soldiers up on the top."

They climbed the slope to where the nine-pound

cannon was located. It was evening and the sun was disappearing over the horizon. They pretended to be stragglers sitting on the grass, enjoying the view.

"Are we sitting in the right spot?" asked Lina.

"Seems so," said Kuan Hee. "The cannon barrel is directly behind me and we are about five feet from the low wall."

"Let's start work," said Tim. "I'll keep an eye out for the soldiers."

They had come prepared with some short wooden sticks, which they were now using to dig the soil in front of them. Kuan Hee and Navin had their backs to the cannon, while Tim and Lina had the cannon in their sights.

Shortly, there was the clanking sound of metal. Kuan Hee and Navin pushed the soil aside and, lo and behold, a round metal plate a metre wide appeared in view. It had two handles on it. Kuan Hee tried to lift it. He couldn't. It was shut fast. Kuan Hee and Navin tried together in vain. Tim was the strongest of the three men. He and Navin heaved and pulled. They gasped and tried again. Years of exposure to the elements had adhered the hatch to the frame. It was a good fifteen minutes before the hatch gave way. It creaked open to the delight of the four friends. The sand around the edges of the hatch fell into the opening.

"Get out your LED flashlights," said Tim. "We are going in. I'll go first."

One after another, they jumped into the tunnel and hunched their way into the small room Mr Hon had described to them. Their LED flashlights lit up the place. It was slightly smaller than Mr Hon's living room. It was concrete everywhere, from the floor to the walls and the ceiling. There were water stains on the ceiling and the walls. Years of neglect had caused damp to build up in the room. The mushy stench of damp air was strong.

"Here, put some tissue paper over your nose," Kuan Hee told Lina.

"Don't close the hatch, or we'll suffocate here," said

Kuan Hee. "I forgot to ask Mr Hon whether there is ventilation in the tunnel."

"If we leave the hatch open, the soldiers might discover us," said Lina.

"Let's leave it open until we have opened the door in this room," said Tim.

"Who's going to try opening the door?" asked Kuan Hee.

"I will," said Tim. "I'm the strongest here. Let me do it."

There was a metal wheel on the wall in the room. It had emblems as Mr Hon had described. Tim followed the instructions Mr Hon had given and part of the wall rumbled open. There were steps going down.

"Let me go first," said Tim.

"Be careful," said Kuan Hee. He and Navin shone their flashlights into the darkness. It was a long tunnel.

"The air seems to be moving," said Tim. He was in the tunnel. "It's not that stale here."

"There must be air coming in from somewhere in the tunnel," said Navin as he and Kuan Hee joined Tim. "It's not that stuffy now." Lina went last. Kuan Hee stood by her side; unlike the three men who had been through national service, she was not used to such living conditions.

"I had better shut the hatch," said Tim. "Wait for me." He went back through the door. Meanwhile, Kuan Hee, Navin and Lina shone their flashlights at the ceiling, the walls and the floor. There were water stains everywhere. But surprisingly, there was no leak. The tunnel had been dug nearly a hundred years ago and it was testimony to the engineering skills of the British in the 1930s.

When Tim returned, the four friends walked along the tunnel. It was wide enough for them to walk abreast. The ceiling was about a metre taller than Tim, the tallest of the group. At regular intervals, there were oil lamps hanging on the walls. Navin grabbed one and peeped inside. There was no oil in it. He put it back on the wall hook. The tunnel meandered for about fifty metres and the four friends found themselves at the other end of the tunnel.

"It's the same type of wheel," said Tim. He pressed hard on the same two emblems and a creaking sound was heard as a door on the wall slid open about a metre from the floor.

"Shush," said Kuan Hee. Beyond the door was the drainage tunnel, and any loud noise they made could possibly echo in the bunker. They had to be careful lest they alerted the soldiers in the bunker.

"So far so good," said Navin. The others nodded in agreement.

"Let me go take a look," said Kuan Hee. "Don't worry, I will be careful." Lina had grabbed his shoulder tightly.

Kuan Hee lifted himself onto the floor of the drainage tunnel. He found himself in a long drain tunnel running perpendicular to the secret tunnel. On the floor, in the middle was a small drain. There was about a centimeter of water flowing in it. He could not stand; he couldn't even sit in the tunnel. There was only enough room for him to crawl through. Luckily, the manhole was less than two metres away. He elbowed his way towards the manhole, holding the flashlight in one hand. There was light filtering through the manhole cover into the drainage tunnel. *Must be from the light in the bunker,* Kuan Hee thought.

Kuan Hee stopped just below the manhole cover. He listened hard for sounds coming from above him. There was none. It was eerily quiet. *There's no one in the passageway,* he thought. *Should I or shouldn't I?*

Perspiration trickled down his forehead. The air was stale in the drainage tunnel. He placed both hands on the metal cover. It was cold. *The air-conditioning is switched on,* he told himself. He pressed against the cover. It moved. He lifted the cover slightly. The light from the bunker filtered through the edges of the cover. He peered through the small opening. There was no one in the passageway. Cool air breezed past his face. It was a welcome change from the humid drainage tunnel. *Must get back to the others,* Kuan Hee told himself. He let the metal cover slip back into position and made his way back to the tunnel.

"So how was it?" asked Tim. Kuan Hee flashed the OK sign with his hand and Tim shut the door.

"Let's talk outside," Kuan Hee said. The four friends walked back to the start of the tunnel and emerged from the hatch next to the nine-pound cannon.

At a McDonald's outlet in the nearby YMCA building, the four friends treated themselves to icy cold soft drinks. It was welcome nourishment after all the hard work they had put in this evening.

"So, are we good to go?" asked Navin in a low voice.

"I am happy to report—the manhole cover can be lifted with the slightest force," said Kuan Hee. "And the manhole opens into the passageway."

"That's what I call real good news," said Tim. The others nodded.

"So when do we strike?" asked Navin.

"Not yet," said Kuan Hee. "I still need to make contact with my mum and dad—confirm where they will be at dawn, and tell them our plan."

"Tell your parents not to leak the news of the rescue," said Tim. "We don't know whether the other researchers can be trusted. Remember—they were kidnapped. One of the researchers could be a spy."

"Tim's right, Kuan Hee," said Navin. "It has to be a surprise lightning operation."

"Yes, Kuan Hee," said Lina. "I agree with the others."

"OK," said Kuan Hee. "Lina and I will make the next trip here. You guys just wait for news. I'll book a room at the hotel across from the exit. Lina and I will spend a night at the hotel. We will observe the Battle Box's exterior for a whole day and night. We need to know the soldiers' movements."

"We can talk to your parents through little Busy," said Lina.

"That's the idea," said Kuan Hee.

"*Wah!* You two so lucky *ah*," said Navin, "having a romantic escapade without us."

"You are bad. Stop teasing us, Navin," said Lina.

CHAPTER 17

The Colonial Hotel stood halfway up the Fort Canning Hill, with its back facing the steep slope where the Battle Box's exit stood. It was originally the administration building of the British Far East Command Headquarters. From the windows of the hotel suite that Kuan Hee and Lina were spending the night in, they had an unhindered view of the bunker's exit. The entire walkway outside the bunker, stretching from the guardhouse on the left to the beginning of the reservoir on the right was within sight.

In the same way, these two hotel guests had no privacy as passers-by on the walkway had a clear view of the interior of the hotel room. But this was of the least importance to Kuan Hee and Lina who were spending the night there solely to watch the bunker. Only they had to be discreet in their activities so as not to arouse suspicion.

The pair took hourly turns to watch the slope and record the activities of the soldiers across from them. They saw soldiers bringing lunch and dinner and noted the times. They counted the number of soldiers on duty for each shift. They jotted down the times the soldiers made their rounds along the walkway. The glaring afternoon sun mellowed into a hazy orange ball before disappearing below the horizon and dark grey clouds swarmed across the skies, bringing evening.

Kuan Hee had left the television on. Channel five was now showing a local drama serial but the pair was not watching.

It was the Ngoh Shi Ping who got the attention of the pair. The former Transport Minister was on the air telling a news reporter he and twenty-three ex-Green Party MPs had joined the Unity Party. They would be contesting the by-elections this month. Next, the Unity Party's secretary-general Tan Eng Chai went on air to welcome the new members to his party. He said Ngoh Shi Ping would take the post of assistant-secretary-general in the party. He called for the public to support the party in the by-elections.

"This guy Ngoh Shi Ping did the right thing," said Kuan Hee. "I am glad he had the guts to stand up to Ong Chwee Seng."

"Will the Unity Party win the by-elections?" asked Lina.

"They will win seats all right. But they must win at least twenty of the parliamentary seats that are up for grabs," said Kuan Hee, "for the Green Party to lose their two-thirds majority in parliament. If it happens, it will be a good thing. At least, the Green Party can't carry on enacting laws at their whim and fancy, disregarding us ordinary folks."

"How many seats does the Green Party need to win to keep their two-third majority?" asked Lina.

"Let's see—four," said Kuan Hee.

"Only four?" said Lina. "Won't that be super easy?"

"Let's cross our fingers," said Kuan Hee, "and hope people will not vote for the Green Party."

"Are we attending the launching of the Unity Party's manifesto at Speakers' Corner tomorrow afternoon?" asked Lina.

"Yes," asked Kuan Hee. "It would be good to hear what the Unity Party has to say. I'll get the others to meet us there."

Soon it was time for Kuan Hee to launch little Busy into action. It was past midnight and the soldiers making their rounds along the walkway had disappeared from view. The pair had half an hour before the soldiers reappeared in front of the exit.

Kuan Hee unfolded the remote control and placed it on his lap. He and Lina sat on the floor in the balcony, leaning on pillows placed against the wall. Through the clear glass panels on the railings, they could see the slope in its entirety.

Little Busy flew out of Professor Wang's pocket, giving the pair a view of the room they were held in. It was about the size of a HDB kitchen. His parents shared the same room. They were asleep on two single beds placed at right angles to each other. Where the beds met was a rectangular table on which stood a table lamp and a clock. Against the opposite wall was a small desk and chair. There were apparently no other occupants.

Kuan Hee was reluctant to wake his parents; he was sure it was difficult for them to fall asleep in such a hostile environment, and if they were already in slumberland, he should not interrupt their sleep.

It was Lina who spoke through little Busy's speakers into Professor Wang's ear.

"Uncle, it's me, Lina," she said. "Uncle, wake up, please."

Professor Wang stirred. He scratched his shoulder and peered through half-opened eyelids. Then he reached for his glasses on the small table.

"Uncle, it's Lina," she said. "Kuan Hee's with me."

Professor Wang sat up and leaned towards little Busy.

"Kuan Hee's with you?" he said in a low voice.

"Dad," said Kuan Hee. "How are you? How's Mum?"

Professor Wang shook his wife. "Dear, Kuan Hee's here," he said. "Wake up, dear."

Mrs Wang turned. Then she sat up and looked at little Busy. She smiled into the little robot housefly's eyes. "Kuan Hee, It's you," she whispered.

"Mum and Dad, I missed you guys," said Kuan Hee.

"So did we, Kuan Hee," said Professor Wang. "Where are you? Are you nearby?"

"We are opposite, in The Colonial Hotel," said Kuan Hee. "We have been here the whole night watching the bunker."

"Uncle and Auntie, did they treat you well?" asked Lina.

"They have been nice to us," said Mrs Wang, "but I don't like it here. This place gives me the creeps."

"Dad, we are going to get you and Mum out," said Kuan Hee. "Listen carefully. The day after tomorrow, just before dawn, we'll come for you."

"What about my staff, Kuan Hee?" said Professor Wang. "I can't leave them here."

"We'll take them with us too," said Kuan Hee. "But, Dad, please don't tell them about the rescue. One of them could be a spy. He could spoil our plan."

"I understand, Kuan Hee," said Professor Wang.

"Dad, are you locked in your room?" asked Kuan Hee.

"They lock us up every night," said Professor Wang. "Then they leave the bunker. But they come in to check on us now and then."

"What sort of lock do they use for the door?" asked Kuan Hee.

"Padlock," said Professor Wang. "Steel padlock."

"Thanks, Dad," said Kuan Hee.

"It's the day after tomorrow—Friday, right?" said Professor Wang.

"Yes, Dad—5:00 a.m. on Friday," said Kuan Hee.

"There are many guards here," said Professor Wang. "And they are armed with rifles."

"Don't worry, Dad," said Kuan Hee. "We aren't going to charge out of the bunker with you. We are taking a secret route below the bunker. It goes all the way to the nine-pound cannon."

"A secret tunnel under the bunker?" said Professor Wang in astonishment.

"Yes," said Kuan Hee. "Tim and Navin are helping me. So is Lina's elder brother. We'll get you and Mum out for sure."

"Kuan Hee, how did you know we are here?" asked Professor Wang.

"Brigadier Walmsley told me," said Kuan Hee. "He's the one who found you. He said he couldn't use the Special Forces to rescue you and the others, but he will back us up on the day of the rescue."

"So the Brigadier has found us finally," said Professor Wang. "Kuan Hee, there's something you must know."

The shuffle of feet echoed in the silence of the night. Someone was approaching the room. The pair was so engrossed in conversation with Kuan Hee's parents that they had forgotten to keep a watch on the bunker's exit.

"Quick, leave, Kuan Hee" said Professor Wang. "They are here to check on us."

"Remember Mum and Dad, 5:00 a.m. Friday," said Kuan Hee.

Little Busy flitted into the professor's palm. He clasped it and placed it in his pocket.

"Kuan Hee, now that your parents are taken care of, let's not waste time," said Lina. "Shall we?"

"Here, on the floor?" said Kuan Hee.

"No *lah*, silly," said Lina. "The big bed's been waiting for us since this afternoon."

"People can see us from the slope," said Kuan Hee.

"Who cares," said Lina. She turned off the lights in the room.

CHAPTER 18

It was the second time that Kuan Hee and Lina were meeting Brigadier Walmsley at ToastBox Café in Plaza Singapura. This time, the Brigadier was waiting for them in the alfresco section of the café. He was the perfect picture of a tourist as he sat wearing his hunting hat and flipping through a tourist guide.

The Brigadier, ever the gentleman, stood up as Lina took her seat opposite him. Kuan Hee ordered beverages for himself and Lina as Brigadier Walmsley had a *kopi oh kosong* in front of him. He returned with the drinks and sat next to Lina.

"You know, I never can get used to the heat here," said the Brigadier. He wiped the sweat off his forehead and behind his ears.

"Mr Walmsley, we can sit in the air-conditioned section of the café," said Lina.

"But I like the sun," said the Brigadier. "I like getting a tan." The pair smiled. They were used to the Brigadier's whimsical mannerisms.

The Brigadier patted the back of his hair as he sat in thought. The two ladies at the next table vacated their seats and a café assistant came to clear the table. Seeing there was no one within earshot, the Brigadier launched into conversation.

"What news do you have for me, Kuan Hee?" the Brigadier asked.

"My parents and the other researchers are indeed at the bunker," said Kuan Hee. "They are safe and sound."

"That's good news," said the Brigadier. "How many researchers?"

"Six," said Kuan Hee, "not counting my mum and dad."

"That's correct," said the Brigadier. "All research staff accounted for. Kuan Hee, what are your plans?"

"Friday 5:00 a.m., that's when we strike," said Kuan Hee. "We'll use a secret tunnel below the bunker." He unfolded a map of the bunker Mr Hon had given him and set it on the small table.

"My parents and the researchers are in these three rooms," said Kuan Hee, pointing them out on the map. "The secret tunnel runs from this manhole to the nine-pound cannon over here." He moved his fingers across the map to the cannon symbol.

"I see," said the Brigadier. "So you avoid the guards altogether. Smart move."

"Mr Walmsley, can you arrange for transport to wait here?" asked Kuan Hee. His finger was now resting on Canning Rise, next to the Gothic Gate.

"May I?" said Mr Walmsley. He took out his smartphone and activated the camera. Kuan Hee nodded and the Brigadier snapped pictures of the map.

"Kuan Hee, I will take care of the transport," said the Brigadier. "My people will take over at the Gothic Gate. They will move your parents and the researchers to a safe place. Do you need firepower?"

"We hope to pull off the whole thing without firing a single shot," said Kuan Hee in an almost inaudible voice. "But we are prepared. We have three SAR21s and a Steyr SSG 69."

"Gosh, how did you get your hands on them?" asked the Brigadier.

"Long story, Mr Walmsley," said Kuan Hee.

"You guys sure are capable. I must take my hat off to you," said the Brigadier. "By the way, do you have a back-up plan?"

"Back-up plan?" said Kuan Hee. He was caught off-balance. He had not thought of a back-up plan.

"Every operation must have a contingency plan," said the Brigadier as Kuan Hee looked uneasily at the Brigadier.

"We forgot," said Lina, racing to Kuan Hee's rescue.

"It's alright," said the Brigadier. "Kuan Hee, keep the communication channel on Google Glass open. Update me as the rescue progresses. If something goes wrong, my people will take over. We will be the back-up plan. You just get your parents and the researchers to safety. And if you hear any noises outside, ignore them. It's my people in action."

"Yes, Mr Walmsley," said Kuan Hee. He had recovered the use of his tongue. "I am sorry I left out a back-up plan."

"No worries," said the Brigadier. "Happens to the best of us. So in a nutshell, I'll take over if something goes wrong. OK?"

"OK," said the pair in unison.

"Godspeed," said the Brigadier.

CHAPTER 19

It was a packed day for Kuan Hee and Lina. No sooner had they checked out of The Colonial Hotel than they met the Brigadier at ToastBox Café in Plaza Singapura. Now, they were on their way to attend the Unity Party's manifesto launch in Hong Lim Park.

Speakers' Corner was a flat open field, almost the size of two football fields. Behind a long concrete platform, across the road were glass-clad high-rise buildings. On the opposite side was a smattering of pre-war shophouses, alongside which was a two-storey colonial-era building now housing a police post.

This evening, the field was flooded with people—office workers from the nearby office buildings and others from across the island. The young and the old—they were all here to listen to what the Unity Party had to offer in the upcoming by-elections. It was a mass of bobbing heads as far as the eye could see. In the warm glow of light globes placed around the perimeter of the field, the spectators stood, eyeing the platform where the Unity Party's leaders sat.

The four friends mingled with the other spectators barely two metres from the platform steps, where party minders kept a wary eye on the crowd. Patches of dark blue marked the positions of policemen in the crowd.

It was a subdued mood that greeted the first speaker on the platform. Tan Eng Chai, the Unity Party's secretary general poured scorn on the Green Party government for restricting people's freedom and creating an atmosphere of fear in Singapore.

Next, Ngoh Shi Ping's voice blared over the loud speakers. He called on the government to arbitrarily release the protesters it had detained and stop the unlawful use of computer judges in the courts to try the detainees. He also condemned the government's house raids on opposition party members.

"I actually came here to hear what Ngoh Shi Ping will do to rein in Ong Chwee Seng if he is elected," said Kuan Hee. "So far, besides complaining, he hasn't done anything else."

"Let's not be impatient, Kuan Hee," said Navin. "The night is young."

"Shush, he's talking about Ong Chwee Seng now," said Lina.

"He's saying Ong Chwee Seng is a two-faced liar," said Tim.

"It's clear to one and all this chap Ong Chwee Seng is a phony," said Kuan Hee.

"He's calling a spade a spade," said Navin.

"He's being frank. Will he get into trouble?" said Lina.

"I hear he and Ong Chwee Seng were schoolmates," said Tim. "Ong Chwee Seng was the one who got him into politics."

"Now they are standing on opposite sides of the fence," said Lina. "Do you think Ong Chwee Seng will turn on his schoolmate?"

"No prizes for guessing," said Kuan Hee.

Suddenly, there was a loud explosion. Plumes of smoke fanned out across the field, blanketing the spectators in the middle of the field. There were cries of pain and panic as shrapnel from the explosion flew. Several spectators were injured. In the ensuing pandemonium, some spectators were trampled over.

Fortunately, the four friends were spared injury; they were standing near the platform. Just then, a score of soldiers filed past them. Some formed a cordon around the platform while others climbed the platform and grabbed hold of Ngoh Shi Ping, Tan Eng Chai and their comrades. The Unity Party's minders could only watch helplessly as the soldiers had brandished their rifles. The soldiers whisked them away in a bus.

"Gosh! The Unity Party leaders have been detained," said Navin. "It's a violation of human rights. This is a peaceful assembly."

"You think the soldiers care a damn?" said Tim.

"Being schoolmates also no use," said Lina.

"It's the politics of power," said Kuan Hee. "Some famous fellow once said: Power tends to corrupt, and absolute power corrupts absolutely."

"What about the by-elections?" Lina asked. "Will the Unity Party leaders be able to participate in the by-elections?"

CHAPTER 20

The sun was descending beyond the blocks of HDB flats in the distance when Kuan Hee and Lina got out of bed. The evening brought a hazy glow that lasted past sunset. It was that time of the year when the burning of forests and peatland in Indonesia ushered in hazy skies across the island. But it was no cause for complaint for the pair this time, for hazy conditions made for better cover when they were mounting their rescue of Kuan Hee's parents and the researchers at the Battle Box.

After dinner, Kuan Hee, Lina, Navin and Tim huddled on the floor of the small room above the shophouse in Realty Park. The smell of lubricating oil punctuated the air. Tim and Navin were cleaning the SAR21s they had retrieved from a hiding place. Kuan Hee was dismantling a Steyr SSG 69 and wiping its parts. He dragged a small rag through its barrel several times and peered inside. Tim and Navin had done a good job oiling the weapons before stashing them away.

"I don't see the cutting tool," said Tim. "Have you forgotten it?"

"My brother will bring it later," said Lina.

"I forgot—he's coming with us too," said Tim.

"He won't go into the bunker with us," said Kuan Hee. "He'll wait in the van on Canning Rise."

"The Brigadier's men will be on Canning Rise too?" asked Navin.

"Yes, they will take my parents and the researchers to a safe place," said Kuan Hee. "And, in case the plan fails, his men will take over."

"It won't fail, will it?" said Lina.

"Of course not," said Kuan Hee. But his voice lacked the brashness it usually displayed.

"Can I go into the tunnel with you?" asked Lina.

"I thought the matter is settled," said Tim. "that you are to stay on the grass slope next to the hatch."

"She insists on tagging along," said Kuan Hee.

"But she can't come with us," said Navin, "It's too dangerous. Besides, she will hinder our work."

"Yeah, I agree with Navin," said Tim. "We can't be looking out for her in the tunnel."

"It's decided then," said Kuan Hee. "You stay on the grass slope."

Lina could not hide her disappointment. But she didn't cry as she usually would. She knew the safety of Kuan Hee's parents depended on the success of tonight's rescue operation. She held back her tears.

"So Lina watches the hatch. Navin stays in the end of the tunnel next to the drainage system. Tim and I will enter the bunker," said Kuan Hee. "Tim will cover me. I will cut the padlocks."

"You sure the cutters can do the job?" said Navin.

"It can cut through steel and titanium," said Kuan Hee. "It cut through the wrist tag the army put on my wrist. Anyway, we've got Alex the robot."

"Gosh, I forgot about the robots," said Tim. "Are you taking both robots along?"

"Yes, of course. But we will only use Alex's laser weapon system if there's no choice," said Kuan Hee. "It's very powerful. It may destroy the entire door."

"Have we forgotten anything?" asked Lina.

"Let's see. Weapons, ammunition, earphones, LED flashlights," said Tim.

"We've got them all," said Kuan Hee.

"Don't forget our Google Glass devices," said Lina.

"What time do we move?" asked Navin.

"My brother says there are roadblocks around the island after midnight," said Lina. "He says it is safer if we travel before midnight. He'll be here at 11:15 p.m."

"That's about an hour from now," said Navin. He fished a pack of cigarettes from his pocket, took out one and lit it. He took a long puff on it. Tim sensed his uneasiness. "We'll be fine. Trust me."

The trees were swaying in the open field across the shophouses as the four friends walked along the five-foot-way towards the van. Some trees were bowing more than the others as the wind swept across the open space. It was too dark to see if the grey clouds were rain clouds. The red tint in the skies gave a hint of the weather to come.

The team squeezed into the rear of Lina's brother's van, next to two large tool boxes which were a fixture in the van. Their weapons and ammo were hidden in their backpacks. Lina's brother sat with his son, Xaden, in front of the van.

"Xaden wanted to come along to help," said Lina's brother. "He will stay in the van with me."

"I am in the National Cadet Corps," said Xaden. "So I know a little about rescue work."

"More hands, less work," said Kuan Hee.

"The more, the merrier," said Tim.

A pair of cutters hung alongside several umbrellas on the metal rack between the driver's section and the rear. Tim took it and placed it in his backpack. It was so long that its handles peeped out of the backpack.

"The wind is too strong for my liking," said Navin. "Maybe, rain is coming."

"Hope not," said Kuan Hee.

The van cruised through the suburban housing estates and arrived at the outskirts of the city where the bright city lights accentuated the redness of the skies.

"Look! The window is misting," said Lina. "It must be too cold in here."

"It's not mist," Kuan Hee said. "It's raindrops." Alas, the rain was here. Within seconds, heavy rain pelted on the windows of the van. The occupants of the van could no longer see the outside.

"So how about the mission?" asked Navin.

"Full steam ahead," said Tim.

"I agree," said Kuan Hee. "There's no turning back." It was too late to postpone the rescue operation, for his parents and the researchers were waiting anxiously in the bunker.

"Lina, you remain in the van," said Kuan Hee.

"But, I want to go with you," said Lina.

"You can't be standing in the rain," said Kuan Hee. "For goodness's sake, we don't know how long it will take us in the bunker."

Lina tilted her head. Her eyes stared upwards at Kuan Hee and her lips tightened into a scrowl. Kuan Hee knew he had to make a concession or the mission could be in jeopardy.

Tim came to the rescue. "Lina, you can hide from the rain in the tunnel," he said. Lina's face lightened up at once. On her, little things worked wonders.

It was pouring cats and dogs when the van came to a stop along Canning Rise. Kuan Hee looked at his watch. The time was 11:55 p.m.

"The good thing about this heavy rain," said Navin, "is nobody comes out for patrol duty."

"Yeah, it's a godsend," said Tim, trying to make light of an unexpected situation.

"Keep your smartphones on," reminded Lina's brother. The team members launched the Zello app on their phone screens. The app provided them with a private channel for communicating with one another.

"Keep your earphones in your ears at all times," said Kuan Hee. "And provide updates to the others in the network." They used rubber bands to fasten the earphones over their ears. It was uncomfortable but necessary. It was simply not practical for them to be holding their smartphones all the time.

Kuan Hee commanded Alex and Xander to come out of the backpacks. The robots climbed onto his lap.

"Kuan Hee, activate your Google Glass," said Lina. "You have to update Brigadier Walmsley during the mission."

"Ten-four," said Kuan Hee.

The team jumped out into the rain, along with Alex and Xander. They were only halfway up the steps along the slope but they were wet to their skin. It was a torrential downpour that had fallen tonight. The rapidly flowing water on the steps made their climb more difficult. Lina slipped and almost fell but for Kuan Hee who was holding on to her arms. It was impossible to see the cannon. Visibility was down to a few metres ahead of them. Tim found the spot where the hatch was. He groped around in the soil for the handles. He found them and, with Kuan Hee, managed to lift the hatch. The rain poured into the hole.

"Be careful, it's slippery down there," said Tim. "I'll go down first."

One by one they entered the hole in the ground. Navin, who was last in, closed the hatch above him. There were puddles of water on the floor in the room below the cannon. But no more water was coming through the hatch opening now. Although they were drenched, they didn't feel cold; it was warm in the room.

Tim walked to the metal wheel on the wall, pressed two emblems on its spokes, and the door on the wall creaked open. The team moved down the steps into the long tunnel.

"Ready your weapons," said Tim. "This is no walk in the park, you know." The three men took out their SAR21s, snapped the magazines into place, and grasped the pistol grips. The SSG 69 was in Lina's backpack.

Kuan Hee ordered Alex and Xander to move ahead in the tunnel. The two robots took long strides to keep ahead of the team, for they were merely thirty-centimetres tall. Speaking with Brigadier Walmsley on Google Glass's communication app, Kuan Hee learnt the Brigadier's men were on site.

At the end of the tunnel, the team sat down together, resting their rifles against the wall. They were about five hours early. It was to be a long wait in the stuffy tunnel. They looked at one another in askance. Kuan Hee took out little Busy's remote and activated the robot housefly. It wriggled out of Professor Wang's pocket. Both his parents were awake. They were sitting on the bed next to each other.

"Kuan Hee, you are here," said Professor Wang. "Your mum and I couldn't sleep. We thought we should wait."

"We are in the tunnel behind the drainage system, Dad," said Kuan Hee. "Lina, Tim, and Navin are with me."

"I told my staff about the rescue at dinner time," said Professor Wang. "They are all excited."

"Have the guards come in to check on you?" asked Kuan Hee.

"Yes, about fifteen minutes ago," said Professor Wang. "Their next round is at 3:00 a.m."

"Kuan Hee, can we move up the rescue operation?" asked Tim. "Now is a good time. It's pouring outside. Nobody in his right mind will come in through the rain."

"Yeah, I agree with Tim," said Navin. "The five-hour wait is too long."

"Let me check with the Brigadier first," said Kuan Hee. He removed his earphones and spoke into the Google

Glass's microphone. Then he turned to his team.

"The Brigadier agrees. We move at 12:30 a.m. His men are in black and wearing balaclava," said Kuan Hee.

He spoke through little Busy's speaker to tell his parents the rescue would be brought forward.

The team spent the next few minutes in nervous concentration. Their hands were clammy on the pistol grips, but it wasn't because of the damp air in the tunnel.

Kuan Hee climbed into the drainage tunnel after Tim had opened the door. With his SAR21 alongside him, he crawled a few metres to the manhole. Alex walked ahead. There was no need for it to bend; the tunnel was twice its height. Tim was next into the tunnel. It was a squeeze for him as he had his backpack on.

Hearing no sound above him, Kuan Hee lifted the manhole cover slightly. The bunker's lights penetrated the drainage tunnel, and Alex's metallic silver body glistened. He looked back at Tim to signal he was going to enter the bunker. He pushed aside the metal cover and let Alex climb on top of him. He lifted himself onto the floor of the bunker and readied his SAR21. Tim climbed onto the floor and knelt in the opposite direction.

"All clear," said Tim. "No cameras."

Alex stayed at Kuan Hee's heels as the two men tiptoed through the passageway towards the room where Kuan Hee's parents were held. It was the first room on the right at the fork in the passageway. The next two rooms were where the researchers were sleeping. The fourth room was where they had seen the guards' rifle rack.

While Tim kept a watch at the fork in the passageway, Kuan Hee sidled up to the guards' room. The door was open. He looked inside. The room was empty. He gave a thumbs-up signal to Tim and Tim came up behind him.

"The soldiers are not in; they must be in the guardhouse," said Kuan Hee.

"I'll watch the exit," said Tim. He passed the pair of long cutters to Kuan Hee.

Kuan Hee instructed Alex to watch the passageway; the robot had heat-sensing capability in his glassy eyes. It could detect anyone coming its way and raise the alarm.

The cutters sliced through the shackles of the padlock effortlessly. Pieces of the padlock fell with a thud. The sound reverberated through the passageway. Kuan Hee hesitated and then opened the metal door. His parents were behind the door. They hugged him; his mother planted kisses on his face. Professor Wang pulled her away.

"Time is precious," Professor Wang told his wife. "These little things can wait."

The couple huddled outside the door while Kuan Hee went over to the next two rooms. Within seconds, he had the doors opened. The six researchers, wearing the look of relief, joined his parents in the passageway. With Kuan Hee leading the way and Tim at the tail of the group, everyone made for the manhole.

Kuan Hee leapt into the drainage tunnel, followed by his mum, dad and the researchers. One by one they crawled to the tunnel doorway. Tim made sure the group had cleared the doorway before jumping into the manhole with Alex. He replaced the metal cover. Perspiration was dripping down his face onto his neck and his hands were wet from sweat. *So far so good,* he told himself.

Lina squealed in delight on seeing Kuan Hee's parents. She went up to his mother and hugged her excitedly. Navin waved his hand to say hello to them.

"No time to lose," said Kuan Hee. "Come, let's go."

With an uneasy gait, the motley group moved to the other end of the tunnel, into the room below the cannon.

Kuan Hee and Navin stepped into the tunnel next to the room. They raised their rifles and pointed them at the hatch. Tim moved past them He placed his hands on the hatch handles. They all paused.

One. Two. Three.

Then the hatch creaked open. Rainwater poured into

the tunnel. The rain pelted Tim. *Good, the coast is clear,* Tim told himself. He lifted himself onto the grassy slope and grabbed the SAR21 Navin had handed him. He knelt next to the opening and held the rifle close to his face, with his hand on the pistol grip. Navin was next to poke his head out of the opening in the ground. He took up position next to Tim. He watched the opposite direction. Then Kuan Hee's parents, the researchers and Lina climbed onto the muddy grass. They wiped their faces. The rain had drenched them. Kuan Hee was the last to come out of the tunnel. Alex was by his side.

Then, without warning, shots rang out in the distance. Some soldiers had appeared on top of the slope, behind the fence. They were shooting at the group.

"Quick! Make a run for it," Tim screamed as he opened fire at the top of the slope. He could hardly see the fence; he was shooting blindly. Navin led Kuan Hee's parents and the researchers down the steps towards the Gothic Gate. Lina refused to move. She wanted to be with Kuan Hee, who by now had climbed onto the grassy slope with Alex. The hail of bullets continued. The pair was in the line of fire. They staggered down the slope, with Kuan Hee pushing Lina in front of him.

There was more gunfire. This time, the shots came from the direction of the Registry of Marriages. They came from high-powered rifles. Some of the soldiers on top of the slope fell. But more soldiers appeared along the perimeter fencing. The whole platoon had congregated at the cannon. Some soldiers had climbed over the fence and were about to jump onto the grassy slope. More shots rang out. One by one, the soldiers fell onto the ground; their lifeless bodies lay sprawled on the grass.

Two vans screeched to a stop along Canning Rise. The doors opened and balaclava-clad men jumped out. They bundled Professor Wang, his wife and the researchers into the backs of the vans. Lina's brother's van was nowhere in sight. Two hooded men, MP5 sub-machine guns slung over their chests, towered over Tim and Navin in front of the vans. They were waiting for Kuan Hee and Lina.

Lina and Kuan Hee reached the vans. Lina's face was a picture of desperation. She was clinging on to Kuan Hee, and crying. Kuan Hee was clutching his chest. He fell in front of the men. There was blood on the back of his shirt; he had been shot. One of the hooded men dashed towards the slope to retrieve Kuan Hee's rifle, while another helped Kuan Hee into the first van. His parents were in it. His mother was hysterical; his father was the picture of calm as he pressed gauze pads onto Kuan Hee's back.

With Tim and Navin on board too, the first van rolled down Canning Rise onto the main road. The second van followed. Behind them, the reports of gunfire continued. The Brigadier's men were still at work on the slope, trying to delay the soldiers' advance.

"Alex. Alex," groaned Kuan Hee. He was delirious.

"Alex is here," said Professor Wang. "It is safe." But Kuan Hee continued mumbling.

The vans raced through Dhoby Ghaut into Selegie Road. Then, at the junction of Selegie and Rochor Roads, they parted ways. The first van, with the team and Kuan Hee's parents cruised into Bukit Timah Road, while the second moved into Serangoon Road. Apparently, they were heading to different destinations.

The first van stopped along the side of the road and a man in the front of the van came over to open the side door. He was no longer wearing a balaclava. The commando was a Caucasian with a tanned face and neck almost the width of a tree trunk. He was holding a longish device in his hand. He waved the device over the occupants of the van and shook his head at the driver, another Caucasian. Once he was back in the passenger seat, the van resumed its journey to an unknown destination.

CHAPTER 21

A popular bible verse goes:

> To every thing there is a season,
> and a time to every purpose under the heaven:
> A time to be born, and a time to die;

In his exploits with his *kakis*, Kuan Hee had had the misfortune to be shot three times. The first time, five years ago, left him with a shoulder wound. The second time, not long ago, saw him injured in the shoulder again. The third time was today. He had been twice lucky the last two times. Would he be able to escape death again? Or was today for him a time to die?

Not if Lina could help it. Not if Brigadier Walmsley had the best that America's special forces could offer.

Kuan Hee, Lina, and his parents were whisked away by speedboat to a ship anchored south of Singapore, near the Indonesian islands of Batam-Rempang-Galang.

From afar, the ship had the outlines of a cargo ship. The US Navy had a fleet of these quasi-civilian ships operating around the world. It had a nondescript name—maritime support vessel—that betrayed its capabilities.

With a displacement of 40,000 tons, the ship could hold two hundred and fifty men easily. It provided the navy with the ability to strike within eight hundred nautical miles of the ship. A helicopter landing pad; a hangar big enough to house Apache attack helicopters and Little Birds; and a rear ramp for vehicles amply qualifed the ship for special operations work.

The ship also had a specially fitted operating theatre and a team of medical personnel. It was this team who attended to Kuan Hee on board the ship.

Kuan Hee woke up on the seventh day of their stay on the ship.

"Where am I?" asked Kuan Hee.

"We are on board the Artemis," said Lina.

"Thank heavens you are alright," said Mrs Wang.

"We are on a ship?" said Kuan Hee.

"Yes, dear. You have been unconscious for a week," said Mrs Wang. She fondled Kuan Hee's hair and stroked his face. "I'm glad you have pulled through."

"Where's Dad? Is he OK?" asked Kuan Hee.

"Your father is with Brigadier Walmsley," said Mrs Wang. "We have been worried sick about you. Lina hasn't slept a wink since you were shot."

Kuan Hee looked at Lina. Indeed, pimples had broken out on her cheeks. There were black rings around her eyes. She had not been sleeping well. But for these, she was a picture of health. Kuan Hee was glad she was unhurt. He had taken a bullet meant for her, but it was his duty to protect her. After all, she was his world.

Kuan Hee tried to sit up. He grimaced. *It must be a pretty bad hit that I took this time,* he told himself. His mother raised the head of the bed so he could look out of the porthole.

"We are in the middle of the ocean," said Kuan Hee.

"No *lah*, we are off Batam," said Lina. "About forty-five minutes away from Singapore."

"Yes, dear. Lina's right. We are on an American

military vessel," said Mrs Wang.

"You are pretty lucky," said a voice from behind his mother.

The Brigadier had entered the room with Professor Wang. He was not wearing his hunting hat. He stood next to Kuan Hee and Lina.

"Three times lucky," said the Brigadier. "You better hope there's no fourth time."

"*Choy!*" said Lina. She glared at the Brigadier. "Mr Walmsley, how can you curse him?"

"Lina, the Brigadier was just jesting," said Professor Wang. "Don't be so serious."

"My apologies, Lina," said the Brigadier. "Don't take this to heart."

"Mr Walmsley, thanks a million," said Kuan Hee. "I couldn't have made it without your help."

"It's the other way round, Kuan Hee," said the Brigadier. "The US government should be thanking you and your friends for helping to rescue the researchers. Well done."

Lina was beaming. *My Kuan Hee is a hero in others' eyes,* she told herself.

"When will I be able to get off this bed?" asked Kuan Hee.

"The doctor says you need a few more days of complete rest," said Mrs Wang.

"Yes, don't stress your body," said the Brigadier. "Don't just think of yourself. Look after your body well too."

"Your mother and I are heading to Fort Bragg in North Carolina," said Professor Wang.

"Is it going to be really safe this time?" Kuan Hee asked himself. His father was a magnet for trouble everywhere he went. *The base in Australia was supposed to be safe,* Kuan Hee thought. *Look what happened there. And the US government was none the wiser for a whole year.*

"Fort Bragg is the headquarters of the US Special

Forces," said the Brigadier. "There's no place safer than that." At once, goose pimples attacked Kuan Hee's arms. It was as if the Brigadier could read his mind.

"Dear, I think you and Lina should come with us," said Mrs Wang.

"Mum, I can't leave Singapore," Kuan Hee protested. "I've lived there all my life. I know of no other place."

"Me too, Auntie," said Lina. "I want to be with Kuan Hee wherever he goes."

"Kuan Hee, there's no place for you on the island," said Mrs Wang.

"Dear, let him do what he wants," said Professor Wang.

"But he's a wanted man there," said Mrs Wang. "If they catch him, there's no telling what they will do to him."

"I'll take good care of myself," said Kuan Hee. He held up his hand slightly and raised his index and middle fingers. "Promise, I will."

"We'll talk about this another day," said Professor Wang. "Let him rest, dear." He did not want the conversation to descend into an argument. The Professor knew his son would not waver once he had his heart set on doing something. Besides, he was doing good things for his country. *Why should I stop him from ridding the country of a tyrant?* Professor Wang thought. *Gosh! I have yet to tell him about the tyrant.*

The Brigadier and Kuan Hee's parents left the room, leaving the pair to themselves. Kuan Hee had many questions for Lina. He had been unconscious for several days and was curious about what had happened after the rescue.

"Where are Tim and Navin? Are they alright?"

"You are the only one injured. I think they should be home now. They were at the jetty to see us off."

"And the researchers?"

"They are on this ship too, except for one. The

331

Brigadier said he was the one who tipped off the soldiers. He activated a GPS tracker when we were in the bunker."

"The devil! He did? Which one is he?"

"The Brigadier didn't say and I didn't ask him."

"Did your brother get away alright?"

"The Brigadier's commandoes got to my brother before we arrived at the Gothic Gate. They told my brother to leave the place. Said they would take care of the transport."

"I didn't notice they weren't at the gate. Everything was moving so fast, and we were dodging bullets."

"You mean—getting in the bullets' way."

"Oh yeah. I guess you are right. Are AleXander with my dad?"

"No, they are under your bed, in your backpack."

"Is that so?" Kuan Hee leaned over the bed, trying to see under it.

"Be careful. You haven't fully recovered." Lina reached for the backpack and handed it to Kuan Hee. He opened it and gently handled Alex. He was looking for signs of damage.

"Don't be silly, Kuan Hee. He's almost indestructible. You said it yourself. He's made of a special titanium and gold alloy."

"Just making sure. Just making sure."

CHAPTER 22

A week later, Kuan Hee was able to move around on his own. The Brigadier showed him around the ship. Kuan Hee felt honoured, for it was supposed to be a secret military vessel. The two of them were now leaning against the railing on the deck of the ship. It was breezy and their hair was in a disheveled mess.

"Was this the ship my dad was taken to five years ago?" Kuan Hee asked.

"Yes, of course. Like you, he was operated on here. This ship is sort of a HQ for our special forces in the region. From it, we stage many missions—for the sake of regional security," said the Brigadier. "You know, Kuan Hee, the United States does not want to be an international policeman. But we have no choice. Tumoil in any part of the world puts democracy at risk. The United States is commited to protecting this fragile thing called democracy, even if people label us *kapoh*." *The Brigadier knows how to use 'kapoh', Kuan Hee thought. He certainly knows quite a few Singlish words.*

"I thought you said you couldn't use your commandoes in the rescue of my mum and dad?" said Kuan Hee.

"That was before the Singapore army's crackdown on

the opposition," said the Brigadier."They went past the tipping point. We had to act. Which is also why we are having this conversation today, Kuan Hee." *The Brigadier wants me to do something,* Kuan Hee told himself.

"The future lies in our hands, Kuan Hee," said the Brigadier. "You and I can change the future, if we want to."

"Yes, Mr Walmsley," said Kuan Hee. He wasn't sure what the Brigadier was getting at. The Brigadier had always been direct—till today.

"I had been wondering how I should put it," said the Brigadier. "Let me quote the words of a famous philosopher." He took a piece of paper from his pocket and unfolded it in front of Kuan Hee. On it, the Brigadier had written:

> There is no crueler tyranny than that
> which is perpetuated under the shield of
> law and in the name of justice.

"Charles de Montesquieu was a French philosopher," said the Brigadier. "I could be wrong, but I think he is the one who gave us the dictionary word 'despot'. The Green Party government is now only a shell of itself. Ong Chwee Seng is the Green Party government and vice versa. Do you copy?"

"You mean he is the one calling the shots?" said Kuan Hee.

"Yes, exactly. He is running the show at his whim and fancy. There is no one stopping him," said the Brigadier.

"You want me to stop him?" said Kuan Hee, with an incredulous gasp.

"Nope, not you—alone, that is," said the Brigadier, "but with other like-minded people. You strike me as someone who will stand up to injustice—correct wrongdoings. I saw this quality in you five years ago, when you led your peers in standing up to the military regime then. You were shot a few times doing it. You attacked an armored personnel carrier to save a fellow protester. In my mind, you have what it takes. Your country needs young people like you to lead it into the future."

"What do you want me to do, Mr Walmsley?" asked Kuan Hee.

"It's not what I want you to do, Kuan Hee," said the Brigadier, "rather what you can do for your country. The United States can give you a leg up. That's all we can do. The rest is up to young people like you—to put things right. Save the country from tyranny."

"I understand, Mr Walmsley," said Kuan Hee. "But, I am only one person. I can't do much."

"Of course, not you alone, Kuan Hee, but together with others," said the Brigadier. "You were once a student leader. I'm sure you can get in touch with many other young people. Get them to do national service. Get them to do something for their country—before it's too late."

"Here, take this note," said the Brigadier. "Reflect on the contents. I'm sure you will understand what it is saying."

Professor Wang appeared on the deck. He was looking for Kuan Hee.

"Ah, your father is here," said the Brigadier. "I'll take my leave. We'll continue this conversation later." The Brigadier left father and son on the deck.

Professor Wang had wanted to get something off his chest. He thought now was as good a time as any to tell Kuan Hee what he needed to know.

"Our arch enemy is alive," said Professor Wang to an unsuspecting Kuan Hee.

"Arch enemy?" said Kuan Hee. "What are you talking about, Dad?"

"Colonel Tee—the scourge of our lives—he is alive and well," said Professor Wang.

"But I thought Jordan killed him five years ago?" said Kuan Hee. "How can it be?"

"Son, I thought so, too," said Professor Wang. "He actually died, but his memories lived on then."

Kuan Hee was having difficulty understanding what his father was saying. He gave his father a blank look.

"Son, Colonel Tee had the master copy of his memories hidden somewhere. His henchmen wanted him back alive, so they kidnapped your mother and me. They forced me to do a memory transfer into another person."

"You mean, the same way you transferred his memories into Jordan?" said Kuan Hee.

"Exactly, son," said Professor Wang. "That's how he came alive again. And he is reprising his evil in the country. Nobody seems to be able to stop him. He is too powerful. I should have destroyed the master tapes when I had the chance. Now, the memory bank is in his hands."

"Dad, so his henchmen got soldiers to kidnap you in Australia and fly you back to Singapore?"

"Yes, son. He has got control of the army—in fact the entire country," said Professor Wang. "You should be able to guess whose body he has taken over."

"There is only one person who's all powerful now— the PM, Ong Chwee Seng?" said Kuan Hee.

"Yes, son. Colonel Tee is Ong Chwee Seng and Ong Chwee Seng is Colonel Tee," said Professor Wang.

"No wonder, this chap Ong Chwee Seng is no longer the person he was before he became PM," said Kuan Hee.

"Colonel Tee's men kidnapped him over a year ago. I did the operation about that time," said Professor Wang.

"So that's why Ong Chwee Seng is doing the same things Colonel Tee did to Singapore five years ago. The country is now totally under his control, Dad," said Kuan Hee.

"I am afraid so, son," said Professor Wang. "And this is only the start. There is no telling what Colonel Tee and his men will do in the coming months. We've got to stop them."

"Couldn't you give this Ong Chwee Seng a dual

personality, like you did with Colonel Tee and his son, Jordan?" said Kuan Hee.

"I couldn't do a Jekyll and Hyde on Ong Chwee Seng then. They were suspicious of me. They suspected I had tampered with Colonel Tee's operation five years ago. They also had your mother. I was afraid for her safety," said Professor Wang.

"He's even more ruthless now, Dad," said Kuan Hee. "His men kill in cold blood. They don't care a damn about human life."

"That's what the Brigadier has been telling me too," said Professor Wang. "Son, I am too old. I don't have the strength or stamina to fight for the country. But you can—stand up to them, for Singapore's sake."

"What should I do, Dad?" asked Kuan Hee.

"Go back. Gather your friends and other like-minded Singaporeans. Get them to support the opposition parties. Join in their activities. Rouse the public into action. Together, you all can be a veritable force the regime has to reckon with," said Professor Wang.

"Will I be up to it?" asked Kuan Hee.

"You can, if you put your mind to it," said Professor Wang. "Don't worry about your mother. I'll convince her. In these difficult times, we have to put country before self."

"I will try my best, Dad," said Kuan Hee.

"One more thing, Kuan Hee," said Professor Wang. "Colonel Tee forced me to work on reproductive cloning of human beings. He wants to create a new race of elite individuals. He wants these clones to inhabit the country in the future. He says Singapore has no place for laggards."

"Laggards?" said Kuan Hee.

"Yes, that's the term he used for people who can't make it to university," said Professor Wang.

"But he was an 'A' level holder. He didn't go to university!" said Kuan Hee.

"Apparently, he has forgotten this or he has gotten

over his inferiority complex. The few times that I met him, he rambled on about how the elite could change the face of Singapore," said Professor Wang. "He wanted me to create an assembly line for cloning human beings. He actually believed the clones could form the new pure race of Singapore, that they would eventually become the ruling race of Singapore."

"You mean, replace the four official races that we now have?" said Kuan Hee.

"Not replace, son," said Professor Wang. "It's going to be the fifth race—and the dominant one."

"That is a preposterous proportion, Dad," said Kuan Hee.

"I know it is a load of bull, but Colonel Tee doesn't," said Professor Wang. "My guess is—since he is no longer human, he wants to create a whole tribe of non-humans like him to populate the island. That way, he won't be a freak."

"We have got to expose him, Dad," said Kuan Hee.

"Son, I have a job for you," said Professor Wang. "Destroy the memory bank. It will put an end to his nonsense."

"Where's the memory bank?" asked Kuan Hee.

"He's hidden it somewhere," said Professor Wang. "It's mobile. It's on a computer. He keeps moving it around."

"How do I find it?" asked Kuan Hee.

"I have placed a tracker on it," said Professor Wang. "It's a robot caterpillar."

"A robot caterpillar?" said Kuan Hee. "I didn't know you had a robot caterpillar."

"Yes, son," said Professor Wang. "It's hiding in the CPU of the computer. They were watching me all the time I was working at the computer. So my only choice was to get a robot caterpillar to crawl inside when no one was looking. You can locate it using the robot housefly's remote control. It's on the same frequency. Have you got the remote with you? I will show you how."

"It's in my backpack," said Kuan Hee.

"Later then," said Professor Wang. "My plan is for you to use the two robots Alex and Xander. Blast the entire computer to kingdom come. That will do a clean job."

"Won't Colonel Tee have made copies of the memory bank?" asked Kuan Hee.

"His men do not have the skills," said Professor Wang. "And I only made a master copy. I have not made any other copies. It's too complicated. There are so many trillions of sequences to map. We still do not have the technology to replicate these sequences in one go. One mistake and the data could be corrupted, rendering the memory bank useless."

That evening, Kuan Hee told Lina what the Brigadier and his father had discussed with him. She was shocked to learn Colonel Tee was alive, that Colonel Tee and Ong Chwee Seng were the same person. He showed Lina the note the Brigadier had given him.

"What is it saying?" she asked.

"That Colonel Tee is using the law and the courts to torment the people and keep himself in power," said Kuan Hee. "Remember—he got rid of the judges and replaced them with computer judges. These machines will do his bidding without question." Then he paused. Seeing the confusion in Lina's eyes, he continued.

"In a democracy, there are three separate entities: the executive, the legislative and the judiciary—meaning the Cabinet, the members of parliament and the court judges. Each entity acts as a check on the other two, so there is a balance of power in the government," said Kuan Hee. "However, in Singapore under the Green Party government, all three entities are actually one. Ong Chwee Seng controls all three pillars of government. That's why he can be so ruthless, yet nobody can stop him."

"How can we stop him if others can't?" asked Lina.

"We gather others—the university alumni," said Kuan

Hee. "Remember the Singapore River protest five years ago? We can get these people back. Just spread the word to the alumni."

"So you are going to lead them?" said Lina.

"Guess I have to," said Kuan Hee. "Dad also wants me to destroy the memory bank."

"Why can't the Brigadier get his men to destroy the memory bank?" asked Lina.

"Because, it's none of their business. It's we Singaporeans who have got to save our country from the claws of tyranny," said Kuan Hee. "We can't very well rely on others to do it for us."

"Yah *hor*," said Lina. "Makes sense."

"Of course *lah*, dear," said Kuan Hee.

CHAPTER 23

The Brigadier presented Professor Wang and Mrs Wang with United States diplomatic passports, for the Professor was doing top-secret work for the United States government. The couple was to fly off to Fayetteville Regional Airport in North Carolina from Hang Nadim International Airport in Batam. Fort Braggs was about twenty kilometres north of the airport. Kuan Hee and Lina had to say their goodbyes to his parents on the Artemis. Both did not have their passports with them so they could not enter Batam.

Mrs Wang was reluctant to leave Kuan Hee behind. She was afraid he would be in danger if he returned to Singapore. But she knew no amount of persuasion could get Kuan Hee to change his mind. After being apart from his parents for more than a year, Kuan Hee was reunited with them for three weeks. He was sad to part with them again. But he was a big man now, with responsibilities on his shoulder. It was no time for second thoughts. He and Lina bade a teary farewell as his parents boarded a speedboat to take them to Batam, fifteen minutes away from the ship. The pair promised to take little Huei Huei to visit her grandparents in the near future.

Kuan Hee had recovered fully. He and Lina were also due to return to Singapore, but before they set sail, the Brigadier wanted a word with Kuan Hee.

"There's someone I would like you to meet when you return to Singapore," said the Brigadier. "He'll be of great help to you."

"Yes, Mr Walmsley," said Kuan Hee.

"Remember the senior police officer who interviewed you at the Police Cantonment Complex five years ago?" said the Brigadier.

Kuan Hee nodded. "You mean, the Superintendent?" Kuan Hee said.

"He is now a Deputy Commissioner of Police," said the Brigadier. "In fact, he is the Acting Commissioner of Police now that the Police Commissioner has passed away."

"I didn't get his name then," said Kuan Hee.

"DC Tangarajoo," said the Brigadier. "He too thought well of you. Well enough to mention your name to me. He isn't a fan of the Green Party government. On the contrary, he wants to put a stop to the injustice the Green Party government is perpetuating in Singapore."

"Will he help restore democracy in Singapore?" asked Kuan Hee.

"He is trying to find a way," said the Brigadier. "But he can't do it by himself. That's why I spoke to you the other day about doing national service, remember?"

"Yes, Mr Walmsley," said Kuan Hee. "You wanted me to bring together young people to oppose the Green party government."

"Yes, that's it," said the Brigadier. "You were one of the student leaders who led the protest at the Singapore River five years ago. Can you do it again?"

"Yes, Mr Walmsley," said Kuan Hee.

"DC Tangarajoo needs the help of people power to topple Ong Chwee Seng's regime," said the Brigadier.

"You mean, like how the Filipino people got together

to bring down the dictator Ferdinand Marcos in the 1980s?" said Kuan Hee.

"I see, you studied history," said the Brigadier. "The Filipinos took to the streets to protest against election fraud. Some army units joined them in rebelling against the Marcos government. Eventually, people power won."

"Is that how we should overthrow the Ong Chwee Seng government?" asked Kuan Hee.

"In a nutshell, yes," said the Brigadier. "Can you do it, Kuan Hee? For your country, for your people?"

"Yes of course, Mr Walmsley," said Kuan Hee.

"Good. I'll tell DC Tangarajoo the good news then," said the Brigadier. "Here's what you need to do, Kuan Hee."

CHAPTER 24

In the small room above the shophouse in Realty Park, Kuan Hee and Lina spent an afternoon calling their old friends at Temasek University. Kuan Hee also contacted the student leaders of other universities he had got acquainted with five years ago at the Singapore River protest.

"What if some of them play us out?" said Lina. "They might report us to the G."

"We have to take the risk," said Kuan Hee. "You were there with them then. Do they look like people who will do us in?"

"I am only saying—what if," said Lina. "I didn't say they would."

"Don't be paranoid, dear," said Kuan Hee.

"Some of the phone numbers don't work anymore," said Lina.

"We can try reaching these student leaders through the alumni pages of the universities on Facebook. We may have some luck there," said Kuan Hee.

"How many people do you think we can get for the protest," asked Lina.

"Hopefully, maybe 30,000," said Kuan Hee.

"The logistics will be mind-boggling," said Lina.

"We have done it before," said Kuan Hee. "My only worry is money."

"We can borrow some of the stuff like megaphones," said Lina.

"We still need money to buy water; make banners and placards," said Kuan Hee.

"Can we crowdsource?" asked Lina.

"That will give the game away," said Kuan Hee. "If the G finds out, they will swoop down on us before we get a chance to take to the streets."

There was the sound of footsteps in the staircase. Kuan Hee got up to open the door. Tim and Navin came in bearing bags of food and drinks.

"Why so late?" said Kuan Hee.

"The queue at Pizza Hut was long," said Navin. "I don't know why there are so many people buying pizza today."

"It's the end of the month, for goodness's sake," said Lina. "People get their pay and splurge."

"*Wah!* Lina," said Tim. "Smart girl, you." Lina blushed. Tim liked to tease her.

"You look OK, man," said Navin.

"It's the seaview," said Kuan Hee, "and plenty of rest and relaxation."

"So lucky," said Tim. "Fancy spending a month on a ship on the high sea, doing nothing."

"Don't jest, Tim," said Lina. "Kuan Hee was recovering from a bullet wound in the back, you know."

"Seriously, how's the injury?" asked Tim.

Kuan Hee pulled off his T-shirt and showed his friends his back. The wound had healed nicely, but there was a four-centimetre scar left behind by the surgical operation to remove the bullet. Otherwise his back was unmarked.

Navin pressed the scar gently. "It's quite near the heart," he said.

"Missed his heart by two centimetres," said Lina. "That's what the doctor said."

"Yes, the bullet was lodged in the muscles near my heart," said Kuan Hee.

"Lucky chap, real lucky," said Tim.

"That's the third time you have used 'lucky' today, Tim," said Kuan Hee.

"With you around, we seem to be falling into adventure every now and then," said Tim. "When will life return to normalcy?"

"Let's get down to business," said Kuan Hee as Lina opened the food boxes and passed around the pizzas and chicken wings.

"I'll take down the minutes," said Lina.

"Putting together the street protest is going to be a nightmare," said Kuan Hee. "There's a lot of preparation work to do. Like the Singapore River protest, we will have a co-ordinating committee with these four groups: media, logistics, security and manpower. Any takers?"

"I'll take security," said Tim.

"Media," said Navin.

"Lina, you take logistics, OK?" said Kuan Hee. Lian nodded. "I will take manpower."

Kuan Hee described the responsibilities for each of the group. When he had finished, he asked for questions. Lina was the first to put up her hand.

"How am I going to get donations for water and bread?" she asked.

"Put up requests for these items on Facebook, but only after the protest has gone underway," said Kuan Hee. "This way, it will be too late to stop the protest."

"So I set up a new WhatsApp account for information sharing?" said Navin.

"Yes. Use it to update the water, phone charging and first aid locations," said Kuan Hee. "Also, to tell protesters where to get umbrellas—it's going to be hot, and the rain could come anytime."

"You forgot another important use of umbrellas—shield against tear gas canisters and pepper sprays," said Navin.

"Agreed!" said Tim. "And I am worried about people smuggling in a bomb in a bag or something. There are so many entry points in the protest. It won't be easy to check everyone."

"Just keep your eyes out for suspicious characters," said Kuan Hee. "And Navin, weed out all false postings on Facebook. We can't have sinister characters scaring the protesters and creating panic with false messages."

"Who's in charge of picking up the trash?" asked Lina.

"You," said Kuan Hee. "It's under logistics." Lina frowned. "Why so many things under logistics?" she complained.

"Don't worry," said Kuan Hee. "I'll get you able helpers from the alumni."

"Have we got everything covered?" said Tim.

"I have to set up a page for information sharing between the protesters," said Navin.

"Use getforme.com's forums," said Kuan Hee. "They have been around since 1999. People trust them. Their moderators will keep an eye on the postings. Give you less work—no need to monitor the postings."

"We will run out of money pretty quickly," said Lina. "There won't be enough to sustain the protest."

"Just hope the public will help," said Kuan Hee, "like they did five years ago. Once we have got a critical mass of protesters, the donations will come pouring in. I'm sure."

"What about the memory bank, Kuan Hee?" asked Lina. "You promised your father you would destroy it."

"I am leaving it on the backburner," said Kuan Hee. "The street protest is more important. We must get Ngoh Shi Ping and the others released first. The by-elections are looming."

"I have created the WhatsApp, Facebook and getforme.com accounts," said Navin, looking up from his

MacBook. "And on channelsingapore.com, there is a news article about the detained opposition leaders."

"Where?" Lina asked. "Turn the screen—I can't see from where I am."

"It says Ngoh Shi Ping is suspected to be involved in a conspiracy to harm Singapore," said Tim, summarizing the article. "It seems the Ong Chwee Seng government is pointing an accusing finger at a foreign government. But it has not named the foreign government."

"Anything on Tan Eng Chai?" asked Kuan Hee.

"It says here that Tan Eng Chai is being investigated for treason—colluding with Ngoh Shi Ping and a foreign government to overthrow an elected government," said Tim.

"It seems Ong Chwee Seng is getting desperate," said Kuan Hee. "He is adamant about keeping these two out of the by-elections."

"But it's unfair," said Lina. "It's downright dirty."

"Welcome to politics, Lina," said Tim.

"Will they be released in time for the by-elections?" asked Lina.

"Fat hope," said Kuan Hee. "Which is why we are pinning our hopes on the street demonstrations—to force the Green Party government to set the opposition leaders free."

"Kuan Hee, we still haven't decided on the venue for the street protest," said Navin.

"I was about to ask you guys," said Kuan Hee, "for suggestions."

"I'm sure you already have a site in mind, Kuan Hee," said Tim.

"Yes, Singapore River, where we held a protest as university students," said Kuan Hee. "We have done it there before, so we are familiar with the place."

"Also, it would be difficult for the army to use its armored personnel carriers there," said Navin.

"I agree," said Tim. "It's also a tourist attraction. The

army will think twice about using force. Too many eyes on them."

"When is the big day?" asked Lina.

"Next Friday," said Kuan Hee. "We can't wait too long. We have to take the G by surprise."

"OK," said everyone in unison.

CHAPTER 25

Deputy Commissioner of Police Ajay Tangarajoo looked different out of uniform. Promotion had come at a cost to his appearance. He was no longer the stern-looking middle-aged man that Kuan Hee had sat across from in the interview room at the Police Cantonment Complex five years ago. Gone was the sleek black hair he had combed neatly into a curry puff pattern. In its place was a mass of frizzy grey hair, which tried hard to conceal a bald patch on top. But DC Tangarajoo was still using Gatsby haircream—its familiar mild aqua smell was unmistakable in the air around him. And he had the same gruff voice.

"Kuan Hee, I saw something in you five years ago," said DC Tangarajoo. 'I was not wrong. You are a promising young man. I heard your father is a brilliant scientist. I think you will be one too."

"Thank you, Mr Tangarajoo," said Kuan Hee. "I was a little apprehensive about meeting you. But, in civilian clothes, you look very fatherly. I am not so nervous anymore."

DC Tangarajoo smiled. His gold teeth shone under the bright halogen lights of the ToastBox café in CHIJMES.

"James Walmsley says you have something to tell me,"

THE MIND CLONES TRILOGY

said DC Tangarajoo. *He must mean the street protest,* Kuan Hee thought. *The Brigadier said he could help me.*

Kuan Hee looked around the café, then at DC Tangarajoo.

"It's alright, Kuan Hee," said DC Tangarajoo. "We aren't speaking in a loud voice. Moreover, everyone here is engaged in conversation. No one will pay attention to what we are saying."

"We are organizing a street protest next Friday," said Kuan Hee. "It's along the Singapore River."

DC Tangarajoo's eyes met Kuan Hee's. "It may not work, Kuan Hee," he said. "The government will not yield." Kuan Hee sank in his chair.

"But, you are welcome to try," said DC Tangarajoo. "Just how many people do you intend to call up?"

"About 30,000," said Kuan Hee.

"That's quite ambitious," said DC Tangarajoo. "It won't be easy keeping order in such a big group. Perhaps, I can help."

"Thank you, Mr Tangarajoo," said Kuan Hee, clasping his hands.

"Keep calm. Don't be alarmed, Kuan Hee," said DC Tangarajoo. "I just want to help smoothen things for you. Let nothing happen that can ruin your event."

"Mr Tangarajoo, my main worry is that the army will send armored personnel carriers to crush our peaceful protest," said Kuan Hee.

"Don't worry, it won't happen," said DC Tangarajoo. "Not if I can help it. Just go ahead."

"Thanks, Mr Tangarajoo," said Kuan Hee.

"You know, these are difficult times for everyone in the country," said DC Tangarajoo. "Some people are hiding behind the law, using it to advance their own selfish causes. And other people who carry out the law are helpless. They can't do anything to stop the first group legally. Do you understand what I am saying, Kuan Hee?"

"Yes, Mr Tangarajoo," said Kuan Hee. He took out the

slip of paper that the Brigadier had given him and placed it on the small table, with the print facing DC Tangarajoo. The Deputy Commissioner of Police glanced at the note.

"Ah yes, you do understand," said DC Tangarajoo. "Kuan Hee, this thing called justice serves not just one side alone. It serves both sides. Justice doesn't protect only the government. It also protects the people. And when one side abuses its trust, the other side can take up arms to protect it, in the same way that justice protects them."

"It's quite a handful you have told me," said Kuan Hee. "I'm trying to fathom the deep meaning behind your words."

"You are a clever chap, Kuan Hee," said DC Tangarajoo. "I am sure you understand what I have just told you. Did you say the protest will take place next Friday?"

"Yes, next Friday along Singapore River," said Kuan Hee.

CHAPTER 26

In its headlines, the local newspapers announced writs of election had been issued. Nomination Day was two days after the planned street protest. It seemed the Green Party government was adamant not to let the Unity Party take part in the by-elections. Perhaps, as DC Tangarajoo had said, the street protest would not result in the release of the Unity Party's leaders in time for the elections. The opposition was doomed to lose the by-elections.

It was against this background that the street protest along Singapore River went ahead. The protest machinery had been cranked up. The volunteers had confirmed their attendance. Water, bread, banners and placards had been requisitioned. Everyone was raring to go. Nothing could stop the planned protest. So the protesters poured into the area around Singapore River.

Facebook postings calling for people to support the protest went viral. Social media was abuzz with excitement. Everyone who came across the posts wanted to come to the Singapore River. They came from all walks of life—the young and the old, the cleaners and the office workers, the able and the differently abled—all coming together with one ultimate purpose in mind, to topple the dictatorship of Ong Chwee Seng. Getting the opposition leaders released was just one of those things that would help the protesters achieve their ultimate goal, so they were for it too.

With the large crowds came the sponsors. Some donated piping hot noodles, some donated water, some donated umbrellas. Soon, more things were being donated than needed. Lina, who was in charge of logistics for the protest had quite a load on her small shoulders.

The police had erected barricades ostensibly to keep protesters reined in, but their real goal was actually to thwart the army's armored personnel carriers.

There was camaraderie among the protesters. Many shared their food and water. They lent their power banks to their fellow protesters. They huddled under shared umbrellas to take shelter from the hot sun.

Singaporeans were supposed to be *kiasu* and *kiasi*, but today, they shed these traits for the common good. They were, perhaps, reprising what their forefathers did when they migrated to Singapore from China, India and other countries, and met in an inhospitable environment—they put aside their differences and got together to build a better future.

Netizens swarmed the protest organisers' online forums to disparate the Green Party government for trampling on the rights of citizens. They shared anecdotes of how the government had come down hard on non-graduates. They also condemned the introduction of newly enacted laws making polygamy legal for graduate men. Navin and his volunteers sat on their backpacks with eyes glued to their MacBook screens. They were busy looking out for false messages meant to cause alarm to the protesters.

The protest was achieving more than what it originally aimed for. People were uniting in adversity. Tim was determined not to let gatecrashing supporters of the Green Party ruin their efforts. He and his security team kept an eagle eye out for these spoilers and spies.

By midday, the crowd had spilled onto the grass verges and the open spaces of nearby office buildings. Everything was proceeding so smoothly that they had all let their guard down. Was this the lull before the storm? Then came the rumbling of heavy vehicles. Then the turrets of the army's armored personnel carriers appeared on one side of Cavenagh Bridge. It was an intimidating presence. It put paid to the protesters' idyllic holiday mood. The roar grew louder as the armored personnel carriers neared the Singapore River. Several drones flew over the protest site. Their silvery blue colour announced their military ownership. These drones became a ubiquitous presence at the Singapore River protest.

On the other side of Cavenagh Bridge, a convoy of dark blue armored carriers roared into view. These belonged to the police. The two rival groups of armored vehicles were now only fifty metres apart on St Andrew's Road, in front of the bridge. They were now facing off each other. It was a tense moment for both groups and the protesters along Singapore River.

Was the situation about to explode into violence? No one knew. Both the army and the police seemed to be wondering which side would blink first.

Kuan Hee's first thoughts were the safety of the protesters. With the armored carriers effectively sealing the Cavenagh Bridge side of the Singapore River, the only means of escape—in case of trouble—was through South Bridge Road, next to Parliament House. Using loudhailers, Tim and his volunteers prepared the protesters to be ready to leave the protest site in an orderly manner.

But some of the protesters were infuriated by the presence of the army's armored personnel carriers. They cajoled others near them to move towards Cavenagh Bridge towards the army vehicles. These protesters had their own leaders now. As they moved into St Andrew's Road, more protesters joined them. Tim's volunteers were helpless; they could not stop the waves of people marching towards the army vehicles.

The presence of protesters around the police armored carriers complicated the situation. Kuan Hee and Tim were worried.

"We've got to get the protesters away from the armored carriers," said Kuan Hee. "It's too dangerous there. The army is ruthless."

Using loudhailers, Kuan Hee and Tim tried to coax the protesters milling around the armored carriers to retreat to the Singapore River.

Just then, a contingent of policemen came up behind the police armored carriers. The policemen kept the protesters behind them, forming a human chain in front of the armored carriers. A red anti-riot vehicle drove up and a senior police officer atop the vehicle ordered the protesters to disperse from the area.

Meanwhile, soldiers were pouring into St Andrew's Road, behind the army's armored personnel carriers. They had their rifles at the ready.

It was indeed a standoff in the making. The minutes ticked by uneventfully. The afternoon heat made standing in the sun unbearable for all parties. Lina's mobile water stations were a welcome respite for the protesters and the policemen who took generous swigs of the liquid.

Kuan Hee, Tim and Navin were now standing next to a police armored carrier, pondering their next move, as the setting sun prepared to make way for the darkness of evening.

"So, do we stay put?" asked Tim.

"Might as well make full use of the situation," said Navin. "With the police protecting us, I am sure the army will think twice about crushing our protest."

"It's your call, Kuan Hee," said Tim.

Kuan Hee combed the back of his hair with his fingers. "We stay for the night," he told them.

Soon the skies above the Singapore River were pitch-black. Instead of thinning, the mass of protesters crept across both sides of the river as youngsters heading outdoors for a weekend of fun joined in the protest. The river glistened as a sea of candlelights and flashlights lit up the promenades alongside the river as far as the eye could see. There had to be at least 50,000 people gathering by the river tonight. They were a formidable force to reckon with.

The four friends had ensconced themselves in the open space next to Cavenagh Bridge. They were seated on the bare concrete screed, having a powwow. Metres away stood the police armored carriers and their attendants.

"Darkness is when the enemy will be most likely to take action," said Kuan Hee. "They may come in when we least expect. Navin, tell everyone to keep an eye out for intruders." Navin typed furiously on his MacBook.

"The army drones have been hovering over us the whole day," said Tim. "They must know we are the organisers."

"Here they come again," said Lina. Two drones were now flying overhead.

"They can't beat our little Busy," said Lina. "No one notices little Busy."

"We may be the army's target," said Kuan Hee.

"Which is why we are sitting here, next to the police armored carriers," said Tim. "The soldiers have to deal with the police too, if they come after us."

"Smart move," said Navin.

"Look! The soldiers are pitching tents on the Padang," said Tim, as the hammering of metal pierced the night in the City Hall area. "There must be at least a dozen of them."

CHAPTER 27

The army commandoes came in the dead of the night. They climbed up the embankment and hid below the Cavenagh Bridge. It had to be just before dawn. It was that time of the morning when even the most alert of men would doze off, yielding to the lure of the cool morning breeze and their dreams.

Kuan Hee awoke with a start. There was cold metal pressing against his throat. Lina stirred beside him. Two men, in aquasuits dripping wet, were squatting in front of him. Tim and Navin were on duty, prowling along the promenade. The policemen were so near, and yet so far away. Kuan Hee dared not let out a cry; Lina's safety was paramount in his mind. He let the figures grab his arms and lead him away.

The three figures were at the edge of the Singapore River when Lina let out a shrill cry. It broke the silence of the night. She had awoken with a start. The river water had seeped through her shorts and she was now wet underneath. She ran after the men, screaming at the top of her voice. Tim and Navin were too far away to be of help. Some policemen gave chase but it was too late. The two commandoes had whisked Kuan Hee away in a rubber dinghy waiting in the water.

Lina and the policemen could only watch helplessly as the boat sped into the darkness. Soon Cavenagh Bridge was a hive of activity. The protesters learnt of the kidnapping and were anxious. The protest was now without a head. It was rudderless. Fortunately, Tim rose to the occasion. He got the volunteers together and made known to them he was in charge till Kuan Hee returned. He implemented a duty roster for the volunteers to keep watch on the river. In their plan for the security of the protest, Kuan Hee and his team had provided for precautions to take in case of a land attack by the soldiers. Never in their mind did it occur to them that the army would use commandoes to deal with them using stealth boats. After all, they were just ordinary protesters.

It was dawn when the protesters settled down. Tim, Navin and Lina sat down to discuss a plan for saving Kuan Hee.

"He's got little Busy with him," said Lina. "We can track him using GPS." She unfolded the remote control card and activated the locate feature. At once, a map of the Singapore River appeared on the screen. A little red dot beeped continually on the screen.

"He's nearby," said Tim. "They didn't go far. Zoom in on the co-ordinates."

"Little Busy is in The Float@Marina," said Lina. "Kuan Hee must be in there somewhere."

"We have to get to him straightaway," said Tim, "before they move him elsewhere. By then it will be too late."

"Someone needs to take charge here," said Navin. "But you and I have to go. Who can do the job?"

"I am going too," said Lina.

"Nope, Lina. You can't go. It's too dangerous," said Tim. "Just stay put and wait for news." Lina knew it was futile to argue with Tim. She realised she would be putting the two men in danger if she went along.

"Who's in charge while you two are gone?" Lina asked.

"You," said Tim.

"But I can't," said Lina. "I am not up to it."

"It's only for an hour or two," said Tim. "Besides it will give you something to keep busy while we are away."

Lina handed the remote to Tim. She took out AleXander the robots and Navin placed them in his backpack.

"AleXander will be enough," said Tim. "Their combined firepower can punch a hole through the enemy."

"Here, bring along Tizzy too," said Lina, placing the robot dragonfly and its remote in Tim's hands.

The two men waved goodbye and made their way through the protesters. They had to take a circuitous route to Raffles Avenue, for the soldiers had blocked off the City Hall area.

Sitting in front of The Float@Marina was a 30,000-seat gallery. It was specially built to host National Day parades. The seating gallery was a simple concrete structure consisting of a hundred-metre-wide concrete stairway tall enough to hold eighty rows of seats. On top sat a reception hall, about seven metres long. Behind the seating gallery was an open-air car park partially shielded from the elements by the slanting gallery structure.

Tim and Navin stood behind a pillar outside Marina Square. From there, they had a clear view of Raffles Avenue in front of them and beyond it, the rear of The Float@Marina.

"The car park looks deserted," said Navin. "The soldiers are congregated on the Padang. Looks like nobody is here. But looks can be deceiving."

"The only enclosed space in the seating gallery is the reception hall on top. The soldiers should be holding Kuan Hee in there," said Tim. "But we can't see from here. It's all walled up."

"Let's make sure," said Navin. He opened little Busy's

remote control and pressed the locate button. "Kuan Hee's still in the building."

"Fly little Busy; take a look at Kuan Hee," said Tim.

Little Busy peeped out of Kuan Hee's pocket. It flitted around him. Kuan Hee was leaning against the wall, staring blankly into space. He seemed to be deep in thought. His hands were behind him, fastened together with plastic cable ties. About three metres away, two men in black were having their breakfast at a wooden table. They wore their pistol strapped under their shoulder. At another table, another man was doing work at a notebook computer. He had his back facing Kuan Hee. There was nobody else in the longish room.

"Fly it to Kuan Hee's ear," said Tim. Navin tabbed on the remote screen and little Busy buzzed near Kuan Hee's ear.

"Navin and I are across the road, outside Marina Square," Tim's voice came through little Busy's speakers. "Tilt your head if you can hear me." Kuan Hee lowered his head slightly; he had woken from his thoughts. His eyes were gleaming. He flashed a weak smile.

"We are coming to get you," said Tim. "Hold tight." Kuan Hee nodded. Tim and Navin were indeed brave. They were unarmed, yet undaunted by their perilous task.

"Ready, Navin?" asked Tim.

"Hold on a second," said Navin. He reached into his pocket for his cigarettes. "Let me take a puff first."

"Later, *lah*," said Tim. "We'll do fine. Don't worry."

Tim and Navin ran across Raffles Avenue to the underside of the seating gallery. There was a lone unmarked van in the car park. Tim placed his hand on its hood. It was cold. The van had been there for at least an hour. There was a lift near the van. Navin pointed to the camera on a pillar.

"The soldiers came here at short notice. I don't think they have access to the CCTV," said Tim. "We take the risk."

"They must have used this lift to go up to the reception hall," said Navin. "The door adjacent to the lift could be the staircase."

"Let's find out," said Tim. Both men moved stealthily into the staircase. There was another door opposite. Navin took a look through a small window slot in it.

"It leads to the floating platform," said Navin. "No one outside." Tim looked up the staircase. There were eight landings.

"The reception hall must be on the fourth level," said Tim. He gave the thumbs-up gesture and they climbed the stairs.

At the top of the staircase, a door opened into an enclosed lift lobby. *There is no one guarding the lobby.* Tim told himself. *These guys are overconfident. They must be thinking no one will ever know they are here. They have forgotten technology works wonders.*

Tim and Navin sidled into the lobby. There was a camera observing their every move, but the two men ignored its presence. There was a pair of doors on one side of the lobby. *It probably leads to the hall.* Tim told himself. Both men took turns to peep through the window slot in the door.

There were the same two men they had seen on the remote screen. They seemed to be in conversation. The third man was still at his table. Kuan Hee was nowhere in sight.

"He must be on the other side of this wall," Tim told Navin. He gave Navin the thumbs-up gesture. *For their own convenience, the soldiers had parked themselves and Kuan Hee next to the lift lobby,* Tim thought. *These guys are either truly unprofessional or utterly complacent. But I thought they are commandoes.*

At once, Navin released AleXander the robots from the confined space of the backpack. He opened their front panels. They were now primed to use their weapon systems. Both robots had been programmed to recognize both men's voices and act on their verbal instructions.

Stunt-hurt-hit-destroy, Tim repeated the commands to himself. The robots would act on these commands to fire their weapons. Tim gestured to Navin to stay behind the door while he entered the room. Xander stood at Navin's heels. His rockets were too powerful to be used this time. He was on standby, for use only as a last resort.

At once, Tim opened the door and rolled on the floor towards where Kuan Hee was sitting. Alex the robot ran into the room and stood ready to fire his laser weapon system. It had the three men locked in its sights. Taken by surprise, the three men drew their pistols, but before they could open fire Tim had shouted 'stunt-fire-3' to Alex.

The electrolaser unit in Alex's laser arsenal shot a powerful electric current at each of the three men in succession. It worked the same way a Taser electroshock gun worked. The electric currents incapacitated the three men instantly. They fell to the ground, writhing in agony. Alex's arsenal was indeed formidable.

Tim had enough time to snatch Kuan Hee to safety. The three friends had a three-minute headstart. Together with the robots, they scrambled down the staircase, not once looking back.

CHAPTER 28

The protesters leaning near the police armored carriers were getting restless by mid-morning. They were preparing to march towards City Hall where the army armored personnel carriers were stationed. Lina and her fellow volunteers could only watch helplessly as the protesters veered off the promenade onto St Andrew's Road.

It was then that Kuan Hee, Tim and Navin arrived breathless at Cavenagh Bridge. Were they in time to stop the protesters from committing suicide?

Kuan Hee took to the loudhailer to calm the protesters. He asked for restrain. Thinking quickly, he jogged their memories of the army's brutal excesses five years ago. Giving a blow-by-blow graphic recount of the army's crackdown on protesters just metres away from where they were standing, he managed to instill fear in their eyes. They viewed the army's armored personnel carriers in different light.

The four friends heaved a sigh of relief. They had averted a disastrous situation—but for how long, it was anybody's guess. It would only take a little poking from a partisan fellow protester to rekindle their rage.

Meanwhile, Lina clung close to Kuan Hee. She had a

million things to tell him, but all these had to wait. Pressing matters of national concern took first place today.

By noon, the police presence along Cavenagh Bridge had grown in tandem with the crowd of protesters. Now, there were Gurkhas in their midst. The policemen were also better equipped today; they were helmeted and carried shields.

Perhaps, it was the heat of the afternoon. The crowd on this second day of the protest had dwindled to about 20,000 people, but it was still large enough to make an impact. Kuan Hee and his team decided that the protesters would march from South Bridge Road to North Bridge Road and Victoria Street instead. They were heading for the Istana, the President's official residence.

The protesters were hungry for action after a morning of inactivity. They knocked on drums, sang nostalgic national songs such as 'Stand Up for Singapore' and rattled sticks in the air. They waved their banners and placards as they moved along the city's thoroughfares. Traffic had slowed to a crawl. Kuan Hee, Lina, Tim and Navin led the march with Alex and Xander the robots walking in front of Kuan Hee. Although he hated for the world to know of the robots' existence, he had no choice. He could not risk being caught by the G operatives again.

At the main intersections of the roads, policemen in riot gear stood watching the procession, but did nothing to stop it. There were no signs of the soldiers along the protest route so far. The army's armored personnel carriers were still parked along St Andrew's Road, facing off with the police's armored carriers.

It had to happen. At the junction of Victoria Street and Bras Basah Road, a convoy of infantry fighting vehicles rumbled into view. Atop their turrets were soldiers who trained their machine guns at the procession of protesters approaching the junction. The soldiers were determined not to let the protesters pass. It was another faceoff in the making.

No sooner had the army's armored personnel carriers taken up positions, then some dark-blue armored carriers pulled up at the same junction from Bras Basah Road. There were Gurkhas manning the machine guns atop the turrets. Behind them was a special operations command vehicle and several armored multi-purpose patrol vehicles. These belonged to the Gurkha police contingent, which had been around since 1949. It had a fierce reputation for strictness and loyalty.

Suddenly it looked as if the police were intentionally creating a head-to-head confrontation with the army. The stakes for control of Singapore had gone up. The Ong Chwee Seng government now had its hands full. Would the Prime Minister order his army into street battles against the police? It would effectively be civil war if he did! It would also plunge Singapore into chaos.

The kilometre-long procession by now was within metres of the junction.

"Looks like the police are on our side," said Tim.

"The police are indeed taking to the streets to revolt against the Ong Chwee Seng government," said Kuan Hee. "We have a fighting chance to overthrow the military regime."

"If civil war erupts, it would be years before we know which side has won," said Navin. "I am not joking."

"Do we turn back, Kuan Hee?" asked Lina.

"We go back to the last junction and turn into Stamford Road. From there to Orchard Road," said Kuan Hee. He was not giving up his plan to lead the protesters to the Istana.

The four friends waded through the thick crowd and arrived outside Capitol Building at the junction of North Bridge Road and Stamford Road. There, they waved the protesters on to Stamford Road.

The sun was now high above the protesters. The umbrellas were not much help in deflecting the heat. The protesters had just passed the Presbyterian Church and were about to turn into the bottom of Orchard Road. Their stomachs were growling for attention. It was time for them to take a break. But they were only a hundred metres away from their destination; they trudged on at the behest of Kuan Hee and his team.

At last, the procession crept to the gate of the Istana. Kuan Hee and his team heaved a sigh of relief. They had seen only policemen along this last part of the march; except for the Istana ceremonial guards, there were no soldiers in sight. The traffic along upper Orchard Road had come to a stop at the junction before the Istana. Policemen diverted the vehicles away from the protesters. A score of policemen formed a human chain across the Istana entrance.

The protest volunteers set up water stations opposite the gates, next to the Istana Gardens. They distributed boxes of noodles and sandwiches to the voracious protesters. The donors were generous to the cause and the protesters were well fed.

Kuan Hee and his team set up base across the road from the Istana. Navin typed away on his MacBook. He was getting status reports from other parts of the procession whose tail trailed to the YMCA Building in Stamford Road.

"Strange! The other reporting centres are saying the soldiers are nowhere near," said Navin.

"They aren't here too," said Kuan Hee. "Could they be preparing to hit us in one fell swoop?"

"Too bad we left no one at Singapore River, otherwise we can get news on the armored personnel carriers there," said Tim.

"Anything on the local news Websites?" asked Kuan Hee. After some minutes, Navin looked up and shook his head.

"Keep trying, Navin," said Kuan Hee. "Something is up. I can feel it in my bones."

Then Kuan Hee, Lina and Tim walked down the road,

past MacDonald's House to Cathay Building. From the front of Cathay Cinema, they had a clear view of the whole stretch of Bras Basah Road up to Raffles Hotel. The traffic was flowing smoothly. The junction at Raffles Hotel was no longer barricaded. The army's armored personnel carriers were nowhere to be seen, so too the Gurkha's armored carriers.

"It's strange," said Kuan Hee, "very strange."

Lina and Tim knew Kuan Hee was now in deep thought. It would be many minutes before he woke from his thoughts. They could only wait patiently. Tim and Lina surfed the Internet on their phones, looking for every piece of news they could find on their protest and trying to locate the soldiers who had been stalking them the past few days.

Then it came. There was breaking news on channelsingapore.com. The Website was exploding with news all of a sudden. The headlines read:

Police Revolt Against Government

There was a blow-by-blow account of the police revolt, which was taking place at several places in Singapore. Police contingents were now attacking the army's infantry regiments at Bedok, Clementi and Bukit Panjang Camps. Over at Kranji and Keat Hong Camps, police armored carriers were engaged in a firefight with the army's armored regiments. And members of the police's Special Tactics and Rescue units were descending on the army commandoes at Hendon Camp.

In a retaliatory move, the army had sent its Leopard main battle tanks to attack the police headquarters at New Phoenix Park in Irrawaddy Road. A news presenter said the Leopard tanks had come up from Balestier Hill Secondary School, behind the police headquarters, and blasted the twin towers of the complex. Numerous injuries were reported at the site of the attack. In a subsequent update, the news presenter reported that the Gurkha police contingent's armored carriers had come racing to the rescue. There was now an intense firefight at the police headquarters. The story was still developing.

"Looks like war has erupted between the police and the army," said Tim.

"The police are no match for the army's Leopard tanks," said Navin. "The tanks can crush them like paper."

"Still too early to say," said Tim. "Don't forget the police's Gurkha contingent. They are a formidable force to reckon with. They go for blood."

"Guys! Breaking news—some Leopard tanks enroute to the Istana," said Navin. "ETA twenty minutes."

"*Wah!* That's too soon," said Tim. "There won't be time to make a getaway if we dillydally."

"We can't fight tanks!" said Lina. "The soldiers have armor protecting them. We only have skin protecting us."

"Don't fret. We've got Alex and Xander the robots," Kuan Hee reminded his friends. Xander can blow a hole through the Leopards."

"Still, we've got to prepare the protesters ahead," said Tim. "We can't take chances with their lives."

"I agree," said Kuan Hee.

"Another update coming up," said Navin. "Boy, these updates are coming fast and furious." The four friends watched a news presenter on channelsingapore.com deliver a live report on the police revolt.

The news presenter said that the police elite units had overrun the infantry regiments at Bedok and Clementi Camps. There was new fighting at Dieppe Barracks in Yishun. She also reported the police headquarters was still under siege, with a fierce battle being fought there.

"Many protesters are leaving," said Navin. "They are going home. These protesters fear for their families. The other centres can't stop them."

"Don't," said Kuan Hee. He had a change of mind suddenly. "The situation is dire. Civil war has erupted. I think it's best we disband the protest. There's no knowing what the army will do. I'm sure they are mad now. Navin, give the instruction to disband."

"OK," said Navin. Tim took to the loudhailer. He thanked the protesters and told them to go home. Before he could finish talking, the protesters were already disappearing in different directions. They too had heard the news of the police revolt.

The MRT trains and buses were packed with people. They were all trying to reach home before it was too late—soldiers were bound to fan out across the island to patrol the streets. There was no telling what these soldiers would do to people still loitering in the streets. Everyone was fearful for his or her life. The good life was about to dissipate. What would the coming days bring to Singapore residents? Nobody could hazard a guess.

When the last of the protesters had left, the four friends crowded into Lina's brother's van and headed home. *Thank goodness Hougang is not a battle scene,* they all thought. *Not yet anyway.*

Along the way, they saw people scurrying through the streets, shops putting up shutters, and shoppers lugging heavy bags of groceries. There was fear in the air. The van did not meet with soldiers during its journey; the soldiers were busy defending their turf across the island.

What a stark contrast in just a few hours! Kuan Hee thought. *This morning, the army seemed to be on top of the situation. Now, their existence is being threatened.*

"Bedok Camp has fallen," said Navin. His MacBook screen shone in the dark interior as it rested on his lap. "The army commanders are frantically looking for men. They are calling up the reservists using Open Mobilisation."

"No use. People are telling their friends on WhatsApp and Facebook to ignore the mobilization exercise," said Tim, taking his eyes off his smartphone to look at the others in the back of the van.

"Let's hope this revolt gathers momentum," said Kuan Hee, keeping his fingers crossed.

"Clementi Camp has been taken too," said Navin.

"The police has the element of surprise going for them," said Tim. "Of course, these two camps will be the first to go. Going forward, it will be difficult to gauge. Once the army collects itself, it will hit back and hard too."

"The army can only depend on the regulars," said Kuan Hee. "How many regulars are there now, Navin?"

Navin scoured the Internet for information on the Singapore army. "According to this US Website, active strength total: 72,000 and reserve strength: 432,000," said Navin.

"Active strength includes those serving national service," said Tim. "So we deduct about 20,000—the annual live births for males. This leaves 52,000 regulars."

"What about the police numbers?" Kuan Hee asked.

"Let's see. Wikipedia has this figure: 38,000," said Navin.

"*Wah!* The army outnumbers the police by 14,000," exclaimed Lina.

"The army also has stronger firepower that the police is hard put to match," said Tim.

"Breaking news again. Soldiers from Amoy Quee and Selarang Camps are on the move," said Navin. "But nothing on their destination."

"They have to or they'll be sitting ducks," said Tim.

"It's one big mess," said Kuan Hee. "Life in the late 2010s was so peaceful." He was reminiscing his childhood days.

"Yeah, I remember everyone in Singapore coming together to celebrate SG50," said Lina. "I was in primary three then."

"I never thought we would come to this," said Navin. "Instead of moving ahead as a people, we now *gostan*."

Certainly, Singapore residents were a hapless lot in the 2030s, falling from one dictatorship into another. But if they had the never-say-die spirits of these four friends too, there was hope yet for the country.

Back in Realty Park, the four friends huddled on the floor in the small room. They were eager for every bit of news that the online Websites and social media threw up on the police revolt. The videos on Facebook were more revealing of the situation than the news channels. Some pro-government news media were selectively providing information on the revolt. The four friends viewed the top videos trending on singaporehappenings.com. Whether shot from the corridors of high-rise buildings, from the roadside, from behind perimeter chain-link fences, or from moving vehicles, together they provided a bird's eye view of the battles being fought for control of Singapore. Citizen reporting was indeed a veritable tool to fight the government's giant fake news machinery.

"The international community is commenting on the police revolt," said Navin. He scrolled down the breaking news on the sidebar of a news Website for the others to read.

> The United States government urges return to democractic process. It calls for restrain on both sides.
>
> Britain supports peaceful resolution to the conflict.
>
> China calls for talks to resolve internal differences in Singapore.
>
> Japan calls for calm in Singapore conflict.
>
> Thailand urges both parties to exercise restrain.
>
> Indonesia calls upon the warring parties to avoid aggravating the situation.

"What about Malaysia and Brunei?" asked Lina.

"Nothing so far," said Navin.

"Both governments must be caught in a spot," said Tim. "Maybe they are waiting for things to become clearer before they say their piece."

"Sitting on the fence?" said Lina.

"A special announcement is being telecast on the official news channel now," said Navin. He turned up the volume on his MacBook.

> The government takes a serious view of the provocations by elements of the police force. It urges the leaders of the unauthorized movement to halt the illegal acts against a popularly elected government. Hostile actions violate our democratic principles, upon which the foundations of our country rest.

> The government hereby orders all police units to return to their barracks immediately. Failure to do so will result in severe disciplinary consequences. Leaders of the police revolt are commanded to surrender to the government immediately.

> All citizens are reminded of their duty to support the government in its efforts to stabilize the situation in the country.

"Bullshit! Look how they sugarcoat their words," said Tim. "Makes the police look real bad."

"Trying to hookwink us citizens," said Kuan Hee. "They must think we are three-year-old kids."

"Guys, they are just putting on a show for the world to see," said Navin. "Everyone knows it's a load of rubbish."

"What's the situation at New Phoenix Park?" asked

Kuan Hee.

"Two gaping holes on the sides of the twin towers. Thirty-eight dead. The battle's still being waged. Looks like a stand-off between the Gurkhas' armored carriers and the Leopard tanks," said Navin.

"The Gurkhas are a truly amazing force," said Tim. "Truly dependable and loyal. We need more like them." The others nodded in unison. Indeed the Gurkhas were the country's saviour in these tumultuous times.

"So what do we do now?" asked Lina. "Wait?"

"We can't," said Kuan Hee. "We move on. Right now, we must destroy the master tapes, which hold Colonel Tee's memories. Without them, he can't replicate himself like he does now."

"The police still needs us to protest in the streets," said Tim. "We can't just let them fight the army alone."

"Yes, I agree, Tim," said Kuan Hee. He turned his eyes on Tim. "I suggest you lead the protesters. I'll find and destroy the memory bank."

"Good idea," said Navin. "Tim and I can take care of the street demonstrations."

"What you say to this arrangement?" said Kuan Hee.

"OK. But can you handle Colonel Tee alone?" asked Tim.

"I've got AleXander the robots. They are enough," said Kuan Hee.

"And me too," chipped in Lina.

CHAPTER 29

That evening, Tim went to spend the night at Navin's home. News on the police revolt was still trickling in, but both men were too exhausted to keep their eyes peeled for it. Their brains were overworked. They could not process what new information was coming in. Sleep was what they urgently needed.

Kuan Hee and Lina finally got their precious moments alone in the small room.

"Kuan Hee, when you were kidnapped, I was so afraid they would do horrid things to you."

"Yes, dear."

"Were you tortured at The Float@Marina?"

"No, dear."

"Kuan Hee, you are not listening to what I'm saying."

"I am, dear."

"But you are not looking at me."

"I'm tired, dear."

"You weren't tired when you and Tim were running around The Float@Marina with the two robots."

"OK, dear. I'm listening, really." He turned his head to look at her eyes. They twinkled beside his face in the faint ambient light. In them he saw a glowing hunger. Lina flashed a mischievous smile.

"You are wicked."

"I know."

At once, she climbed over him and pressed her body against his. She was breathing heavily. He knew he had to fulfill her immediate needs.

The couple ignored the hard floor beneath them as they wrapped themselves around each other and entered each other's worlds. Relishing their fantasies together was their way of partaking in a sorely needed respite from the mundane world. It was a long night, but much too short for their liking.

It was early afternoon when the pair woke. It was Kuan Hee who was shaken out of slumber by the ringing of his smartphone. He groped for his smartphone on the floor next to him. It was Tim on the line. He had grabbed his forty winks and was on the Internet surfing for tidbits of information on the police revolt the whole morning.

"The Gurkhas have repelled the Leopard tanks," said Tim. Kuan Hee sat up at once.

"It's good news," said Kuan Hee. "Jolly good news."

"The Gurkhas braved the machine guns atop the tanks and launched TOW anti-tank missiles on them," said Tim.

"They sure are a fighting machine," said Kuan Hee. "How did they manage to get their hands on the US-made anti-tank missiles?"

"Search me," said Tim. "Must be the Americans, I guess."

"When did this happen?" asked Kuan Hee.

"At the crack of dawn," said Tim. "But the news only came in just now."

"Can you find out how they have divided the island?" said Kuan Hee. "For our own safety, we can only protest in police-protected areas."

"OK," said Tim. "I am with Navin now."

"Where are you guys?" asked Kuan Hee.

"In his study," said Tim.

"Lina and I will hop over later," said Kuan Hee.

After a late lunch, Kuan Hee and Lina flagged down an Uber taxi along Upper Serangoon Road. They were expecting roadblocks along the way to Sengkang, but fortunately it was an uneventful ride. Hougang had not been marked as an army or police zone yet. They did pass some police minibuses packed with policemen racing through the streets in Sengkang.

Navin lived with his mother in a four-roomed HDB flat in Sengkang, north of Hougang. His father passed away five years ago. His elder brother had moved to a new flat in Punggol when he got married so there was an extra room available. Navin had turned it into his study. It was where Tim and Navin were camped the whole day today.

"Auntie!" Kuan Hee and Lina greeted Navin's mother in unison. She broke into a broad smile as she opened the gate to let them in and then went back to the kitchen to continue her cooking. The heady smell of fish curry permeated the air as the pair entered Navin's study.

The couple threw themselves onto the large cushions on the ceramic floor. Navin resumed the commentary on the police revolt that he had been giving Tim.

"As far as we know, the police have got control of the downtown area, Geylang, Bedok, MacPherson, Serangoon, Hougang," said Navin. "The army controls Changi, Tampines, Jurong, Yishun and Woodlands—especially the outlying areas."

"This means the causeway in Woodlands leading to Johor Bahru, the Tuas Second Link connecting to Tanjung Kupang in Johor, and Changi Airport are under the army's control," said Kuan Hee.

"Effectively, all routes into and out of Singapore are blocked by the army," said Tim.

"Except the harbour," Navin corrected him.

"Oh yeah, I forgot about the harbour," said Tim.

"What if the navy blockades the harbour?" asked Lina.

"The police have got the coastguard," said Kuan Hee. "But their vessels won't be of much use against the navy's destroyers."

"We can only hope the navy won't get involved in the fight," said Tim. "So far the navy and the air force have remained neutral."

"I'm sure their top brass aren't happy about Colonel Tee taking charge of the armed forces," said Kuan Hee. "They are torn between duty and allegiance—duty to their superiors and allegiance to the country. They are merely biding their time now."

"Will the police be able to convince the navy and the air force to take their side?" asked Lina.

"Hard to say," said Kuan Hee. "They need a push. We can push them. The people of Singapore can push them over to the police's side."

"You mean our protest?" said Tim. Kuan Hee nodded.

"Now where would be a good place to stage a protest?" asked Navin. Any suggestions?"

"Must fulfill these conditions: safe, easy to access, maximum exposure," said Kuan Hee.

"How about Chinatown? Along New Bridge Road?" said Tim. "The Police Cantonment Complex is nearby. It's in the middle of town and many people frequent the place, expecially tourists."

"Mmm. The whole stretch of road is wide enough to hold a large procession," said Navin. "The overhead bridge between People's Park Complex and Chinatown is suitable for a look-out station—to spot soldiers."

"It's within the police protected zone. The army won't get in easily," said Kuan Hee. "Any objections?"

None of the four friends voiced disagreement to the suggestion. Just then, the aroma of whole-wheat flour being toasted on the griddle wafted into the study. Soon, Navin's mother appeared at the doorway. In her hands were a plate of chapati and a bowl of fish curry. Lina stretched her hands to receive them. Before she could lay them on the desk, the men had snatched some chapatti from the plate. They were indeed famished. Navin's mother certainly knew how to make delectable chapatis.

"It's set then, New Bridge Road it is," said Kuan Hee. The others nodded in unison. With the chapatis happily devoured, the four friends hunkered down to discuss the protest details.

CHAPTER 30

Colonel Tee's ability to live in another's mind depended on the master tapes hosting his memories. It was Kuan Hee's job to locate the memory bank carrying these tapes and destroy it. Now was the right time to carry out the task. Kuan Hee recalled his father telling him he had placed a robot caterpillar in the memory bank's CPU. Little Busy's remote control could locate the robot caterpillar's position.

Kuan Hee unfolded the remote control in his hand. The screen glowed into life. He recalled his father's instructions as he delved into the hierarchical menu and tapped on different icons. The remote control was indeed complex for the tiny state-of-the-art robot. *Will I be as good as Dad some day?* Kuan Hee wondered. *These nano robots require delicate engineering.*

He brought up the dedicated screen for the robot caterpillar. In a second, the screen switched to a map on which a blinking orange dot stood. *It's somewhere in Sembawang,* he told himself. He pinched the map and spread two fingers to enlarge it. *Let's see now. Sun Plaza…Old Nelson Road,* he muttered under his breath.

He heard faint footsteps in the corridor. Then the door creaked open and Lina came in carrying their breakfast.

"How's the situation outside?"

"People going about doing their own things."

"Any soldiers?"

"Nope. What's that?"

"Getting a fix on the robot caterpillar's position. It's at Old Admiralty House."

"Gosh! That's the PM's residence."

"Yes, seems Colonel Tee only trusts himself. He keeps the memory bank near him."

"It will be heavily guarded. It's dangerous going there." Lina unwrapped the disposable chopsticks and handed a pair to Kuan Hee. They ate fried beehoon together.

"It's on a hill. It is difficult to recce, even more difficult to infiltrate. Anyone up there can see us immediately."

"We've got little Busy."

"But I still have to get up there."

"Oh! I forgot."

"I will do a search on Old Admiralty House. It's a national monument so there should be plenty of information on the place online."

Lina left Kuan Hee alone. She knew he hated to be disturbed when he was on to something. She spent the morning cleaning the room and washing their laundry.

An hour later, she came up behind Kuan Hee. "So how's the progress."

"There's speculation about a secret tunnel somewhere under the house. Seems it leads to Sembawang Shipyard."

"Really? Could be leading us on a wild goose chase."

"I know. But in 1990, during excavation work on the grounds, the contractors discovered an underground bunker—World War II period."

"For real?"

"Yes. It says so in the online national library archives."

The evening brought updates on the police revolt situation on the island. The navy and air force commanders had gone on air to state their neutrality in the on-going conflict. That the news media had given them a chance to air their views on national television spoke volumes about the volatile situation. It was a slap in the face for the Ong Chwee Seng government.

"The police can breathe more easily now."

"Yes. And I can't keep putting off my mission. Time is of the essence. Colonel Tee could move the master tapes anytime. It could go into an army base. That will make finding it more difficult."

"You going to give up looking for the secret tunnel on Old Admiralty House?"

"I have been looking high and low. It's thrown up nothing but dead ends. I don't have the luxury of time. Besides, it might not exist."

"What have you found out so far?"

Kuan Hee and Lina browsed the Websites he had bookmarked in his search. They examined the pictures of the various rooms in the big house and the surroundings.

Lina fingered a large room on the second storey. "So Queen Elizabeth II stayed in this room when she visited Singapore. I bet Colonel Tee must be sleeping in this room too."

"For sure. The memory bank could be in this room. We will send little Busy into the room to look around."

"When are we going to Old Admiralty House?"

"I have completed the research. We can go tomorrow. Remember to bring pen and paper. We are going to sketch a plan of the house."

Early next morning, an Uber car took Kuan Hee and Lina to Sembawang. The driver avoided Sembawang Road where several army camps were sited. Instead, he took them through Yishun Avenue two, which ran smack in the middle of an HDB estate. They passed soldiers guarding MRT stations along the route. There were no roadblocks.

On arrival, the pair staked out Old Admiralty House and watched from a safe distance. They squatted in a drain on the bottom of the hill, outside the perimeter fencing on the far end of the sprawling grounds. It was difficult to see the top of the hill through the trees and the bushes. *Good. People up on the hill can't see us too,* Kuan Hee told himself. He unfolded the remote to reveal the control panel for the robot caterpillar. He tapped on the camera icon. At once, the screen went into video mode. But all the pair could see was a darkened screen.

"Kuan Hee, is the screen working? It's blank."

"Of course, it's working. It's just too dark, I guess. I can't see anything."

"Switch on the caterpillar's lights." Kuan Hee tapped on a flashlight icon. At once, the caterpillar's eyes shone. Its home for the past year lit up.

"Looks like a computer server. We are looking at the innards. Let me try to get out of this contraption." Kuan Hee let the caterpillar wriggle along the metal frame of the computer and then out through a small opening on one side.

"It is inside a metal cabinet of some sort. *Aiyoh*, this caterpillar sure is slow. Little Busy could have done the job in a few seconds."

"Don't complain, Kuan Hee. Your father must have had a good reason for making the caterpillar like that."

"I see marking on the metal wall of the cabinet. Let me zoom in. Says C-H-U-B-B. Gosh! It's a Chubb safe." Kuan Hee stared in disbelief. Then he spoke. "I was going to steal the master tapes. Now, it looks like I have to destroy the whole safe instead. There's no way to get inside the safe."

"So we are looking for a safe? A Chubb safe?"

"Yes. Alex's laser weapon will come in handy."

"But the robot caterpillar's in the safe."

"It's a pity, but I have no choice. It's either the robot caterpillar or the country. I'm sure Dad will understand. Anyway, he's the one who is adamant about destroying the memory bank. He must have known he was putting the robot caterpillar in a death mission."

"You speak as if the caterpillar is alive."

"Finding the master tapes is of paramount importance. Let's release little Busy." Kuan Hee switched to the main menu on little Busy's remote.

Little Busy flitted up the slope. It flew over bushes and trees till it was hovering over a large flat open ground on the top of the hill. A stately old mansion—with wide verandahs on its upper floor, long wooden louvred windows and a gable roof—took centre stage, with two smaller buildings on its right and a swimming pool next to it. Adjacent to them stood a newer building standing on lower ground. Beyond the buildings, on the horizon, a long line of tightly packed blocks of HDB flats met the sky. Two armored personnel carriers dotted the open space near the mansion. There was a smattering of soldiers moving around the grounds.

Lina sketched the layout as the scene played out before them. Kuan Hee manoeuvred little Busy towards the big house. It flew into a large sitting room on the second level. No one was in it. The robot housefly flitted through a long corridor where sunlight glared through tall windows on one side. There were two doors opposite the windows. At the end of the corridor, next to the staircase was another door. According to a Website, this was the room Queen Elizabeth had stayed in when she visited Singapore. Kuan Hee switched to the map screen for the robot caterpillar. The orange dot on the map was flickering in greater intensity.

"The memory bank should be inside this room. But there's no gap for little Busy to sneak through."

"Fly outside the house to the windows of the room."

"Yeah. I forgot about the windows."

"You always do."

Kuan Hee instructed little Busy to fly out the windows up over the roof to the other side of the house. Soon it hovered outside the room's two windows. They were shut.

"The gaps between the lourves are too tiny for little Busy to slip through. Its heat sensors are telling me the air-conditioning is not on. I think nobody's in. At least, we know the tapes are somewhere inside."

"Kuan Hee, move around the place so I can complete my map." Kuan Hee let the robot housefly explore the premises. As it moved around, Lina sketched details onto the map she had drawn.

"The soldiers are concentrated at the entrance on top of the hill. Mark their positions. Also draw circles where the machine guns overlook the bottom of the hill."

In an hour, Lina had finished with the sketched map. They were tired after being in a constricted position for so long.

"We'll come back tomorrow to take care of the memory bank. I miscalculated. I can't tackle the hill alone."

Just then, a motorcade roared into the compound. The Mercedes-Benz moved away from the two Volvos and stopped in the porch. Little Busy reversed direction and flew over the porch. A seventyish man, pompous and rotund, stepped out of the back of the vehicle. He paused to survey the surroundings and then entered the house with two men in army fatigues following him.

"Ong Chwee Seng. That's him all right."

"Are we staying or going?"

"Let's observe him for a while. I will send little Busy after him." Little Busy flew into the house, trailing the men through the corridor on the upper floor. The men went into a room at the other end of the corridor. It perched itself on a painting in the longish room. A large desk and an oversized armchair stood on the side of the door and facing them, across the room, were two tall windows. A settee and armchair occupied the space at the far end of the room.

Ong Chwee Seng sank into the armchair behind his desk. His two lieutenants stood across the desk. Both looked glum. Ong Chwee Seng drew a breath. "Wipe them off the face of the earth."

"But, sir. Who will take charge of the police then?" said the man nearest him. He wore the epaulettes of a Lieutenant General.

"We can put them under the MPs," said Ong Chwee Seng.

"But it's still the military police, sir. People will think they are under military rule," the man protested.

"Aren't they now?" said Ong Chwee Seng. "Look, Warren. We can drop the pretence since some of them no longer support us. Anyway, we don't need them. I will do away with the polls. This police revolt has given me the perfect opportunity."

Warren Tan, a major who followed Colonel Tee into power five years ago was now a Lieutenant General in the army. Somehow, he had escaped the scalping of Colonel Tee's followers, which took place when the Tee Dynasty fell.

The three men huddled over a large map on the desk.

"Pound their positions. Pulverize them," said Ong Chwee Ong, slapping his palm on the map.

"Yes, sir," the two men chorused in unison.

Kuan Hee and Lina had no inkling what the men were discussing. But they were sure it had something to do with the police strongholds. It was too dangerous for little Busy to fly over the men for a closer look.

"Time to withdraw." Kuan Hee got little Busy to fly out of the room back down the hill to where they were squatting. The pair climbed out of the drain clumsily. They had spent an eternity in the drain; their legs were numb.

CHAPTER 31

On the other side of town, along New Bridge Road, a huge procession had taken shape. People from all walks of life had flocked to Chinatown to stand as one against the authoritarian regime of Ong Chwee Seng. They had had enough of his regime. They didn't want to wait four more years for the ballot box to take him down. They wanted him to step down straightaway. The police revolt was timely. It acted as the catalyst for Navin to cobble together a coterie of groups with the common aim of bringing down his regime. From political parties to non-government organisations, almost everyone who's anyone in society was represented.

From Outram Road MRT Station all the way to the Speakers' Corner in Hong Lim Park, it was a sea of faces. It was not easy for Navin to keep the different groups together. Each group's leaders had its own agenda; this uneasy union between the groups at times threatened to throw the protest into disarray. Fortunately, they all hated Ong Chwee Seng enough to keep their differences beneath the surface—for the time being. How did Ong Chwee Seng's popularity spiral downwards in a short span of less than a year? For the answer, look no further than ancient philosopher Aristotle's words:

> "No notice is taken of a little evil, but when it
> increases it strikes the eye."

"You managed to get these disparate groups together? Impressive. I couldn't have done better myself," said Kuan Hee. Navin beamed.

"It's indeed an achievement, getting First People's Party, One Singapore Party and Unity Party to bury their differences," said Tim.

"*LOL!* The common good makes the difference," said Navin.

"How's the going, Kuan Hee?" asked Tim.

"Not so good *lah*. Need your help. Not now. Tonight," said Kuan Hee. "I can't make it up the hill alone." Kuan Hee described the situation on the hill to the two men. "But I guess Navin's got his hands full here."

"You and I should be enough," said Tim. "But we need hardware. Let me retrieve them first." His eyes did not betray fear.

For their own reasons, the police were anxious to let the protest go smoothly. They were not taking any chances. Their commanders stationed armored multi-purpose vehicles at the junctions along the protest site. Gurkha policemen stood atop their turrets. Their no-nonsense looks reassured the protesters of their safety.

Over at the Gurkha's Mount Vernon Camp—the home of the contingent, the mother of battles had begun. It started with the army's howitzers pounding the grounds. These were self-propelled howitzers mounted on tracked vehicles called Primus. The army had sent two of these vehicles to Vernon Park. Then Bionix armored fighting vehicles rolled up Mount Vernon Road. The Gurkha guards on duty fought a hard fight, trying to keep their attackers at bay. There was no let up in the army's attack. Fortunately, the Gurkha contingent's families were not on site. They had been relocated days before on fears that the army would mount retaliatory action. Nevertheless, there were casualties from the howitzers' pounding. The howitzers did not play fair; they targeted the highrise living quarters of the Gurkhas, blasting holes through the walls.

If the Gurkha policemen along the protest route in New Bridge Road were unsettled by the news of the intense firefight, they certainly did not show it in their faces. They stood steadfast atop their vehicles. For them, allegiance to Singapore came first.

The embattled Gurkhas on Mount Venon did not have to wait long, for the police commanders had sent a convoy of Tenix S600 armored carriers to the rescue. Policemen in them were armed with TOW anti-tank missiles, powerful enough to blow the howitzer-mounted Primuses to smithereens.

The arriving Tenix armored carriers locked the attackers between them and the Gurkhas on Mount Vernon. Policemen leapt out of the vehicles, carrying TOW missile launchers and wielding MP5 sub-machine guns. They fanned out across the slope in front of Mount Vernon Road and stealthily they ascended it. Some fired their TOW anti-tank missiles at the army's Primuses and armored personnel carriers, while others sprayed bullets at the soldiers along Mount Vernon Road. The attackers found themselves stuck between a rock and a hard place.

Taken by surprise, the soldiers yelled in pain, dropping like flies to the ground. Their mission was in peril. Soon the Primuses and armored personnel carriers were but a shell of themselves with plumes of smoke billowing from them. Remnants of the invading force surrendered to the Gurkha policemen.

News of the police's success in fending off the army attack at Mount Vernon Camp spread like wildfire across the protest site. The protesters looked at the Gurkha guards with renewed respect; for the Gurkhas had not flinched from duty.

Standing next to a Gurkha armored carrier stationed outside the historic Yue Hwa Building, the four friends mingled with fellow protesters in the dwindling evening light. The event had gone without a hitch all day. Perhaps, the presence of the fierce-looking Gurkhas had something to do with it. No one knew or cared. Everyone was having a good time, oblivious to the dark clouds looming overhead. *These are night clouds,* the protesters reasoned to themselves.

CHAPTER 32

With nightfall came the city lights, which illuminated the dark skies. Floodlights from portable towers lit up the intersections of roads along the protest site.

It was time for Kuan Hee and Tim to make a move. Leaving Navin and Lina behind, they scrambled into Lina's brother's van parked along Upper Cross Street. Xaden had come along for the ride. He sat in front, next to his father. With its human load tucked in the back, the van cruised along Clemenceau Avenue, heading first to Paya Lebar, where it stopped by Tim's family-owned warehouse. Tim alighted to pick up a large tennis bag. It held two SAR21s and ammunition.

"So this is where you have been hiding the weapons all along."

"It's so big, there's no way anybody will notice a small bag hidden in some nook."

"*Wah!* You are really clever." Tim's face reddened. He took out the SAR21s. These came with 40mm underbarrel grenade launchers locked into place.

"How did you get your hands on these M203s?"

"You like them?"

"Of course *lah*. They are a godsend."

Both men did a quick cleaning of the rifles. Then they slapped the magazines into the magazine well of the rifles and slid the M203 barrel forward. They slotted in a grenade and glided the barrel backwards. Their rifles were now primed for action. They slipped a spare clip and two grenades into their backpacks.

"Two clips—sixty rounds altogether. Should be enough."

"I'll take Alex; Xander will follow you. Here's the headset. It's been programmed to communicate with Xander directly. Kuan Hee retrieved AleXander the robots from his backpack and opened their front panels.

"Follow," Kuan Hee spoke into the headset he had plugged into his ear. "This ensures Alex stays by my side all the time." Tim did the same with his headset.

The van arrived at a desolate road behind the hill.

"We'll be back soon," said Kuan Hee to Lina's brother. Her brother waved them on as he and Xaden surveyed the surroundings.

With their backpacks strapped firmly to their backs, Kuan Hee and Tim climbed the slope together with Alex and Xander, stopping every few steps to watch for the slightest movements on top of the hill. They could not afford to be sloppy, for mistakes could cost them their lives. Kuan Hee released little Busy into the air. The robot housefly flew upwards towards the light. On reaching the top of the hill, little Busy wasted no time in surveying the perimeter of the grounds, looking for machine-gun nests. It found three, one overlooking the open field across the road, another looking down at the overhead MRT tracks and a third only metres on top of them.

Kuan Hee shut the remote and gestured for Tim to move sideways. They inched nearer to where they had started the climb. "We are outmatched."

"It's going to be damned hard to come out of this alive. I'm having second thoughts."

"Don't. Even if we die martyrs, we still have to do the

job."

"*Wahseh*, you haven't even seen your little Huei Huei and you are talking nonsense like this. Cut it out."

"Shush!" Kuan Hee placed a finger over his lips. "Let me think." Minutes slipped by as Kuan Hee contemplated their mission. Then he spoke.

"I'll go up alone. You keep watch here. If I don't return in fifteen minutes, leave this place." Without waiting for a reply, Kuan Hee snuck up the slope with Alex, stealing a quick glance back at Tim before resuming his climb. Then he heard a faint sound behind him. It was Tim. He had changed his mind.

"For better or for worse," Tim whispered. Kuan Hee nodded.

There was no turning back now for the two men. They understood their country came first. They stole past two soldiers manning a machine gun on their right. They crouched down and duckwalked through the verandah of a small building next to the swimming pool.

Seeing no one in the open space between the mansion and them, they sprinted across the open space. They spied a guard at the porch. Kuan Hee gestured for them to take the opposite direction. They crept around the mansion to the back. Kuan Hee tried a door. It opened into a large room empty of people. They sidled to the opening at the other end and peeped into the foyer. The coast was clear. A stately staircase stood on their left. The two men climbed the stairs to the second level. Colonel Tee's bedroom was on their right, next to the staircase. They tried the knob; the door opened and cool air met their faces.

Kuan Hee surveyed the large room while Tim kept an eye on the corridor through a crack in the door. Kuan Hee had precious minutes to complete his task. He could not dillydally. He had to take a risk. "Time for the robot caterpillar to make a noise." He tapped on the loudhailer icon on the remote. At once a piercing beep resonated in the room. It seemed to come from the king-sized bed. He walked to the bed and knelt beside it. There was nothing suspicious about the divan or the mattress. The large wooden headboard had to conceal something. He leaned the rifle against the wall and pushed the bed away from him.

Embedded in the wall was a rectangular old-world safe. It had an oval brass plate with the words C-H-U-B-B emblazoned on it. Directly below the inscription, there was a combination lock and a handle. *This is it,* Kuan Hee told himself. *The memory bank must be in it.*

There was no way Kuan Hee could open the safe. Even if he could pry it off the wall, it looked too heavy to lug away. *Have to say goodbye to the robot caterpillar,* he told himself. *Sorry, old chap. I have no choice.*

He thought about using the M203 on his rifle, but decided against it. It might not be able to blast the safe to bits. He did not have time for a second try. He had to make the first work. He grabbed his rifle and stood away from the safe. Then he retreated to the far end of the room, next to Tim. *Play safe,* he told himself. He tapped Tim's shoulder. Tim nodded. They braced themselves for the explosion that would follow.

"Destroy-fire-1," he commanded Alex. He had used Alex's most potent weapon. It had the power to tear a gaping hole through a tank. Alex remained standing with his feet apart. It had readied itself for action, but nothing happened.

"Kuan Hee," Tim whispered. "What's wrong?"

"*Alamak!*" Kuan Hee blurted out. "Did I forget something?" He had been nervous and didn't realize he had forgotten to open Alex's front panel. It was a safety feature that his father had incorporated into the two robots.

"*Ah!*" Kuan Hee exclaimed. He knelt next to Alex and opened its front panel. "Alex, destroy-fire-1."

At once, Alex's laser weapon system went into gear. It

unleashed a blinding beam that illuminated the whole room. Its high-energy laser hit the Chubb safe, combusting it in seconds, and ripping a large hole in the wall. All that was left of the safe was a melted heap of white-hot metal.

There was the sound of footsteps running outside the room and in the compound outside. Their rifles at the ready, Kuan Hee and Tim dashed out of the door, with the two robots at their heels.

They returned fire at the soldiers running through the corridor. They clambered down the stairs, firing at the soldiers below. Tim lobbed a grenade with his M203. The soldiers at the porch fell.

The whole hill had awakened. Soldiers were running across the compound. They came out of nowhere. *There has to be a garrison stationed here,* Tim told himself. The two men ran like they never ran before, back to the small building next to the swimming pool, and then the grassy verge.

Behind them, bullets rained. Then the two men crouched below a low parapet wall. Machine gun fire was spraying the walls with holes. They had forgotten about the nest ahead of them. While Tim was firing at the soldiers behind them, Kuan Hee released the M203's safety catch and lobbed a grenade into the machine gun nest. At once there was silence in the darkness ahead.

The two men scurried into the darkness, and clambered down the slope, leaving their pursuers bewildered.

Suddenly, Kuan Hee fell and rolled down the slope. He had been shot. By then, Tim had almost reached the bottom of the slope; he was a better runner. He heard a loud thud sound behind and turned to take a look. Kuan Hee was not to be seen but there was a limp figure on the grass up ahead. He retraced his steps towards where the figure lay. But it was too late, for soldiers were hovering around the figure. In the darkness, he could not take them alone, not without harming Kuan Hee.

Tim retreated down the hill and ran towards the parked

van. With him safely inside, the van sped off.

When Kuan Hee came to, he found himself seated in a chair in a small room. He felt faint. His hands were tied behind him. He felt cold metal pressing on his wrists. Blood seeped through a hastily bundled bandage wrapped across his back. Standing in front of him was a soldier in fatigues, wearing the epaulettes of a Colonel. He had a thick round face, unshaven at the chin.

"Ah, I see you are conscious now," the Colonel said in a gruff voice. He pulled a chair in front of him and sat in it. His eyes met Kuan Hee's. "Very brave chap, you. Young too. Who sent you?" There was silence in the room. Then the Colonel broke the silence by slapping Kuan Hee's face with a heavy calloused palm. He repeated the slaps. Kuan Hee's lips bled, but he remained defiantly quiet. The pain was also gnawing at the flesh in his back. *I have to remain strong,* he told himself.

The door opened and Ong Chwee Seng stepped into the room. Behind him was Lieutenant General Warren Tan.

"Did you get anything out of him?" Ong Chwee Seng asked.

"No, sir. Not yet. This young chap is stubborn, very stubborn, sir," said the Colonel.

"Is he badly hurt?" Ong Chwee Seng asked.

"Bullet lodged in his back. I've stopped the bleeding for the time being, sir," said the Colonel. "He's got gunshot scars on his body. Looks like he's battle-hardened, sir."

"What? Really? He's such a young lad," said Ong Chwee Seng. "Amazing." He stooped to take a closer look at his prisoner. "You look familiar. I've seen you before, somewhere." He grabbed Kuan Hee's hair and tilted the young intruder's head.

"*Ah.* I remember now. I have seen your picture somewhere. Yes, you are Professor Wang's son—his only son." He let go of Kuan Hee's hair and stood in front of him, hands clasping both sides of his waist.

"No doubt about it. You are Professor Wang's son, all right. Your father escaped from me and went into hiding. I thought all was lost." Ong Chwee Seng let out a haunting laugh. "Your father will come running back to me once I let word out you are in my custody."

"Sir, he must have come for the master tapes," said Lietenant General Warren Tan. Ong Chwee Seng's face contorted with fury. He grabbed Kuan Hee's sides and lifted him off the chair. Kuan Hee grimaced in pain. His back was hurting badly.

"You destroyed my memories, you little devil," Ong Chwee Seng screamed.

Suddenly, he recalled seeing Kuan Hee at Singapore General Hospital where his son had been warded five years ago. Pain tore through his heart when he realized Kuan Hee was the one who was responsible for his son's death.

"You—you are the one who killed my son—my precious son."

"No! You killed Jordan," said Kuan Hee in a weak voice. At once, he poured out his grievances. "You killed your own son! It was your greed. For the sake of power, you lived in his mind. You tormented his mind with your evil deeds. He wanted you to repent but you became worse. The only way to deal with you was for him to kill himself. He saved Singapore."

"No! No! You are lying. You are lying through your teeth. I will teach you a lesson today or my name is not Tee Bak Chai."

"Of course you aren't Tee Bak Chai. You are Ong Chwee Seng."

"Smart aleck!" Ong Chwee Seng screamed. He reached for the Colonel's holster. He pulled the pistol out and pointed it at Kuan Hee's head.

"Jordan. My son, can you hear me?" Ong Chwee Seng wailed. "I will avenge you today, Jordan." His finger squeezed the trigger.

Kuan Hee's face turned white with fear. In a second, he would be dead. He braced himself for the bullet he would take in his head. Then he spied Alex lying on the floor in a corner, with its front panel resting at an angle against the floor. He screamed his lungs out. "Alex, arouse-hit-fire-3."

At once, Alex woke up. It rolled onto the floor, kicked itself into an upright stance, and sprang into action, firing its lasers at the three men in the room. They fell into a heap on the floor, their bodies smouldering through their tattered clothes.

It was all over. Ong Chwee Seng and his minions had been killed. Singapore was free again.

Kuan Hee fell off the chair. He got up and staggered to the door. With his hands still handcuffed behind him, he tried to open the door. He was too weak to turn the knob. "Alex, hit-fire-1." Alex's laser blasted the door open. Kuan Hee poked his head outside. He was in the verandah, on the ground floor of a small building. He wobbled along the corridor towards the grassy slope with Alex at his heels. Soldiers were running towards him. He had hardly any strength left to run; he was a sitting duck. *My mission has been accomplished,* Kuan Hee told himself. He was resigned to his fate. *I am at peace.* He fell to the ground.

CHAPTER 33

Kuan Hee heard voices around him. Some sounded familiar. *Am I dead? Am I in heaven or in hell?* His thoughts tormented him. His eyeballs moved erratically. *Lina. My Lina. Huei Huei. Where are you?* He cried out in his thoughts. He saw them in front of him and tried to reach out to them. They were so near, yet so far away. He tried to grab their hands but no matter how hard he tried, he could not move an inch. Something was holding him back. He was moving farther away from his beloved Lina and Huei Huei. *It's the shackles. It is pulling me back everytime I try to move forward.* He tried with all his might. At last, he broke free of the shackles. At once, darkness turned into daylight. *How wonderful,* he told himself. But it was too bright. His eyes were uncomfortable in the bright light.

Kuan Hee squinted his eyes. Then he opened them. He saw Lina by his side. She was cuddling a baby—his beloved Huei Huei. He glanced around the room. He saw Tim and Navin. "Where am I?"

"Kuan Hee, you are awake. Thank heavens you are awake at last," said Lina. She leaned against him and planted a kiss on his forehead.

"I knew you would pull through," said Tim. He was

fighting back tears. "I'm so sorry I left you behind."

"Kuan Hee, so good to see you again," said Navin. He slapped Kuan Hee's shoulder playfully.

"What happened?" said Kuan Hee. He realized he was in a hospital ward. Navin cranked up the head of the bed so Kuan Hee could sit up. He looked out of the tall window on his left. The sun was gawking at him. *It must be indignant that I have slept so long, while it has to work hard to keep the world bright,* he told himself.

"How long have I been out?" Kuan Hee asked. His three questions had gotten no answers so far. He tried again.

"I thought I was dead," Kuan Hee said. "How did I get here? Won't someone tell me?"

At this moment, the door opened and Brigadier Walmsley stepped into the room. He stood next to Lina.

"By George, you are all right," said the Brigadier. "Sure got all of us worried sick. Don't do it again, young lad."

"Mr Walmsley, you are here," said Kuan Hee.

"You are looking good, old chap," said the Brigadier. "Let me see now. If I am not wrong, it's the fourth time you have been shot. You should be getting a medal for every one of your bullet scars."

"Mr Walmsley, you are horrid, simply horrid," said Lina. She was close to tears.

"Lina, he's only jesting," said Tim. "Anyone can see he's joking."

"My dear girl, you are indeed too sensitive," said the Brigadier. "Kuan Hee's in for hard times, for sure."

"Mr Walmsley, do you know what happened to me?" asked Kuan Hee. "I've been trying to get them to tell me, but no one has said anything."

"Kuan Hee. It's a long story," said the Brigadier. "In a nutshell, the delta force got you out of a jam."

"Delta force?" said Kuan Hee. "You mean they were around when I fell?"

"Of course, old chap," said the Brigadier. "To tell you

the truth, I didn't really trust you to get the job done. So I got them to tail you—report your every move. The commandoes were nearby when you and your friend here tried to be heroes on your own."

"You mean, they were on the hill too?" said Kuan Hee.

"Well, not at first. They came a little later," said the Brigadier. "I'm sorry we took so long. You know, taking action in a foreign land is a complicated thing. Need to get permissions from the top and all that. But it didn't really take that long. Our Apache helicopters took care of things on the hill that night. Our commandoes cleaned up the mess after you fell. The important thing is. All's well right now."

"Yes, Mr Walmsley is right," said Tim. "What counts is we are all together safe and sound."

"How about Singapore?" asked Kuan Hee. "Who's in charge now?"

"We are," said Tim. "The people of Singapore are finally in charge."

* * * * *

Dawn Breaks

CHAPTER 1

It was the clang of metal that woke Kuan Hee. He opened his eyes and took in his surroundings. He found himself in a small room, lying on a thin shabby mattress laid next to a louvred window. Except for this spongy spread, the room was bare. Even the floor was bare screed. A battered wooden door stood about two metres across from him. Sunlight filtering through the shutters above him told him it was day outside. The air was musty; he detected a stench of rotting fish wafting in through the window. He had to be near a wet market or some big rubbish bin. There was a cacophony of noises on the other side of the wall he was now leaning against. It was difficult to make out the voices from the noise.

It had to be early morning, for the wall behind him felt cold against his back. His nose itched, but he could not scratch it. His hands were tied behind his back. He felt pricky fibres poking his wrists. He could only wriggle his legs. They had been bound with a rope. He took a deep breath and sighed heavily. He couldn't open his mouth; it had been taped shut. Soon he got used to the bad odour in the room; he took no notice of it anymore.

Where am I? This is definitely not an HDB flat, Kuan Hee

murmured under his breath. He tried hard to recall what had happened. His mind was still hazy. *Have I been fed with some stupefying drug? What mindless creeps have done this to me? Don't they know it's a capital offence kidnapping someone in Singapore?*

He looked down at his pants. His pockets were not bulging—his iPhone and wallet had been taken from him. There was no way for him to get help. Then he remembered Little Busy was with him. *Where is it now?* The happenings of the recent past slowly drifted into his consciousness.

He had left for work at the university. It was a rainy day and traffic was heavy on the road outside the university. He recalled getting out of his car in the car park. All of a sudden, someone had grabbed him from behind and...

The door creaked open and two men entered the room. One knelt beside Kuan Hee and pressed a moist cloth over his face.

Try as he might to hold his breath, Kuan Hee couldn't stop the involuntary muscles in his body from doing its work. He gasped and took in air. The chloroform finally had its chance to work its magic. He struggled to keep awake. "Lina. Lina," he yelled, but only muffled sounds were heard. He succumbed to the drug and slumped onto his captor's knee. "Lina, where—"

CHAPTER 2

It was as if Lina had heard Kuan Hee's desperate call for help. Or perhaps, it was a loved one's sixth sense. Lina felt a tingling sensation grip her, jolting her thoughts. Something had happened to Kuan Hee. She could feel it in her bones. It wasn't Huei Huei. Huei Huei was in front of her, watching her favourite cartoon on the iPad in their house at 79 Jalan Nuang. She reached for her Samsung smartphone and dialed his number. There was no reply. She tried again several times in vain. Kuan Hee should have reached his office at the Cyborg Intelligence Unit of Temasek University. She called up the reception desk. Kuan Hee had not reported for work today. It was unusual for him to skive. Like his father, Professor Wang, he was a stickler for schedule. And he was also in his element at work. He enjoyed his work in nanotechnology so much that he would forget everything else. Many times, Lina would complain that he had neglected her and Huei Huei. This time, he wasn't in his laboratory. He had no other work place. Kuan Hee also wasn't a social creature. He didn't like to make conversation. Save for Tim and Navin who were his *kakis*, he had a handful of friends. Lina called up every one of them. None could tell her where he was.

Just then the doorbell rang. Lina opened the door to let Xaden in. Eighteen-year-old Xaden was Lina's nephew. It was the school holidays and he had volunteered to fetch lunch for his aunt.

"Aunt Lina. You look flustered."

"I can't get hold of your uncle. I'm afraid something has happened to him."

She took the tiffin carrier from Xaden and spooned out Huei Huei's lunch. With Huei Huei happily enjoying her food and watching YouTube on the iPad, Lina could resume her search for Kuan Hee.

Ignoring Xaden, she sat on the sofa in the living room, hands clasped over her knees, and eyes closed. She took a deep breath. She had to think clearly and not let her muddled thoughts affect her.

"That's it. Why didn't I think of it?"

"What? What is it, Aunt Lina?"

"Little Busy. Your uncle has Little Busy with him. I forgot about it. Now where's the remote?" Little Busy was a metallic robot housefly drone.

Xaden helped her to look for Little Busy's remote control card. They searched the whole house but nothing turned up.

"Look after Huei Huei. I'll go down to the cellar. It should be there."

Lina walked into the study and retrieved a ladder from a hidden corner. She placed it against a floor-to-ceiling bookcase on one wall and climbed it. She tapped on an end panel, which slid open to reveal a small knob. She turned the knob and at once the bookcase rumbled to one side. There was an opening on the wall wide enough for two people to enter. The interior was stark dark. She turned on some switches and light flooded the cellar. She walked down the steps into the secret room, which Kuan Hee's father, Professor Wang, had constructed to hold his inventions. The air was stuffy and warm. The room was slightly smaller than the living room. It held some cupboards, two standing fans and chairs. A large table took centrestage.

Lina opened one of the cupboards and AleXander the two metallic robots glistened in the light. She ignored them and bent down to look at the lower shelf of the cupboard. She spotted two remote control cards. One was Little Busy's and the other Tizzy's. Tizzy was a metallic robot dragonfly drone. She pocketed the two cards.

"Tizzy must be somewhere here too." She opened the small boxes on the shelf. In one, she found the robot dragonfly. She placed it in her other dress pocket and grabbed AleXander the robots.

She paused for a moment, asking herself what else she needed from the cellar. Satisfied she had had everything, she climbed up the steps and returned the bookcase to its original position.

"Aunt Lina, why have you brought out Alex and Xander?"

"In case I need their help. I have a funny feeling we'll soon be falling into adventure again."

"What? Can I join in?"

"Don't interrupt my thoughts. I need to think."

CHAPTER 3

Kuan Hee jolted awake. He opened his eyes. He was feeling drowsy so he saw only floating images. He blinked several times and squinted at his surroundings. He seemed to be in the back of a van. There were windows at the back and on the sides but these were heavily shaded. The vehicle rocked back and forth as if it was in the middle of the ocean. But there wasn't the familiar smell of sea air. And this wasn't a Hippo—one of those amphibious crafts; it was plainly a small van he was in so he was definitely on the road somewhere. But what road in Singapore was as rocky as the one the van was moving on? Kuan Hee searched his memories but could not recall any. *Perhaps, I am on Pulau Ubin.*

Kuan Hee flitted in and out of consciousness. As the drug wore off, he gathered his thoughts. His body was sore all over. He had to have been tied up for many hours. Parts of his arms were numb from resting too long on the floor of the van. He wriggled left and right. He began counting numbers in his mind. He had to keep alert. He couldn't doze off again. He had to be on the lookout for landmarks, if at all he could make out any in these darkened surroundings. He could not see the driver's section. The window separating the two parts of the van had been blocked with an opaque plastic film.

Then the rocking stopped. The van had not stopped moving, but the ride was smooth now. *We are no longer on a kampong track.* Kuan Hee estimated the journey thus far had taken at least three hours. *What journey in Singapore would take so long? Am I in Malaysia? Have they smuggled me across the causeway? Why? How did they do it? How did they manage to get past the eagle-eyed custom officers at the Singapore checkpoint? For sure, these guys couldn't be bribed.* There were so many questions in Kuan Hee's mind but he had no answer for every one of them.

Strangely, his stomach was not grumbling. Was it the sedative effect of the drug? Kuan Hee swallowed his saliva. He had not had a drop of water in ages. *What day is it?* Then the van jerked to a stop. He could hear some people talking outside the van. It was minutes before the door opened and someone jumped into the van. With his eyes shut, Kuan Hee feigned unconsciousness. Through the tiny slit between his eyelashes, he could make out a burly Chinese man with close-cropped hair. He wasn't the same one who came into the room to take him away. Even with his hands free, he was no match for these men, and what's more, his hands and legs were bound. He decided to continue his act.

Kuan Hee allowed the men to heave his limp body onto a metal trolley. They wheeled him along a concrete pavement. Soon this forked into a wooden platform. He could hear the men's boots stomping on the timber floor, which reverberated in sync. *Golly, it's hollow underneath. Am I on a wooden bridge?*

The pungent smell of vaporizing diesel in the air overwhelmed Kuan Hee's senses momentarily. Then the breeze brought a strong musty odour. It conjured up memories of fishing trips with his *kakis*, Tim and Navin, at Changi Point. He had to be close to the sea, but the smell of seawater was absent in the air.

Kuan Hee squinted his eyes. He saw a huge expanse of water in front of him. *Am I near the sea?* There was a long stretch of undulating land in the distance beyond the water. He was not familiar with Malaysian shores and islands but he surmised the land ahead could be an island off the Malaysian coast.

His captors bundled him into a boat, which resembled a small ferry. The boat chugged towards the island.

At last, one of the men spoke. It was a smattering of Mandarin, not of Malaysian-accent variety. Certainly, it wasn't Taiwanese Mandarin. It was Mainland Mandarin he was speaking. He mentioned something about buying *hé fàn*. In Taiwanese Mandarin, boxed meals were *biàndang*.

From the men who delivered a new fridge to his house to the hawker assistants at the neighbourhood coffee shops, Kuan Hee had heard Mainland Mandarin enough times to be able to identify the accent unmistakably. *Why are the Mainland Chinese interested in me?*

Kuan Hee allowed his thoughts to wander. Why had he been kidnapped? He was not rich or influential. Then he remembered Colonel Tee, the late dictator of Singapore. Was it the remnants of his men exacting revenge on their master's behalf? It couldn't be his dad they were after. His dad was safe and sound halfway around the world—in Fort Bragg in North Carolina, the headquarters of the US Special Forces. Professor Wang was doing secretive work in nanotechnology for the United States government.

Then it dawned on him. *They must want something from Dad.* His father was privy to sensitive US state secrets. Just what did they want? Three years ago, he had blasted to smithereens the disks holding the memories of Colonel Tee, so the Colonel could not resurrect himself even if his minions desired to help him do so.

First he had to find out where he was and where he was being taken. It would soon be dark and it would be difficult to make out any landmarks. These Mainland Chinese had the audacity to haul him into the boat in clear view of any passers-by who might be around. But then he had yet to see any passers-by. It had to be a desolate area, Kuan Hee surmised. How was he going to get help? There was not a single soul around to help him. He was resigned to his fate.

The boat reached shore shortly. It was a wooden jetty that the two men disembarked with Kuan Hee in tow. An acoomplice was waiting on the jetty. Rotund and fair, the middle-aged man was starkly different from the able young men who had kidnapped Kuan Hee. He seemed to be in charge, bellowing instructions and waddling about the jetty.

The taller one heaved Kuan Hee over his shoulder and lumbered off the jetty and up the slope to a meandering concrete pavement with the portly supervisor tailing them. Kuan Hee spied a huge house at the top of the slope. As they approached the house, he could see it was a grand old two-storeyed mansion with a large compound. There were Chinese men milling around in front of the building.

Just then a horrifying thought crossed his mind. He had been shanghaied to China. He had landed in some remote part of China, far away from his beloved Lina. She would never be able to find him this time. How did he get himself into this mess?

CHAPTER 4

Little Busy's remote control held the answer to Lina's pressing question—Kuan Hee's whereabouts. It had a feature that could track the robot housefly's position, no matter where it was in the world. The Polaris satellite— that secret American spy satellite in the sky powered the feature. Professor Wang had access to the satellite, courtesy of the United States government for whom he was working. Lina flipped open Little Busy's remote. There was no beeping dot on the map of Singapore, which occupied the entire screen. She pinched the screen to zoom out of the republic. As the map widened to reveal stretches of the Asian continent and part of the South China Sea, she saw something blink on the Indonesian Archipelago, off peninsular Malaysia. She stretched the screen with her fingers. She blinked several times. She couldn't believe her eyes. The blinking dot was hovering over—Lake Toba! Lake Toba in Northern Sumatra was a tourist attraction. It was an idyllic spot for vacation and— trysts!

"That Kuan Hee! He has the gall to drop everything he's doing to hop over to Lake Toba for sexation!"

"Really?" Xaden passed the crayon he was holding to Huei Huei and crossed the room to where Lina was sitting. He stooped next to her, looking at the map on the screen.

"Yeah, *hor*. Uncle Kuan Hee's on Lake Toba."

"Here I am tending to our little baby, and there he is gallivanting around with some hothead."

That night, Lina turned in early. But she could not sleep a wink. She tossed and turned in bed, conjuring what Kuan Hee was up to. *Why should I care? He's likely having a swimmingly good time with some old flame of his this very moment.* Still, she could not bring herself to accept this truth. All along she had thought she was the only world Kuan Hee knew—until little Huei Huei came along. Now, she had to come to terms with some third party sharing this intimacy.

Just then, Lina's smartphone rang. Tim was on the line.

"So, have you found Kuan Hee?"

"He—He's having a secret tryst with some lover."

"Whaaat?"

"He's enjoying himself with his lover somewhere far away."

"Come on, Lina. Don't speak in crypted lingo."

"I'm not. That's what I just said in plain English. That good friend of yours is having the time of his life with another woman in his lap."

There was a long pause.

"You're joking, Lina. You must be. Kuan Hee's not the type, man. I mean, he's a nerd. Nerds don't go fooling around. Hahaha."

"Don't laugh. It's the goddamned truth."

"*Wah piang!* You must be really mad. Fancy you letting foul language out of your mouth. This is—a first!"

There was another long pause.

"Where did you say Kuan Hee's fooling around at?"

"Lake Toba."

"So far away?"

"Yeah. You can't believe it too?"

"No. Not that. It's just not like Kuan Hee. Besides, he's

not been there before. Why should he go to a faraway place he's never been before to do such a thing? I mean, he can go to somewhere nearby—like Geylang."

"Tim! I hate you." She almost wanted to bang down the phone.

"*Alamak!* Lina. Sorry. I didn't mean that. So sorry."

"You men are the same. Always harbouring the thought of having trysts."

"Lina, not me. Certainly, not Kuan Hee."

"I am furious. He has no respect for me. After what we have been through together, after what I've done for him—"

"Lina, pipe down. For goodness's sake, be sane. Kuan Hee is not a Casanova. Think! Something must have happened to Kuan Hee. He doesn't just take off in the middle of work for some fling. He's not that kind of guy. You and I know it. For God's sake, wake up."

The words made some sense to Lina. They quietened her raucous mind. She no longer let expletive-laden language come out of her mouth. What was boiling rage had now turned to simmering fear.

There was another long pause.

"Tim. Could something bad have happened to him?"

"Hey! Lina, why are you blowing hot and cold over Kuan Hee? He's your man. Don't you trust him at all?"

"Tim, I am worried. Has something happened to Kuan Hee?"

"Let's meet, Lina. I'll get Navin. Tomorrow at 10:00 a.m.?"

"Tim, I—alright, 10:00 a.m. here."

CHAPTER 5

It was with a sense of urgency that Tim and Navin stepped into the living room at 79 Jalan Nuang. Lina's harried demeanor added to the tense atmosphere. Little Huei Huei was sitting at the coffee table, busily halving some toy vegetables with a plastic knife.

"Where's Kuan Hee's car?" Tim asked.

"The WheresMyHonda app pinpoints its location at his workplace in Temasek University," Lina said. "The engine monitor says it's been idle for twenty-six hours."

"That's not good news," Tim said, tapping a finger on his forearm. "What does Little Busy's remote say?"

Lina passed the remote to Tim. It was showing the map of North Sumatra, with a blinking dot hovering over Lake Toba.

"The blinking dot hasn't moved?" Tim asked.

"Been like that since yesterday," Lina said.

"What time did you first know Kuan Hee's in Lake Toba?" Navin asked.

"I don't know. I think. Yes. Yesterday afternoon. Xaden was here, delivering lunch," Lina said.

"And you didn't tell us until late last night?" Navin said.

"Sorry. I couldn't think clearly," Lina said. She was almost in tears. She blamed herself for wasting precious time tending to her doubts.

"Let's put the pieces together, before we decide on a plan of action," Tim said. "Kuan Hee's not at the office. His car is at the university. He's uncontactable. Little Busy's GPS shows it's been in Lake Toba since early yesterday afternoon. The lake is two hours away by air."

"No doubt about it," Navin said. "He's got to be there."

"Yes, looks like it," Tim said. "We need to go there right away—before his captors have a chance to act."

"Time is of the essence," Navin said. "He could…" He stopped short of telling them the dire consequences of their late action; Lina was in no state to hear such things.

"Let me check the next available flight to Medan," Tim said. He took out his iPhone and spent the next few minutes browsing the flight apps.

"There're two flights—1:40 p.m. today and 7:40 a.m. tomorrow," Tim said.

"We can't wait till tomorrow," Lina screeched. "It might be too late!"

"Let's go today, then," Navin said.

"That gives us less than three hours," Tim said.

"Let's do it," Navin said.

"I'll book the tickets. Get your passports—and Kuan Hee's too," Tim said. "How did they get him out of Singapore without a passport? Never mind. We won't have time to purchase rupiah. We'll do it in Medan. Anyway, it's cheaper there."

"I will take Huei Huei over to my mother's place," Lina said. "Shall we meet there?"

"Have we forgotten anything?" Tim said.

"How are we going to the airport?" Navin asked.

"I'll uber a ride for us," Tim said.

"I'll bring along the robots and Tizzy too," Lina said.

"Don't forget to book hotel rooms," Navin said.

"No need," Tim said. "I'll call my uncle afterwards. We'll stay with him. He lives in Medan."

"You have a relative there?" Navin said. "You never said anything about having relatives overseas."

"You know I'm not a blabbermouth," Tim said. "Let's get going."

CHAPTER 6

As Flight MI234 descended over Medan in Indonesia, it gave its occupants a sweeping close-up view of the low-lying mishmash of residential districts encircling Polonia Airport.

Polonia Airport was a world away from Changi Airport. Stepping into the airport was akin to stepping back into Singapore of the early 1980s. While Singapore's Changi Airport had improved by bounds and leaps, Medan's Polonia Airport had stagnated. You could say Polonia Airport was only a provincial airport, but the stark difference between the two airports was revealing of faultlines in management.

Flight MI234 taxied to a stop outside the terminal. Tim, Navin and Lina stepped out of the aircraft onto a boarding staircase. Together with the other passengers, they climbed down the flight of steps and packed into a coach, which unloaded them at the arrival section of the terminal building.

Tim kept an eye out for his uncle and cousin. They were supposed to meet him at the airport today. It was difficult to make them out in a sea of faces. Polonia Airport was humming with passengers and visitors today.

The customs officer attending to the trio removed a carton of cigarettes from several that Tim had brought into the country for his uncle. Tim protested in vain. Perhaps, it was this that led to the trio being detained at the arrival terminal. A customs officer said Tim had come too often to Medan. He took the three friends to a small room in a corner of the arrival hall.

Half an hour later, he released them. They found themselves standing in front of Tim's uncle and his cousin. The three friends exchanged greetings with Uncle Kenny and Harry. Uncle Kenny was middle-aged and balding. He was Tim's mother's elder brother. Harry was Uncle Kenny's only son. He was a twentysomething tanned and handsome lad. He had his father's high forehead. He was also almost as tall as Tim.

"Uncle Kenny, the guy at the counter confiscated a carton of Marlboro I brought in for you," Tim said.

"It's OK," Uncle Kenny said. "Don't let it bother you too much."

"The immigration chap also said I had come here too often. I told him I visited you once every few months but he was adamant that I had an ulterior motive for coming here so he detained us," Tim said.

"He just wants coffee money," Uncle Kenny said.

"Did you give him any?" Tim asked.

"One million rupiahs," his uncle said.

"What? That's corruption," Tim said.

"It's a way of life here, Tim," his uncle said. "We are used to it. Anyway, it's just peanuts. Don't let it bother you."

"Uncle Kenny, such things don't happen in Singapore," Navin said.

"Of course. That's why Medan is so underdeveloped," Uncle Kenny said. "The good thing is—we can get things moving fast this way."

"Luckily, they didn't query us about AleXander the robots," Tim said.

"Robots? What robots?" Harry asked.

"Erh. It's a long story, Harry. I'll tell you later," Tim said.

"Uncle Kenny, thanks for putting us up," Lina said. She wanted to put a stop to the conversation about the two robots; they were within earshot of everyone in the arrival hall of the airport.

"It's our pleasure," Uncle Kenny said. "I'm sorry to hear about your husband. We'll find him if he is in Lake Toba. Harry will be your guide in town. You'll all be in good hands with him around."

"Yes, I know North Sumatra like the back of my hands," Harry said.

"Thanks," the three friends chorused in unison.

Everyone packed into a Toyota Camry which cruised through rickety neighbourhoods till it came to a stop on the side of a small road—more like a lane—straddling rows of tightly packed concrete shophouses, some of which were shorter than the others, but all of which were no taller than four storeys.

"Harry, why don't you have auto-pilot for the Camry?" Navin asked.

"Such technology has yet to trickle down to us here," Harry said. "Perhaps, in ten years, if we are lucky."

"You must be joking," Navin said.

"Navin, Indonesia is a big country, unlike Singapore," Tim said. "There are over one hundred million people. It's not an easy job managing such a big population."

"Besides," Harry said. "We don't need the latest technology. It's not really useful here because we don't have the infrastructure to support high-tech stuff." He pointed at the road ahead. "My house is just in front—on the left."

228A Jalan Muara Takus was a three-storeyed shophouse unit but unlike other units along the row, its first storey was vacant. It was the Camry's garage. The Chen family lived on the upper floors of this unit. Next door to this unit was Toko Harry, a modern provision shop housed in a double-unit shophouse. The shop, run by Harry, catered both to the neighbourhood and the expatriate community.

"*Wah!* Tim, your uncle must be rich," Navin said. "He owns three units here."

"He doesn't just own the units here," Tim said. "He has other properties in Medan. He has businesses catering to the American expatriate community for which he gets paid in hard United States currency, not rupiah."

"Come, let me show you your rooms," Harry said. He led the visitors up a narrow concrete staircase located on one side of the shophouse. The third storey was where Uncle Kenny and Harry lived. The second storey had two rooms—both vacant. Lina was to occupy one and the two men the other.

"My father's gone to the restaurant. He wants to check for himself things are in shipshape order," Harry said. "Make yourselves at home." He excused himself and disappeared downstairs.

Lina was in a hurry. She wanted to throw her things down and get down to searching for Kuan Hee at once, but it was not possible. This was Medan, a city of three million people. It was strange territory for the three friends. They were helpless without Harry and he needed time to make arrangements for their trip to Lake Toba.

Noticing her impatience, Tim said, "Lina, we are in a foreign land. This is no walk in the park."

"Kuan Hee is still in Lake Toba. The blinking dot hasn't moved," Lina said. "I haven't let my eyes off the screen since we left the Polonia Airport."

"Don't fret, Lina," Navin said. "We'll find Kuan Hee, if it's the last thing we do. We're best friends right?"

Lina allowed a smile to peep out of her face. But it quickly deflated with Tim's next remark.

"Harry says we can only set out early next morning," Tim said. "He can only lay his hands on a van tonight."

"We can set off tonight then," Lina said.

"Lina, this is not Singapore," Tim said, "where the street lights go on at a flick of a switch and everywhere is in brightness. Here, most of the roads do not have any streetlights. And many of them have potholes. It's too dangerous to travel in the dark."

"Yeah. Tim is right," Navin said. "Let's wait for Harry to get back."

That evening, Harry returned with—not a van—but a minibus he had borrowed from a friend. It had ample space for all of them and Kuan Hee too when they rescued him. Harry was busy washing the minibus on the side of the road when Navin popped downstairs.

"Can I lend you a hand?" Navin said.

"No need," Harry said. "Almost finished. Had your dinner?"

"Yes," Navin said.

As the water splashed onto the sidewalk and into the drain, Navin could see the water in the drain glistening under the streetlight. Curious, he stooped to take a closer look.

"It's mosquitoes," Harry said. "Mosquito larvae and pupae."

"*Ha*?" Navin said. "But the whole drain is glistening."

"Yes, they are all over the drain," Harry said. "But nobody bothers here. You don't get fined here."

With the cleaning done, Harry knelt down by the drain and motioned for Navin to join him.

"Here, we have our little conversations while squatting along the sidewalk," Harry said. "It's our way of life."

"Oh, really?" Navin said. "Well, as the saying goes, when in Rome do as Romans do." He squatted next to Harry who offered him a cigarette.

"No thanks," Navin said. "I don't smoke. We don't smoke."

Harry took a long puff and expelled the clove-flavoured smoke away from Navin but some of it wafted into Navin's nose. "Where's your missus?" He asked.

"Gosh! I'm not married yet," Navin said.

"Why do Singapore men marry late?" Harry asked. "Tim is also unattached. I've asked him several times, and each time he tells me he hasn't met the right girl."

"You ask so much about us. You must be married right?" Navin said. "But I don't see your wife."

"She's visiting her parents in Jakarta," Harry said. "She'll be back in two weeks."

"When did you get married?" Navin asked.

"Five years ago," Harry said. "My daughter is already four years old."

"You have a four-year-old daughter?" said Navin in disbelief. "Indonesian men do marry young."

"Our girls marry even younger," Harry said. "If they are not married by the time they are twenty-three, they will be left on the shelf forever."

"S-e-r-i-o-u-s?" Navin said.

"It's the truth," Harry said. "You still haven't told me why you are still single."

"Actually, I will be getting married next year," Navin said.

"That's great news. What is your girlfriend working as?" Harry said.

"I don't know," Navin said. "I haven't met her yet." "Really?" Harry exclaimed. "How come you're marrying someone you haven't even seen?"

"It's our custom," Navin said. "My mother arranged this marriage for me. The girl lives in Hyderabad in South India. She's working for my mother's cousin who runs a business dealing in pearls."

There was a moment of silence while Harry digested the explanation.

"I wouldn't marry someone I don't love," Harry said, "let alone someone I haven't even met."

"As I have said," Navin explained curtly, "it's our

Indian custom. It's been like this for a thousand years."

"Is she a child bride?" Harry asked.

"*Alamak!* Nothing like it," Navin said. "She will be twenty-one this December."

"I see," Harry said.

"Actually, we Chinese also had arranged marriages in the past," Tim said. He had just come outside and saw it fit to wade into the conversation to save the situation. "In fact, for thousands of years, it's been like that. Even now, it's happening in some places."

"What's that you were saying about robots?" Harry asked. He had suddenly remembered Tim's remark at the airport.

Tim was glad the conversation had taken a turn. He regaled Harry with an account of the adventures of Alex and Xander the robots.

"Wow! I thought such things only happened in comics and movies," Harry said. "Can they really do the things you just said? Can I see them in action?"

"Come on up to our room," Tim said. "We'll show you. I mean—we'll let Lina show you. She's their master."

"You mean, half their master," Navin said.

"Oh yeah, Kuan Hee's the real owner," Tim said.

Soon Harry was enjoying the antics of the two robots in the company of the three visitors.

"This is their latest feat," Lina said. "Alex and Xander can climb walls." She uttered an order to the two robots. At once, they ran up the wall of the room. Then they were dangling from the ceiling.

"Wow! How do they do it?" Tim asked. "They are defying gravity."

"Kuan Hee's father has fitted their feet with millions of special microscopic hair," Lina said.

"Hair can stick on the wall?" Harry asked in disbelief.

"You mean the same type of hair found on lizards' toes?" Navin said.

"Not really," Lina said. "But the properties are similar."

"Spectacular. Simply spectacular," Harry said.

"Yeah. I agree," Navin said.

"One question, Lina," Harry said. "Can they fly?"

"Hey Harry, that's asking too much of them," Tim said.

"I've asked Kuan Hee this question. He says it's still in science fiction realm," Lina said.

"What's that?" Harry asked.

"Lina means it may be possible in the near future," Navin said. "It is not impossible."

"I see," Harry said.

"Have you got the hardware I was asking you for?" Tim said.

"Er. Yes," Harry said. He got up from the floor and excused himself from the room.

"What hardware?" Lina asked.

"I didn't tell you guys earlier," Tim said. "I asked for some weapons."

"Aren't Alex and Xander enough?" Lina said. "They are pretty powerful, you know."

"We don't know who or what we are dealing with," Tim said. "We need to be well-prepared. We can't afford to fail. Kuan Hee's life is at stake."

"Is it easy to get guns here?" Navin asked.

"Nope, not guns. Rifles," Tim said. "It's easy to get these here. Money talks."

Harry returned hauling a longish bag. He fished out three Steyr AUGs and handed them to the three friends.

"Three enough?" Harry asked.

Tim took the olive green Steyr AUG in his hands and examined it carefully. Then he pulled the charging handle. It snapped into place. He pressed the rifle stock against his shoulder and grapped its fore grip. "An A3 M1. Compact. Short barrel. The charging handle is not obtrusive, unlike the original AUG. Allows one-handed shooting just in case. Love the pistol grip. Pretty old, but will do the job. I like it."

"It's light and fits into a backpack easily," Navin said.

"How do I use this contraption?" Lina asked.

"It's not for you," Tim said. "You just sit around and look pretty." Lina at once contorted her face. *Tim always annoys me.*

Harry poured out six loaded magazines onto the floor.

"Each magazine holds ten rounds," Harry said.

"Should be enough," Tim said.

"You can get assault rifles here?" Navin asked.

"We need some protection in the city," Harry said. "Just in case of unrest."

"Unrest?" Lina said. "What type of unrest?"

"Civil unrest," Harry said. "It happens once in a long while. People attack businesses and loot shops."

"*Wah!* That's serious," Navin said.

"Happened here?" Lina asked.

"Yes, in Medan not too long ago. Thousands of students and local residents swooped down onto the neighbourhood. They threw stones and looted shops," Harry said.

"So the government allows you to buy such weapons?" Navin said.

"No," Harry said. "We get them through illegal channels. These are a must-have. We hide them away."

"What if they do a spot check?" Navin asked.

"They will never find the weapons," Harry said. "Besides, money settles everything."

"What caused the unrest?" Lina asked.

"Steep price rises," Harry said. "Such things are out of our control, but people blame us businesses."

"But it looks so peaceful outside," Lina said.

"Looks can be deceiving," Harry said.

"How far away from Medan is Lake Toba?" Navin asked.

"One hundred and eighty five kilometres," Harry said. "It will take half a day to travel there by road."

"So, when are we leaving for Lake Toba?" Lina asked.

"At dawn," Tim said. "We'd better get some sleep. It's

going to be a long day tomorrow."

CHAPTER 7

"Finally!" Lina exclaimed as the minibus pulled off from the side of the road and drove past the rows of shophouses that lined Jalan Muara Takus. It was dawn and the neighbourhood was still asleep. As the minibus reached the junction, Harry slowed down to allow two men time to pull aside a wooden barricade to let them through. He waved to them and they waved back. The minibus drove into Jl. Kh. Zainul Arifin, a thoroughfare in Medan.

"Why is the street barricaded?" asked Navin.

"To keep unsavoury elements away from the neighbourhood," Tim said. He was in the front seat with Harry.

"Yeah, we pay these thugs to protect us," Harry said.

"These are gangsters?" said Lina. Harry nodded.

"Harry. Is your mother out of town?" Lina asked.

There was a long silence in the driver's section of the minibus.

"Our mothers died in an air crash years ago," Tim said. "We were toddlers then."

An uneasy silence fell in the minibus.

"I'm terriby sorry," Lina said. "Kuan Hee didn't tell

me. I didn't know."

"It's alright," Tim said. "Happened so long ago."

"How did it happen?" Navin asked.

"They were returning to Medan from Jakarta. There was bad weather and visibility was poor. The plane crashed into the woodlands near Polonia Airport," Harry said. "I was too young then. I can't recollect the happenings, but I daren't ask my father. I don't want him to be sad."

"Your father didn't remarry?" Lina asked.

"Lina!" Navin interrupted.

"Lina, you just don't know when to shut your gap," Tim said.

"Oh sorry," Lina said. "I didn't think."

"It's alright, Lina," Harry said. "Honest, I'm fine."

"Just don't bring it up again," Tim said.

Silence returned to the minibus for the next few minutes.

"Don't say a word," Harry said. "Let me handle the police, if they turn up."

"Aye. Aye. Captain," Navin said. Lina broke into laughter. The uneasy silence that reigned moments ago was soon forgotten. In its place was animated chatter. Everyone was excited about the mission.

"We'll stop over in Brastagi. I need to pick up a friend. He knows Lake Toba well. He has contacts there," Harry said.

About two hours into their journey southwards, the three friends realized they were heading into the highlands. The roads were cobbled and the ride was bumpy. Lina opened a window and poked her face out to take in the fresh morning air. At once, cold air descended on her face, caressing it.

"It must be below sixteen degrees Centigrade outside," Lina said. "My face feels like it's been in a freezer."

"Brastagi is 1,300 metres above sea level," Harry said.

"*Wah seh*, that's really tall," Lina said. "Bukit Timah Hill is only one hundred plus metres."

"Lina, Bukit Timah Hill isn't a hill—more like a slope," Navin said.

Ahead of the minibus, a tanned handsome lad with a shock of messy hair and an impish grin waved. He looked like he had yet to do national service. Harry stopped the vehicle by the side of the road. Everyone got down for a breather. They had been crammed into the vehicle for too long and needed to stretch their legs.

The air in Brastagi was indeed cold. It had the three friends wishing Singapore weather could be like this every day. Not freezing cold—that would be too uncomfortable, but cold enough to enjoy the day without reaching for some tissue paper to absorb the sweat. The three friends rubbed their hands as they surveyed the surroundings. Except for a lone ramshackle shack, it was all undulating greenery around them and some peaks—great places to watch sunrise. The road was no more than sandy track beatened by years of use.

Harry was busy chatting with his friend in Bahasa Indonesia. They seemed to be catching up with each other. Then he brought the others into the conversation. Alfredo was a Batak. He had lived in the highlands all his life. He listened intently and nodded as Harry introduced his three friends from Singapore. But he really didn't understand English. All he knew was a smattering of English words such as 'thank you', 'good' and 'goodbye', phrases he had picked up over the years from acquaintances.

"Alfredo knows Lake Toba like the back of his hands," Harry said. "We'll be safe in his hands."

"How come he's got a Christian name?" Navin asked.

"He's a Christian," Harry said.

"I thought Indonesians are Muslims," Lina said.

"He's a Batak Karo—they're mostly Christians," Harry said.

Just then, Alfredo waved to someone passing by on a motorized pushcart. The vendor stopped his makeshift stall and placed skewered ears of corn atop a charcoal-fired grill. Minutes later, he handed the sticks of toasted, lightly blackened corn to the visitors.

The corn was deliciously sweet. "These have been buttered," Harry explained. "It's a local favourite. Cheap and nourishing."

The three friends were glad for the treat. They hadn't had a bite all morning and were ravenous. They devoured almost an entire basket of corn on the cart.

"Tim, you ride in the back," Harry said. "Alfredo will take the front with me. He will guide me all the way to Parapat."

"Where's Parapat? Is that our next stop?" Lina asked.

"Parapat is the gateway to Lake Toba," Harry said. "We take a boat to Lake Toba from there. By the way, Lake Toba is known as Danau Toba here. The island on the lake is Samosir Island."

With its occupants' stomachs satiated, the minibus continued its journey along the hilly terrain southwards towards Parapat town.

CHAPTER 8

Magnificent Samosir Island loomed into view across a large expanse of water on the right as the minibus wound its way along a small road hugging the contours of the hilly terrain near the banks of the lake.

Lina shuddered as she peered out of the window. Each time the minibus perilously negotiated a bend on the small road, she shut her eyes. A mere metre of ground stood between the road shoulder and the edge of the cliff. There were no guardrails on the lake's side to guide the driver's eyes. It was a sudden drop from a great height if the minibus careened off the road. Alfredo was at the wheel. A seasoned driver along this part of the country, he effortlessly guided the minibus along the long and winding road towards Parapat.

Lina did not have the mood to take in the spectacular view of the lake or the longish island. She was now near to her beloved who was somewhere on the island. Unfolding Little Busy's remote, she pinched and dragged the screen to enlarge the map of North Sumatra on it. As Samosir Island grew bigger on the screen, roads and places appeared out of nowhere. They dotted the entire island. The blinking dot hovered over a spot near Pondok Wisata

Lagundi Samosir on the west of the island.

"Kuan Hee hasn't moved," Lina said. "He's still near this place Pondok something."

"I still can't figure out why these people brought him here," Tim said. "Doesn't make sense to me."

"We'll find out soon enough," Navin said.

"Alfredo is taking us to a place where we can put down our things and take a rest," Harry said.

"We aren't going to the island right now?" Lina said, disappointed.

"In good time, Lina," Tim said. "Anyway, we're already here, right? Kuan Hee's within sight, right?"

The minibus pulled into Parapat town and cruised through its narrow roads along the banks of the lake. It drove up a slope, past a sign saying Atsari Hotel and stopped in the driveway of a two-storeyed building overlooking the lake.

"This is the place," Harry said. "The jetty's a walk away and we can rent a speedboat at this hotel."

"I like it," Tim said. "It's away from prying eyes of locals and others."

"It looks modern," Navin said. "No more than twenty years old."

The five friends checked into two rooms on the second storey of the hotel. From the rooms, they had a paranomic view of the lake and Samosir Island. Below, the shore was only a stone's throw away. In front of them, idyllic Danau Toba masked the danger the visitors were heading into.

"We need to feed our stomachs first," Tim said, "before we have a powwow." He ordered room service through the phone in the room. "They serve Western food too."

"Why can't we stay in a hotel on the island?" Lina asked. "There are a few spread throughout the island."

"We need a getaway hideout," Tim said. "A safe spot far from the place where these kidnappers are holding Kuan Hee."

Lina nodded. Now she understood. It was for everyone's safety that Tim had made the arrangement to stay in Atsari Hotel instead of on the island. She was secretly glad Kuan Hee and she had levelheaded Tim as their close friend.

It had taken the three friends four days to get this close to Kuan Hee. They had to plan carefully; his safety was in their hands.

Everyone crowded around a twin bed in the men's room. Lina unfolded Little Busy's remote and pointed to Kuan Hee's current location on the map. The screen was too small for everyone to take a good look, so Tim laid down his iPad for Lina to swipe the map from the remote onto the iPad. He enlarged the map of Samosir Island. At once, buildings and roads popped up on the map.

Next Harry explained the local terrain to the group. He told the group that the place Kuan Hee was being held in was a desolate area, off the tourist track.

"Lina, can we get 'live' pictures of Kuan Hee?" Tim asked.

"I'll try," Lina said. She turned on the camera feature on the remote. At once, the iPad screen turned stark black.

"It's been like this all the while," Lina said. "No matter what I do, I cannot get the screen to light up."

"It's not working?" Harry asked.

"Little Busy is in a darkened place—perhaps in Kuan Hee's pocket," Tim said. "Lina, get it to fly around."

With Lina at its controls, Little Busy flitted into action and hovered in the contained space it was in.

"Use its night-vision feature," Tim said. In her anxiety, Lina had forgotten the robot drone could see in the dark. She tapped an icon and at once warm reds and cool blues competed for screen space.

"Little Busy is in some tight spot—like a cabinet," Lina said.

"Looks like a drawer to me," Navin said. "The contours are narrow. Little Busy can only move forward or backward."

"Navin's right," Tim said. "Little Busy's stuck in this place. We have to wait till someone opens the drawer."

"The robot can't drill through the drawer?" said Harry.

"It's not designed for that," Lina said, disappointed. She had been hoping to see Kuan Hee's face.

"Lina, don't fret," Tim said. "Keep trying." Lina nodded.

"We're all behind you, Lina," Navin said.

"Let's discuss our plan of action," Tim said. "First, I would like to say this—it's near impossible to succeed on a first attempt." He paused for a moment as if to catch his breath. Then he continued. "But, we are here to do the impossible—and succeed the first time."

Everyone nodded in unison. Alfredo merely imitated the others. He actually didn't understand a word Tim had said. He was glad Harry was doing the translation for him.

Tim shared his plan for rescuing Kuan Hee. They would go to the island in a speedboat and alight at Pondok Wisata Lagundi Samosir—a jetty on the island. From there, they would make their way on foot. Navin and Lina were to wait in the speedboat at the jetty. Tim, Harry and Alfredo would set off to save Kuan Hee.

Then Tim lugged a big bag onto the bed and fished out the Steyr AUGs. At the same time, Alfredo drew a rifle from the backpack behind him and placed it on the bed.

"M16. May I?" Tim said. He lifted the rifle and made a few snap motions with it. "Solid dependable piece," he declared to his audience.

"What about Alex and Xander?" Lina asked.

"Alex will follow me," Tim said, "and Xander will be with you and Navin. We also need to bring Tizzy along, Lina." Tizzy was a robot dragonfly drone. Both Little Busy and Tizzy were Professor Wang's creations.

"Don't worry," Lina said. "I won't forget."

"When do we move?" Navin asked.

"Tomorrow, at the crack of dawn," Tim said. "Harry,

how about the speedboat?"

"Settled," Harry said. "I'm getting it tonight."

"OK! Let's get down to cleaning the weapons," Tim said.

CHAPTER 9

Lake Toba looked the picture of calm and serenity this morning as the five friends crowded into a speedboat at the jetty. Not a sound pierced the still morning air. Nothing stirred at such an unearthly hour in the idyllic surroundings.

Alfredo proved he was not only a good driver, but also a capable speedboat pilot. He seemed to be a jack-of-all-trades. It was simply handy having him around. He seemed to be at home at the wheel of the speedboat. The speedboat broke the silence of the night as it spurted and hummed its way through the placid waters of the lake, leaving a trail of white as it sped parallel to the island, heading for its destination south of the island.

It was a twenty-minute ride to the jetty on Samosir Island. There was not a soul in sight as the speedboat slowed to a stop at the jetty. The moonlight was the only illumination on the entire stretch of shore.

On the jetty, Navin was careful to conceal his Steyr AUG in his bag. It was cocked and ready for action. Xander stood at Lina's side while she kept her eyes trained on Little Busy's screen—just in case. They could see each other, but anyone farther away from them could only make out their shadows, for it was too dark.

Tim and Harry followed Alfredo along the jetty to a wide walkway hugging the slope of a hill. Visibility was poor so they had to stay close to one another. Alfredo gave the signal for them to get down on their knees. They crouched down in single file and retrieved their rifles from their bags.

A footpath, which wound with the contour of the hill, stood metres above these intruders. It led to a big house perched on top of the hill.

The intruders needed eyes on the hilltop, so it was time for Tizzy to do its work. Tim released the robot dragonfly into the air. It flapped its wings and flew upwards towards the house on top. As it ascended the slope, its cameras gave the intruders a bird's eye view of the elevated grounds. Young trees dotted the slope with small open spaces between them.

As Tizzy flew higher, a large compound appeared on the screen. Wall spotlights lit part of the compound, leaving the other parts in darkness. There was a driveway in it. At one end of the driveway stood a large two-storeyed house with a gabled roof and red brick walls. A wide verandah hugged the perimeter of both floors of the building. In the verandahs, white-painted French windows lined the walls. On the upper floor, a lone Chinese guard sat huddled in a chair. A rifle rested on the balustrade parapet in front of him. The guard had the entire compound in his sights, but he appeared to be dozing.

Tizzy flitted along the verandah on the ground floor, peeping through the glazed French doors as it flew past them.

"We're going nowhere letting Tizzy fly all over the place," Harry said. "It's too big and we don't have time."

"Ah! I forgot I have the coordinates of Little Busy's location," Tim said. He fished out of his pocket a slip of paper Lina had given him. In it, she had written the information.

"Let's compare coordinates," Tim said. He swiped the screen and tapped the set of numbers onto the screen's search box. At once a grid appeared, superimposing a blinking dot onto a map of their immediate surroundings. Now there were two blinking dots. One showed Tizzy's real-time position, the other Little Busy's.

"The dots are very close to each other," Harry said. "Both are in the building."

"Yes, we need more details," Tim said. He enlarged the map so that it zoomed into the big building. He tapped an icon and the infrared scanner in Tizzy threw up a skeleton plan of the entire house on the screen with both dots blinking in different spots.

Tim pointed to the screen. "This blinking dot is where Tizzy is—in the verandah, west of the house. The other dot seems to be in the second last room on the east end. Question is—upper or lower floor?" He tapped on the screen again to bring up a front elevation of the house.

"Wow!" Harry said. "How did you do that?"

"Magic," Tim said as he fingered the blinking dot on the screen. "Ground floor—second last room. Time for Tizzy to get moving again." He manoeuvred Tizzy to the other side of the house.

"How can we be sure Kuan Hee is in the same room as Little Busy?" Harry asked.

"We can't," Tim said. "We can only hope he is."

Tizzy was now hovering outside the room. It swerved downwards to the bottom of the door and crawled through the small opening between the door and the floor. Then it flitted upwards, propelling itself towards the centre of the room.

"There's Kuan Hee!" Tim said. He piloted Tizzy towards a dark figure on a mattress laid on the floor. He switched on Tizzy's spotlights. At once the area in front of the robot dragonfly lit up. Kuan Hee's dishevelled hair shone in the light. In sleep, he looked tired and bedraggled.

"Kuan Hee. Kuan Hee," Tim called out through the

tiny speakers on Tizzy's head. Kuan Hee stirred. Then he opened his eyes and blinked several times. Tizzy's tiny lights had blinded him momentarily. He squinted and allowed his mouth to widen into a weak smile.

"Tim, is that you?" Kuan Hee said. He tried to get up but fell onto the mattress. It was a difficult act as his hands were tied to his back and his legs were bound too.

"Take it easy, old chap," Tim said. Kuan Hee tried again and this time succeeded in raising himself against the wall.

"Lina, where's she?" Kuan Hee asked. "Lina, are you here too?"

"Lina is nearby," Tim said. "She's down at the jetty with Navin. I'm here with my cousin and his friend. We are below the hill now."

"Where am I?" Kuan Hee asked. "Where's this place?"

"Lake Toba," Tim said.

"Lake Toba in Indonesia?" Kuan Hee said. "I'm not in China?"

"No time for small talk now, Kuan Hee," Tim said. "Let's get you out of here first. Hang on! We are coming up the hill now." Tim pocketed the remote and discussed a plan of action with Harry and Alfredo. Then he took out Alex from his backpack. The men cocked their rifles and began climbing the hill with Alex at their heels. They had not seen any other guards through Tizzy's cameras. It was apparent Kuan Hee's captors were not expecting an intrusion. Their guard was down; it was the best time to strike.

From the edge of the compound, the three intruders could make out the Chinese guard on the upper floor. He had yet to wake from his slumber. There was no one in the open area. However, there were two CCTV cameras perched on the pillars of the house. Together, they gave a complete coverage of the compound. Someone could be monitoring the cameras. They had to knock out the camera watching the east side of the house.

The intruders trod as lightly as they could to the corner of the building. Tim pressed a protruding button on the back of the robot and its front panel opened. He whispered some commands. At once, Alex leapt onto the wall and shuffled up to the second level where the CCTV camera was perched. It released a short burst of laser beams, which melted the camera lens. Then it returned to where Tim was standing.

"Let's go do our job," Tim said. The three men stalked through the verandah in single file. Outside the second last room, Harry and Alfredo kept the verandah in their rifles' sights while Tim got down to breaking open the door with Alex's help. In seconds, the robot burned a hole through the lock with its laser. Tim pushed the door open and all three moved swiftly into the room with Alfredo keeping watch at the door.

"Tim!" Kuan Hee whimpered. "Thank goodness you are here."

Tim was all smiles as he unfastened the ropes on Kuan Hee's hands and legs. Kuan Hee wobbled as he struggled to stand. His legs were numb from disuse. Tim and Harry had to help keep him stable on his feet.

"My iPhone…Little Busy…They're in that drawer," Kuan Hee said. He was too weak to reach the drawer. Tim opened the drawer and retrieved the iPhone and a wallet. Before he could grab Little Busy, it flitted into the air, prancing and dancing as if it was delighted to be free at last. In fact, it was Lina at the controls. She had been glued to the remote's screen and was hopping with joy when the screen finally played 'live' images of a limping Kuan Hee.

"Look at the way Little Busy's buzzing through the air. Lina must be elated," Tim said.

"Kuan Hee. Meet my cousin Harry and his friend Alfredo," Tim said. Kuan Hee smiled at the two men.

"We must hurry," Harry said.

The two men slung their rifles and helped Kuan Hee out of the room and through the verandah, with Alfredo and Alex behind them.

"So far so good," Tim muttered under his breath as they scrambled down the slope towards the jetty. It was too good to believe. They had not fired a single shot in their rescue mission. Would luck turn against them now, just when they were relishing success?

Lina and Navin ran towards the three men as they hobbled onto the jetty. Lina flapped around Kuan Hee. She had missed him so much.

"Lina, wait till we put him down," Tim said.

The group hurried to the speedboat with Navin and Alfredo covering their backs. Once everyone was safely in the speedboat, Alfredo shifted the control handle forward and at once the speedboat sliced through the calm waters as it raced towards the mainland.

"Kuan Hee, I missed you so," Lina cried as she hugged Kuan Hee. Tears were welling in her eyes.

"Aw! I can't *tahan* this," Tim said. "It's overwhelming my senses."

"For goodness's sake, stop teasing her, Tim," Navin said.

Kuan Hee blinked. He was relishing his newfound freedom. He squeezed Lina's hand. It was good she was at his side again.

CHAPTER 10

It was almost noon when the six friends gathered in Lina's room. Kuan Hee had regained his strength and could move about unaided.

"It's good to see you guys again," Kuan Hee said.

"Yes, thanks to you all," Lina added.

"How did they get you into Indonesia?" Navin asked.

Kuan Hee shook his head. "I really have no idea. When I woke up, I was already somewhere in Indonesia, I think. I actually thought I was in some part of China."

"Actually, nothing's impossible in Indonesia," Harry said, "with money, of course."

"Is that so?" Navin said.

"It also helps if you have connections," Harry said.

"You mean anyone can be smuggled in and out of the country just like that?" Navin snapped his fingers to make his point.

Harry nodded. "We have a long coastline. It's difficult for the authorities to monitor."

"Then there is another question—how did the kidnappers smuggle you out of Singapore, Kuan Hee?" Kuan Hee shook his head again.

"It's rare that you do not have answers to my

445

questions," Tim said. "You always have a ready answer for everything."

"They didn't even use his passport," Lina said. "It's with me." She waved his passport for everyone to see.

"It can't be that the kidnappers bought off the immigration officers," Tim said.

"Yeah," Navin said. "For sure, you can't buy off our immigration officers."

"I don't know how I can get home," Kuan Hee said. "I don't think the Indonesian immigration officers will let me leave. There's no arrival *chop* in the passport."

"It's an easy problem to solve, Kuan Hee," Harry said. "I'll get your passport stamped."

"Just like that?" Navin said.

"Yeah. It's that simple," Harry said.

"Thanks, Harry," Tim said. "I owe you one."

"No sweat. We are cousins, Tim," Harry said.

"Thanks for coming to my rescue," Kuan Hee said.

"*Aiyah*," Navin said. "Can we stop all these 'thank you' stuff? We are good friends, aren't we? And good friends help each other. Period."

"Navin's right," Tim said.

Alfredo finally spoke—in Bahasa Indonesia.

"Alfredo is curious. He wonders why they kidnapped Kuan Hee," Harry explained.

There was silence in the room. Everyone was in deep thought. Then Kuan Hee broke the silence.

"Might have something to do with my dad," Kuan Hee said. "The kidnappers might want something from my dad."

"Kuan Hee, have you heard from your father?" Tim asked.

"Not since I was kidnapped," Kuan Hee said. "They took my iPhone. By the way, where's my iPhone?"

"It is being charged," Lina said. "The battery has gone flat."

Kuan Hee put out his hand and Lina passed the

smartphone to him. He scrolled to see the call log. Several entries caught his eye.

"My dad called me," Kuan Hee said. "He's been trying to reach me."

"Did you tell Dad about me?" Kuan Hee asked Lina.

"Sorry, it didn't cross my mind," Lina said. "Everything was in a whirl. I didn't know what to do. I merely called Tim and Navin."

"It's alright," Kuan Hee said. He tapped his dad's number to call him. Soon father and son were in animated conversation.

"My Dad's in town," Kuan Hee said. "He's staying at Siantar Hotel."

"Where's Siantar Hotel?" Tim asked.

"It's only about five hundred metres away from here," Harry said.

"I've been here for four days, waiting for the kidnappers to call me," Professor Wang said.

"I'm OK, Dad," Kuan Hee said. "I am safe. In fact I am nearby."

"I'm glad you are out of harm's way," Professor Wang said in a voice thick with emotion. "Your mum will be so happy too."

Kuan Hee ended the call. "Room eighteen," he said. "Let's go."

Kuan Hee had gotten excited at the prospect of seeing his father again. He had forgotten they were in the middle of a discussion. He wanted to fly over to Siantar Hotel this instant.

The six friends could walk to Siantar Hotel, but it was faster using the minibus so they scrambled into the vehicle with Alfredo at the wheel. The minibus turned back towards the town centre.

Room eighteen was in the middle of a row of rooms on the second level of the Siantar Hotel. No one answered the door when Kuan Hee rang the bell. He knocked on the door several times.

"Dad has to be in," Kuan Hee said. "We just talked minutes ago."

"Perhaps, he's in the toilet," Lina said.

"Let's wait a little longer," Tim said.

The minutes passed and the knocking continued, still there was no response from the inside of the room. Harry walked down to the reception counter to enquire while the others waited outside the room.

Harry came back with a woman service staff. She knocked on the door and waited for a response before using a card key to open the door. Signalling the visitors to wait, she entered the room alone and returned to the door pronouncing the hotel guest was not in.

Despite protests from Kuan Hee, she refused to let them into the room. Then she promptly locked the door and left.

"Doesn't make sense," Kuan Hee said. "I was on the line with him just now. He said he would wait for me."

"Kuan Hee," Tim said. "I have a horrid feeling something's happened to Professor Wang."

"No! Can't be," Kuan Hee said.

"There's a CCTV camera overlooking the passageway," Tim said, pointing upwards at a camera perched in a corner below the ceiling. "There's no way anyone can steal past its eyes undetected."

"Let me handle this," Harry said. "I'll speak to the manager. Wait here for me." He and Alfredo disappeared down the staircase.

Just then, a figure appeared at the top of the staircase. He strolled down the passageway towards the group.

"It's Brigadier Walmsley!" Kuan Hee exclaimed. It was the Brigadier all right. Except for a slow gait and more wrinkles across his face, nothing had changed. He still had the same hunting hat, straggly beard and beer belly.

"Hallo Kuan Hee and Lina," Brigadier Walmsley said. "Fancy meeting you here—of all places. These must be your friends. Hi!"

"Mr Walmsley, you must be looking for my dad too," Kuan Hee said.

"Yes, afraid so," Brigadier Walmsley said. "Why are you guys standing outside? Isn't your father in?"

"We are trying to find out what has happened to my dad," Kuan Hee said.

"It's pretty stuffy here," Brigadier Walmsley said. "Why don't we go down to the lobby? It's much cooler there and there are seats too."

The Brigadier took the lead and the group of friends followed him down the stairs to the hotel's reception area. It was air-conditioned, unlike the passageway they were in earlier. Harry and Alfredo were at the counter with the hotel manager.

"Harry seems to be having difficulty at the counter," Tim said.

"What's going on?" Brigadier Walmsley asked.

"Mr Walmsley, my friend is trying to get permission to view the CCTV video footage for the passageway upstairs. We suspect something has happened to my dad," Kuan Hee said.

"I see," Brigadier Walmsley said. "You guys take a seat. Let me give him a helping hand." The Brigadier strode over to the counter.

"Will he succeed?" Navin said. "Harry and Alfredo are locals, yet have no luck."

"Don't forget he's an *Angmoh*," Lina said.

"So?" Navin said. "It's no longer the twentieth century. We're no longer under colonial rule. Being an *Angmoh* doesn't help."

"You spoke too soon, Navin," Tim said. "Look over there." The Brigadier was now standing next to the manager behind the counter looking at a monitor. He was also using his phone.

"He's an old hand at this," Kuan Hee said.

"I agree," Tim said.

Minutes later, the Brigadier returned to the group with

Harry and Alfredo. He took a seat next to Kuan Hee.

"Guess I came too late," Brigadier Walmsley said. "Should not have stopped for lunch before coming here."

"Did you see my dad coming out of the room?" Kuan Hee asked.

"Seems two men—of Chinese origin—took him away," Brigadier Walmsley said. "Just before you guys arrived. You were three minutes late."

"Three minutes?" Kuan Hee said in a tremulous voice. "We could have stopped them if we had hurried over."

"Kuan Hee, stop blaming yourself," Tim said. "Nobody knew these guys were coming for your father. Stop being hard on yourself."

"Your friend is right, Kuan Hee," Brigadier Walmsley said. "What we must do now is find your father as soon as we can—before he falls into danger."

"Mr Walmsley, what do these men want with my father-in-law?" Lina asked.

The Brigadier looked around the lobby. Then he turned his eyes on Harry and Alfredo. Finally, he looked at Tim and Navin. He seemed to be scrutinizing Kuan Hee's friends.

"Mr Walmsley, what are these people after?" Kuan Hee said.

The Brigadier leaned back on the sofa and twiddled his thumbs. "Shall we order some coffee? I'm thirsty."

A service staff brought beverages for all of them. In between sips of his favourite *kopi oh kosong*, the Brigadier chatted with Tim and Navin. It seemed he wanted to know them better. Both men had heard Kuan Hee and Lina speaking about the Brigadier so many times that they knew all about him and what he did.

"Who's he?" Harry asked Kuan Hee.

"Brigadier Walmsley is an American operative," Kuan Hee said. "My dad works for him. Mr Walmsley works for the American government. Special Forces."

"Special Forces?" Harry exclaimed. "Delta Force?"

"Right," Kuan Hee said. Harry translated their conversation to Alfredo, who looked in amazement at the Brigadier. Apparently, Alfredo had not seen a real American spy before.

"Kuan Hee, aren't we wasting precious time here?" Lina said in a low voice. "We should be out looking for your father."

"The Brigadier must have his reason for remaining here," Kuan Hee said. "Let's wait."

"Kuan Hee, I see you have been to the house on Samosir Island," Brigadier Walmsley said.

"Erh. Yes. Mr Walmsley," Kuan Hee said. "I was kidnapped and held there the past few days."

"I see," Brigadier Walmsley said. "Your friends have been there too?"

"They—they went there to rescue me," Kuan Hee said.

"Mr Walmsley, I went there too," Lina said.

"Lina, really?" Brigadier Walmsley said. "Gosh! You are a brave girl. Indeed very brave."

The main door opened and a tall Caucasian man with the demeanor of a warrior stepped into the hotel lobby. He walked over to the Brigadier and whispered into his ears.

"Kuan Hee. Apologies. I need to take my leave," Brigadier Walmsley said. "Have to settle an urgent matter." He bade goodbye to the group and left quickly with his escort.

"Just like that?" Lina said. "He's gone just like that. Without a word about your father, Kuan Hee."

"I know. I know," Kuan Hee said. "He'll be back—soon."

"But, he doesn't know where we are staying," Lina said.

"I think he does, Lina," Kuan Hee said. "For sure, he already knows what we have been doing on the island."

"Really?" Tim said.

"One hundred percent," Kuan Hee said. "He didn't look surprised when I told him I had been kidnapped.

451

Don't forget. He spies on others for a living."

"Why didn't we follow him?" Navin asked.

"We can't," Kuan Hee said. "We'll only be in the way."

"Maybe these Chinese men have taken your father to the island," Tim said.

"Yeah. Tim is right, Navin said. "Let's go save him now."

"Damn it, why didn't I think of it?" Kuan Hee said. "Are we too late?"

"Not if we go now," Tim said. "Everyone for it?"

The six friends nodded in unison.

"Let's go get our hardware," Tim said.

The sun was high in the sky when the speedboat cut through the calm waters of the lake, heading towards the same jetty the six friends had left that morning. This time everything was in clear view—the island with its lush vegetation and tall hills that jutted into the clear skies like the serrated edge of a knife.

At the jetty, the group left Navin and Lina behind to look after the speedboat. They were careful not to take out their rifles, for it was broad daylight and Samosir Island was teeming with tourists at this time of the day.

Climbing the hill was easier this time as the group was familiar with the terrain. Little Busy flew up to the house to provide them with an aerial view of the surroundings. There was no one in sight. The intruders readied their rifles and scrambled up the slope. When they reached the compound, they fanned out with Kuan Hee and Harry taking the lead in approaching the verandah. At one end of the verandah, the two men crouched down and kept out of view.

"It's eerily quiet," Kuan Hee said. "Like they are lying in wait to ambush us."

"Could they have abandoned the hideout?" Harry said.

"You mean they have taken my dad to a new hideout?"

Kuan Hee said. "Let's find out for sure." He raised his hand to signal to the others he was starting the search. At once, Tim and Alfredo aimed their rifles at the upper floor of the house. Both found each other unlikely partners; they were unable to communicate with each other. Both had to use hand gestures and hope the other could read the signal. A mistake could cost them their lives.

Kuan Hee and Harry checked the rooms one by one. Then they climbed the stairs to the second storey. The rooms upstairs were also vacant. Harry slung his rifle and leaned out of the parapet. He signalled to the others to come up. They were now all standing in the verandah on the second storey.

"The house is deserted," Kuan Hee said, dispirited. "It's only been half a day and they have managed to clear out so quickly."

"The rooms do not appear to have been lived-in," Harry said. "It is likely the kidnappers were using it as a hideout—nothing more. Once they were found out, they merely abandoned the place."

"But it's so big," Tim said. "Who in his right mind would spend so much money renting such a big place only to use it as a hideout?"

"You have a point, Tim," Kuan Hee said. "They might return."

"Let's see if we can find out more about the kidnappers from the things they left behind," Tim said.

"Alfredo will keep watch," Harry said. "Just in case."

Alas, they found no clues. Dejected, they trudged back to the jetty. Their looks told Navin and Lina plenty.

"Indonesia is so big," Kuan Hee said. "Where can my dad be?"

"He's got to be nearby," Tim said. "It's only been a few hours. He can't be far. We'll find your father." The others nodded in agreement.

CHAPTER 11

In their hotel room that evening, Kuan Hee and Lina received an unannounced visit from Brigadier Walmsley. The Brigadier lumbered to the balcony. He swept his hand in front of him. "Such a picturesque view. Kuan Hee, there are many more such views in this world of ours. So many that there's hardly enough time for us to enjoy all of them even if we visit one every day. Yet, man isn't satisfied. He wants to control the world."

Turning to face Kuan Hee, Brigadier Walmsley said, "Talented people like your father are always a target of unscrupulous villains in our world. These villains want to control mankind. It's been like that for thousands of years. Our history books attest to their misdeeds. Power is what they seek." He leaned towards Kuan Hee. "That is why we need to keep people like your father out of their hands. But it's difficult. These unscrupulous people attack your father's Achilles' heel—you—and force him to do things against his will."

The Brigadier sank into a cane settee and the weight of his back squashed the cushion, curling it inwards. He clapped his hands on his lap and gazed into Kuan Hee's eyes. "I'm getting on in years, Kuan Hee. I'm almost

454

seventy-nine years old. Age is catching up with me. I can't do the same things I did three years ago when we last met."

"Mr Walmsley, you still look hale and hearty," Lina said. "You don't look your age."

"Yes. Lina's right," Kuan Hee said.

"Lina. My mind is young," Brigadier Walmsley said. "But my body is old—very old. His father is even older. He's—I think he should be eighty-one?"

"My dad will be eighty-one in January," Kuan Hee said.

"At our age, your father and I should be spending our twilight years taking care of our grandchildren. Instead, we are looking out for mankind. Your father has this special gift of knowledge. He knows it and he's been spending his entire life furthering his discoveries of the human mind and the technologies behind reproductive human cloning. He knows he is not a good father or grandfather in many people's eyes. But the fact is—his discoveries propel man into the future. He exists to help us live better." The Professor paused to collect his thoughts.

"Kuan Hee, do you understand what I'm saying?" Brigadier Walmsley said.

"Yes. Mr Walmsley," Kuan Hee said. "I've never doubted my dad's love for me. In fact, Mum and I always knew we had to share Dad with his work. He is his work and his work is he. We know it very well."

"Yes. That's right. Realising he hasn't got many years of his life left, your father copied his memories into an optical storage cartridge. You know very well, transcribing the data into another human brain is akin to creating another Professor Wang. Your father hoped, perhaps, some day in the future, you or some others could make use of these memories to further the progress of science," Brigadier Walmsley said.

"Was I kidnapped because of the mind clone cartridge?" Kuan Hee asked.

"Yes, I am afraid so, Kuan Hee," Brigadier Walmsley

said. "These men have evil designs for the mind clone cartridge. They will stop at nothing to get their hands on it."

"How did my captors know of it?" Kuan Hee asked.

"I'm not proud to say this—even our spy agency has moles inside working against our interests," Brigadier Walmsley said. "Your father is always a target for evil men who seek to control others. Yes. I hate to say it, but it's true. Man's greed is as wide as the ocean."

"So they wanted the mind clone cartridge in exchange for me?" Kuan Hee said.

"Yes. Kuan Hee. Your father travelled thousands of miles to come here to save you," Brigadier Walmsley said. "He snuck away when his minders were distracted. He didn't even tell me. That shows you are very important to him—more important than his work."

"Is the mind clone cartridge in their hands now?" Kuan Hee asked.

"I'm afraid so, Kuan Hee," Brigadier Walmsley said. "Both your father and the mind clone cartridge have fallen into their hands. Even if your father refuses to cooperate with them, they still have the disk. I believe the perpetrators have skilled scientists who can transcribe the data into a human brain. I seriously think they have the means and capability to do so."

"I'm curious. How do such things work?" Lina asked.

"Well, it's beyond me. But, in a nutshell, the neuro-scientist fortifies and impedes specially picked synaptic connections in the brain. This way, he creates and erases memories at will—at least that's what I remember the Professor telling me," Brigadier Walmsley said. "Kuan Hee, do you understand what I just said?"

"Yes. Mr Walmsley," Kuan Hee said. "Using some high-frequency light pulses, the scientist can stimulate synaptic connections in the brain, causing a change of state, thereby influencing memory. In short, it's memory control. A skilled scientist can manipulate a person's memories—for instance, erase, change or replace."

"Yes, Kuan Hee. Very well said," Brigadier Walmsley said. "You do take after your father. You've got his brain."

"Of course. He has," Lina said, beaming.

"Someday, we could use you," Brigadier Walmsley said.

"I'm nowhere near my dad in skills," Kuan Hee said, blushing.

"That's because you are still young, Kuan Hee," Brigadier Walmsley said. "You have untapped talent." He took out something from his pocket and thrust it into Kuan Hee's hand.

"With this you can return to Singapore," Brigadier Walmsley said. "Go back. It's not safe here."

"It's a passport," Lina said, grabbing it from Kuan Hee's hand. "A United States passport."

"Yes, with it you can travel anywhere—it's a diplomatic passport," Brigadier Walmsley said. "We give it to certain individuals who work for the US government. But it doesn't grant citizenship. That's another matter."

"You mean Kuan Hee's working for the US government now?" Lina said.

The Brigadier nodded. "It's time I take my leave. I'll get in touch with you shortly. Do you still have the walkie-talkie I gave you?"

"It's at home—in Singapore," Kuan Hee said.

"Never mind," Brigadier Walmsley said as he ambled into the corridor. "Goodnite. And don't lose hope."

CHAPTER 12

Loud knocks on their hotel door woke Kuan Hee and Lina that night. It was Alfredo at the door. His face was contorted in fear. He was rattling off long strings of words in Bahasa Indonesia. They had no idea what he was saying to them. He pointed to the next room. The pair looked inside—it was empty.

"What are you trying to tell us?" Kuan Hee said. He gave up talking to Alfredo and instead used hand gestures to communicate with him. Still he could not decipher what their Indonesian guide was trying to tell him.

"They went out? Why?" Kuan Hee said in response to Alfredo's waving of his hands. Clearly, Alfredo didn't understand a word he was saying.

"Alfredo wants me to follow him—at least, I think that's what his hand gestures are saying," Kuan Hee said. "You stay in the room. Something has happened to the others."

"I want to tag along," Lina said.

"Not this time, Lina," Kuan Hee said. "It's too dangerous. We're in a foreign land."

Kuan Hee grabbed his iPhone and backpack. He peeped inside the bag. *The Steyr AUG should do the job.*

To Lina's protests, he scrambled down the stairs with Alfredo.

Alfredo took the wheel and led the minibus out of the hotel compound into the darkness, with the vehicle's headlamps providing much needed illumination. There were hardly any streetlights on the long and winding road and it took Alfredo's driving skills to negotiate the bends without the vehicle veering off into the darkness. Kuan Hee did not know where the minibus was heading; he could hardly see the road. Even if there were landmarks, he had no inkling where he was.

Fifteen minutes into the journey, the minibus turned into what seemed like a plantation. There was row upon row of palm trees lining both sides of the road. The minibus came to a stop and Alfredo beckoned Kuan Hee to get down. He pointed to a row of houses ahead of them. In the darkness, they looked like a cluster of buffalo horns poking the grey skies. As the duo drew nearer, they saw wooden thatched houses on stilts. Two lampposts with light globes provided the only illumination in the area. Instinctively, Kuan Hee reached for the Steyr AUG. He readied his weapon as Alfredo led the way towards the buildings. The air was silent.

The two men were now at the corner of the nearest house. Kuan Hee patted Alfredo's shoulder and the guide turned to face him. Kuan Hee wanted to ask him where their friends were but didn't know how to do it. He stretched out open palms facing upwards, hoping Alfredo would understand. Alfredo pointed to the house in front. In his haste, Kuan Hee had forgotten to bring Little Busy along. The robot housefly drone could have allowed them to suss out the place. Now, they had to rely on themselves.

The men crouched between the stilts propping the house. Kuan Hee signaled he was climbing up to the verandah above them. Alfredo put out a hand so Kuan Hee released his grip on the Steyr AUG and clambered up the wooden pole. The rifle would have weighed him down for he was not good at climbing such things; he was not commando-trained.

Kuan Hee heaved himself over the wooden railing and steadied himself. He was about to stretch his hand for his rifle when someone grabbed him from behind. The man's heavy hands made light work of subduing Kuan Hee. It was then Kuan Hee realized there were two Chinese men, lean and mean, looking down at him.

"Run, Alfredo, run," Kuan Hee shouted at the top of his voice as the men dragged him away from the railing.

CHAPTER 13

There were loud knocks on the hotel door again. Lina grimaced. *Should I open the door? What if the kidnappers are out there? Kuan Hee said to wait. He didn't tell me what to do!* Her friends were missing and Kuan Hee had gone to look for them. There was nobody else that they knew here in Indonesia. Her mind was in a whirl.

"Kuan Hee. Kuan Hee. Lina. Are you in?"

It's Tim's voice! He's back! Lina rushed to the door.

"Why did you take so long?" Tim said, annoyed. Navin and Harry were standing next to him.

"You are safe!" Lina exclaimed. "You are all safe!" She let her tears fall.

"Why shouldn't we be?" Navin asked.

"What's happened?" Tim asked.

"We…we thought you were taken," Lina said.

"We merely went out for a drink," Navin said.

"Why didn't you tell us?" Lina said. "We were so worried."

"Our door was open. We saw the Brigadier walking past. We figured he wanted to have a long chat with you privately. So we thought we'd leave you guys alone with

461

him. That's why we did not say a word," Tim said.

"We left Alfredo behind," Harry said. "Didn't he tell you? Oh! I forgot. He doesn't speak English."

"Alfredo?" Lina said. "But Alfredo said—I mean he gestured that something had happened to you."

"He did?" Tim said. "Where's Kuan Hee? Has he gone to look for us?"

"He and Alfredo left," Lina said. "Alfredo knew where you were."

"That's nonsense," Harry said. "Alfredo said he was tired, so we left without him."

"You could have called us," Tim said, waving his smartphone in the air.

"The phone! Why didn't I think of using the phone?" Lina said.

"How long have they been gone?" Tim asked.

"Er…about an hour ago, I guess," Lina said. "It wasn't long after the Brigadier left."

"Something has happened to Kuan Hee again," Navin said. Lina put her hands to her face and started crying. She wailed into Tim's shoulder.

Tim shuddered. The sudden turn of events was frustrating to him—to say the least. *Just when things are going right,* he muttered under his breath.

All eyes were now trained on Harry.

"He's a familiar face in Parapat," Harry said. "I spoke to my friends. They highly recommended him. I didn't know it would turn out like this. I'm sorry. Very sorry."

"It's alright, Harry," Tim said. "Nobody's blaming you."

"Did Kuan Hee take Little Busy with him?" Navin asked.

"Nope. He only took his backpack—with the Steyr AUG in it," Lina said.

"FindMyiPhone app," Tim said. "I forgot the iPhone's got this app."

Lina retrieved Kuan Hee's MacBook Air from a bag and powered the device. Then she stopped. She contorted her face and covered it with her hand. "I forgot. We haven't been using the FindMyiPhone app for years. Kuan Hee feared the government was spying on us. He deliberately kept off using it. We have been relying on Little Busy and Tizzy since." She was near tears again.

Tim patted her shoulder. "It's alright. It's alright."

"I tried reaching Alfredo," Harry said as he expelled clove-flavoured cigarette smoke. "He's not answering my calls." He stubbed out the cigarette and reached in his pocket for another.

There were many minutes of silence in the room as the four friends pondered the situation.

Then they heard a tap on the door. They had not ordered any room service. At once, Tim strode across the room to his backpack and took out a Steyr AUG. Navin and Harry followed suit. The knocks grew louder. With his rifle at the ready and Navin opposite him, Tim turned the door handle and let the door creak open.

"Gosh! It's Mr Walmsley!" Lina exclaimed from the far end of the room. The men relaxed their grip on their weapons.

"What are you young men doing?" Brigadier Walmsley said.

"Mr Walmsley, we thought—" Tim said.

"Seriously, do I look like an intruder?" Brigadier Walmsley said. Then he started coughing and fanned the air in front of him. "What smell is this?"

Harry flicked the cigarette in his hand and crushed it with his foot. "Sorry. Mr Walmsley."

The four friends crowded around the Brigadier. As he took his seat, Lina explained what had happened since he left earlier in the evening. The Brigadier rolled his eyes in disbelief. "Your lives are more interesting than a spy's."

The Brigadier twiddled his fingers. "Can someone get

me a *kopi oh kosong*?" he said. Lina called room service.

In between sips of the hot beverage, the Brigadier eyed the four friends—one by one.

"So this chap—Alfredo—took Kuan Hee for a ride and they didn't return?" Brigadier Walmsley said. They nodded.

"So Kuan Hee's got his iPhone with him?" Brigadier Walmsley said. "The one with the Polaris SIM card?"

Lina nodded. "Kuan Hee's been using this SIM card the past few years."

"Now, we have a way to locate father and son," Brigadier Walmsley said.

"Really, Mr Walmsley?" Lina said. Her face lit up.

Ignoring Lina, the Brigadier excused himself and plodded to the balcony where they saw him using his smartphone.

"I'm afraid I have to go," Brigadier Walmsley said as he pocketed his smartphone. "Lina, I will get Kuan Hee back safely. Trust me."

"Mr Walmsley, you found out where he is?" Lina asked.

"Let me handle it," Brigadier Walmsley said. Then he looked at the men. "All of you stay put. Hear? Don't be a hero."

Everyone nodded in unison reluctantly.

CHAPTER 14

What a turn of events! First, he was kidnapped. Then, his friends rescued him from the clutches of his captors. Now, he had landed in his captors' hands again. Kuan Hee shook his head as he pondered his misfortunes in the darkened room. *Alfredo will get help. Alfredo must get help. Where are they holding Tim, Navin and Harry? They don't seem to be here.* His mind was in a whirl. He opened his eyes. *Dad! Dad must be somewhere near!*

Kuan Hee shivered. He was unaccustomed to cold weather. In Singapore, he would pat his forehead and neck continually as he got about his tasks in the midday heat. He would wish for cool temperatures all year round. Here, he had gotten his wish, but he felt uncomfortable. It was colder than the air-conditioned environment he worked in.

It's too cold here. I must be in the highlands. I must be somewhere in Brastagi. Alfredo must have driven us back to Brastagi.

The door opened and the same two men ambled up to him. With his mouth taped, and his hands and legs bound, Kuan Hee was powerless to resist. One lifted him over his shoulder with the help of the other. With the heavy load bearing on him, the man shuffled into a corridor and then out into the open area in front of the house. It was even colder outside in the early morning air, but Kuan Hee took no notice; he had other things weighing on his mind.

The men unloaded their human cargo into a van and drove out of the plantation. There was no knowing where Kuan Hee's captors were taking him. *Perhaps, they are taking me to Dad. I will be meeting him soon.* As the van rocked along the uneven road, a sense of foreboding overcame Kuan Hee. It shook his consciousness.

About an hour into the journey, the van screeched to a stop. Then it moved again, albeit at a slower pace. Sunlight peeped into the back of the van through the opening behind the driver. It was noisy outside. Carhorns blared intermittently; loud voices rang out now and then. *I must be in some town.*

The van stopped again. This time, Kuan Hee heard the front doors creak open. Then the back door slid open and sunlight flooded the interior. The two men dragged Kuan Hee out into what looked like a room. *No! It's a garage, like the one in Harry's house.* Kuan Hee realized he was in a shophouse. The men heaved their hostage up a flight of stairs to the second level and into a room at one end of the building. Kuan Hee looked up at his new surroundings. He shouted at the top of his voice, but only muffled sounds came out. *Dad! Dad!* The elder Wang was right in front of him.

The men let go of their load and Kuan Hee fell onto the floor next to his father. Then they left. Kuan Hee crawled up to his father. He pressed his shoulder on him. The elder Wang glowed as he felt the warmth of his son's body on his. He too had been gagged and bound. Deep ridges of wrinkled skin formed along the edges of the duct tape fastened across his mouth. His eyes were heavy with sleeplessness. He was visibly tired and gaunt. His usually neatly combed hair was in a disheveled mess, exposing bald patches of scalp on top of his head. At his advanced age, he was too frail to take the knocks of captivity.

466

Though down-and-out, he flashed a weak smile. He was glad his son was unharmed. It had been a nerve-racking experience for father and son, and it was set to get worse.

There was so much that both wanted to tell each other, but all they could do was look into each other's eyes. They had to let their eyes do the talking for them. Both were not shy to let the tears flow down their face.

Gunshots echoed through the shophouse. Then came the sound of running footsteps and stomping. More gunshots rang out in quick succession. *Quick bursts. These have to be automatic rifles. Help is here!*

The Wangs huddled together under the window, their eyes trained on the door. Footsteps thundered in the hall outside. Then they drew nearer. The door flung open and a balaclava-clad figure towered in the doorway. He was wielding a Heckler & Koch UMP40 submachine gun. He shouted to someone outside and hastened into the room to cut the ropes bounding the two hostages. He beckoned them to follow him. Kuan Hee helped his father out of the room. With their rescuer covering them, they staggered across the hall to the staircase. At the bottom of the stairs was a slumped figure, lying in a pool of blood. A tall balaclava-clad man was standing next to the body. He waved them down. The smell of gunpowder punctuated the air. The garage walls and van were riddled with bullets. Another body lay on the floor. Father and son wobbled past it to the entrance.

Outside, a minibus was waiting with a third member of the rescue party at the wheel. There were faces peeping at the rescuers and hostages from behind windows and doors on both sides of the narrow road. But no one dared come outside; everyone was afraid of being caught in the firefight.

With Kuan Hee and his father safely in the minibus, the vehicle sped off, leaving the neighbourhood in a tizzy.

As the minibus cruised through the streets, the rescuers

took off their masks, revealing young, tanned and taut facial features. *Caucasians. They must be Delta Force. Brigadier Walmsley had come to their rescue again!*

The commando sitting in front of the Wangs retrieved something from his jacket and pressed it in Kuan Hee's hands. "I believe this is yours."

Kuan Hee beamed. It was his iPhone. "Thank you."

"We got your location with its help," the commando said.

The elder Wang leaned on his son. He was delirious. The ordeal had taken its toll on his health. Kuan Hee placed his hand on his father's forehead. "It's hot. My dad is having a fever."

"We'll arrive at our destination shortly," the commando said. "There will be a doctor to attend to him."

"Step on it," the commando in the front section of the minibus told the driver. The minibus accelerated towards Medan.

As the minibus pulled into a driveway, off a busy thoroughfare in the city, Kuan Hee saw the Brigadier, Lina and his *kakis* standing in the porch.

On hand to attend to the elder Wang was a doctor and a nurse. They promptly sat him in a wheelchair and pushed him into the building. The Brigadier followed them. The commandos straggled behind the Brigadier.

Lina flew into Kuan Hee's arms. She was delighted he had come to no harm. The others patted Kuan Hee's shoulder. They were grinning from ear to ear.

But poor Kuan Hee was in no mood to rejoice or answer their questions. Only one thing occupied his thoughts—his father's condition. He hurried into the building with the others tagging behind.

It wasn't a clinic or hospital they were in. It was a support centre that the United States government had set up to bolster its consulate in the city of Medan. The consulate, a stone's throw away from here, had been serving Indonesians in Sumatra since 1949.

"How's my dad?" Kuan Hee asked.

"Professor Wang has pneumonia," the doctor said. "There's fluid and pus in his lungs. We need to get him to a hospital straightaway."

"Go ahead," Brigadier Walmsley said. "I'll arrange security for him." The doctor nodded and excused himself. The Brigadier conferred with the commandos who had gathered around him.

"I'm going to the hospital with Lina," Kuan Hee said.

"We'll be at Harry's place," Tim said. "Keep in touch."

Professor Wang was admitted into the Intensive Care Unit at Rumah Sakit Polonia, a private hospital in Medan with English speaking doctors and staff. In the corridor outside the ICU, the Brigadier's two commandos stood watch, while Kuan Hee and Lina, looking forlorn, sat on a long wooden bench.

"Your father's in a coma," Brigadier Walmsley said as he emerged from the ward. He leaned over to place his hand on Kuan Hee's shoulder. "We have to prepare for the worst, Kuan Hee."

Lina burst into tears. "Oh. Kuan Hee. What shall we do? What can we do?"

Kuan Hee was a picture of calm outside, but inside he was crying his heart out. He was not one to openly display his emotions, but his wobbly voice betrayed his staid exterior. "I—I got to call Mum. Got to tell her."

The minutes stretched into hours. The Brigadier uttered some apologies to Kuan Hee and lumbered towards the lift; he had to get some sleep. The night was long and the wait frustratingly uneventful.

Lina curled up on the bench for some shut-eye, while Kuan Hee drifted in and out of sleep. He rubbed his eyes; he had to keep them peeled for news from the ICU. Then he slumped onto the bench.

Kuan Hee awoke with a jolt. He had heard his father shout his name. *Aiyah! I was dreaming.* Lina was fast asleep next to him and the commando on watch duty was at the far end of the corridor, leaning on the wall near the lift. Kuan Hee tapped the iPhone screen. It was showing 2:18 a.m. He took a deep breath. The air-conditioning was cold. He thought of putting his jacket over Lina, but realized he was not wearing one.

Then came the shuffling of feet along the corridor. Kuan Hee looked up. A doctor was rushing into the ICU. A nurse met him at the door. Kuan Hee's hunches went into overdrive. Goose pimples broke out all over him. He shook Lina awake. When the doctor came out of the ICU and approached him, Kuan Hee already knew what he was going to say—his father had left for a new world.

Lina cried uncontrollably. Kuan Hee wrapped her in his arms; he too let his tears run freely. It was a bad end to a long bad day.

CHAPTER 15

Morning came, gloomy and chilly. The dark clouds gathering in the sky outside the funeral parlour looked threatening. Another face of humid Medan was about to show itself.

The elder Wang's body lay in an open wooden coffin, bereft of embellishments and supported on a pair of short wooden benches laid perpendicular to the coffin. The hall was a non-descript one-storeyed concrete structure with a corrugated steel roof. The coffin took centre place, facing rows of benches and a wide entrance, flanked by folding metal doors. The parlour was typical of funeral parlours in the city.

Professor Wang was not of any religion, but he was not agnostic either. The scientist in him reasoned that the myriad intricate and delicate processes that supported life on earth were beyond the realm of science. So unlike the astrophysicist Stephen Hawking, who famously declared there was no god, he believed somewhere in the universe, some magical source had created the earth and every living thing on it. He believed life itself was a miracle and that the miracle was beyond man and nature. He believed somewhere out there, there was a superior life. Perhaps, it was God. But he stopped dwelling on this curiosity of his, for the scientist in him also argued that there had to be a scientific explanation for existence. With his death, the question of existence in his mind remained unanswered and his unadorned wake properly reflected this impasse.

"Mum's flying over," Kuan Hee said. "She won't be here so soon. Fort Bragg is almost two days away from here by plane."

"Kuan Hee. I'm lost," Lina said. "Terribly lost." It was the first time someone close to her had passed away. She didn't know how to handle the situation. Neither did Kuan Hee. Just how would one handle the loss of a loved one? Hours ago, his father was sitting next to him in the minibus, snuggling his warm body against him. Now he was cold and stiff in the coffin. Kuan Hee's thoughts drifted to the previous day's events—to the Chinese men who kidnapped him and his father. As their faces loomed in his mind, he boiled with anger. *Even if I have to go to the ends of the earth, I'll make them pay dearly.*

"Lina, I've never told anyone before," Kuan Hee said. "Dad and I were not close. He spent most of his time in his lab. It was his baby. I was not. But he came thousands of miles to save me. He died doing it. I hate myself. I really hate myself. I should have treated him better." His vision blurred as tears enveloped his eyes and drained down the sides of his face. Some landed in his mouth. They were salty. With tissue paper, Lina wiped the tears off him.

The rain came suddenly and in torrents. It whipped the metal roof, beating it relentlessly as if heaven was meting out justice on the perpetrators of his father's tragedy. How Kuan Hee's father would rejoice knowing heaven was on his side.

"Kuan Hee, why aren't you flying your father's body back to Singapore?" Navin asked as he and Tim joined the pair on the bench.

"My mum says it doesn't matter where we hold the funeral," Kuan Hee said. "My parents don't have many friends in Singapore."

"So your father's getting a quiet sendoff?" Tim said.

"It's what he wanted, really," Kuan Hee said. "My dad doesn't mix around. All he knows—and cares about—is his work. He never got around to making friends. He seldom received invites for weddings and gatherings."

Though the elder Wang lay lonely and lonesome in the coffin, his son Kuan Hee was in the company of his beloved life companion Lina, and his closest friends Tim and Navin who were here at the parlour to grieve with him.

Harry arrived with Uncle Kenny, bearing umbrellas, dripping wet. They paid their respects to the elder Wang before taking their seat on a bench.

"My father says you can stay as long as you wish," Harry said.

"Yes, Kuan Hee," Uncle Kenny said. "Find the ones who caused your father's death. Come to me if you need help."

"Uncle Kenny, these kidnappers may come looking for me at your house," Kuan Hee said. "You'll be in danger."

"Kuan Hee, I'm not afraid of danger. I have been through turmoil," Uncle Kenny said. "People came bearing lit torches. They looted my shops and then burnt them down. My friend had rocks thrown at him. He was hit with metal pipes till he died. He was on his way to his factory to save it from looters. Medan is no stranger to riots. We have come so far because we stick together. We go through weal and woe as one community. That's the reason why I'm around today. I'm alive because I never caved in." Uncle Kenny had gotten emotional. Kuan Hee's remark had triggered memories long buried in his mind. He was now reliving them.

Harry placed his hand on his father's arm. "Pa, it's the past."

"No. It may happen again, just as it did years ago," Uncle Kenny said. Lina passed a packet drink to Harry who placed it in his father's hand. Uncle Kenny's hands shook as he tore the straw off the packet.

"Why can't they leave us alone?" Uncle Kenny said. "We're only trying to make a living."

"Pa, it's over. Forget it," Harry said.

At that moment, Brigadier Walmsley stepped into the parlour. Drenched, he trudged to the side of the coffin to take a good look at his bosom friend. He took off his hunting hat, lightly shook off the water away from the coffin, and holding it against his belly, slid into a long silent conversation with the late Professor, shaking his head at times, and raising a hand to wipe his tears.

"Dad and the Brigadier have been working together for as long as I can remember," Kuan Hee said. "In fact, Mum says their relationship goes back decades."

"He looks very sad," Navin said.

"I believe Dad and he were best friends," Kuan Hee said. "Mum told me the Brigadier looked after Dad's interests well."

The Brigadier, having bidden a teary farewell to the Professor, took a seat next to Kuan Hee. He let out a long sigh. "Kuan Hee, I'm sorry that things have come to this state—very sorry. You see, after you were taken, instead of rescuing you straightaway, my men followed you, hoping your captors would lead them to your father." The Brigadier paused as if in thought. "But, never did I expect this operation would cost him his life. I'm sorry, very sorry, Kuan Hee."

"It's not your fault, Mr Walmsley," Kuan Hee said. "Those men dumped him in a room and left him to die. They're the ones responsible. They have to pay a price."

"Kuan Hee, let me take care of them," Brigadier Walmsley said. "Don't get involved. Return to Singapore after the funeral."

"Mr Walmsley, he's my dad," Kuan Hee said. "As his son, I have a duty to avenge him."

"But these are no ordinary men," Brigadier Walmsley

said. "They're professionals—sent by powerful people."

"Let me think over what you've said, Mr Walmsley," Kuan Hee said.

"Lina, make sure he doesn't get himself into trouble," Brigadier Walmsley said.

"I will. I will, Mr Walmsley," Lina said. Kuan Hee glared at her.

The Brigadier hauled himself from the bench and plodded to the entrance with Kuan Hee and Lina at his tail. Outside, the rain had petered out. The pair watched as the Brigadier, in his hunting hat, waddled into the back of a waiting car.

CHAPTER 16

After a day of rain, the skies over Medan cleared and the streets basked in the sunlight. The midday heat resumed its embrace of the city. In her haste, Kuan Hee's mother had dumped only the bare essentials in a Duffel bag, which she carried with her onto the plane. Tim and Harry met her at Polonia Airport and they arrived at the funeral parlour in Uncle Kenny's car.

Mrs Wang flew to the coffin where the Professor's body lay. She reached inside to touch his face and hair. She mumbled into his ears. She was crying inside her; she was not one to show her feelings openly.

Kuan Hee pulled Lina aside. He knew his mother wanted to be alone with his father. There were so many things that she would have to say to him. Kuan Hee had to let his parents have their last private moments together.

"Now that Mum's here," Kuan Hee said, "Dad won't be lonely anymore."

The funeral, which took place the next day, was a simple affair and the Professor's body was cremated in the afternoon.

"Your father left so suddenly," Mrs Wang said, staring into space. "I can't believe he's gone." Then she looked into Kuan Hee's eyes. "I've to return to Fort Bragg with your father's ashes. There is a memorial for colleagues and friends to attend. Once I have settled matters, I will fly home."

"Mum. I may not be home soon," Kuan Hee said. "Lina and I have to remain here for a while."

"Your father's gone," Mrs Wang said. "I don't want you gone too. Leave things be. Return to Singapore and wait for me. Besides, you can't be leaving Huei Huei with your in-laws."

"It's alright, Mum," Lina said. "My mother won't mind. In fact, she loves to take care of Huei Huei."

"Kuan Hee, did you hear what I just said?" Mrs Wang asked. Kuan Hee nodded. That was all he could do. It was the only thing he could do. He knew talking back to his mother would result in a never-ending tirade. That would bring her to tears and his plan would be ruined.

That evening, Kuan Hee's mother left Medan. She had no wish to stay longer in this place, which held nothing but bad memories for her. In her parting words, she pleaded with Kuan Hee not to disappoint her.

Kuan Hee was in two minds as he and his *kakis* milled around in the living room on the second storey of Uncle Kenny's house. Should he remain in Medan to track his father's killers and retrieve the mind clone cartridge that they had stolen from his father? Or should he do as his mother wanted—return to Singapore? He didn't want his mother to despair further. He opened the United States diplomatic passport issued in his name and flipped through it. On one page was an arrival stamp bearing a Polonia Airport immigration officer's signature and serial number on it. It seemed genuine. The Brigadier had everything arranged for him. He would be letting the Brigadier down too if he remained here.

"I've found him," Harry said, stumbling into the living room. "I know where he is hiding."

"What the dickens?" Kuan Hee said, as the four guests turned to look at their host, perplexed.

Catching his breath, Harry eyed the others in the room. "Alfredo! He's still in Brastagi."

"*Wah seh*, that's the best piece of news I've heard in ages," Tim said as everyone huddled on the floor.

"He's been staying with his sister in a village in Brastagi," Harry said. "If we hurry, we should be able to catch him."

"How long will it take on the road?" Tim asked.

"An hour or so," Harry said.

"It's already past eight o'clock," Lina said. "Will it be too dark out there?"

"No matter how late, I'll go meet him," Kuan Hee said. "You stay here, Lina."

"I want to go with you," Lina said.

"Shall we take the hardware?" Navin asked.

"We have to," Tim said. "Alfredo has an M16 with him."

"And my Steyr AUG as well," Kuan Hee said.

"My minibus's ready," Harry said, as he retrieved some flashlights from a cabinet in the room.

With everyone crowded into the minibus, Harry drove off. The minibus cruised past the city lights into the dimly lit rural roads towards Brastagi. It was a bumpy ride but the Singaporeans were no longer feeling nauseous.

After meandering along a track off the main road, the minibus came to a halt. The moon was conspicuously absent. The minibus's headlamps lit up the bushes in front of it. Elsewhere it was darkness. Yet Harry seemed to know his way around. Kuan Hee tapped his smartphone screen. At once, the OLED screen lit up showering light into the darkened surroundings. It was showing 8:23 p.m.

The occupants poured out of the minibus, slinging their backpacks and fumbling for flashlights. With Harry in front, they trod into the darkness. One by one, shabby huts appeared in the glow of the flashlights. These were obscured by vegetation and sometimes, the five friends had to stumble along narrow paths. They were deep in a village, which lacked the convenience of streetlamps. Suddenly, Harry stopped and the intruders knocked into one another. He gave the signal for them to switch off their flashlights. Apparently, they had arrived at their destination. The home of Alfredo's sister was metres ahead of them, but it was pitch-black everywhere. Tim and Harry drew their rifles and prowled through the darkness.

The minutes passed slowly as Kuan Hee, Lina and Navin crouched in the vegetation. Mosquitoes were having the feast of their lives, delighted by the unannounced arrival of their human guests. The intruders cursed and swore as they scratched their necks, arms and legs.

Then ahead, leaves in the bushes rustled and branches snapped. Someone was approaching. The intruders froze. They were unarmed. In front of them, three figures appeared, two flanking one who seemed to be staggering. It was Tim, Harry and—Alfredo!

Tim and Harry let go of Alfredo and he fell onto the grass. Harry shone a flashlight onto Alfredo's face. The Batak native was distressed. Both Indonesians unleashed a torrent of Bahasa Indonesia, which pierced the silence of the night.

"What's he saying?" Tim asked.

"What are both saying?" Kuan Hee asked. They had to wait a while longer for their answer, for the two Indonesians were still in animated conversation.

Then silence reigned. Harry stared into Alfredo's eyes. It was some moments before Harry spoke.

"He says he needed money for his mother's hospital bill," Harry said. "He says he had no choice. His mother needed treatment."

"He could have come to us," Tim said. "We could have helped."

"That's what I told him," Harry said. "I believe he's not telling the whole story."

"Ask him who got him and me to go to your rescue," Kuan Hee said.

"I already did," Harry said. "He says an acquaintance brought a Chinese man to him. He didn't want to do the job at first, but the Chinese man threatened to harm his family. So he went along."

"Who's the man?" Kuan Hee asked. "Where can we find him?"

Harry rattled off in Bahasa Indonesia to Alfredo.

"He says the Chinese man who contacted him did not give any name," Harry said. "But he found out from his acquaintance the man's name is He Bin. He doesn't know where he is. But, he thinks his acquaintance knows."

"We've got to find his acquaintance first," Tim said.

"Question is—will Alfredo help us find him?" Kuan Hee said.

Harry resumed his conversation with Alfredo. Alfredo kept nodding. There was hope yet.

"Alfredo understands he needs to help us," Harry said. "He has no choice. Otherwise, I'll tell everyone in Brastagi what he did. He won't be able to make a living here anymore."

"Can we trust him?" Navin asked. "I'm not sure I want someone who has betrayed us around us. He could betray us again."

"Navin's right," Tim said.

"But, we've no choice. The acquaintance is our only lead," Kuan Hee said.

"Yeah, afraid so," Tim said.

"Then we've got to keep an eye on him," Navin said. "A real close eye."

"It's set," Kuan Hee said. "Harry, tell him we won't let him off if he tells on us again."

"Do we take him back with us?" Navin said.

"Yes," Harry said. "He's agreed to come with us."

"My Steyr AUG's with him," Kuan Hee said.

"He's hidden it somewhere," Harry said. "He'll take us

480

to it now."

Lina was most glad to be moving again. Those horrid mosquitoes had left itchy bumps all over her arms and legs.

With its human cargo laden, the minibus weaved its way out of the village and emerged on the main road.

"We're going to Alfredo's home," Harry said. But they did not visit the house. They stopped on a track behind the house. Harry, Tim and Alfredo alighted to retrieve the two rifles, which were concealed in a small shed away from the house.

CHAPTER 17

The sun peeped over the low buildings in Medan. As it made its ascent, its warmth enveloped the city and its rays shone into the windows of homes. Its glare caressed Lina's face and she opened her eyes. It was morning, yet Lina felt tired. She had not had her full forty winks. The previous night had taken a toll on her. She felt the mattress next to her. Kuan Hee was not in bed. *Has he left without me?* She shook off the blanket and strode out into the living room.

"Ah! You're finally awake," Kuan Hee said, looking up. He had been poring over a map of the city. "I'm studying the map. Need to familiarize myself with the city."

"Where're the others?" Lina asked.

"Downstairs," Kuan Hee said. "Did you think I was going to leave you all alone here?"

"You dare?" Lina said as she sat next to him.

"We're going to Sun Plaza, an old shopping centre," Kuan Hee said. "Alfredo's acquaintance works there—in the cinema."

"When?" Lina asked.

"After breakfast," Kuan Hee said. "Tim has bought some packets of fried *kway teow* from the market behind."

It was 10:00 a.m. when the men and Lina packed into

the minibus parked outside the shophouse. They had not taken along their rifles, for the Provincial Governor's Office was a minute's walk away from the mall; they didn't want to risk being found with firearms in the city. In Indonesia, unauthorized possession of firearms warranted a maximum jail sentence of twenty years. It might even attract the death penalty. But this did not deter many from carrying firearms. It was only a problem if they were discovered doing so. Even then, money quickly settled things.

The minibus pulled into the car park outside Sun Plaza, which was a walk away from Jalan Muara Takus.

Alfredo pointed to a middle-aged man in a plain blue long-sleeved shirt and grey pants, squatting against the parapet on the roadside pavement, puffing away at his *kretek*. He was oblivious to the happenings around him; he seemed deep in thought.

"Let's sidle up to him, pretend we are buying food from the cart vendor next to him," Tim said.

"Don't," Kuan Hee said. "We'll stand out like a sore thumb. Don't forget we're foreigners here."

"I'll go," Harry said.

"Look! He's got up. He's moving," Navin said.

"Let's follow him," Kuan Hee said.

"Looks like he's going back to work," Tim said, "in the cinema."

Alfredo's acquaintance entered Sun Plaza with his tail trailing at a safe distance. He took the escalator up to the fourth storey and disappeared into the Cinemaxx theatre. The posse lingered on the floor directly below, leaning on the glass railings and glancing up at the theatre entrance occasionally, but the man was nowhere to be seen. It was a fruitless watch that day.

"I vote we keep watch on this guy for a few days," Kuan Hee said, "till we find a lead."

"But, it'll be like looking for a needle in a haystack," Navin said.

"Do we have a choice?" Kuan Hee said. All shook their heads in agreement.

"This is a big mall, but we can't be standing here the whole day," Navin said. "People will take notice for sure."

"We'll take turns then," Tim said.

"The mall is about five hundred metres away from my house," Harry said. "It will be a breeze walking over."

It was Kuan Hee and Lina who were to do duty at Sun Plaza the next day.

"Let's take a *becak* there," Lina implored.

"But it's so near," Kuan Hee said. In the end, he hailed a *becak* and the pair scooted off, with the owner peddling the contraption from behind them and ringing a bell intermittently as the *becak* moved alongside hordes of motorcycles, with their horns blaring. It weaved through the traffic effortlessly, letting the pair take in the sights and sounds of the neighbourhood. They never felt this close to the road before; their feet were dangling inches above the asphalt.

"What if it rains, Kuan Hee?" Lina asked, peering at the flimsy canvas overhead sheltering them from the sun. "We'll get wet."

"Don't be silly," Kuan Hee said.

Upon arrival at the mall, the pair scouted for a suitable spot to keep watch on the theatre. Finally, they settled on a familiar name—Killiney—located on the third level. The Singapore homegrown coffeeshop chain had an outlet in Medan.

The pair took seats at a table overlooking the wide concourse, ordered coffee, and settled down for the long haul. Lina had brought along something to read. Kuan Hee, ever the perfectionist in whatever he did, proudly proclaimed, "I've got Little Busy with me." He placed the robot housefly and its remote on the small table. Poor AleXander the robots had to contend with the dark interior of Kuan Hee's backpack.

It was a good half hour before their target appeared. There he was, riding the escalator up to the fourth level. Apparently, he was still wearing the same clothes they had seen him in the day before.

Kuan Hee glanced around the shop before releasing Little Busy into the air. The robot housefly darted and danced forward and then flew upwards towards the theatre level. Then it disappeared out of sight into the theatre and the pair had to manoeuvre it using the remote.

They found the man, broom and dustpan in hand, pacing through a cinema hall, cleaning the place. Little Busy perched itself on a wall light to conserve power. The dim lights in the hall could not generate enough energy for the tiny solar panels on its body to absorb.

His work done, the man found a spot on a staircase landing next to the cinema hall exit and promptly made himself comfortable. In minutes, he was lying sprawled on the bare concrete floor, taking a snooze. Little Busy rested on a railing, not taking its eyes off the slumped figure.

"It's been a boring morning," Kuan Hee declared over the phone to Tim, who was back at the shophouse.

Lunchtime found the pair partaking of *mee siam* and *mee rebus* at the coffeeshop. Harry and Alfredo came up to them and took their seats.

"He's moving again," Lina said. The posse glued their eyes on the screen, watching their target move around the theatre. Finally, he appeared at the entrance of the theatre.

"Must be looking for food," Kuan Hee said. "Time for us to move too." He let the robot housefly hover behind the man and attach itself to his belt. "There! I've my hands free again." Then he folded the remote.

Outside Sun Plaza, the man approached a street vendor who had parked his motorized cart by the roadside. He was soon tucking into a bowl of *mee soto*. When he had finished with lunch, he whipped out his *kretek* and took long drags on it. Then he squatted down by the roadside and busied himself with his phone.

"This is frustrating," Kuan Hee said.

"Are we really going to be doing this for the next few days?" Lina groaned as the posse followed the man back into the mall.

All of a sudden, Kuan Hee stopped, and those behind him knocked into one another. Their target had turned back and was heading in their direction. *Good Lord! Has he seen us?* Kuan Hee wondered.

The posse turned their backs to the man, pretending to be in conversation with one another. But the man did not walk past them. Kuan Hee looked back. The man was nowhere to be seen.

"*Alamak!* He's disappeared," Kuan Hee said. They took to their heels, striding to where they had last seen him.

"Look! A door," Harry said. "He must have gone that way."

They scrambled through the door and out into a service road. There was no sign of their target.

"Drat!" Kuan Hee said. Then he realized Little Busy was on the man. *All is not lost!* He drew its remote and fingered the icons on the screen. "We have him. He's gone in that direction." They ran in the direction Kuan Hee had pointed.

"He's gone into Jalan KH Zainul Arifin," Harry said. "He's trying to hail a taxi."

"We need the minibus," Kuan Hee said. "We can't compete with a taxi."

"Wait here for me," Harry said. He grabbed Alfredo's arm and both men sprinted back to the car park where he had parked the minibus.

When he returned in the minibus, Kuan Hee and Lina got inside.

"The taxi went that way. It's a blue taxi with a bird on top," Kuan Hee said. "The map shows him moving along Jalan Pangerang Diponegoro. He's moving south towards Jalan Jendera Sudirman."

"Got it," Harry said. "Don't worry, I won't lose him."

"He's moved into Jalan Masdulhak," Kuan Hee said.

"I think I see the blue taxi ahead," Harry said.

"Yeah. That's it alright," Kuan Hee said. "It's the same toys hanging on the back window."

Harry stepped on the throttle and the minibus was soon tailing the blue taxi. "The taxi's turned into Jalan Walikota. It's—it's entering a car park. K-F-C. It's a KFC restaurant." Harry parked the minibus away from the entrance of the restaurant.

The KFC restaurant was a stand-alone single-storeyed building with alfresco dining on the side facing Jalan Walikota.

Harry pointed to their target. He was sitting under a big umbrella, enjoying his *kretek*. He kept looking at his phone. He seemed to be waiting for someone.

The posse took their seats eight tables away from their target.

"No need to be too near him," Kuan Hee said. "As long as we can see him. We've got Little Busy on him."

"Where's this place anyway?" Kuan Hee asked.

"We are near the Chinese Consulate-General's office in Medan," Harry said. "It's just around the corner."

As Harry spoke, a man ambled past their table. The man moved farther away from them towards their target and promptly took a seat next to him. He had his back to his watchers. They only saw he was short and stout.

"Time for Little Busy to do its work," Kuan Hee declared. He turned up the microphone in the robot housefly. At once, the remote reverberated with the conversation between the two men. They were talking in Bahasa Indonesia. It was Sanskrit to the Singaporeans so Harry did translation on the fly.

"He wants money from the stout man," Harry explained. "He claims Alfredo needs to run and hide from his pursuers."

"That's nonsense," Kuan Hee said. "Alfredo's right here with us."

"They don't know that," Lina said.

Alfredo rattled off something in Bahasa Indonesia.

"Alfredo says his acquaintance is lying through his teeth. He says they hadn't been in touch since the incident."

"This slacker must want easy money," Kuan Hee said. "He's a parasite."

"The other man is taking something from his pocket," Lina said. "I can't make out what it is."

"He's actually paying off the fellow," Kuan Hee exclaimed.

"How much?" Lina asked. But they were too far away to see the transaction. "Did they say how much?"

"Ten million rupiahs," Harry said.

"How much's that?" Lina asked.

"Five hundred Singapore dollars," Harry said.

"Only five hundred dollars?" Kuan Hee said. "That lowlife arranged my kidnapping for such a small sum?" He could hardly believe his ears.

"It's actually more," Harry said. "This five hundred dollars is a subsequent payment."

"Ask Alfredo how much they paid him to do the job," Kuan Hee said.

"Sixteen million rupiahs. Eight hundred Singapore dollars," Harry said, after conversing with Alfredo.

"That's a paltry sum," Kuan Hee said, "to play out a friend."

"Remember, Kuan Hee. Indonesia is a poor country," Harry said. "It doesn't take much to arrange a hit."

"The stout man is leaving," Lina said. "He's—he's walking this way."

The posse pretended to be in conversation with one another. The stout man veered near them as he made his way towards Jalan Walikota. He took no notice of them; his eyes were staring into the distance. They could see him clearly now. He was Chinese, fair and had a big beer belly. He was possibly in his middle forties.

It was the way the Chinese man walked that jogged Kuan Hee's memory. He took short swaying steps as he moved. Kuan Hee recalled seeing similar gait. *Now where did I see this?* Suddenly he realized the man was the one on the jetty shouting orders to his kidnappers on Samosir Island.

"He's the one," Kuan Hee stammered. "He's one of the kidnappers."

"What?" Lina said.

Alfredo mumbled something in Bahasa Indonesia to Harry.

"Alfredo says this man is He Bin. He's the one who threatened him into betraying you," Harry said.

"Quick! We've got to follow him," Kuan Hee snapped. At once, the group sprang to their feet.

"What about the other fellow?" Harry asked.

"Forget him," Kuan Hee said. "It's He Bin we're after." As the group strode towards the main road, Kuan Hee ordered Little Busy to detach itself from the Indonesian and return to base. Soon the robot drone was flitting over the remote in Kuan Hee's hand.

The posse's new target, He Bin, was about thirty metres ahead of them. He was walking along the side of a two-laned road lined with big trees, which hid the road from the sun's glare. There was a long line of motorcycles on the opposite side of the road, with scores of young Indonesian men huddled in casual conversation outside zinc-roofed shanties.

"I think he's heading for the Chinese consulate," Harry said.

Their target turned left and entered a gated compound, unaware he had been tailed. As the group approached the gate, they saw a single-storeyed bungalow with a thatched roof peeping over a row of tall bushes, which lined a low wrought-iron fence facing the road.

The group stood beside a huge tree with a massive trunk, pondering their next step.

"This is not the Chinese consulate," Harry said. "The

next building's the consulate." Harry pointed to a big three-storeyed building with an imposing portico jutting out in the middle. A gold ornate wrought-iron gate stood at both entrances to the compound, with a tall concrete wall, topped with ornate wrought-iron spikes, tucked between the gates.

"*Wah!* So opulent," Lina exclaimed.

"Is this a Chinese neighbourhood?" Kuan Hee asked.

"No," Harry said. "See the Indonesian men across the road? These men live around here. We Chinese live only in certain areas of Medan, like Jalan Muara Takus, where we're the majority. It's safer this way."

"You're saying, then, that He Bin is linked in some way to the Chinese consulate next door," Kuan Hee said.

"Likely," Harry said. "I don't see any other reasonable explanation."

"So, the Chinese consulate is smack in the middle of my kidnapping," Kuan Hee said.

There was silence in the group as they took in the severity of Kuan Hee's revelation.

"Let's go back to your house," Kuan Hee said. "We need to powwow."

"What about He Bin?" Lina asked.

"I think he's stationed here," Kuan Hee said. "In fact, I'm quite sure. We won't lose him. Let's come back another day."

CHAPTER 18

That evening, in the second storey living room of Uncle Kenny's shophouse, the four Singaporeans and their two Indonesian friends gathered. They snuggled down on cushions laid on the cold ceramic floor.

"We have to crack our heads over this matter," Kuan Hee said. "The Chinese government has entered the equation."

"People's Republic of China?" Lina said. Kuan Hee nodded.

"You are saying the Chinese government wants your father's mind clone cartridge?" Tim said. Kuan Hee nodded.

"That's espionage," Navin said.

"Did the Brigadier say anything about this?" Tim asked. Kuan Hee shook his head. "I have yet to talk to him."

"So this chap, He Bin, you saw this afternoon is the same person who kidnapped you?" Navin said.

"For sure," Kuan Hee said. "My kidnappers thought I was unconscious, but the stupefying drug had worn off. I was as alert as any of them. It's the same man all right. Same clumsy walk. Same bloated face. His chin seemed to blend with his neck. I'll never forget his pudgy chin."

"Question is—who's this fella He Bin?" Navin said.

"We can assume he belongs to the Chinese consulate," Tim said. "He's got to be one of their employees."

"He's definitely not an Indonesian Chinese," Harry said. "He's a foreigner."

"Tim, google the Chinese consulate in Medan," Kuan Hee said.

"Already done," Tim said as he tapped on his iPad to bring up the browser. "Did all the work while you were still on the road. Here!" He laid the iPad on the floor for all to take a look. They huddled closer.

"The Chinese consulate office serves the different provinces in North Sumatra. Besides the Consular Affairs Office, it also hosts the Science and Technology Office," Navin said.

"Science and Technology Office?" Lina parroted.

"Yeah," Navin said. "I figure this He Bin you tailed is connected in some way to this office."

"He didn't look like a diplomat," Kuan Hee said. "More like a runner. Those men with him at the jetty looked like thugs."

"Probably they are the ones doing the ground work," Tim said. "We need to locate the point man. He is the one with the answers we seek."

"He must be the one who ordered the kidnappings," Kuan Hee said, his voice croaking. "He's the one who killed my dad." Lina grasped his arm and squeezed it gently.

"Could it be—these men are part of a triad, eager to lay their hands on your father's mind clone cartridge so that they can sell it to the highest bidder?" Navin said. "And the Chinese government is not involved?"

"It's possible," Kuan Hee said, "that these people are only interested in money. To them, it's just a commercial transaction. They gang up for mutual benefit. Their pay's much lower than ours. They have to find a way to feed their vices."

"We are guessing. We need more information," Tim said. "We have to recce the place."

"I agree," Navin said.

"Let me google a map of the road," Tim said. He opened the Google Maps app and typed the road's name. Then he switched to a street view of Jalan Walikota. He scrolled through the street. "Where's the house He Bin went into?"

Kuan Hee took over the iPad and dragged the images on the screen till it showed the bungalow. "That's the house. And this grand building next to it is the Chinese consulate."

"It'll be difficult not to be noticed," Harry said. "The shops opposite are frequented by young locals. You can't watch from there. You will stand out."

"Can we use your minibus?" Kuan Hee asked. "We can stake out the place in your minibus instead. See the cars parked along the road?" He fingered the vehicles on the roadside. "A minibus will not look out of place here."

"No problem," Harry said. "No problem."

"Harry, is it OK for you to be spending so much time with us?" Tim asked. "How about your shop?"

"No worries," Harry said. "My staff will look after it. Anyway, Chloe will be back soon. She can take over then."

"Who's Chloe?" Lina asked.

"His wife *lah*," Tim said.

"I forgot," Lina said. "She's visiting her parents right?" Harry nodded.

"We'll let Little Busy and Tizzy do the work for us," Kuan Hee said. "Little Busy will explore the house, and Tizzy will take a look inside the consulate."

"I'll take charge of Tizzy," Navin said.

"Why can't we go into the consulate?" Lina asked. "We can pretend to be looking for information."

"I've thought of it," Kuan Hee said. "But I don't want to take chances. These men may already know our faces. For sure, they can recognise me. They could have been watching us in Parapat or the funeral parlour. I don't want to alert them."

The next morning saw Jalan Walikota teeming with motorcycles. Hordes of young Indonesian men were ensconced on motorcycles and wooden benches on the sidewalk, chattering away amid the hum of motorcycle engines.

Harry parked his minibus opposite the bungalow, away from the rows of motorcycles lining the roadside. Alfredo was next to him. In the back, the four Singaporeans sat two abreast, peering across the road at the bungalow.

The bungalow looked lonely next to its neighbour, which had a steady stream of visitors the whole morning.

"It seems deserted," Lina said. "There's not a soul around."

"You spoke too soon," Tim said, pointing to a familiar figure sauntering along the sidewalk across from them.

"It's He Bin," Kuan Hee said. "He's got to be working here. I'll get Little Busy after him." He slid open a window to let Little Busy out of the minibus. It soared into the air and flitted across the road towards its target, He Bin. Soon it was no more in sight; it had disappeared behind the tall bushes with the Chinese operative.

On Little Busy's remote, Kuan Hee and Lina watched He Bin walk up to a man at a small desk in the porch.

"It's not really deserted after all," Lina said.

"Yes. There's someone guarding the compound," Kuan Hee said. He was giving a running commentary to the others who were seated away from the remote's screen. "Chinese. Early thirties. Close-cropped hair. Burly. Wait, there's something under the desk. It's—it's a short assault rifle."

"Let me take a look at the screen," Tim said. Kuan Hee held up the remote. Tim and Navin, who were seated behind the pair, analysed the silhouette in the image.

"QBZ-95," Tim declared. "A bullpup assault rifle used

by the People's Liberation Army."

"Why do they need assault rifles to guard the bungalow?" Lina asked.

"Might be something secretive they're doing inside," Kuan Hee said. "Otherwise, they don't need an armed guard."

"He Bin has gone inside the house," Navin said. "Quick! Let Little Busy go after him."

"All in good time," Kuan Hee said. "It's a small place. He can't go far."

"Yah *hor*," Navin said. "I forgot."

"No need to get excited so early," Tim said, smiling.

"Navin, I'm beginning to think my kidnapping is sanctioned by the Chinese government. It's not these guys moonlighting," Kuan Hee said.

"I agree. I made a wrong guess yesterday. You don't see moonlighters brandishing assault rifles in broad daylight next door to a consulate," Navin said. "The Chinese government must be behind your kidnapping."

Kuan Hee let Little Busy slip under the front door into the house. The remote's screen fogged immediately. As the robot drone acclimatized to the cool temperature inside the house, a wide corridor stretching the width of the house appeared on the screen. At the end of the corridor sat a large man next to the back door. He was guarding the door. There was a QBZ-95 resting on his lap. Little Busy flitted through the corridor to a window on the right. Its cameras peeked through the clear glass panel.

"It's a lab all right," Kuan Hee screeched.

"What?" Tim exclaimed, as he and Navin craned their necks to take a closer look. There were big pieces of equipment in the large room, which occupied half of the house. At the far end of the room, two men in lab whites were at work at computer monitors on a long table, flanked by racks of computer servers. Beyond them was a small partitioned area with glass windows. It was difficult to see what was inside.

"It's got robotic assemblers and DNA Molecular Assembly units," Tim said. Both he and Kuan Hee were specialists in nanotechnology, so they were familiar with the equipment.

"It's a cloning laboratory," Kuan Hee said, "albeit a small one."

"Yeah," Tim said. "Still, it must cost a bomb to set up."

"The evidence is piling up. It has to be a government operation," Kuan Hee said. "The Chinese government is behind my dad's death."

"Where's He Bin? Navin asked.

"He's got to be on the other side of the house," Kuan Hee said. He commanded the robot housefly drone to fly to the fork in the corridor. There were five doors in this part of the corridor—three on the side facing the front of the house. "The doors are shut and there are no openings under three of them for Little Busy to go through. We'll try the first door on the left."

Little Busy landed on the floor next to the door and crawled through the small opening into the room. On the remote's screen, a water closet loomed large above the robot housefly.

"Drat! It's a toilet," Kuan Hee said, as he manoeuvred Little Busy out of the small room.

"See if we have better luck with the next," Kuan Hee said as he let the drone squeeze under the door of the next room. "It's a changing room with lockers, a small table and chairs. There's a pantry at one end."

"We have to wait for someone to come out from the other three rooms," Lina said.

"Or go in," Kuan Hee said.

They didn't have to wait long, for the bungalow was a hive of activity today. The door opposite the changing room creaked open and a gaggle of men in lab whites poured into the corridor.

Little Busy darted through the air into the room.

"It's a conference room," Lina said. "They must have

been attending a meeting."

"Two more rooms left and both are at the end of the corridor," Kuan Hee said, as he let the robot housefly perch itself on the wall at the end of the corridor. "He Bin could be inside either room."

Finally, the door on the drone's right opened and out stepped He Bin and another man—middle-aged and bespectacled. Part of a desk and wall cabinet peeped through the opening in the doorway.

"Another office," Kuan Hee said. "Wonder who this chap next to He Bin is."

"Might be the man in charge of this place," Tim said. "Look at the way he swaggers in the corridor."

"Then he's He Bin's boss?" Navin said.

Little Busy darted above He Bin and the man as they walked towards the large room. The man looked into a square screen mounted on the wall beside the door. At once, the door slid open and both men entered, with Little Busy flitting overhead. The robot drone suddenly rocked and wobbled before recovering its balance.

"There's something in the air over the doorway," Kuan Hee said. "Something at the door could be spraying vaporized hydrogen peroxide to decontaminate visitors."

The room was alive with activity. There had to be a dozen people in it. He Bin's boss chatted with a wizened man in lab white as they stood next to the partitioned area.

Little Busy flew over their heads and hovered next to the glass partition. Its cameras took in the view of the room's interior.

"There's a man lying on a gurney inside. He's got a maze of wires all over his scalp," Lina said. "They connect to this big apparatus that looks like a hairdressing salon's hair perming machine. There are monitors around the room—like those you see in the hospital."

"His eyes are closed," Kuan Hee said. "Could be unconscious or sleeping."

"What are these men saying?" Harry asked. Though an

Indonesian Chinese, he didn't understand a word of Mandarin. The schools in Medan did not offer Chinese as a subject. His father spoke to him in *Hokkien* at home so there was no urgent need to learn his mother tongue.

"The man in lab white says the patient is in stable condition," Kuan Hee explained. "He says the transplant will be completed in two days."

"What transplant is he talking about?" Lina asked.

"Beats me," Kuan Hee said. "He used *yí zhí*. I think it means transplant."

"What kind of transplant takes two days?" Navin said. "A patient can die in the process. Perhaps, he means the operation will be carried out in two days."

"It's not what he said in Mandarin," Kuan Hee said.

"Let's not bicker," Lina said.

"Look! He Bin's boss is leaving the room," Tim said.

He Bin and his boss walked out of the house with Little Busy tailing them. They sauntered through the compound and out into the sidewalk.

The posse looked out of the minibus. He Bin and his boss were walking into the Chinese consulate next door.

"Let's go home," Kuan Hee said. "We've found enough information for today. We need to analyse our findings." He directed Little Busy back to its remote and the posse headed back to Jalan Muara Takus for lunch. Everyone was glad to get out of the minibus; they had been crammed inside the entire morning.

CHAPTER 19

Evening found the six friends in a room above Harry's provision shop. They lined the floor along the perimeter of the room, resting their backs on the wall, watching television on a wall-mounted screen as they discussed the happenings of the day.

"We still don't know the name of He Bin's boss," Kuan Hee said.

"But I can guess he runs the show there," Tim said.

"And there are so many men in lab whites," Lina said. "I counted eight."

"I think they are scientists," Navin said.

"The outside looks deserted," Lina said. "Yet it's such a busy place inside."

"Why did the Chinese government pick Medan for the lab?" Kuan Hee said. "Doesn't make sense. It's so laid-back."

"I guess it's a perfect cover," Tim said. "I mean, no one walking past the house would suspect anything. Their activities are so well hidden."

"And the laws are lax here," Harry said. "It's easy to get things done."

"I'm still trying to figure out what they are doing with

the man on the gurney," Kuan Hee said. "And why here of all places. Singapore has everything—the latest technology. And it's only an hour away from here by air."

"Just imagine, they take two days to do an operation on the man," Navin said.

"It might have been longer," Lina said. "We don't know how long he's had the wires on his head."

"Wires on his head," Kuan Hee parroted. "That's it. Why didn't I think of it before?"

"Think of what?" Navin said. "You're not making sense, Kuan Hee."

"The man with the wires on his head," Kuan Hee said. "He's undergoing a memory transfer process. They are either wiping his memories or transcribing new ones."

"You mean, like Colonel Tee and Jordan?" Lina said.

"Yes, exactly," Kuan Hee said.

"So the Chinese scientists are experimenting with memory control too," Tim said. "The same thing your father was doing."

"No wonder they are after your father's mind clone cartridge," Navin said.

"What did you just say, Navin?" Kuan Hee said.

"Huh?" Navin said.

"Navin said that's why they are after your father's mind clone cartridge," Tim said.

"That's it," Kuan Hee said. "That's got to be it."

"What?" Navin said. "You've got this bad habit of keeping us in suspense over your words."

"It's my dad's memories that are being transferred into that man's brain," Kuan Hee said.

"S-e-r-i-o-u-s?" Navin stammered. He sat upright. The others followed suit.

"That man lying on the gurney in the room is receiving my dad's memories," Kuan Hee said.

"He's like another Colonel Tee?" Lina said.

"Yes." Kuan Hee said. "My father's memories are going into his head."

"What you guys talking about?" Harry said. He was unable to keep up with their conversation.

"Now I understand everything," Kuan Hee said. "The Chinese government has got some willing scientist to be a guinea pig. It got my dad's memories transplanted into his brain." He paused in thought. "Horror of horrors! This chap can do what my dad can do. He is my dad—resurrected!" Kuan Hee's face reddened.

"We've got to stop them," Tim said. "With your father's knowledge falling into the wrong hands, there's no telling what evil they will do."

"We've got to terminate this man," Kuan Hee said. "At all costs."

A loud thud above them, followed by the sound of scurrying feet, sent goose pimples rippling down Lina's spine.

"It's rats," Harry explained, pointing to the ceiling boards. "There is a whole family up there."

"Don't tease her," Tim said. "She's very timid."

Lina leaned against Kuan Hee's shoulder, seeking relief, but he was oblivious to the distraction. He was deep in thought, plotting revenge.

"Kuan Hee," Lina cried out.

"Sorry," Kuan Hee said as he caressed her in his arm. "Sorry."

"We have to get rid of the man with the wires on his head," Tim said.

"Yes, we can't have another Colonel Tee in this world," Navin said.

"He's not another Colonel Tee," Kuan Hee blared. "He's my dad. My dad doesn't do evil."

"Kuan Hee, pipe down," Tim said. "Navin didn't mean it that way. He's right. Your dad's memories in this man's brain can cause a lot of harm to the world. There's no telling what evil these people are up to. We've got to stop them."

"That's what I mean," Navin said. "No offence meant,

Kuan Hee."

"I'm sorry I got all worked up," Kuan Hee said. Tears were welling in his eyes. "I never thought I would ever see my dad again. But this man has got his memories. He'll behave like my dad. It will be like seeing my dad alive again." Lina grasped his arm. She saw the hurt in his eyes as he grappled with the stark truth. He had to kill the man.

"Now we need to ponder the big question. Where's the mind clone cartridge?" Tim said.

"Yeah *hor*," Lina said. "We need to destroy the disk."

"Nope," Kuan Hee said. "I got to get my hands on it. It holds my dad's memories. His thoughts. His ideas. His lifetime of work—everything! I can't bear to see it destroyed."

"The mind clone cartridge should be in the house," Navin said. "They had to have used it to carry out the memory transfer."

"We need to go to the house again," Tim said, "when nobody's around."

"Night time's the best time," Navin said.

"What say you, Kuan Hee?" Tim said.

"OK," Kuan Hee said. "And we must work on the man on the gurney."

"What work?" Tim said.

"Perhaps, perhaps, we can reverse the process," Kuan Hee said. "Erase my dad's memories from the man."

"Do you know how to do it?" Tim asked.

"Er…nope," Kuan Hee said.

"You have no inkling?" Tim said. "Stop dwelling on this idea. We're running against time. We need to do the necessary."

"Kill him?" Kuan Hee said.

"That was the original plan, right?" Tim said. "You were the one who said—kill him at all costs, remember?"

"I haven't forgotten," Kuan Hee said.

"Look, Kuan Hee. He isn't your father," Tim said. "Your father's left this world. You've got to accept this fact."

"I know," Kuan Hee said. "OK. Let's do it."

"That's the Kuan Hee I know," Tim said.

"We'll go back to the house tomorrow night," Kuan Hee said. "We'll prowl the premises tomorrow night."

CHAPTER 20

It was a beaming moon that greeted the adventurers as they climbed into Harry's minibus. Having rested the whole day, they were refreshed and raring to go. So with weapons laden and the team seated, the minibus screeched into the dimly lit neighbourhood.

"Remember our mission's goals tonight," Tim said.

"Get rid of the man on the gurney," Kuan Hee said.

"Find the mind clone cartridge," Navin said.

"But we don't know what the mind clone cartridge looks like," Lina said. "Or where it is."

"We'll play by ear," Tim said. "I'm pretty sure it's in there somewhere."

"Lina, you stay in the minibus," Kuan Hee said. "I don't want to have to worry about you." Lina nodded. This time she did not protest. Kuan Hee already had a load on his mind. He had to save his dear father's mind clone cartridge. She shouldn't make matters worse for him.

"Navin, you keep watch in the minibus with Lina," Tim said.

"But I can't drive," Navin said.

"This isn't a heist," Tim said. "We aren't making a getaway. Also, the solar film on the windows is nearly opaque. No one can look inside. You don't have to worry about a police spot-check. Just stay in the back of the minibus." Navin nodded.

"I'll take Alex with me," Kuan Hee said as he fished the two robots out of his backpack. "Xander will stay behind."

"I'll let Little Busy follow you," Lina said. "So I'll know you are OK."

Kuan Hee nodded. "Don't worry. Everything will go smoothly." But the tremulous tone of his voice betrayed his rhetoric.

"Kuan Hee and I will take the front," Tim said. "Harry, you take the back."

"How about Alfredo?" Harry asked.

"He'll come with us too," Tim said. "We need all the hands we can get," Tim said.

The minibus pulled to a stop along Jalan Walikota. It was just steps away from the front gate of the bungalow. Except for a few cars parked along the roadside, the street was deserted.

"It's too bright here," Tim said. "People can see us from a mile away. Is there a back lane, Harry?"

The minibus moved along the road and turned left. More big houses came into view. Then a grassy patch of land loomed on the left. It was infested with unwieldy low-lying vegetation. On their left, bounding the greenery were houses. One of them stood out with its massive size.

"It's the Chinese consulate," Tim said. "The building next to it must be the bungalow." He pointed to a single-storeyed building adjoining the massive building.

"Harry. Stop here," Tim said, "in front of the overhanging branches." The vehicle slowed to a halt by the side of the road. "Prime your weapons."

With the bolts of their rifles snicked into position, the team dismounted and stole into the knee-high grass in single file. There was an uneasy sense in each of the adventurers as they prowled in the darkness.

They crouched past the towering consulate building and arrived at its humble neighbour. Then they sprang into action, stepping on one another's shoulders and hauling one another over the low concrete wall into the compound of the bungalow. Within the grounds, they stooped, looking out for CCTVs on the walls and pillars. Unlike its snazzy neighbour, which gleamed under big floodlights perched on towers, the bungalow glowed faintly in the light provided by small spotlights. But it served the purpose of the four intruders well.

The back door to the house was about two car-lengths from the wall where the intruders huddled, hidden by overhanging branches, pondering their next move.

"We're lucky these branches block the light," Tim said.

"I'll get Alex to neutralize the CCTV cameras," Kuan Hee said as he released the robot from its darkened quarters. Its front panel flipped open when he pressed a button on its back. At his command, Alex leapt across the compound and up one wall. Then it released a stream of laser beams, vaporizing the camera. With the job done, it ran across the wall to the other cameras, its tiny suction pads gliding it effortlessly over the rough surface, and put the cameras out of action in no time.

"Time to move," Tim said.

As Kuan Hee prepared to come face to face with the man who was usurping his father's memories, a sense of uneasiness overwhelmed him.

What if he has become Dad? What if he speaks like Dad? What should I do? These were questions lingering on Kuan Hee's consciousness. He shuddered to think of the repercussions of him facing off against this malevolent manifestation of his father. He might not have the courage to kill the man.

Tim nudged Kuan Hee on his arm. "Kuan Hee, time to move." Kuan Hee woke from his thoughts. "Sorry, Tim."

Tim circled the perimeter of the house. There was no one guarding the place. He returned to where the other intruders were kneeling in wait. At Kuan Hee's order, Alex burned through the back door lock with his laser beam. Then, one by one, the intruders entered the premises, rifles at the ready. The house was in darkness. The air was still and stuffy. They groped their way to the fork in the corridor. Then they fanned out, with Kuan Hee and Tim checking out the laboratory, and the Indonesians looking through the other rooms on the other side.

Tim produced a flashlight and shone it around the big room. Both men sidled to the partitioned room. Through the window, they saw the silhouette of the gurney. Kuan Hee opened the door. They saw nothing on the gurney. Tim trained the flashlight on the gurney. It was indeed empty.

"Drat! The man with the wires on his head is not here," Kuan Hee said.

Just then, Harry and Alfredo came up behind them. Their long faces told Kuan Hee and Tim what they didn't want to hear. The house was empty of people. *Had they got wind of tonight's operation? Did Alfredo betray him again?* These were thoughts running through Kuan Hee's mind as he stared into Alfredo's eyes. Alfredo rattled off a string of Bahasa Indonesia words.

"He says he has nothing to do with this," Harry explained. "He did not tip them off."

"Important things first, Kuan Hee," Tim said. "Find the mind clone cartridge first."

"My dad's mind clone cartridge must be in here somewhere," Kuan Hee said.

The intruders spread out across the empty house, ransacking the cabinets and drawers.

"One room left to check out," Kuan Hee said as the intruders moved to the last room on their right. "This is the one we didn't see the other time."

"It's only a storeroom,' Harry said. "Alfredo and I went

through it just now."

Kuan Hee turned the knob and they entered the room. It was big for a storeroom. There were tall shelves lining both sides of the wall with laboratory equipment neatly stacked on them. There were cell disrupters, desiccators and analysers. One shelf stored cleanroom wipers, frocks and facemasks. Three nitrogen generators lined the end wall.

"These are state-of-the-art stuff that they got here," Tim said. "This is serious stuff they are doing here."

"My dad's mind clone cartridge," Kuan Hee reminded Tim. "Find it first."

"Sorry, Kuan Hee," Tim said as the four men fingered the shelves and equipment in the room. They even checked the walls.

"It's got to be here somewhere," Kuan Hee said. "All the expensive things are stored in this room." He bent down to examine the floor. "Shine a light on the floor, Tim." But it was a futile search.

"We've got to go," Tim said. "We can't stay here for too long. Someone may come back."

"But we haven't found my dad's mind clone cartridge," Kuan Hee protested. "We didn't get the man with the wires. We found nothing."

"We'll find them sooner or later," Tim said. "Let's get out of this place first. We've been here too long." He slung his rifle, grabbed Kuan Hee's arm and ushered him out of the storeroom with the Harry and Alfredo following them.

Indignant at the prospect of failing their mission, Kuan Hee unleashed his fury, shouting commands to Alex, the last to leave the room. At once, the robot released a torrent of laser beams at the equipment in the room, burning to a crisp everything in it, and sending the place up in flames.

"We've got to make a run for it," Tim said. "The whole house is on fire." He pulled Kuan Hee out of the house with Harry and Alfredo flanking them, and Alex at their heels. In the compound, the four intruders came face to face with a Chinese guard, who had apparently been out on an errand. The guard drew a pistol from his waist and fired at them.

"Kuan Hee!" Alfredo shouted as he lunged forward. A hail of bullets dug into his back. He slumped into Kuan Hee, uttering something in Bahasa Indonesia.

Harry shot back at the guard, felling him. Kuan Hee knelt beside Alfredo, who was grimacing in pain. Kuan Hee kept shaking his head. "Alfredo. Alfredo."

"We've got to move," Tim said. "Help me lift him up." Kuan Hee, shaken by the sudden turn of events, turned somber. He heaved Alfredo over Tim's shoulders and the intruders staggered towards the rear of the house, to the back gate. Behind them, the fire was devouring the house. Flames leapt into the air. The air was intensely hot.

Alex's laser beam burned through the metal gate lock and the intruders scrambled into the darkness.

Suddenly, the bungalow was no longer a pale shadow of its brightly lit neighbour. The flames over it glared proudly over the massive building beside it. Like a supernova, the bungalow seemed to be enjoying a sudden burst of attention, before it was reduced to rubble.

Lina and Navin were waiting at the side of the road. Lina had been impatient, fearing the worst, when she saw the fire raging over the bungalow. She insisted on getting out of the minibus and Navin couldn't stop her. He did manage to hold her back when she tried to wade into the low vegetation.

Tim and Kuan Hee came out of the bushes, panting. A bleeding Alfredo was strapped to their shoulders. Harry appeared a moment later, bearing rifles on his shoulders.

The intruders bundled into the minibus, which sped off into the dimly lit neighbourhood.

"Quick, hide the weapons," Harry shouted from the driver's seat. "There may be police on the road."

Tim stashed the rifles below the seats, using some rags

to cover them.

"Is he dead?" Lina asked.

"His chest is moving," Tim said. "He's not dead."

"Don't say such things, Lina," Kuan Hee stammered. "He saved my life." He was frantically piling tissue paper over Alfredo's back. The Indonesian was incoherent and shivering. Kuan Hee's eyes were welling. He was feeling the strain of their failed mission.

"We're going to my family doctor," Harry said. "He lives three streets from here. We'll be there soon. How's Alfredo."

"I don't know," Kuan Hee said. "He's drifting in and out of consciousness."

"Look! A police van ahead," Navin called out from the front passenger seat. The occupants of the vehicle froze for a moment. It was Tim's quick thinking that saved the day.

"Here, pass me the tin of diesel," Tim said, pointing to the metal tin hanging on the rack separating the driver's section from the back of the minibus. Lina grabbed the tin beside her and handed it to him.

As the minibus slowed to a stop along the side of the road, Tim unscrewed the tin of diesel while the others looked questioningly.

"Surely you aren't going to pour it on the police!" Navin said.

"Boy! I must say. You do have great imagination," Tim said. "We can't have the minibus smelling of gunpowder or blood, you know." He poured diesel into some rags. He hung the rags on the rack. At once, the strong smell of diesel overwhelmed the air-conditioned air in the minibus, camouflaging all other smells.

"Kuan Hee, rest his head on your shoulder," Tim said. "Pretend he's drunk." He signaled to Harry to drive off. The minibus proceeded at a slow pace towards the roadblock. There were two policemen standing next to a police van whose strobing lights lit up the darkness.

A policeman waved the minibus to a halt. He ambled up to Harry, and with the deftness of a seasoned sentry, shone his flashlight into the driver's section and then into the back of the minibus at its occupants. He walked back to the driver's section.

At once, Harry fished some currency notes out of his pocket and pressed them into the policeman's free hand. He spoke in Bahasa Indonesia. There were smiles between him and the policeman, who waved him on. The Singaporeans' hearts skipped a beat as Harry stepped on the throttle and the minibus continued its journey along the darkened road.

"It's that easy?" Tim said.

"Yeah," Harry said. "Money is king here."

"What did the policeman say?" Lina asked.

"He asked what we were doing so late at night," Harry said. "I told him we'd just left a party."

"He didn't suspect anything?" Tim said.

"He only sees money," Harry said. "That's all he's interested in."

The minibus turned into a lane and pulled to a stop. Tim slid open the side door and helped Kuan Hee bring Alfredo down. Together, they hobbled towards the back of a shophouse. A man was waiting for them at the door. He led them through the corridor into a room where they carefully rested Alfredo on an exam table.

Then he cut through the shirt Alfredo was wearing and worked his way around his wounds expertly, looking out for entry and exit wounds. He turned him over and opened his mouth to check his airway for breathing. He pressed fresh gauze pads onto the four gaping holes on Alfredo's back. Alfredo was convulsing. He was suffering from shock as he had lost a lot of blood. With deft fingers, the doctor filled a syringe and plunged it into Alfredo's chest. Next, he tried to resuscitate him. But all was in vain. Alfredo was gasping his last breath. Then he turned silent. The long silence in the room was broken by Lina's sobs.

She had realized he had left them. Kuan Hee folded her in his bosom and let her cry in it. He held back his tears. He blamed himself for Alfredo's death. If only he had not been reckless that night. Alas, it was too late. But, whatever wrongs Alfredo had done, the Indonesian had redeemed himself by taking the bullets meant for him. Kuan Hee scolded himself for suspecting Alfredo had betrayed him again.

CHAPTER 21

In the minibus parked outside the funeral parlour where Alfredo's body lay, Kuan Hee and Lina sat. He could not summon the courage to enter the hall to pay his last respects to the fallen Indonesian. Tim and Navin came out of the nondescript building and boarded the minibus.

"Harry's with Alfredo's parents," Tim said.

"He's barely twenty," Kuan Hee croaked. "In the prime of life. Gone. Just like that."

"It's not your fault," Navin said. "Quit blaming yourself."

"Yeah. It's a twist of fate," Tim said.

Just then Harry emerged from the parlour. He climbed into the driver's seat and looked back at his friends in the back of the vehicle. "It's all done. Alfredo's family will take over from here." That said, he started the engine and manoeuvred the minibus into the traffic.

Kuan Hee was silent in the journey back to Jalan Muara Takus. In his eyes, two deaths in a week were too much to stomach. First, it was his dad. Now it was Alfredo. He wondered if his persistence would cost them more lives.

Back on the narrow kerb outside Uncle Kenny's shophouse, the remaining five adventurers lingered, leaning against the shophouse wall, or sitting on the parked motorcycles, staring into space. Harry flicked a smothering *kretek* stub into the air. It joined the dozen others littering the ground around his feet. The night was young, but they had too many things on their mind to enjoy themselves.

It had been a trying day for them. Kuan Hee had stared death in the face. Their mission was in tatters. It was Harry's first time witnessing someone dying.

"The mind clone cartridge must have been destroyed in the fire," Tim said.

"But we can't be sure," Navin said.

"Shall we stop here and return home?" Lina said.

"Let me think," Kuan Hee said.

"Your mother will be home soon," Lina said. "And she'll be worried sick if we are not home."

"Give me some time to decide," Kuan Hee said.

"Tim?" Lina said, looking at him for support.

"Guys, we came here to rescue Kuan Hee," Tim said. "That, we have done. And in all probability, his father's mind clone cartridge has been destroyed. There's nothing left here for us to do."

"Yeah. The police may be on to us, man," Navin said. "If we don't leave now, we may never get to leave. I don't want to spend the rest of my life in an Indonesian prison."

"And we may have worn out our welcome," Tim said. "We keep getting into trouble. I don't think Uncle Kenny likes the idea of Harry falling into trouble."

"My pa understands what we are doing," Harry said. "He is a little worried, that's all. Otherwise, he's OK with me hanging around with you. It's all right." In a way, what Harry said was true. His father was worried he would suffer the same fate as Alfredo. He was beginning to regret encouraging Kuan Hee to pursue his agenda. But he stopped short of telling the Singaporean visitors to halt what they were doing and return to Singapore.

"Shall we give it two days more?" Kuan Hee said. "Then we wrap things up and head home."

"Why, Kuan Hee?" Lina asked.

"Cos I want to find out what's happened to the man with the wires," Kuan Hee said. "He's got my dad's memories. I don't want him doing evil using my dad's memories."

"I plain forgot about the guy with the wires on his head," Tim said.

"Me too," Navin said.

"What say you guys?" said Kuan Hee. "We stay two more days. I promise we'll leave after that."

The other adventurers nodded in unison.

With long faces, the adventurers trooped into Harry's house. They settled themselves down on the floor of the second storey living room. Harry translated a newspaper article on the fire at Jalan Walikota.

"So it's just two short paragraphs on the fire?" Tim said.

"That's all they wrote," Harry said, holding up the newspaper in his hand. "See?"

"Nothing on the guard you shot?" Kuan Hee said.

"No mention at all," Harry said.

"The Chinese consulate must be anxious," Tim said. "They deliberately withheld important information."

"If the guard died, surely they had to report it," Navin said. "Did he die?"

"Everything was in a whirl," Tim said. "I didn't have time to check. In fact, I didn't even think of it."

"I think the Chinese consulate didn't want anyone to know about the goings-on in that house," Kuan Hee. "That's why they played down the fire as an accident." He paused. Then he continued, "We've got to keep a close watch on the Chinese consulate. Find out what happened to the man with the wires on his head."

"From the looks of it, the police won't be looking for us," Navin said, heaving a sigh of relief.

"Two things we've got to do," Kuan Hee said. "Tail He Bin's boss. He's got to know where the missing man is.

And find out just what they are up to. There has to be an evil scheme in this whole thing. I can feel it in my bones."

"Harry, when do you need to return the minibus?" Tim asked.

"No hurry," Harry said. "My friend doesn't need it back so soon."

"Let's go recce the consulate first thing in the morning," Tim said. "Shall we?"

"OK!" the others screeched in unison.

CHAPTER 22

Today, the Chinese consulate in Jalan Walikota was abuzz with activity. Next to it stood the lonely charred carcass of the bungalow that had occupied the interests of the adventurers the previous few days. Security seemed tight at the main gates. Milling around were men in plainclothes who looked more like members of the triad than visa-seeking visitors.

Little Busy hovered over the consulate's compound, giving the adventurers ensconced in the back of the minibus across the road an aerial view of the grounds. A covered car park stood on the left of the large building. The housefly drone flitted between two-storey-tall fluted columns adorned with ornate renderings emulating Greek architecture. It flew into a window on the second storey.

"We've got to find the man's office," Tim said. "Kuan Hee, throw up a picture of He Bin's boss." Kuan Hee swiped an image off Little Busy's remote onto Tim's iPad. Then he changed back to video mode on the remote.

"Let's see. He looks about fifty years old. Wears glasses. Broad face. Small eyes under bushy untidy eyebrows," Tim said.

"He's pompous," Kuan Hee added. "Remember the

way he swaggered in the house?"

"Yeah," Navin said. "Carried himself around like some VIP."

"Where's Little Busy now?" Tim said.

The robot housefly was exploring the corridors on the second storey. Its cameras captured some people seating on benches here and there placed against the wall. Some others were standing around, papers in hand, resting their arms or backs against the wall. On a wall, a TV screen perched, with a programme plying Chinese attractions to the visitors as they waited their turn.

The doors in the corridor took turns opening and closing, providing an erratic rhythm in an otherwise monotonous atmosphere.

The adventurers took turns manning the remote's screen. It was an hour later that something stirred their attention. On the remote's screen, a heavyset bespectacled man plodded into the corridor from the stairs. It was the same man on Tim's iPad. The man stopped at a door, inserted a key into a lock and turned it. Little Busy flew after the man and followed him inside the room.

The man settled himself in an armchair behind a small desk, next to a tall draped window. A nameplate on the desk read:

Cao Kun
Head, Science & Technology Office

Little Busy landed atop a tall cabinet across from the desk and the spies in the minibus prepared for the long haul.

"Finally, we know his name," Kuan Hee said.

"And what he does at the Chinese consulate," Tim said.

The morning was uneventful. He Bin's boss busied himself with some paperwork and phone calls. In between, he took a short nap. The minutes droned on for the spies

518

watching him on the remote's screen.

"He seems to be in a fit," Navin said. "Look at the way he slams things on his desk.

"Must be sore about losing the house next door," Tim said.

"Look! Someone is entering the room," Kuan Hee said.

"It's not He Bin for sure," Tim said. "This guy is tall."

The visitor's back was facing the screen. He slumped into a chair opposite Cao Kun. Then began a long animated conversation in Mandarin between the two Chinese men.

"What are they saying?" Harry asked. Like most Indonesian Chinese in Medan, he did not understand Chinese. Bahasia Indonesia was the only language he studied at school. Indonesian Chinese residents could only learn Chinese through private tutors, but Harry faltered in the language. It was alien to him and the family gave up trying to get him to learn the language.

Navin was in the same boat. Years of mingling with Chinese friends yielded some simple Chinese words such as *xiè xie* (thank you) and *bào qiàn* (sorry). Tim and Kuan Hee, though Chinese, fared only slightly better. They failed their Chinese subject at school. They were the *chia kantang* type of Singaporeans.

It was left to bilingual Lina to do the translation for the other adventurers.

"Cao Kun is telling the tall guy his superiors are angry that the lab has been razed," Lina said. "The fire has put everything behind schedule. His superiors want him to find out who's behind the attack on the lab. They want him to nab them."

"No wonder he has a black look," Navin said. "Serve him right."

"We still don't know who his superiors are," Kuan Hee said. "Someone high in government, I suspect."

"Remember. It's the Chinese government which is behind all the happenings," Lina said.

"That's what we thought," Tim said. "Now, I'm not that sure."

"Why?" Lina asked.

"We were hasty, jumping to conclusions. So much has happened recently. Logically—"

"Shush," Navin said. "They are talking again."

"Quick, Lina," Tim said. "Tell us what they are saying."

"I've got to listen first, right?" Lina snapped.

"Don't let's bicker," Kuan Hee said. "Lina, continue."

"They are making small talk," Lina said.

"It's going to be a long morning," Kuan Hee said.

"Cao Kun is telling the other man to look after things here," Lina said. "Says he's leaving tomorrow for Singapore."

"Did he say why?" Kuan Hee said.

"Nope," Lina said. "They are now discussing matters which need to be attended to here."

There was a knocking sound. The remote's screen showed the door opening and a stout man moving towards Cao Kun's desk. He stood next to the other visitor.

"It's He Bin," Kuan Hee said.

"Cao Kun is entrusting He Bin with an errand," Lina said. Cao Kun rose from his chair, walked over to a tall fireproof metal cabinet adjacent to his desk, and worked his hand at the combination lock. He opened the door and retrieved a slim rectangular metal box, the size of a paperback book.

"It's a hologram-encoded multi-mode ODS," Tim said.

"A what?" Lina screeched.

"What's ODS?" Harry asked.

"ODS stands for Optical Data Storage," Kuan Hee explained. "Essentially, it's 3D images storing vast amounts of information. It's an encrypted ultrahigh-storage device."

"That's a load of information," Harry said. "But I don't quite understand what you are saying."

"Kuan Hee is simply describing a storage medium—

like a flash drive, but stores a huge amount of information," Tim said. "Pay no attention to him. He likes to impress us with his deep knowledge and bombastic words."

"OIC," Harry said.

"Guys, you are interrupting my ears," Lina said. "I can't tell what they are saying."

"Sorry!" the men chorused in unison.

"Cao Kun's handing the ODS device to He Bin," Navin said.

"He wants He Bin to take the thing to Jakarta and hand it over to a man called Guo Wei at the embassy," Lina said.

"It must be my dad's mind clone cartridge," Kuan Hee said. "It's been here all along, not in the house next door. Why didn't I think of it?"

"From the size of the device, I can tell it contains exabytes of stuff in it," Tim said. "It can map the entire brain a few times over."

"Your father hasn't shown this ODS device to you?" Navin said.

"Never seen it before," Kuan Hee said. "My dad's always been secretive about his work. Even Mum doesn't know much about what he does."

"Does it mean you don't know how to repair AleXander if they are injured—I mean damaged?" Navin said.

"*Yah hor*," Kuan Hee said. "I never thought of it. I never thought they would come to harm one day."

"We must take good care of AleXander," Lina said. "We can't use them for dangerous missions any more, or we might lose them."

"Quiet!" Tim roared. "Listen to what they are saying."

There was silence in the minibus.

"I forgot to pay attention to them," Lina said. "Sorry."

"He Bin is leaving the room with the device," Navin said. "Shall we follow him or stay?"

"My dad's mind clone cartridge is more important," Kuan Hee said. "We've got to get it back." He commanded Little Busy to tail the stout man.

He Bin left the building and climbed into a car at the covered car park. Someone else was in the driver's seat. The car rolled out of the compound into Jalan Kalikota, sped past the KFC restaurant and turned into Jalan Polonia, with the minibus tailing it.

"He's going to Polonia Airport," Harry shouted into the back of the minibus.

"Huh? The airport's so near?" Lina said.

"We have to stop him before he gets to the airport," Kuan Hee said.

"The airport is two minutes away," Harry said. "There's no time."

"That means only one thing left to do," Kuan Hee said as he fumbled in his backpack. His hand emerged, clasping Xander.

"Surely, you aren't going to use Xander's rockets on He Bin," Tim said. He spoke too soon.

"What about your father's mind clone cartridge?" Lina asked. "All his hard work is in it. You can't just destroy it. You'll regret it the rest of your life."

"Hobson's choice," Kuan Hee retorted. "At least, having it destroyed is better than letting it be used for evil again and again." His mind was set. Lina knew it was futile trying to persuade him.

Perhaps, in his muddled mind, Kuan Hee had his answer to William Shakespeare's poser in *The Merchant of Venice*, the play that he studied in secondary school:

> If you prick us do we not bleed? If you tickle us do
> we not laugh? If you poison us do we not die? And if
> you wrong us shall we not revenge?

"I'll blow the car the smithereens," Kuan Hee said. "With He Bin and the mind clone cartridge in it." He pulled open the side window of the vehicle, unfastened Xander's front panel and uttered some commands to the robot. At once, Xander climbed onto the roof of the minibus and, standing with its hands on its waists and feet apart, fired a rocket at the car in front, blasting it to kingdom come instantly.

The minibus swerved to avoid the burning vehicle. There were more explosions as the flames shot up several storeys high. Pandemonium reigned in the street as motocyclists and drivers alike manoeuvred their vehicles to avoid the burning heap of metal.

"This time, I know for sure the mind clone cartridge is gone forever." Kuan Hee said, looking out of the back window with his *kakis*. "There goes my dad's life work."

"You have avenged your father," Tim said. "He should rest in peace."

"This is only the beginning," Kuan Hee promised. "I still have Cao Kun and his masters to deal with." Perhaps he had yet to hear Mahatma Gandhi's sobering words:

An eye for eye only ends up making the whole world blind.

"Oh no. There'll be no end to this," Lina said. "Kuan Hee is fuming mad."

CHAPTER 23

Brigadier Walmsley waddled up to the four Singaporeans and their Indonesian friend as they stood on the kerb outside Toko Harry under the glow of the streetlamps. The air was cooler now but the heat of the day had yet to dissipate from the wall behind them. The adventurers had been waiting for him. He was, as usual, punctual. It was his trademark.

"Glad to hear you guys are leaving for Singapore," Brigadier Walmsley said. The Singaporeans smiled at him.

"Me too. Never did like this place," Brigadier Walmsley said. "There aren't any lifts. I've to climb the stairs all the time everywhere I go. At my age, it's a chore."

"Mr Walmsley," Lina said, "you still look fit. Should be no problem at all." The Brigadier beamed.

"Kuan Hee, come with me," Brigadier Walmsley said. He pulled Kuan Hee aside and both men took a stroll together along the roadside.

"Kuan Hee, you have caused enough trouble here," Brigadier Walmsley said. "Make sure you leave tomorrow. I won't be around to get you out of a spot; I, too, am leaving Medan tomorrow."

"Yes, Mr Walmsley," Kuan Hee said.

"Your father left some things behind in the hotel at Parapat," Brigadier Walmsley said. "My men picked them up while clearing the place. I've sent them to your mother."

"Yes, Mr Walmsley," Kuan Hee said.

"He also left behind a note," Brigadier Walmsley said. He fished out something from his pocket and handed it to Kuan Hee. "Here. I'm sure your father wants you to have it. Read it later, when you are alone." Kuan Hee nodded.

"Kuan Hee," Brigadier Walmsley said. "Those Chinese men whom you tangled with are not to be trifled with. One slip and all of you could lose your lives."

"But, Mr Walmsley," Kuan Hee said. "I've to avenge my dad's death."

"Let me deal with them, Kuan Hee," Brigadier Walmsley said. "I promise you I will make them pay for what they did to your father."

"Yes, Mr Walmsley," Kuan Hee said.

"There. I've said my piece," Brigadier Walmsley said. "When you have landed safely, give me a call—so I'll have piece of mind." Kuan Hee nodded.

The Brigadier got into a waiting car and waved goodbye to Kuan Hee. The car sped off into the dimly lit neighbourhood.

Kuan Hee unfolded the piece of paper and held it up under the streetlamp. It was a letter addressed to him. It bore his father's handwriting.

> *My son,*
>
> *I had hoped I would not need to write this letter to you. But circumstances dictate that I should. I don't know whether you will get to read it; I don't know whether you will make it safely out of the*

kidnappers' hands. I don't even know whether I will get out of this alive.

All I know is, I've to tell you this—I have created a mind clone of myself. Remember the robot tank I showed you eight years ago—the one in the cellar of the house? In it exists my mind clone. It is essentially a copy of me minus the physical body. I've kept it updated regularly through the years using Polaris File Transfer Protocol. I didn't tell you earlier. I thought I would do it at a suitable time. Alas, I can't wait. The next few hours are crucial.

If I have to leave this good earth, I want you to protect the robot tank with your life. In it is my life's work. With it, you can help mankind.

Everything you need to know is in the robot tank. The mind clone cartridge I am using to exchange for your safety is a copy. The robot tank holds the master copy and more.

Take care of your mother, Kuan Hee. Take care of yourself, too. I am afraid I might not be around for Lina and Huei

Huei. Take care of them too. I love you.
Goodbye.

Your father

It was Kuan Hee's father's last words. He had scribbled them hastily just before the kidnappers paid him a visit in Parapat that night. Kuan Hee's vision turned blurry. It was as if someone had splashed water on his eyes. He wiped off his tears. He couldn't let the others see him cry. It would be unbecoming of him. But try as he might, his eyes stayed red.

Kuan Hee pocketed the note and rejoined the other adventurers who were waiting eagerly for him to update them on his conversation with the Brigadier. He merely waved them into the shophouse.

In the second storey living room, everyone sat in anticipation for Kuan Hee to begin talking. But he remained silent.

"What's wrong with you?" Tim said. "Were you crying?"

"Nope," Kuan Hee said. "It's the haze. It got into my eyes."

"Tell us what the Brigadier said, Kuan Hee," Lina said.

Kuan Hee took out the tear-stained note and passed it to her. She read it and handed it to Tim. The next couple of minutes went by with nary a word spoken as the adventurers took turns to read the note.

"I guess your father sort of knew he was heading into trouble," Tim said. "But, he didn't flinch. You were important to him."

"Yeah. Kuan Hee, your father was a brave chap," Navin said.

"I know," Kuan Hee said.

"All is not lost," Tim said. "Your father has the master copy of the mind clone cartridge." Kuan Hee nodded.

"You were so adamant to destroy it," Navin said. "Yet, it's still around. It's heaven's will. Definitely heaven's will."

"Yeah, Kuan Hee," Lina said. "Your father's work lives on. Use his knowledge to make him proud."

"Let's book tickets to go home, shall we?" Kuan Hee said.

"Yeah. Let's," Lina said. There was a chorus of approval.

"Harry, I'm sorry we've inconvenienced you and Uncle Kenny for so long," Tim said.

"What? Inconvenience? Nothing of the sort, Tim," Harry said. "It's been a pleasure hosting you."

"Come visit us," Lina said. "We'll show you around town."

"I will," Harry promised.

The four Singaporeans followed Harry upstairs to tell Uncle Kenny their decision.

CHAPTER 24

Flight MI234 left idyllic Medan for pristine Singapore with the four friends safely on board. Three of them had come to Medan seeking the fourth. Kuan Hee arrived in the city packed in diplomatic luggage. Today, he left it as a paying passenger on a commercial flight using a United States diplomatic passport. Such a twist in events, a staple in spy thrillers, followed Kuan Hee wherever he went. His life wasn't—ordinary.

The airplane landed on Changi Airport's third runway, used previously for military aircraft in the early noughties. The four friends deplaned at Terminal five, a mega passenger complex built in the late 2020s.

"So glad to be home—finally," Lina screeched.

"Yeah. We've been away too long," Navin said.

"No more *kretek* smoke following me wherever I go," Tim said."

"And an end to the honking and tooting noises in the streets," Kuan Hee said.

After breezing through the automated checks in the arrival hall, the four adventurers made a beeline for the shops. It was their chance to buy duty-free merchandise. Navin hunted for perfume for his mother. Tim headed for the alcohol aisle to get his father's favourite Johnny Walker Black. As for Kuan Hee and Lina, they were just glad to be together, windowshopping—their favourite pastime.

As they were sauntering under a humongous Moby Dick artpiece, something caught their eye. It was Navin's eagle eyes that alerted them. A chubby man was bending over a showcase looking at watches. It was Cao Kun! He had arrived in Singapore.

The adventurers were torn between wanting to go straight home to see their loved ones and following their only lead. It was Lina who spoke from the heart first.

"Huh? But I miss little Huei Huei," Lina protested. "I haven't seen her in ages."

"Look! Singapore is so small," Kuan Hee said. "He can't be spending a whole day travelling around Singapore. It'll only take us an hour or so. Be a sport, Lina."

"Our guy is moving down the travellator," Navin said. "Should we follow or not?"

It was Kuan Hee who lunged across the aisle after their target first. The others followed suit.

Cao Kun walked up to a taxi stand and took his place in the queue. Fearing he would recognize them if they stood behind him in the queue, the adventurers kept away from the taxi stand. Meanwhile, Tim booked an Uber ride with his smartphone.

"There's our ride," Tim said, pointing to a Mitsubishi Lancer, which had stopped at the road shoulder along the terminal entrance. The adventurers piled into the vehicle and sat waiting for Cao Kun who had now reached the front of the taxi queue.

Soon, the taxi Cao Kun was in cruised along the expressways into the affluent Bukit Timah district. It turned into Shelford Road and disappeared into a driveway at the end of the long road.

The adventurers remained in the Uber vehicle, plotting their next move. With the exception of Kuan Hee, all had luggage with them. If they disembarked here, it would be difficult for them to lug their luggage around Shelford Road, a magnet for upper-class residents. They would also stand out like a sore thumb.

"Let's see if he's merely paying a visit," Tim said. He asked the driver to let them wait in the vehicle.

There was no sign of Cao Kun after fifteen minutes. The Uber driver showed impatience, so the group decided to end their surveillance and head home.

"Never mind, at least we know where Cao Kun's living," Kuan Hee said, as their vehicle left for the main road.

With the adventurers safely dispatched to their homes, the Uber driver resumed his cruise for paying customers along the roads.

The first thing on Kuan Hee's mind when he reached home was to look for the robot tank, while Lina only thought of seeing her darling Huei Huei. In the end, Lina's tears won the battle, albeit for a short while only.

A day went by as Lina busied herself catching up with little Huei Huei at their house in Jalan Naung. Tim kept to his room, taking long naps to make up for the lack of sleep the past few weeks. Navin's mother kept him constructively occupied, discussing his wedding plans. She thought the sooner he settled down, the earlier he would stay put at home. In short, she thought it would get rid of his travelling itch.

What was Kuan Hee doing this while? He had rushed into the secret cellar to look for his father's robot tank, but it wasn't there any more. Instead, he found it nearby—it was sitting on an upper shelf of the bookcase in the study. Slightly longer than two palms of a hand, it was a scaled model of a main battle tank. He wiped the dust off with a cloth. It glistened. Its body was of a gold-titanium alloy, the same material that protected AleXander the robots. Then he got down to work on the tank. Try as he might, Kuan Hee simply could not get his hands into its innards. He was careful not to go overboard in meddling with the tank, for like his father's other robot inventions, it could possibly fire deadly live projectiles. He gave up in exasperation that evening. *What's the secret behind this robot tank?* His father's note left no clues; it had been prepared in haste.

Then Kuan Hee thought of his mum. Surely she should know how to unlock the robot tank's secrets. She was still in Fort Bragg in the United States, so he telephoned her. Alas, she too was none the wiser. The suspense was killing him. In desperation, he took to reading his father's note line by line, again and again, hoping somehow it would trigger some part of his memory.

"Take a break, Kuan Hee," Lina said. "It'll do you a world of good. Refresh your mind and then start looking at the robot tank again."

Reluctantly, Kuan Hee placed the robot tank on the desk. The pair passed time reminiscing their adventure in Medan. Just when they were marvelling at the rollicking good times spent there, loud beeping sounds interrupted their conversation.

The robot tank had sprung into life. It was beeping and whistling away on the desk. It took the pair by surprise.

"What happened, Kuan Hee?"

"The robot tank woke up."

"How did it happen?"

"Beats me. It came alive all of a sudden."

"But, we didn't do anything, or did we?"

"It could be something we said. Something either you or I said activated it."

The pair walked up to the desk.

"Gosh! The model soldier's eyes are beaming. I think it moved just now."

"Now what was it we were saying just now—before the tank started beeping?"

"You mean, something we said activated the robot?"

"Just what were we talking about?"

"We were just making casual conversation."

Suddenly, the toy soldier on the turret spoke. "At your command," it said.

"It's speaking to us."

"Why didn't I think of it before? Like AleXander, we talk to it. We give verbal commands to it. It can communicate with us verbally."

"But what activated the robot tank. One of us must have said something."

"Let me give it some commands. Let's see. What shall I say?"

Looking to the toy soldier, Kuan Hee uttered a string of commands which he had used on AleXander the robots. At once, the robot tank rumbled forward, then turned right and moved towards the wall.

"Stop!"

The robot tank halted in its tracks.

"It's responding to your verbal instructions, Kuan Hee."

"Yes, but for how long. Once it rests, I will need to utter its name again for it to wake up. But, we don't know its name."

"Think, Kuan Hee. Think of the names that we used in our conversation just now. That must be the answer."

"But we didn't mention any names—at least that's what I think."

"We must have said a name. The robot tank responded to its name being called."

"*Aiyah!*" Kuan Hee paused for a long while, trying to recall their conversation.

"I only said 'AleXander' once or twice, I think. I can't think of any other names."

He tried calling 'AleXander' but there was no response from the robot tank. An hour passed without any success. By then the robot tank had settled into a rest state. The toy soldier's eyes were no longer bright with light.

"For the life of me, I just can't think of its name no matter how hard I try."

"It's OK, Kuan Hee. Take a rest. Let's try later."

But Lina knew too well that it was no use telling Kuan Hee to give up. Once his mind was set on something, he would not stop till he reached his goal. So she got little Huei Huei to doodle on drawing block paper while she watched her. Kuan Hee settled into a long silence.

"That's it!" Kuan Hee's voice pierced the silence in the study.

"What? Kuan Hee. For goodness's sake, don't startle me and Huei Huei."

"Lina. I remember now. We were talking about AleXander. You were saying: AleXander. The great thing about—" The toy soldier atop the turret started moving again. Its beaming eyes flickered.

"There. The robot tank is responding to its name again."

"So what's its name? AleXander?"

"It's Alexander the Great, my dear." At once, the robot tank chirped and tooted again.

Lina's face lit up. "You're right, Kuan Hee. It's indeed Alexander the Great." The robot tank squealed a response.

"I never imagined Dad would come up with such a name."

"No one would think of it. They would be so confused. They would never think the name would come so close to Alex and Xander."

"Such an apt name for a robot tank. You know, Alexander the Great conquered much of the world then." The robot tank whistled and tooted in reply.

"See? The robot tank agrees."

"Now what next?"

"Find out how to access Dad's mind clone, of course. It must be inside."

"It will be like looking for a needle in a haystack."

"Yes *lah*."

Lina left Kuan Hee staring at Alexander the Great. It was time for Huei Huei to take a bath.

It was a good hour before Kuan Hee made his first move. He had spent the time visualising in his mind the possible ways that his father could have used to provide access to the robot tank's interior. He fiddled with the contraption, holding it in his hands and turning it upside down, fingering and pressing every part of it. He even tried pulling up the toy soldier. Still, he could not find a way to get inside. Frustrated, he put it down and sat gawking at it with furrowed eyebrows. *It's damned difficult to find out its secret.*

Then Kuan Hee thought of the Brigadier. *Yes, Mr Walmsley must have the answer. He knows Dad so well.* He contacted the Brigadier via telephone. Alas, like his mother, the Brigadier had no inkling. So it was back to the drawing board for Kuan Hee.

Kuan Hee was so engrossed that he didn't notice Lina slipping up next to him. "Any luck?" she said. Jolted out of his thoughts, he glared at her.

"You don't have to get angry with me, Kuan Hee. I didn't do anything wrong."

"Sorry."

"I was just thinking. Remember the tunnel at The Battle Box?" He nodded.

"Remember how we opened the tunnel door?" He turned to look in her eyes.

"Yes. We had to press two buttons simultaneously for the door to unlock itself."

"That's right, Kuan Hee. Is it just possible that your father designed the opening mechanism this way too?"

"Yeah *hor.* Dad was an iPhone fan like me. To grab a screenshot on iPhone, one had to press the side button and volume-up button at the same time. Perhaps, he used this idea on the robot tank too."

Kuan Hee pecked Lina on her cheek. "Thanks, dear." Then he went back to work, meddling with the robot tank again. He started from the turret and, using fingers of both hands, pressed every raised surface on the tank.

Soon he got to the front headlamps. He depressed both headlamps simultaneously. At once, two panels on the tank above the headlamps flipped open, and a screen rose, unfolding itself as it did so. The screen was now thrice the length it was. Delirious with excitement, Kuan Hee brought the robot tank towards his face and gawked at the screen. Then he placed the tank down and felt the screen with his fingers. *It's an OLED touch screen display.*

"Lina. Lina. Come quick!"

Lina practically flew into the study, with flannel in hand. She had been cleaning the stove in the kitchen. Seeing his excitement, she could not resist wrapping herself around him, wetting his back with the soiled flannel.

"Yikes! What's that on my back?"

"Sorry, Kuan Hee. I forgot. It's a cleaning cloth." She released her grip of him.

"My, really great job you have done. Fancy finding the secret in such a short time."

"Short time? My foot. It took me an entire day."

It also went on to take an entire night of his time as he tinkered with the hierarchical menu on the screen. He delved into the different layers of the menu and deep below, chanced upon one bearing his name. He tapped on the only file in it.

It was a video that played. In it, his father was addressing him. He listened in earnest in the privacy of the study. He came to the part about human cloning.

"You see, Kuan Hee. I can replicate a human body, but I can't grow a human mind. That part of the process of creating a real human being, though not fantasy, is still in the science fiction realm. That's why I call my creations clones, not human beings.

"My invention merely reads data off a human mind and copies these into another medium for easy transfer into another human mind. This is mind cloning. But to be sure, I can't call it mind growing. Mind cloning only maps a human mind at a particular instance in time. So the information is dated. It is not updated in the sense it doesn't keep up with the growth of a human mind.

"But my mind clone is up to date. I continually update it with readings of my own mind and then upload these wirelessly via the Polaris satellite into Alexander the Great. There are about five petabytes of data, which represent a scan of my entire mind, in the Optical Data Storage drive. It's my gift to you. Keep it safe from prying eyes. Use it for the benefit of mankind.

"I know it's information overload for you. You're a clever boy. Play this video a couple of times, and you will fathom my intentions. Go to Brigadier Walmsley for help if you need."

Kuan Hee sat in deep thought in the silence of the night, digesting the contents of the video.

CHAPTER 25

The four adventurers pored over the map of residential Shelford Road that Kuan Hee had swiped off his iPad onto the large TV screen in the living room of 79 Jalan Naung.

"There's nothing for us to watch over in Shelford Road," Tim said. "It's only a residential area. It's where Cao Kun stays."

"I agree with Tim," Navin said. "We should focus on his workplace—the Chinese Embassy. Stake him out there."

Kuan Hee sat with crossed arms facing the TV screen, contemplating his fellow adventurers' remarks. He pursed his lips. "We are staking out Cao Kun because he has a secret to hide. So if it's a secret thing he is doing, do you think he will do it at the Chinese Embassy in broad daylight? He would be in pretence there."

"What if the Chinese government is in the secret?" Lina said. "What if the devious scheme is cooked up by the government? Then they will do it openly—at the embassy."

"I know. I know," Kuan Hee said. "But remember the house in Medan—the one next to the Chinese consulate?

They were carrying out some clandestine operation there. Perhaps, they are using the same method here too. They could be using the residence in Shelford Road."

"Logical assumption, but far-fetched," Tim said. "What was the first thing we did when we landed in Singapore? Head for home, right? That's probably what Cao Kun had been doing—heading for his home in Shelford Road."

"Let's stop bickering," Lina said.

"We aren't bickering, Lina," Kuan Hee said. "We are merely reasoning things out."

"Alright," Tim said. "Let's do it this way. We'll keep watch over both places. See what our guy is up to. But, we'll do it like this. Follow him wherever he goes. Not stake out the two locations. We don't have the manpower."

"Good idea," Navin said. "This way, we'll always be in the action."

"I vote we start with the Chinese Embassy," Tim said. "Wait there for Cao Kun to turn up." The others nodded their heads in agreement.

"The Chinese Embassy is not like its laid-back cousin in Medan," Kuan Hee said. "There are eyes everywhere in the compound. We have to be extra careful."

From Tanglin Road, the Chinese Embassy is an imposing sight. At first look, its fortified façade and overarching front gate entrance is a modern take on provincial gates in ancient Chinese cities. Granite slabs form a common theme, lining its façade and the perimeter wall along the road. Tanglin Road is a tree-lined two-laned road, which forks into a busy arterial junction serving the upper-class residential districts on one side and the urban shopping district of Orchard Road on the other.

The four adventurers stood at a sheltered bus stop across the road from the Chinese Embassy, pondering their next step.

"*Wah seh!* It's awfully big," Lina exclaimed. "It must be

at least four times the size of the consulate in Medan,"

"Yeah. It's huge," Tim said. "And it's on a slope. It will be difficult to watch this place without being noticed. I mean—anyone up there can easily spot us loitering around. There's hardly a soul out here."

"Let me release Little Busy first," Kuan Hee said. He opened his palm and the robot drone flitted into the air, glad to be soaking in the sunlight, its energy source. The drone flew across the road and up past the granite façade into the centre of the embassy grounds. The adventurers packed in front of the remote's screen.

The housefly drone landed on top of a CCTV camera perched on one of four tall spotlight towers on the premises. Its cameras beamed live pictures to the remote's screen, giving the adventurers an aerial view of the embassy.

"*Wah!* I was wrong," Lina said. "This place is six times bigger than the consulate in Medan."

"It's really big," Tim said. "It even has a swimming pool."

"Now, where is Cao Kun?" Kuan Hee said.

"He's got to be in one of these buildings," Navin said. "But, it will take ages to scour through them."

"Let's start work, then. Kuan Hee. Let Little Busy fly through the main building," Tim said. The robot drone flew past several large buildings and entered the biggest. It flitted through the corridors of the third storey, avoiding capture by CCTV cameras installed on pillars.

"*Alamak!* Why didn't I think of it earlier?" Kuan Hee said.

"Think of what?" Lina said.

"Cao Kun's Head of Science & Technology Office. This means he's got to be in the Science & Technology Office here too."

"Yah *hor*," Tim said. "Quick! Kuan Hee. Locate the office. We've wasted precious time already. We can't be standing here for too long. A few buses have passed us and we've not gotten on any. People in the embassy across the road will get suspicious of us."

At Kuan Hee's direction, Little Busy flitted from door to door looking for the Science & Technology Office. It was the third door on the second storey of the main building. The robot housefly crawled under the door into the room. There were four low-height cubicles in the room, which was about the size of a classroom. In each cubicle, stood an L-shaped desk. The remaining open space in the room held a round table and accompanying chairs. Little Busy hovered over the cubicles, one by one.

"Cao Kun's not in the first two cubicles," Kuan Hee said. "Let's take a look at the third." Little Busy flitted over the third cubicle.

"Kuan Hee. It's him alright," Tim said. Cao Kun was using the computer. The monitor was showing a page, which had Chinese words all over it. It was unintelligible to the three men.

Little Busy perched on a picture frame on the wall behind Cao Kun. Then Cao Kun's smartphone rang and he started speaking into it.

"Lina. Our Chinese is not good," Tim said. "We need you to be our ears."

"Sure thing," Lina said, smiling. She was happy she had a skill the others appreciated.

"I think the caller asked him to get the first batch ready in two days' time," Lina said. "He's asking for more time."

"First batch of what?" Kuan Hee asked.

"Didn't say," Lina said.

"Any names mentioned?" Tim asked.

"Nope," Lina said. "But, I think the call is from overseas. Cao Kun is talking about airport clearance for the stuff. Something about diplomatic cargo."

"So he's sending some stuff overseas," Kuan Hee said.

"Sounds like it," Lina said. "Cao Kun is speaking in accented Mandarin. It is difficult to catch what he's saying."

"He's put down the phone," Tim said. "Nope, he's calling someone now."

"He's relaying the earlier caller's message to the other party," Lina said. "He's telling him to hasten the work. By hook or by crook, the first batch has to be ready by Wednesday."

"He's put down the phone again," Tim said. "Kuan Hee, can you get Little Busy close to the screen? See what he's doing now?"

"No need," Kuan Hee said. "I'll zoom in on the screen from here. Little Busy's got telephoto lens." Kuan Hee tapped on the remote's menu and pinched the screen.

"Lina, do your work," Kuan Hee said.

"It's an air freight schedule," Lina said. "He's ticked departure for Thursday 8:00 a.m. Destination: Shanghai."

"So the stuff is heading for Shanghai?" Lina said.

"Seems so," Kuan Hee said.

"Look! There's a pickup ferrying workers into the embassy," Lina said, pointing to a blue vehicle moving through the front gate. "It says 'Johnson Painters' on the side."

"I know. I'll pretend to be a painter," Tim said. "It'll be better than loitering out here. Lina. Did you say 'Johnson Painters'?"

"That's what it says on the side panel," Lina said.

"I'll try to get into their team. I'm sure they need more helpers," Tim said.

"You sure or not?" Navin said. Tim nodded.

"Let me join you, then," Navin said.

Just then two uniformed men turned out of the embassy compound. They looked like security guards making their rounds along the perimeter of the premises.

"Let's get out of here," Kuan Hee said. Across the road, the adventurers shuffled along the sidewalk heading towards the busy junction. Minutes later Little Busy flew into Kuan Hee's hand. "We'll return tomorrow," he said.

CHAPTER 26

The Cherry Blossoms Apartments is a freehold property occupying two hectares of prime residential land in sub-urban Shelford Road. Once you enter the gate, you find yourself in a large garden replete with a winding driveway and dozens of large mature trees. A two-storeyed I-shaped building takes centre-stage. Its façade with arched French windows harks back to the colonial era, with its understated whitewashed walls, red-bricked pillars and an imposing gable roof. A porch, offering shelter from the elements for two cars, protrudes prominently from the middle of the building. But nothing in the premises gives any hint of association with cherry blossoms. Perhaps, some time in its past, there were many cherry blossom trees growing in its grounds.

Kuan Hee and Lina hunched on the floor in the back of a Fiat Doblo, a cargo van, which he had rented a day earlier. The van was parked on the side of Shelford Road facing the Cherry Blossoms Apartments. Apparently, Kuan Hee was adamant about staking out the place where Cao Kun stayed. While Tim and Navin were at work painting some part of the Chinese Embassy in Tanglin Road, Kuan Hee and Lina had planted themselves on Shelford Road.

They were keen on the secrets that the private apartments might hold.

"We've been here since 8:00 a.m. and Cao Kun hasn't come out yet," Lina said.

"Be patient," Kuan Hee said. "He has to go to work, right?"

"He might not be here," Lina said. "Then how?"

"Don't worry," Kuan Hee said. "Tim and Navin are at the Chinese Embassy right?"

"Yah *hor*," Lina said.

"Just relax," Kuan Hee said.

"I can't," Lina said. "I don't know why, but I'm getting the jitters."

"It's just your imagination, Lina," Kuan Hee said. "Don't worry. We'll be fine. We won't be in any danger sitting out here."

"It's getting warm and stuffy," Lina said.

"I'll let in more air," Kuan Hee said. He pulled the side panel door farther, making a bigger gap between it and its frame. "We can't be turning on the air-conditioning. People will know we're inside."

"I know, I know," Lina said.

Soon the two-laned road was receiving less traffic, signaling the start of a lull period until lunchtime. Most residents in the neighbourhood had left for work. But, nothing seemed to have stirred at Cherry Blossoms Apartments. There was no movement in or out of the premises.

"Can it be no one's living there?" Lina asked. There was silence in the van.

"Why haven't you released Little Busy into the place?" Lina asked again. She was getting impatient at the lack of progress in their stakeout.

"I'm doing it now," Kuan Hee said.

"Look! There's a car turning into the place," Lina said. The pair pressed their faces against the translucent glass window.

"It's Cao Kun," Kuan Hee said. "I was wrong. He's not living here after all."

"He's coming to work?" Lina said.

"Looks like it," Kuan Hee said. "There is more than meets the eye at Cherry Blossoms Apartments." He let Little Busy out through a tiny slit in the window. The robot housefly soared into the air and flew over the wall into the sprawling grounds, heading towards the moving car, which came to a stop at a covered garage next to the far end of the building.

Little Busy's cameras captured little activity in the compound. Except for one man, presumably a security guard, manning the front gate, it was empty of people.

However, inside the long building, it was a hive of activity. There were people—men and women—busily striding the verandahs and corridors.

"There has to be at least a score of people here," Kuan Hee said.

"But, we didn't see anyone coming in through the front gate," Lina said.

"Perhaps, they used the back gate," Kuan Hee said.

"There's a back gate?" Lina said.

"Don't know," Kuan Hee said. "We'll find out afterwards. Let's follow Cao Kun first."

"No need to wait. I'll fly Tizzy into the place," Lina said. "It will find out for sure." She released Tizzy the robot dragonfly into the air outside the van. It flitted over the young trees on the sidewalk into the apartments. It flew over the compound towards the perimeter fencing beyond it, looking for a gate. Finally, it found one behind the long building. The metal grille gate was at the bottom of a slope, level with the basement floor of the building. There was someone sitting at a small table on a verandah. He seemed to be watching the back gate.

"They must have come in through the back gate," Kuan Hee said. "It's strange that they don't use the front gate. Very strange indeed."

"Perhaps, they don't want to attract attention," Lina said. "After all, this is a residential estate." She let Tizzy land on a small tree near the gate.

"Now we have more eyes on the compound," Lina proudly declared.

"These people are up to something," Kuan Hee said. "It's beginning to look like a factory here."

"The whole building is air-conditioned, Kuan Hee," Lina said, glancing at the temperature gauge on Little Busy's remote. "Where's Cao Kun?"

"We were so busy sussing out the back gate, I plain forgot about him," Kuan Hee said. "He was at this spot just now." He manoeuvred Little Busy through the corridor on the first storey. Then the robot housefly flitted past a lift and up the staircase at the end of the building. On the second storey, its cameras saw a set of double-leaved glass doors adjacent to the lift. It led to an entire floor of platformed workspace stretching all the way to the other end of the building. There were men and women in lab whites at work on big machines here and there.

"I was wrong. It's not a factory after all," Kuan Hee said. "It's a lab—and a very big one. We'll wait for someone to let Little Busy in."

It wasn't a long wait, for every few minutes, the doors flipped open automatically when someone went near it. Little Busy took the chance to slip in unnoticed. It wobbled and wavered before balancing itself and then fluttered through the large laboratory.

There were all sorts of equipment, ranging from the very small to the very large—DNA stabilisers, scanning electron microscopes, spectrometers, nitrogen generators, multi-purpose X-Ray diffractometers, cryogenic systems, tissue replicators and fabrication systems—the works!

There were several partitioned areas, one of which looked like an operating theatre in a hospital with its large operating table and overhead lights. On one side in the room were electrocautery machines and tanks containing possibly oxygen or anaesthetic gases. Some men and women in lab white uniforms crowded around the operating table. It was difficult to see what they were doing. Standing outside the operating theatre were robotic assemblers and DNA Molecular Assembly units.

Along one wall of the laboratory was a nest of servers on racks. Next to them, on long tables laid against the wall were computer monitors and keyboards. More men and women were at work here.

It was indeed a big operation unlike any other that Kuan Hee and Lina had laid eyes on.

"Such a large-scale operation only means one thing," Kuan Hee said. "People at the top of the Chinese government are involved."

"It's way over our head," Lina said. "We're powerless against them, Kuan Hee. Shall we get help?"

"You mean, Brigadier Walmsley?" Kuan Hee said.

"Yes. He's the only one who can handle them," Lina said. "He's got the United States government behind him."

"Let's get more evidence before we alert the Brigadier," Kuan Hee said. "I want to be sure first. I want to find out exactly what these guys are up to." Lina nodded.

"By the way, where's that guy Cao Kun?" Kuan Hee said. "I don't see him anywhere."

"Try downstairs again, Kuan Hee," Lina said. Little Busy flew behind a man in lab white and followed him out of the laboratory.

Downstairs, the robot housefly flitted from door to door, looking for openings under the door. But it found none. The pair resigned themselves to letting Little Busy perch itself atop a CCTV camera mounted on the wall.

It wasn't long before a door below the robot housefly opened and out stepped a familiar face. It was Cao Kun all right. Little Busy hovered above the Chinese man, following him as he lumbered along the corridor, carrying some files in one hand. He entered a room at the end of the corridor with Little Busy at his tail.

It was a large room with a long table and a dozen chairs. There was no one else in it. He strode to the head of the table, dumped the files on it and slumped into the chair.

Minutes passed. Some men and women in lab whites streamed into the room and took their seats. When all the seats were occupied, Cao Kun started speaking.

"What's he saying?" Kuan Hee asked.

"Shush!" Lina said. "Let me hear some more first." She scribbled on a notepad as she listened to the meeting.

"Lina, tell me what they are saying," Kuan Hee snapped. He was getting impatient.

At last, Lina spoke. "They are discussing a delivery schedule for human clones."

"Human clones?" Kuan Hee parroted.

"That's what Cao Kun is saying. They have to get ready eight human clones over the next four weeks."

Just then, the door opened and a man in a wheelchair entered. He wheeled himself to an unoccupied space along the table.

"It's him. It's the man on the gurney in the house," Kuan Hee stammered.

"You mean the one with the wires on his head?" Lina said.

"Yes. But, he's in a wheelchair this time," Kuan Hee said.

"Shush!" Lina said. "Let me listen in to their conversation."

There was silence in the van for the next few minutes.

"The man in the wheelchair," Lina said. "His name is Wei Xin. He is telling the others the mind swapping is on schedule."

"He—his mannerisms are familiar," Kuan Hee said. "He gestures like my dad."

"Remember? He's got your dad's mind," Lina said. "They cloned your father's mind into his brain."

"But, he's not my dad," Kuan Hee said. "I've got to

destroy him before he commits more evil."

"Are you serious?" Lina said. "You want to kill him?" Kuan Hee nodded. "What about your father's mind. It is in his brain. If he dies, your father dies too."

"I've got my dad's mind clone data in the robot tank," Kuan Hee said. "My dad's memories are safe."

"Oh! I forgot about that," Lina said. "But, we still don't know how to make use of it, Kuan Hee."

"I can ask the Brigadier for help," Kuan Hee said. "He's got a whole lab behind him—and my dad's staff too."

"We've been here ages, Kuan Hee," Lina said, fisting her bended knees. "I'm hot and tired."

"Time to pick up Tim and Navin at Tanglin Road," Kuan Hee said. "Let's go."

The pair made an awkward attempt to get down from the back of the van. They had been sitting for hours and their legs were numb from inactivity. They climbed into the driver's section and Kuan Hee set the vehicle to autonomous mode. He tapped Tanglin Road on a virtual map on the front panel. Then they settled down in the cool airconditioning as the vehicle cruised down Shelford Road and turned into Bukit Timah Road.

On autonomous mode, the van moved at a leisurely pace as it negotiated traffic along the roads, but the pair did not complain. They were not in a hurry to get to their destination. They were relishing the air-conditioning.

Kuan Hee took over the wheel along Tanglin Road. Tim and Navin were waiting for them along the sidewalk. They had gotten down from the contractor's pickup when it left the embassy. The two men slumped into the back of the van, resting against its frame and the van resumed its journey.

Lina broke the silence. "Did you guys find out anything at the embassy?"

"Give us a minute to cool down," Tim said. "No. Five minutes."

"I've never been so tired before," Navin said.

"Yeah. It was solid work, painting the swimming pool area," Tim added. "It was hot, real hot. The reflection from the water in the pool made things worse. I think I'm having a headache now."

"Gosh! It's not that bad," Kuan Hee said. "You guys are army trained, you know."

"What's that got to do with painting the place?" Navin said. "It was sheer hard work. My muscles are aching."

"I thought it was a simple job," Kuan Hee said.

"Next time, you do it," Tim said. "Then you'll know."

"OK, guys. Quit bickering," Lina said. "So what did you find out?"

"We didn't get to see Cao Kun the whole day," Navin said. "Perhaps, we missed him."

"He was at the apartments all day," Kuan Hee said as he placed the van in autonomous mode again, indicating Upper Serangoon Road as destination on the screen.

"So did you find anything suspicious?" Lina said.

"There's nothing secretive in the embassy grounds," Navin said. "Just people going about their work. There doesn't seem to be any covert thing happening."

"Any areas off-limits? Tightly guarded?" Kuan Hee asked.

"Nope. No part of the embassy was out of bounds to us," Tim said. "Nobody bothered about us. We were free to loiter around."

"And no plainclothes guarding the grounds," Navin said. "Just the usual uniformed CISCO guards at the gates."

"That's strange," Kuan Hee said.

"Yeah. We thought it was strange too," Tim said. "We expected them to be hiding things there. It was a disappointment."

"What about you two?" Navin asked.

Lina beat Kuan Hee to the punch. "Loads happening." Like a machinegun, she rattled off in quick succession what they had seen at Cherry Blossoms Apartments, pausing at times to catch her breath. She didn't give Kuan Hee any chance to add his two cents' worth.

Then she sat back in her seat to let the two men in the back digest her stakeout report.

At last, Tim spoke. "Something fishy is going on at the apartments."

"It's all happening in Shelford Road," Navin said, "and not at the Chinese Embassy."

"Same modus operandi as in Medan," Kuan Hee said.

"Let's put everything together, shall we? Kuan Hee said.

"What we do know is they are manufacturing eight human clones," Tim said.

"Two of which they are sending over to Shanghai on Tuesday," Kuan Hee added.

"We don't know for sure where the other clones are going," Navin said. "But I can guess it's also Shanghai."

"We don't know the purpose of these clones," Tim said.

"Or what they look like," Navin said. "Do they look more like robots or human beings?"

"Exactly," Lina said. "Also, can they think like us?"

"Maybe they are only slightly better than robots," Kuan Hee said, "and their AI is only good enough for them to react to situations. They can't reason."

"So many unknowns," Lina said. "Just what is the truth behind these human clones?"

"Beats me," Kuan Hee said.

"May I also add—we don't know who's behind this machination," Tim said.

"So what we need do now," Kuan Hee said, "is to find the answers as quickly as possible. Solve the riddle and put an end to their evil scheme."

"Yeah. Kuan Hee's right," Tim said. "We can't rest till that happens." The other adventurers nodded in unison.

"I suggest we move in two directions," Tim said.

"One—follow the trail of the human clones. Two—track Cao Kun and whom he meets or talks to."

"Good idea," Kuan Hee said.

"I agree," Navin said. "Both directions will eventually meet somewhere along the way and we'll get our answers."

"I'll take care of the human clones," Tim said.

"Then I'll follow Cao Kun," Kuan Hee said, "with Lina."

"I'll partner Tim," Navin said.

"Everything's settled then," Kuan Hee said.

CHAPTER 27

The Brigadier was unassuming as he sat across the table from Kuan Hee and Lina in the ToastBox outlet at the basement level of NEX, a shopping mall in Serangoon Central.

"It's a little warm today," Brigadier Walmsley said as he fanned himself with his hunting hat. "I'm still not used to the tropical heat." Kuan Hee and Lina grinned. The airconditioning had been working extraordinarily well that afternoon.

"Your mother's taking a little longer in Fort Bragg," Brigadier Walmsley said, "because she and your father spent a good few years there. She needs to sort out his things first. You know he's got a lot of research notes she needs to gather." Kuan Hee nodded.

In between sips of his favourite *kopi oh kosong*, the Brigadier regaled Kuan Hee with anecdotes of his adventures in Southeast Asia and finally got to the part about meeting Kuan Hee's father the first time. Then he launched into another long rendition expounding the firm friendship that the two men had forged over the years. Kuan Hee and Lina sat giving attentive ears for the next hour.

The Brigadier was tearing. It was the first time the pair had seen his vulnerable side. He wiped his eyes with a handkerchief.

"Kuan Hee, your father was a noble man," Brigadier Walmsley said. "He had high hopes for his inventions." He paused and then continued. "Alas, he went before his time."

The Brigadier leaned forward and twiddled his thumbs. It was a long minute before he collected his thoughts.

Kuan Hee was anxious to seek the Brigadier's help in putting to practical use his father's mind clone. He could hardly wait longer. But wait he had to, for the Brigadier had started another round.

"You know, Kuan Hee," Brigadier Walmsley said. "Your father believed that we human beings were manufactured by alien beings from a faraway galaxy. That was what got him started in this cloning research. He wanted to replicate the aliens' feat. He wanted to prove this theory—we human beings were clones made by aliens far more advanced than we are."

Without being prompted, the Brigadier had now delved into Kuan Hee's pet question for him. The Brigadier had read his thoughts almost effortlessly. Kuan Hee gazed in amazement.

"Kuan Hee, you are a smart chap," Brigadier Walmsley said. "You take after your father. You should be able to understand what I have just said."

"Yes, Mr Walmsley," Kuan Hee said.

"Fortunately, you father's precious mind clone is safe in your hands," Brigadier Walmsley said. "His life's work is in it. With it, you have the ability to inherit his skills and vast knowledge—instantly." Kuan Hee nodded.

"But, it is a double-edged sword, Kuan Hee," Brigadier Walmsley said. "You gain something precious; you also lose something equally precious."

"Mr Walmsley, that is what I'm curious about," Kuan Hee said. "How do I make use of Dad's mind clone? I don't have the equipment or the expertise."

"That's what I just said, Kuan Hee," Brigadier Walmsley said.

Kuan Hee pondered over what the Brigadier had been rambling about the last few minutes. He stared blankly at the wizened face with the scraggly beard opposite him.

"Kuan Hee, if you are thinking of implanting your father's mind clone in your brain," The Brigadier said, "I'd advise against doing it."

"But, why, Mr Walmsley?" Kuan Hee asked.

"Because—" The Brigadier brought his face close to Kuan Hee's, "—you'll lose your memories once you do it. You will have no knowledge of your past. Everything—Lina, Huei Huei, your friends and your favourite things—will cease to exist in your mind. They will become strangers to you. In their place, new thoughts and feelings, alien to you now, will take over your most intimate spaces." The Brigadier leaned back in his seat.

"Kuan Hee, is that what you want?" Brigadier Walmsley said. "Is it worth sacrificing all that you love?"

"Kuan Hee. It's a horrid idea," Lina lashed out. "You can't do it. You can't forget me. You can't forget Huei Huei. I won't let you." She was almost in tears.

Kuan Hee wrapped his arm across her shoulder. "It's alright. Nothing's happened. We're just talking, that's all."

To inherit all his father's skills and knowledge, Kuan Hee would have to wipe out all his memories. That meant Lina would cease to exist as his beloved. Instead, his mother would be his one and only love. Kuan Hee agonised over this decision he had to make in the coming days.

"Not only will you forget me and Huei Huei. You will even forget your buddies!" Lina said.

"And you won't even remember you want to avenge your father," Brigadier Walmsley said. "So, do you still want to go ahead with it?" He looked at Kuan Hee in the eyes, expecting an answer but receiving none.

"Kuan Hee. Much as I want your father to come alive again," Brigadier Walmsley said. "I can't be selfish and think only of using his knowledge. I have to spare a thought for you. You are his only son—his precious son. I'm sure he'll never want you to take over his mind and lose your own. Not in a million years." The Brigadier paused to take a sip of his coffee. "We'll find another way to sieve his knowledge from his mind clone. Our scientists may be able to do it. It just takes time. Trust us. Trust me, Kuan Hee."

CHAPTER 28

A metallic-silver Mercedes-Benz turned out of the Chinese Embassy gates into the road. Behind its headlamps, a fluttering Chinese stateflag atop a tiny mast announced to one and all the country's top diplomat, the Chinese ambassador, was on an official journey in the back of the limousine.

Two car-lengths behind it, in a rented van, Kuan Hee and Lina kept the limousine in sight.

"Kuan Hee, why are we tailing the ambassador?" Lina asked.

"Cos what the Chinese are doing at Shelford Road setup is just too big for the Chinese ambassador to this country not to know anything about," Kuan Hee said. "He must figure in this somewhere. I can feel it in my bones."

"What if you are wrong?" Lina said.

"Then—it's back to the drawing board," Kuan Hee said. "But, I can bet you I can't be wrong this time round."

The Mercedes-Benz breezed through Orchard Road and entered a service road in front of Paragon, an upper-end mall in the shopping district. It came to a stop in front of the side entrance. Kuan Hee promptly dispatched Little Busy after a stocky balding man in a navy blue business suit who emerged from the back of the limousine.

"Aren't we going to follow him in?" Lina asked.

"It will take time to look for a parking space in this upscale mall," Kuan Hee said. "We can't afford to lose sight of him."

"But I can keep watch on him," Lina insisted.

"Nope. It's not safe for you to do it alone," Kuan Hee said.

The matter settled, Kuan Hee drove the van into the basement car park as Lina watched the Chinese ambassador's movements on the remote's screen.

"The ambassador's entered a bespoke tailor shop on the second level," Lina said.

"OK. Luckily I sent out Little Busy after him. I can't seem to find a vacant lot," Kuan Hee said as he manoeuvred the van around the car park.

"It's Orchard Road, for goodness's sake, Kuan Hee," Lina said. "Everyone comes here to shop."

"Where's the ambassador now?" Kuan Hee asked.

"Still inside," Lina said. "Someone's coming out now. Looks like the ambassador, but dressed differently. He's in an oversized flowery shirt and Bermuda shorts."

Kuan Hee craned his neck to look at the remote's screen. "It's him alright. He's changed out of his office wear. Strange!"

"He's going down the escalator, heading for the taxi stand," Lina said. "He looks grim."

"Gosh! He's leaving the mall," Kuan Hee said. He revved up the van's engine and shot out of the basement car park, oblivious to the honking of several drivers whose right of way he had ignored.

"Where's he now," Kuan Hee asked as he emerged from the car park.

"In a Comfort taxi, moving along Bideford Road towards the Istana," Lina said. "Little Busy's perched itself on the taxi sign."

"Don't tell me he's going to the Istana dressed that

way," Kuan Hee said. Lina shrugged her shoulders in reply.

"The blue taxi in front. That's the one," Lina said.

"Don't worry. I've locked it in my sights now," Kuan Hee said. "We won't lose the ambassador this time."

The Comfort taxi turned left into a road just before the Istana and entered Bukit Timah Road, an arterial road. Then it cruised up the plush residential district.

"He could be heading for Shelford Road," Kuan Hee said.

Just as Kuan Hee had predicted, the blue taxi made a U-turn and glided down the opposite direction, turning into Shelford Road.

"We've hit pay dirt," Kuan Hee said. "He's got to be in the evil scheme too. Cunning devil! Fancy using that switcheroo trick to disguise his tracks."

The taxi unloaded its paying passenger at Cherry Blossoms Apartments and promptly left. Meanwhile, Kuan Hee had parked the van at a shady spot outside. He didn't want the van's metal frame to bake in the searing midday heat; he didn't know how long they would be stationary.

"You guys are in Shelford Road too?" Tim said into his smartphone.

"Yeah," Kuan Hee said into his iPhone. "Whereabouts are you two?"

"On a bench somewhere outside the back gate," Tim said. "We're walking over to you now."

Tim and Navin climbed into the back of the van and settled on some cardboard laid on the floor.

"*Wah!* Nice airconditioning," Navin said as the two men savoured the cool air.

"We were practically melting out there in the sun," Tim complained. "You two are really lucky." Kuan Hee and Lina grinned.

"Seems all directions turn into Shelford Road," Kuan Hee said. "This must be the nerve centre of their operations."

"For sure," Navin said. "Things are getting clearer now. We know the Chinese ambassador figures in this scheme."

"How did you know the ambassador's in it?" Tim asked.

"Lucky hunch, I guess," Kuan Hee said. "Cao Kun's here too?"

Tim nodded. "We have been staking out the place since early morning. Tizzy has its eyes on him right now."

The two insect drones were now perched on different spots in the same place—the conference room. The Chinese ambassador was calling the shots in an armchair at the head of the long table in the room. Around the table sat men and women in lab whites, with Cao Kun on the ambassador's right. Wei Xin was conspicuously absent.

The stocky man roared at his charges. He demanded they quicken their paces. They were behind schedule. Their deadline was drawing near and the people at the top were getting impatient for progress. It was astonishing watching him admonish his audience; they said nary a word.

"What deadline is he talking about?" Kuan Hee asked.

"He didn't say. He merely used *jiézhǐ rìqí* without any elaboration," Lina said.

The adventurers abruptly turned their attention to the meeting, for a sudden loud thud had rung out in the room. The Chinese ambassador had just slammed a pistol on the table. Apparently, he had drawn the weapon he had concealed in his waist.

"What's happening?" Navin asked.

"He's saying if they can't make the deadline, they'll have to face the pistol," Lina said.

"S-e-r-i-o-u-s, man," Tim said.

"I think he means it," Kuan Hee said. "Look at his face. It's fuming red." With the two remotes' screens to watch, the adventurers had two different views of the meeting room; the robot drones had the entire room covered from where they were perched.

"What's Cao Kun saying?" Navin asked.

"He's giving the rundown of the revised schedule for the human clones to leave the lab," Lina said. "Shush! I need to listen."

Just then, the door opened. Wei Xin wheeled himself into the room and stopped on the left of the ambassador. When Cao Kun had finished his presentation, Wei Xin spoke.

"Wei Xin says the first batch of human clones has left safely for Shanghai," Lina said. "He personally saw them off."

The Chinese ambassador broke into loud clapping and the rest of the room followed suit. He was grinning from ear to ear now. It was an abrupt change of mood from earlier on. His pistol was nowhere to be seen on the table.

"What's the schedule?" Kuan Hee asked. Lina referred to her note before replying.

"Total of eight clones to be delivered in four batches. Each batch consists of two clones. Let's see. Delivery of one batch every Thursday starting from today."

"That means—in a month their mission's complete," Kuan Hee said.

"We've got to stop them before then," Tim said. "Before they do more damage."

"Too late to deal with the first batch," Navin said. "It's out of our hands now."

"Shall we tell the Brigadier?" Lina said. "Perhaps, he can help."

"No. Not yet, Lina," Kuan Hee said. "When the time is ripe, perhaps." He wanted to do the crooks in personally; sweet revenge was on his mind. He wasn't going to let anyone or anything stand in his way—not even the Brigadier! It would be better if the Brigadier had no inkling of his selfish plan. But, it was wishful thinking on his part.

"We've got to destroy the human clones en route to the airport," Kuan Hee said. "We don't have the manpower needed to take down this place. There are too many people here. There's also no telling what weapons they've got hidden in the premises. It's too risky to launch an attack here."

"I agree," Tim said. "This place is too big for us four amateurs to handle."

Lina couldn't help but let out a guffaw. The men stared at her in bewilderment.

"The things we've done in the course of our adventures over the years certainly make us much more than amateurs, Tim," Lina explained. "We're virtually experts in the art of spying!" The entire van broke into laughter.

CHAPTER 29

The plan was straightforward. The four adventurers were to waylay the truck conveying the two clones in the vicinity of a fringe road leading to the airport. AleXander the robots with their deadly laser beams and armor-piercing rockets were to figure prominently in the attack plan.

The problem was finding out the truck's route so that the adventurers could lie in wait in a secluded spot. They didn't want to stir up attention by attacking the truck in thick traffic.

"The only way is to tail the truck as it leaves Cherry Blossom Apartments," Tim said. "But, we may be discovered before we can make our move."

"It's a risk we have to take," Kuan Hee said.

"Why can't we attack the truck outside the apartments, say along Shelford Road?" Lina asked.

"Cos then they will know their lab's secret location has been exposed. They will move elsewhere," Tim said, "and we'll never be able to find them again."

"Then we strike them in one fell swoop at the apartments," Lina said.

"Gosh! Lina, you think too highly of us and our abilities," Navin said.

"We'll be dead meat before we get near the clones, Lina," Tim said.

"Lina, this is a big group we're up against," Kuan Hee said. "It's not like our previous adventures."

"Kuan Hee is right," Tim said. "So a surprise attack is the best choice."

"Correction. It's the only choice," Navin said.

Next Thursday morning found Navin and Lina staking out Cherry Blossoms Apartments from behind a bush along Shelford Road. They let Little Busy fly into the compound to look for the truck, which would deliver the two clones to the airfreight multiplex at Terminal 5 in Changi Airport.

It seemed the two adventurers were too early. The truck was parked in the front porch, but its back doors were wide open. There was nothing inside. But the compound was abuzz with activity. In the driveway, there were men with menacing looks lingering around two cars. At the front porch, men in lab whites were hauling large boxes out of the front entrance. Soon, they were loading these into the truck. Wei Xin appeared at the front door. He barked orders to the men in lab whites. Little Busy hovered in the air near the walls of the building.

"I don't see human clones anywhere, do you?" Navin said.

"Don't tell me they are in the boxes," Lina said.

"One. Two. Three. Four. I count four boxes," Navin said. "Three in the truck and one on the porch."

"Two of the boxes are large enough to hold an adult in a sitting position," Lina said. "They've got 'Diplomatic Bag' stickers on them."

"Yeah. The clones could be in them," Navin said. "There's nothing else going into the truck."

"They're shutting the doors," Lina said. "We must be right."

"Quick! Get Little Busy on top of the truck," Navin

said.

Lina let Little Busy fly over the truck and attach itself to the top of the driver's cabin.

"Little Busy's in position," Lina said. "I'll WhatsApp Kuan Hee to let him know." She started tapping on her Samsung smartphone.

"Now. We wait," Navin said. "I think the two cars are going together with the truck."

"I'll turn Little Busy's cameras on them," Lina said.

They saw two men helping Wei Xin into one of the cars. Then all the men boarded the vehicles and the convoy of three vehicles rolled out of the driveway into Shelford Road.

"Wei Xin's in the first car with two men," Navin said. "Another two men in the driver's cabin of the truck and two more in the car behind."

"OK. I'm sending the info to Kuan Hee right now," Lina said.

The vehicles moved past the hidden adventurers and disappeared into a bend in the road.

"There's nothing more we can do here," Navin said. "Let's go. It's going to be a long walk to the main road from here." They patted the grass off their clothes and trod down the road. Lina kept her eyes on the remote's screen. She needed to update Kuan Hee on the route taken by the convoy.

Meanwhile, Kuan Hee and Tim had parked the van along Tanah Merah Coast Road, just before it forked into Changi East Drive. The two men started their long wait for the truck to travel from the middle of the island to the east coast.

"Don't turn off the engine," Tim said. "It's a hot day. I don't want to melt in the van."

"The truck is moving along the Pan Island Expressway," Kuan Hee said, looking at Lina's WhatsApp message on his iPhone.

Tim brought up a map of the island and zoomed in on

the Pan Island Expressway. He fingered the roads in Changi East, which the Pan Island Expressway connected to. "The logical choice would be for the truck to turn right into East Coast Parkway after the Pan Island Expressway. From there, it will do two left turns, first into Tanah Merah Coast Road and then into Changi East Drive. Thereafter, it'll turn left again into the Cargo Terminal Megaplex, where the airfreight terminal is located."

"I think so too," Kuan Hee said. "We're here, at the junction of Tanah Merah Coast Road and Changi East Drive. The truck has to pass us to get to the airfreight megaplex in Terminal 5. We'll ambush it here." He took AleXander the robots out of his backpack. They stood with their arms at their sides, as if ready to move off at a moment's notice. Kuan Hee pressed a button on the robots' back and their front panels flipped open. Both robots were now armed and primed for action.

Kuan Hee's iPhone chimed again. It was Lina on WhatsApp. The convoy had turned into East Coast Parkway. It was only minutes away from Kuan Hee and Tim.

Kuan Hee got down from the driver's seat and climbed into the back of the van while Tim slid over to take the wheel.

"We don't have any hardware with us," Tim said. "So we have to be extra careful."

"Don't worry, I'll keep Alex by our side. Its laser beams will protect us," Kuan Hee said. "Xander will work his rockets on our target."

At Kuan Hee's command, Xander leapt out of the van and stood with its feet apart about a metre into the road, ready to pounce on its unsuspecting victims who would be coming up on the road behind them. The robot was only thirty centimetres tall; no one would notice it.

By now, the convoy had turned into Changi East Drive. Kuan Hee could see the vehicles from the back window of the van. Little Busy had already lifted itself into the air and flown to safety. It was time for Xander to do its work.

"I'll let the first car pass," Kuan Hee told Tim. He dragged the glass window open and waited for the precise moment before shouting some commands to Xander.

At once, Xander leapt into the path of the truck and launched two rockets successively from its arsenal. Though tiny, the rockets packed a punch. Each one could blast a hole through an army tank. The rockets hit the truck, sending it up in smoke in seconds. It was now a burning heap of metal. The car behind the truck could not stop in time to avoid a collision. It exploded into flames instantly.

By now, Xander had jumped into the van, which roared away from the burning wreckage. From the back window, Kuan Hee saw the lead car in the convoy stop in the middle of the road. Two men were helping Wei Xin out of the car. Wei Xin was gesticulating frantically. He was hopping mad.

Kuan Hee allowed a wicked smile to betray his abhorrence of the scene of carnage behind him.

"It's a piece of cake," Tim declared. Kuan Hee could not agree more.

"I could have sent Wei Xin up in flames too," Kuan Hee said. But he didn't. Say what he would, Kuan Hee didn't have the heart to set Wei Xin ablaze, for doing so was akin to destroying his father, whose mind had been installed in the evil scientist's brain.

CHAPTER 30

That evening, the four adventurers sat in the living room of 79 Jalan Nuang, pondering their next move.

"The Chinese aren't going to take this lying down," Tim said. "We've struck at their heart. They will hit back—and hard. We've got to be ready for the backlash when it comes."

"But we have an advantage," Kuan Hee said. "I don't think they know who hit them yet. By the time they do, we'll have destroyed the rest of the human clones."

"Too bad I wasn't there when Xander launched his rockets," Navin said. "I bet it was fun."

"The flames shot up a few storeys high," Tim said.

"Wei Xin's jaw practically dropped open," Kuan Hee added.

"But people died you know," Lina said.

"They deserved it," Kuan Hee said. "Doing evil doesn't pay."

"Couldn't we have just destroyed the clones without killing the men in the truck too?" Lina said.

"If the truck had reached the cargo megaplex, it would have been too late to stop it," Kuan Hee said. "Lina, these people's heinous plot—if successful, could put many more people's lives in danger. Besides, the men in the truck looked like thugs. At the very least, we had stopped them doing more evil. Goodness knows how many people they have killed in their lives."

"Let's not dwell on it," Tim said. "What's done is done."

"Yeah. We've got to figure out how to deal with the next batch of human clones," Navin said. "I don't think these guys will use the same route to the airport."

"I vote we stake out Shelford Road again," Tim said. "Find out their plans."

"Won't they be on the alert?" Lina said. "It'll be dangerous getting so near to them."

"We have no choice, Lina," Kuan Hee said. "Perhaps, you should stay out of the next mission."

Without a word, Lina stormed out of the room. Then she returned and glared at him. "I'll do no such thing. You're horrid, Kuan Hee."

"Pipe down, guys," Tim said.

"Look! The burning inferno's on TV," Navin said.

The adventurers' attention turned to the large wall-mounted television set in front of them. The seven o'clock news was airing and a female news presenter was shown, on site, reporting the incident. They heard her saying that four charred bodies—beyond recognition—had been dragged out of the debris. A representative of the Chinese Embassy appeared on the news clip telling the presenter the embassy's truck had been en route to the airport when it suddenly exploded. When asked for a possible reason, he replied he was clueless.

"They are covering up the incident," Tim said.

"For obvious reasons, they want to keep it under wraps," Kuan Hee said.

"Wei Xin's nowhere in sight," Kuan Hee said.

"It's a secretive project," Navin said. "I'm sure they don't want him showing his face on national TV."

"I still can't figure out why he's in a wheelchair," Kuan

Hee said. "It is one of two burning questions in my mind."

"So what's the other, Kuan Hee?" Navin asked.

"Huh?" Kuan Hee said. "Oh! How should I put it? I don't know how he managed to control my dad's mind in him. I mean, my dad's mind went into his brain right? So his own mind should have been wiped out. So how is it he's still in control of his own mind?"

"You're not making sense, Kuan Hee," Lina said.

Tim came to Kuan Hee's rescue. "Remember Jordan? His father erased his memories and installed his own memories in Jordan's brain. Look what happened then. Jordan wasn't himself. He couldn't recognize us. He had become his father."

"What Kuan Hee wants to say is Wei Xin shouldn't remember who he really is—but he does," Navin said.

"Kinda complicated, isn't it?" Lina said.

"I guess so," Kuan Hee said. "In Jordan's case, there was a Jekyll and Hyde moment. Sometimes, Jordan would wake up and assume control of his own mind. Other times, his father reigned in his mind. So I thought in Wei Xin's case, things would pretty much be the same. But they aren't. That's the problem. I just can't figure out why it's different this time and how the Chinese scientists managed to let Wei Xin control his own mind—not let my dad's mind take over totally."

"Amazing. Simply amazing," Tim said. "The Chinese must have some pretty talented people in their payroll."

"Of course they do," Navin said. "With a population of nearly two billion people, finding talented people should be a breeze."

"We are Chinese too," Lina said. "We Chinese are good at science and technology."

"And we Indians are good at mathematics and computer programming," Navin added.

"Guys. Stop typecasting our races," Tim said. He was the voice of reason in their group. "Don't generalize our talents into the moulds you think they fit. Talented people exist everywhere—in every race."

"Tim's right," Kuan Hee said. "We shouldn't be sterotyping people. It's mean."

"OK. OK," Navin said. "Now, where were we? How did we get sidetracked?"

"Beats me," Kuan Hee said.

"So what were we talking about?" Tim asked.

"Kuan Hee's two burning questions," Lina said.

"Oh. Yes. My two burning questions," Kuan Hee parroted. "I wonder—the reason Wei Xin's in a wheelchair. Maybe the operation on him went awry. That's the only plausible explanation I've been able to come up with."

"Wah! Even with these scientists' brilliant minds, things can go wrong," Lina said. "Kuan Hee. Your father must be the best scientist around." Kuan Hee smiled. "No, *lah*."

"That's humility for you," Navin said.

"Plain flattering to me," Tim said. "Wife buttering up husband." Everyone broke into laughter. The mood in the room had lightened up.

"But, the Chinese scientists must have found a way to inhibit certain portions of my dad's mind," Kuan Hee said, "so that Wei Xin still has some control over his mind. This explains why Wei Xin didn't come looking for me and Mum. My Dad's mind isn't in control. Wei Xin's not my Dad."

"Kuan Hee, you were telling us you want to install your father's mind in yours," Tim said. "Is that for real?"

"He's not going to do it," Lina said. "Not ever—if I can help it."

"I was just exploring the idea," Kuan Hee said. "But, I don't think I can go far. I can't even make a copy of my own mind. The whole process is beyond me. I'll need my dad's—the Brigadier's research team. It's not even a possibility."

"Thank heavens for that," Lina said.

"Kuan Hee, did you speak to the Brigadier about it?"

Tim asked.

"I sure did," Kuan Hee said, "when Lina and I met him at NEX recently."

"So did he warm up to your idea?" Navin asked.

"On the contrary, he kept trying to talk Kuan Hee out of it," Lina said.

"No. He didn't," Kuan Hee said.

"He did," Lina said. "I should know. I was sitting beside you when he lectured you on the dangers of mind cloning."

"What exactly did the Brigadier say, Kuan Hee?" Tim asked.

"The Brigadier told me that human cloning is outlawed by the United Nations. It prohibits all forms of human cloning. He went on to say everyone's doing it, turning a blind eye to the law in the interest of science. Cos the lure of making a real live human clone in our lifetime is simply irresistible."

"I remember the Brigadier advised you against it," Lina said. "I distinctly remember him asking you whether it was worth sacrificing everything you love for it." Kuan Hee was silent for the next few minutes. Lina had hit paydirt with her words. The other adventurers looked at each other, not knowing what to say.

It was Tim who broke the uneasy silence in the room. "Maybe, in time, you will learn how to do it. Then you can harness his skills and knowledge. It won't be too late."

"Yes. Tim's right," Navin said. "You can wait, can't you? You are still young. We're all still young."

"Perhaps, you guys are right," Kuan Hee said. "Perhaps, I was a little rash. I should be glad my dad lives on in the 3D images etched in the holographic optical data storage drive." He paused. "What matters is—this data storage drive is safe in my hands. Nothing else matters."

"Yeah. Kuan Hee, nothing else matters," Lina echoed.

"What's our next move?" Navin asked. He was eager to move on with the discussion.

"Guess we continue to stakeout Shelford Road," Tim said. "It's the only way to keep abreast of their development."

"Not so," Navin said. "Remember the Chinese Embassy?"

"Oh yeah. I forgot," Tim said.

"For sure, they will make changes to their schedule," Kuan Hee said.

"Why not you and Lina keep tabs on Cao Kun and the Chinese ambassador? Navin and I will keep an eye on Shelford Road," Tim said. The adventurers nodded in unison.

CHAPTER 31

The Chinese Embassy in Tanglin Road was crawling with plainclothes when Kuan Hee and Lina arrived for a day of reconnaissance in their rental van. Except for their civilian attire, the plainclothes looked like they belonged to a uniformed corp.

"Must be Chinese agents," Kuan Hee said. After releasing Little Busy into the air, he drove the van away from the embassy, parking it along the road a hundred metres away from the embassy gates. "It's safer here."

Little Busy busied itself following the ambassador as he went about his business. The ambassador was in a bad mood today, ranting and raving as he negotiated the corridors of the embassy with his minders at his heels.

"What's he complaining about?" Kuan Hee asked.

"I can't hear him clearly," Lina said. "Let me get Little Busy nearer to him." At her direction, Little Busy sped after the ambassador. It was now hovering above him.

A minder came up to the ambassador with news of the arrival of visitors from Beijing. They were waiting for him in his office.

"The ambassador is rushing to his office," Kuan Hee said. "Must be important visitors. Let's see who they are."

Flitting into a large room at a secluded corner of the ground floor, Little Busy saw two visitors rising from a sofa to shake hands with the ambassador. All three sat down to conversation. The ambassador's minders had excused themselves from the room.

"The visitors are from the Central Government Investigative Unit in Beijing," Lina said. "They are here to probe the case of the burning truck. The older man is Zhang He Jun and the other Wang Chen Ming."

"They do work fas—"

"Shush!" Lina said. "Let me hear them talk first."

The minutes passed. To Kuan Hee, these were agonizing minutes. He longed to hear what Lina had to tell him about the men's conversation.

"Lina, just what are they saying?" Kuan Hee asked.

"It's strange. They aren't talking about the human clones," Lina said. "Instead, the ambassador is telling them a short circuit in the electrical wiring of the truck caused it to go up in flames. He deeply regretted the loss of four lives."

"*Wah seh*," Kuan Hee said. "Why is the ambassador hiding the truth? These visitors are not in cahoots with the ambassador after all."

"The four dead men are from the Military Attache Office," Lina said. "The investigators are asking what they were escorting to the airport."

"So what did the ambassador tell them?" Kuan Hee asked.

"He claims he needs clearance from Beijing to release the info to them," Lina said. "But these men are from Beijing. I'm confused."

"I think he's playing for time," Kuan Hee said. "The investigators' visit must have taken him by surprise."

"If the Chinese government has sanctioned the human clones, why does he need to hide things from them?" Lina asked.

"Search me," Kuan Hee said. "Could be these

investigators have not been cleared to receive top-secret info. The human clones are a top-secret project."

After the investigators from Beijing had left the room, Cao Kun came in, shoulders hunched. Something had cowed him into reticence. This time, when he spoke, it was in a subdued tone. But he didn't get a chance to say much, for the ambassador was in a fiery mood, waving his hands in the air as he reprimanded the man.

"Their plan is in disarray. They need time to manufacture replacement clones. The ambassador says their master is furious," Lina said.

"Master? They have a master?"

"*Zhŭzi.* That's what the ambassador said," Lina said. "It means 'master'."

"Lina, every word they say is important," Kuan Hee said. "Don't miss a single word."

"Don't worry. I won't," Lina said. She was glad her mastery of Chinese was proving useful to Kuan Hee. She was a valuable asset to him after all.

"*Alamak!* We forgot to tail the investigators," Kuan Hee said.

"But, we only have Little Busy with us," Lina said. "Tizzy is with Tim and Navin."

Meanwhile, on a grassy verge outside the back gate of Cherry Blossoms Apartments in Shelford Road, Tim and Navin sat. Tim was fiddling with his iPad while Navin kept his eyes glued on Tizzy's remote control. Tizzy was on duty in the apartments' compound, taking in the activities of the Chinese operatives. It had to be careful not to be spotted today, for there were two drones hovering over the premises. Plainclothes were milling around in the compound. The Chinese were taking no chances.

"Are these drones able to sense Tizzy's presence?" Navin asked.

"I really don't know," Tim said. "The drones are unlike those we see in the shops. They could be used for military surveillance. They might be able to sense heat from the equipment in Tizzy's body. Just keep Tizzy away from them."

"Don't worr—"

There was a commotion where the two adventurers sat. Someone had come up behind Navin and wrapped him in his arms. Navin let out a cry, but it was too late. He passed out from a knock on the nape of his head. Tim wriggled out of the strong arms of another man. He staggered to his feet and made for the bushes below, with the man barely metres behind him. Suddenly a shot rang out. Tim fell and rolled down the slope. The man who fired the shot stumbled down the slope after him. At the bottom of the slope, Tim heaved himself up and wobbled towards the busy Bukit Timah junction. His first thoughts were to get to where people were clustered. He was oblivious to the intense pain radiating down his back. *The hawker centre— must reach the hawker centre.* In the car park outside the hawker centre, he collapsed. Quickly, people milled around him. Someone stooped to lend a helping hand, while another pressed some tissue paper on his bleeding back. A third called for an ambulance.

Back in the van parked along Tanglin Road, Kuan Hee and Lina had no inkling of the drama unfolding behind Shelford Road.

"Tim is not updating the WhatsApp group chat," Lina said. "Navin's not answering either."

"Keep trying," Kuan Hee said. "Maybe, it's a network problem."

But the minutes passed uneventfully. Both Tim's and Navin's smartphones were not responding to their calls. Kuan Hee feared the worst.

"Quick! We've got to go to Shelford Road," Kuan Hee said. He revved the van's engine and it roared to life. It sped off towards the Chinese Embassy. The pair had to pick up Little Busy first. With the robot drone safely on board, the van raced towards the plush Bukit Timah district.

The mood was somber in the van. Silence prevailed the entire journey. Soon the van reached Lornie Road, which faced the back of the Shelford Road residences. Kuan Hee stopped the van along the road and, leaving a reluctant Lina behind in the van, clambered up the grassy slope to where Tim and Navin were supposed to position themselves. There was no one in sight. He scanned the grassy verge. The grass was flattened at one spot. *Tim and Navin had to be sitting here.* Kuan Hee moved around the spot, kicking the grass as he hovered over it. There was nothing lying in it. Tim and Navin were nowhere to be seen. So were their backpacks and Tizzy's remote control. *Where have they gone?* He looked down the slope, trying to find clues. Then he retraced his steps to the main road below. Near the bottom of the slope, he saw what looked like bloodstains on the grass. He knelt beside the stains for a close look. *It's blood all right.* At once, he felt a shiver down his spine. *Something has happened to them.* He ran back to the van.

"Kuan Hee, look—across the road," Lina screeched.

Kuan Hee turned his eyes to the car park across the road. There were scores of people—under trees, on pavements, among parked cars—everywhere. Something had happened.

"Wait here. Don't you dare move," Kuan Hee shouted. He dashed across the road to where the crowd had gathered. He elbowed his way through the throng of people, to the focus of attention. There, lying limp in a man's arms was—Tim! Kuan Hee dropped to his knees and cradled his bosom friend in his arms.

"I'm here, Tim," Kuan Hee said. "Hang on, dear friend."

"We're waiting for the ambulance," the man who had been holding Tim said. "Are you his friend?" Kuan Hee nodded. He was tearing. He took a wad of tissue paper from his pocket and pressed it on Tim's back.

"The ambulance's taking ages to arrive," Kuan Hee complained. Tim was delirious. He was mumbling away.

Finally, the ambulance pulled into the car park. Attendants packed Tim into the ambulance and, sirens wailing, the ambulance sped into the traffic. But not before Kuan Hee found out where it was taking Tim.

Kuan Hee sprinted back to the van across the road. On seeing his bloodied hands and shirt, Lina screamed. He folded her in his arms and comforted her. She was too squeamish to handle traumatic situations. It was minutes before her cries petered out. It was time to rush to Tan Tock Seng Hospital, where Tim had been taken.

At the Accidents & Emergency department of Tan Tock Seng Hospital, the pair loitered, waiting for news of Tim. It was to be a long wait. Tim had been rolled into an operating theatre. Doctors were now operating on him.

Images of the day's happenings flitted past Kuan Hee's mind as he sat slumped in a chair beside Lina. *I should have been more careful. I'm to blame.* His thoughts wandered to Navin. He sat up suddenly. *Navin's been caught.* He scanned his iPhone for messages and missed calls; there were none. *Navin must be in their hands.* Fear gripped his consciousness. He lingered in a state of shock. *What can I do? What must I do?*

Kuan Hee's best pals Tim and Navin were in trouble. He had no one to turn to. Lina was no help in this chaotic situation. The least he could do was to keep her calm. He had to compose himself or he risked getting her going emotional again. *I must rescue Navin. They'll torture him for sure. I must get to him before it's too late.* He never felt more helpless.

"Tim is safe now," Kuan Hee said. "The doctors are attending to him." He was trying to pacify Lina.

"Lina, you stay here. Wait for news," Kuan Hee said. "I need to go look for Navin."

"No! Kuan Hee. No! It's too dangerous," Lina

squealed. "You can't go alone. You could be killed."

But Kuan Hee's mind was set. He was adamant to save Navin no matter what he took—even if he had to die, he would not have any second thoughts. He pulled her away from him. "Listen, Lina. Pull yourself together, for goodness's sake. I—we can't very well let Navin die. I've got to save him. You look after Tim here. I'll be back soon. Trust me." Not looking back, Kuan Hee tore off through the hall, heading for the van in the basement, leaving behind a wailful Lina.

CHAPTER 32

As the van raced through the suburban district towards Bukit Timah, Kuan Hee's thoughts were on Navin. *He must be alive. He's got to be somewhere in Cherry Blossoms Apartments. I'll find him if it's the last thing I get to do.* The minutes fleeted past. Kuan Hee didn't know where Tim had hidden the SAR21s. The rifles, which hadn't been used in the past three years, had to be in deep storage in Tim's father's warehouse in Paya Lebar. Kuan Hee had to mount the rescue without them. He inhaled deeply. He had arrived outside the apartments in Shelford Road. It was time for action. Kuan Hee let Alex and Xander out of his backpack. They were his weapons. They would protect him from harm; they would help him rescue Navin safely.

Leaving the van by the roadside, Kuan Hee stole along the perimeter wall of the apartments, with the two robots at his heels. He set Little Busy into the air over the wall and watched the drone housefly broadcast live images of the compound on the remote's screen. Little Busy's work wasn't as easy as before. Now it had to hide from the two drones circling the air over the compound.

There was no time to lose. Kuan Hee had to find Navin quickly. There was no telling what these evil men would do to his best pal.

Little Busy flitted into the long building and explored the corridors on the upper floor. It entered the laboratory easily, for men and women in lab whites, wearing anxious looks, were scurrying around. But there was no sign of Navin. There was a line of gurneys with people lying on them in a corner of the laboratory. Kuan Hee piloted the robot housefly over them. At first look, the people on the gurneys were unfamiliar middle-aged Chinese men to him. They appeared to be asleep. Then one face stood out from the rest. There was a hint of recognition in Kuan Hee's eyes. He paused Little Busy over the figure. Kuan Hee's face lit up. The figure had the unmistakable broad cheeks. It was the Chinese President! Or was it? *Oh no. It's a clone of the President! Gosh! It so resembles the President. There's no way to tell them apart.* There was a moment of silence as Kuan Hee took in the full impact of his discovery. *Horror of Horrors! These evil men intend to usurp power. They are using human clones to take over the Chinese government!* Kuan Hee sank against the perimeter wall. *I was wrong. It's not the Chinese government that's stealing Dad's secrets. It's someone or some group that's intent on replacing China's top leaders with lookalike human clones. I've got to stop them before they can do harm.*

Kuan Hee knew he had to make a decision. Carry on looking for Navin or destroy the human clones. He could only do one. He was sure Navin wasn't on the upper floor, so he barked orders to Alex and Xander. All three climbed over the wall. Once they landed on the ground inside the compound, Kuan Hee threw all caution to the wind. The three intruders sprinted to the end of the building and entered a door. Then they climbed the stairs to the upper floor and stopped at the double-leaved glass doors. At Kuan Hee's command, Alex the robot burned a hole through the lock on the door. Kuan Hee opened the door and all three ran through the laboratory to the astonishment of the men and women in lab whites who tried to stop them. Seeing the gurneys ahead of them,

Kuan Hee uttered a string of orders to Alex. At once, the robot directed a stream of laser beams at its target. The first few gurneys lit up in flames. Before Alex could shoot another volley of laser beams, some men had grabbed hold of the remaining two gurneys and whisked them out of firing range of Alex's laser weapons system.

Shots rang out in the laboratory. Men were shooting at Kuan Hee. He threw himself onto the ground, narrowly escaping a bullet. At his insruction, Xander the robot leapt onto a table and launched a rocket at their attackers. A loud boom rang out. Windows shattered and body parts splattered across the room. Xander's rocket was menacingly powerful. Ahead of the intruders was a mangled mess of metal and human flesh. Fire had broken out in the laboratory. The intense heat activated fire sprinklers on the ceiling. In seconds, sprinkers were spraying copious amounts of water all over the laboratory, causing the floor to be flooded.

Kuan Hee picked himself up. In the chaos, he and his robots made their escape through a window, leaping one floor onto the grassy patch behind the building. He sprained his ankle on impact with the ground. Alex and Xander, being virtually indestructible, landed without incident. He limped towards the back gate with Alex and Xander flanking him. There, a guard raised his gun at the trio. Alex stopped him in his tracks. Its laser beams reduced him to a smouldering heap at Kuan Hee's order. Such was the price of incurring Kuan Hee's wrath, which knew no bounds when stoked. It was a simple task for Alex to break open the back gate. Without once looking back, the party of three fled the scene.

CHAPTER 33

After his successful operation to remove a bullet lodged in his back, Tim spent the next four hours under observation in a ward next to the operating theatre, out of sight of visitors.

Lina was leaning on the back of a chair, eyes closed, in the wide corridor outside the operating theatre when Kuan Hee came up to her and pecked her forehead. She opened her weary eyes. Glad to see Kuan Hee safe and sound, she lurched forward and grabbed his waist, sobbing into his shirt. He patted her back.

"How's Tim?" Kuan Hee asked.

"He hasn't woken up yet. He's in a room over there," Lina said, pointing to one end of the corridor, "waiting for the anaesthetic drug to wear off. The doctor says he'll be fine."

Kuan Hee sat next to Lina. "Where's Navin? Did you find him?" She asked.

Kuan Hee brought clasped hands over the back of his head and rested them against it. "I didn't manage to find him. They had hidden him somewhere else. But, I did manage to destroy some of the human clones."

"Where can they have hidden Navin?" Lina asked.

Kuan Hee shook his head. "I have no idea. I really have no idea. I'll try looking for him tomorrow. The embassy should hold some clues."

The windows at the end of the corridor began to darken. Soon it was brighter in the corridor than outside the window, which turned black in the dwindling light. Slowly, tiny lights of different hues of the rainbow sprouted all over the window. The night cityscape had come alive as a kaleidoscope of colours outside the windows.

Visiting hours had ended. But for Kuan Hee and Lina, it marked the start of their ward visit; Tim had just been wheeled into a four-bedded ward on the second level.

Tim forced a weak smile to peek out of his face. He tried to sit up, but Kuan Hee wouldn't allow it. Kuan Hee placed another pillow below Tim's head to prop it up.

"I say, you're looking good," Kuan Hee said. "Better than I looked when I was lying there three years ago."

"Aw, Kuan Hee," Lina said. "Don't tease him."

"I'm sorry Navin got taken," Tim said. "I was too careless."

"It's over, Tim," Kuan Hee said. "It's not your fault. These men are professionals. We can't beat them at their game."

"Do you know where they have taken him?" Tim asked.

Kuan Hee shrugged his shoulders in reply. "I didn't find Navin at Cherry Blossoms Apartments, but I got wind of the Chinese ambassador's heinous plot," Kuan Hee said.

"Heinous plot?" Tim repeated. "What heinous plot?"

"In the laboratory, on one of the gurneys lay a human clone with remarkable resemblance to the Chinese President."

"He looks like him?" Tim said.

"To a T," Kuan Hee said. "It's my deduction that these evil men have hatched a plot to take over the legitimate

Chinese leadership. They plan to usurp power."

"The Chinese President is on par with the United States President," Lina said. "If they succeed, they will control half the world."

"Precisely," Kuan Hee said. "We've destroyed four clones. They are left with four, including the Chinese President lookalike."

"But they still have the most powerful clone with them," Tim said. "They can do a great deal of damage with just that one."

"So I have to find out where they have hidden the Chinese President lookalike," Kuan Hee. "I won't rest till I do."

"How will you do that?" Tim asked.

"By shadowing Wei Xin," Kuan Hee said. "I have a strong feeling he will lead me to the clones. But, I will also go looking for Navin again—first thing tomorrow. I promise."

"Don't worry, Tim," Lina said in a tremulous voice. "Kuan Hee will bring Navin back. We'll be all together again—for sure."

CHAPTER 34

The next morning found Kuan Hee fiddling with his iPhone. He had spent a good hour downloading an app and testing it on his iPhone. Looking pleased with himself, he settled down for breakfast with Lina.

"I've found a way to understand what the Chinese are saying without you as a go-between," Kuan Hee said, raising his iPhone in the air. "See? This app is the answer. It provides translation on the fly. We'll use it afterwards."

"You mean, you don't need me anymore?" Lina lamented.

"No. Lina, not like that," Kuan Hee explained. "It's just that you won't need to waste time translating for me. The app will do it as it hears the person talk. It will free you for more important things."

"More important things?" Lina's face lit up. She was no longer cross. Kuan Hee heaved a sigh of relief. It wasn't easy for him living with Lina's temperamental nature.

"I'm leaving for the Chinese Embassy," Kuan Hee said.

"I'm coming with you," Lina said.

"But it's dangerous," Kuan Hee said. "Look at what happened to Tim and Navin. I don't want anything happening to you."

"Take me along, Kuan Hee," Lina said. "I promise I won't be in the way. I'll listen to you."

At the Chinese Embassy, the ambassador was in conference with his lieutenants. Listening in on the conversation from his van parked half a street away, Kuan Hee delighted in his success with the new app he had downloaded into his iPhone. The translation was almost seamless.

"It might be impossible to salvage the situation. Li ZhanNan is flying into town tomorrow morning," the Chinese ambassador said. "We've to be ready with answers, or our heads will roll." At once, his audience stood up and bowed their heads low.

Next to speak was Wei Xin. He assured the ambassador that nothing would happen to the remaining two human clones in his custody. "The two clones will leave for Shanghai the next morning. I'll personally accompany them."

"So will I," Cao Kun said.

"The young man you caught outside the apartments," the ambassador said. "Have you gotten anything out of him?" Kuan Hee and Lina cocked their ears. Kuan Hee brought his iPhone closer to them.

"He's a stubborn guy," Cao Kun said. "Give me a few more days. I'll have him eating out of my hand."

"Remember, I don't want him dead—yet," the ambassador said. "I want to find out who are behind this scheme to destroy our human clones. I want them to pay dearly for what they have done."

"Rest assured, I'll get him talking," Cao Kun said.

"So Cao Kun's the one holding Navin captive," Kuan Hee said. "Follow him and we'll find out Navin's whereabouts."

"Who are we following? Wei Xin or Cao Kun?" Lina said. "We can't follow both of them. We don't have the manpower." Kuan Hee scratched his head, trying to think of a solution, but found none.

"Look! Wei Xin's leaving the meeting," Lina said.

"He could be going back to his office," Kuan Hee said. But he didn't. He wheeled himself out of the building to a waiting van. There, two men pushed him up a ramp into the vehicle, which moved out of the embassy with all three on board and Little Busy clinging on the roof above the windshield.

"Aren't you going to tail Cao Kun?" Lina said. "He knows where Navin is."

"But we've got to find the human clones before they leave Singapore," Kuan Hee said as he kept Wei Xin's van in sight.

"Isn't Navin more important than those clones?" Lina said. "He's our good friend. We can't leave him in the lurch."

"I won't. I promise," Kuan Hee said. "The clones are leaving tomorrow. Once they leave, we are powerless to stop them. Navin can wait a little while. Didn't you hear the ambassador? They won't do anything to him yet."

"I can't believe you, Kuan Hee," Lina said. "Is revenge that important to you? More important than your best friend?"

"Lina, we've got to see the big picture," Kuan Hee said. "We've got to rid the world of these human clones—before they can do damage."

"Kuan Hee, you have changed. You are blinded by revenge," Lina said.

Knowing it was pointless to continue the debate with Kuan Hee, Lina did the only thing she could—she sulked.

CHAPTER 35

The two vans cruised along the traffic-heavy expressways in the heart of Singapore. Kuan Hee was careful to keep three car-lengths behind Wei Xin's van. *Nothing must spoil my plan to destroy the clones.*

The vans filtered into a sub-urban road. At a junction stop, Kuan Hee grabbed Alex and Xander the robots. He punched a button on their back and a panel on their chest opened. They were now primed for firing.

The two vans resumed their journey eastwards towards Upper Changi Road and then Simei Avenue, where they turned into an industrial park.

"They are not using a house this time," Kuan Hee said. But Lina was not listening.

The first van entered a gate and came to a halt in front of an old single-storeyed concrete building with a flat roof and casement windows. There was a man behind a small desk outside the front door. He rose to greet the visitors.

Little Busy lifted itself into the air and surveyed the premises. Used vehicle parts lined one end wall. The entire place looked more like a workshop than a sophisticated laboratory. Its neighbours were grimy workshops dealing with car repairs and auto spare parts. Loud knocking sounds pierced the air intermittently in the neighbourhood.

Kuan Hee and Lina sat in the van, which he had parked diagonally opposite the building. He turned up the volume on Little Busy's remote and his iPhone. The clanging of metal in the workshops around them made listening to conversations difficult. Luckily, the translation app had no difficulty picking up the conversation.

"This place is too noisy for work," a man said. "It's also dirty and greasy."

"I couldn't come up with anything better at short notice," Wei Xin said. "Just bear with it. Make do with what you have. Anyway, we'll be leaving here tomorrow."

"Is the equipment packed and ready?" Wei Xin asked.

"Almost done," the man said, pointing to a row of crates on one side of the workspace. "What about the rest of the stuff in Shelford Road?"

"Leave them there," Wei Xin said. "I'll be able to get another place ready by next week. You can move them then." He wheeled himself to the back of the building. "Let's take a look at the clones."

In a large air-conditioned room, three men in lab whites were at work—one in front of a computer, and the other two connecting wires to two figures on gurneys.

"How are the memory tests?" Wei Xin asked.

"The scans indicate their brain waves are regular," one of the men in lab whites said. "The explosion has done no damage to them. But we need another twenty-four hours before we can give an all clear."

"We can't wait," Wei Xin said. "The flight is at 9:00 a.m. You can continue your tests when we arrive in Shanghai. The master is getting impatient."

"Lina, wait here," Kuan Hee said, getting down from the van. "I'm going inside the building." Lina grudgingly obliged. She still wasn't talking to him.

"Alex and Xander, heel," Kuan Hee said. It was the command for them to stay at his side.

All three sidled up to the building on their left.

"Kuan Hee!" Lina screamed. Before Kuan Hee could react, a man had come up behind him and wrapped him in his arms. Another man placed a hand across his mouth, preventing him from making any sound. They took him into the compound. A third man emerged from the front gate, looking for Lina. Instinctively, she locked herself in the van and crammed her petite body into the small space below the dashboard. She was shivering with fear—not just for her safety but also for Kuan Hee's. She did not expect things to turn up this way, not when she was blowing hot and cold with Kuan Hee.

The two men bundled Kuan Hee into a small room at the side of the building. They forced him to kneel and kept their hold on his arms, which they pushed behind him.

"Now what have we got here," Wei Xin said, entering the room.

"You can speak English," Kuan Hee said.

"Of course. I can," Wei Xin said. "I spent many years in London as a student. So you are part of the group that's been destroying my labour of love."

"Labour of love? Bullshit!" Kuan Hee said. "You are bent on monopolising the world with your evil deeds."

"That's a laugh!" Wei Xin said. "We're merely orchestrating a change of leadership in our government. That's all we're doing—till you came into the picture. You idiot!" He leaned forward and slapped Kuan Hee in the face. "You destroyed five years of my work!"

"It's not your work," Kuan Hee screeched. "It's my dad's. You merely copied his ideas."

"Your dad?" Wei Xin said. "Now who exactly are you?" He stared up Kuan Hee's face.

"So you are Professor Wang's little boy, aren't you? You know, I've got your father's mind in here." He raised a finger and pointed it at his head. "Hahaha! I'm half your father!"

Kuan Hee spat in his face. "No. You're not! Not in million years. You're just a crook—a low-down dirty conniving crook. That's what you are."

Wei Xin wiped the saliva off his face with his hand. "You little brat! I'll teach you to destroy my best work of art."

He stretched out his hand and opened his palm like a lotus flower. The man next to him thrust a pistol into his palm.

"You will pay dearly for what you did," Wei Xin stammered. "You will die just like your father did."

He brought the pistol to Kuan Hee's eyes. "That's right. Keep staring. Stare at death in the face—your death." He let out a guffaw and squeezed the trigger.

Forcing his eyes shut, Kuan Hee screamed his lungs out and prepared to take the bullet. "Alex, destroy-fire-1."

The metallic-silver robot somersaulted into the room and landed in an upright position, legs apart and hands at its hips. The gears on its chest whirled rapidly and a laser at its epicentre unleashed a blinding beam that illuminated the small room. Its high-energy laser hit the man in the wheelchair, combusting him in seconds. Both Wei Xin and his wheelchair fused into a mass of white-hot substance.

Wei Xin's two minions were shell-shocked. Never before had they seen anything as deadly as this. They dropped Kuan Hee to the floor and scrambled for the door. Xander leapt into the room and stood guard at the door, legs apart and hands at his hips. It was the robots' programmed posture for attack situations.

Kuan Hee staggered to his feet. "Alex and Xander heel." He stumbled out of the room. In the open workspace of the building, Wei Xin's men had gathered. Some were brandishing pistols in their hands. It was six against one. Nope. It was six against three (one man and two thirty-centimetre-tall robots).

Suddenly shots rang out in the workspace. They weren't from Wei Xin's men. They came from the main entrance. In a split-second, a group of men in balaclavas had the entire workspace in their rifles' sights.

"It's the Brigadier's men! Hurray!" Kuan Hee shouted. Then he stopped in his tracks. The masked men were holding QBZ-95 assault rifles—the standard issue of the People's Liberation Army!

Alamak! I've gotten myself out of the pot into the frying pan.

Wei Xin's men dropped the weapons in their hands and squatted on the floor, with folded hands on their heads.

The masked men rounded their captives into a corner and stood guard over them.

Two men appeared at the front doorway. One was unmistakably familiar to Kuan Hee.

"Gosh! Mr Walmsley. It's you," Kuan Hee screeched.

"Ah. Kuan Hee. You are still in one piece. Thank goodness," Brigadier Walmsley said. He went up to Kuan Hee and patted him on the back. "Look at who's with me." He stood aside to let Lina face Kuan Hee.

Petite Lina threw herself into Kuan Hee's arms. She was gleeful with joy. She wasn't in tears! This had to be the first time she didn't cry in such a tense situation.

"Kuan Hee. Meet my counterpart from the Chinese intelligence," Brigadier Walmsley said. He ushered Kuan Hee in front of a tall brawny close-cropped man who had come in with him.

"Zhou Meng. This is the promising lad I've been talking to you about," Brigadier Walmsley said. "Professor Wang's son, Kuan Hee."

Zhou Meng proffered a hand and Kuan Hee shook it. The man had a strong grip.

"Thank you for bringing us to the human clones," Zhou Meng said. "We've been on their trail for some time. It's been difficult locating these clones. They've been hiding them in different countries."

Kuan Hee beamed. "Mr Walmsley, how did you find me here? Was it a coincidence?"

"Coincidence my foot, Kuan Hee," Brigadier Walmsley said. "It was you who brought us here."

Kuan Hee gave the Brigadier a look of surprise. "Have you been following me?"

"Perhaps, you didn't know, Kuan Hee. AleXander the robots and the drones broadcast their locations to the Polaris satellite 24/7," Brigadier Walmsley said. "That's how I know where you are every time all the time. So there's no need for me or my men to follow you."

The Brigadier paused for a breath. "What you see on the drone's remote screens, I see too. What AleXander the robots see, I also see. Every single frame and image is recorded in our servers."

"You mean—you have been privy to what we have been doing all along?" Kuan Hee exclaimed.

The Brigadier nodded.

"No wonder! You always arrive in time to save the situation," Kuan Hee said. "No wonder. You didn't need me to explain myself."

"Yes. Kuan Hee. Also no wonder why you are standing here safe and sound," Brigadier Walmsley said. "It's all thanks to your father."

"Dad? Why?" Kuan Hee asked.

But the Brigadier had no time to give him a reply.

"Kuan Hee. Zhou Meng and his men are on official business here. Let's leave them to do their work," Brigadier Walmsley said. "We've got to leave quickly. Don't want to attract attention from the neighbours."

The Brigadier waved to his counterpart and left the building with Kuan Hee and Lina in tow.

"Kuan Hee. Zhou Meng and I are doing our work without the knowledge of the Singapore government," Brigadier Walmsley said. He put a finger to his lips. "Shush!"

There were two vans parked in front of the main door. A tanned Caucasian was standing next to a car at the entrance to the compound.

"Follow me," Brigadier Walmsley said. He led Kuan Hee and Lina to the waiting car. "We're going to meet someone."

"Who is it?" But the Brigadier kept mum.

"I bet it's your mother. She's returned from Fort Bragg," Lina said.

Everyone piled into the car. Alex and Xander sat on the pair's laps.

"Let's move off," The Brigadier told his driver.

CHAPTER 36

The pair walked through the corridor on Level 2 of Tan Tock Seng Hospital with the Brigadier leading the way.

"We're going to visit Tim," Lina whispered.

"It's not a surprise after all," Kuan Hee said. "Perhaps, the Brigadier doesn't know we have been here before."

The Brigadier ushered the pair into Ward 5. There, lying on their beds were Tim and—Navin!

"Navin! You are safe!" Lina cried. She rushed to his bed to give him a hug.

"Not so tight, Lina," Navin said. "Kuan Hee will get jealous."

"Never you mind, Navin," Lina said. "He deserves it." She thought of telling their best pal about her fight with Kuan Hee over his rescue earlier today. Then she had second thoughts. In the end, she said nothing. *Let sleeping dogs lie.*

Kuan Hee and Navin gave each other a high five and the four adventurers cheered. They were all together again!

"How did you escape?" Kuan Hee asked.

Navin threw a glance at the Brigadier.

"You forgot what I told you, Kuan Hee," Brigadier Walmsley said.

Kuan Hee furrowed his brows. Then he spoke. "Oh. Yes. I understand now," Kuan Hee said. "It's Tizzy. The drone broadcast its location to the Polaris satellite."

"Of course. It is, Kuan Hee," Brigadier Walmsley said. "Otherwise, Navin would have ended up being dead meat." He chuckled. The adventurers roared with laughter.

"Mr Walmsley. Have you and the Chinese operative, Zhou Meng, been in touch over the human clones?" Kuan Hee asked.

"Well, it's a long story, Kuan Hee," Brigadier Walmsley said. "In a nutshell, the Chinese central government has been wise to the perpetrators' machinations. Zhou Meng is leading the central government's investigations into the plot to usurp power from the Chinese government."

The Brigadier paused to collect his thoughts. "This dastardly plan is the brainchild of Sun Zehao, a member of the Politburo Standing Committee—the highest decision making body in the Chinese government."

"All his underlings are being rounded up as I speak," Brigadier Walmsley said.

"The Chinese ambassador too?" Kuan Hee asked.

"Yes, he too," Brigadier Walmsley said. "The United States government is only lending the Chinese government a helping hand in this matter. We share the world stage. It is only right that we pool our resources."

The Brigadier surveyed his audience.

"The greatest achievement has been carried out by you guys," Brigadier Walmsley said. "Kuan Hee, Lina, Tim and Navin—you are all heroes. You discovered the evil plot. You went all out to destroy the human clones before they could do evil. You are all willing to place your lives at risk for justice."

He paused again. "That's highly commendable. Highly commendable indeed." All four adventurers blushed.

"Kuan Hee. Remember I gave you the diplomatic passport?" Brigadier Walmsley said. "I didn't do it for no rhyme or reason. It was with a specific purpose in mind."

Kuan Hee looked blankly at the Brigadier.

The Brigadier turned his gaze to Kuan Hee.

"Get ready for the next stage of your life, Kuan Hee," Brigadier Walmsley said. "You'll be using this passport regularly from now on."

"Huh?" Kuan Hee muttered.

"The sky is the limit," Brigadier Walmsley said. "Kuan Hee, fly as your father flew. The United States' Special Forces is behind you all the way."

"Hurray for Kuan Hee," Tim and Navin shouted.

"I'm happy for you, dear," Lina said.

CHAPTER 37

The Uber taxi pulled up at the gate of 79 Jalan Naung. Kuan Hee and Lina disembarked wearily. It had been a long day. The front door was open.

"Mum!" Kuan Hee shouted. The pair ran through the living room into the kitchen. The smell of food cooking on the stove led the way.

"Mum. You're back," Kuan Hee said. "Is that pork chops and baked potatoes with apple sauce?"

"Yes. It is, Kuan Hee—your favourite food," Mrs Wang said, smiling. Turning to Lina, she said, "I've cooked *meesuah* for you."

"*Wah!* It's got two hard-boiled eggs! Thanks Mum," Lina said. "It's my favourite."

"Have you guys been up to mischief again?" Mrs Wang said.

Kuan Hee flashed her a cheeky smile. "Aw. Mum. It's nothing like that. Honest. Lina and I were just watching 'Dawn Breaks' the movie at Cathay Multiplex."

The End

Some of the places mentioned in this book are real.

Temasek University in Yio Chu Kang is a figment of the author's imagination. So is the Colonial Hotel.

SINGLISH AND OTHER TERMS USED

Ah Kong: Hokkien for grandfather
Ah Ma: Hokkien for grandmother
aiyoh: expressing shock or astonishment
alamak: expressing regret, shock or astonishment
Angmoh: Caucasian
Becak: Indonesian for pedicab
Chia kantang: Westernised
chop: official stamp/seal
enche: Malay for Mister; a senior NCO in armed forces
hah: expressing disappointment
Hock Chew: a Chinese dialect
Hokkien: a Chinese dialect
hor: added to the end of a sentence for emphasis
huang ah ma: Chinese for Empress Dowager
hor: added to the end of a sentence for emphasis
huh: expressing disappointment
kiasi: aversive to risk taking
kiasu: afraid of losing out to others
kakis: Malay for buddies
kampong: Malay for village
kaypoh: a busybody
kopi oh kosong: Malay for black coffee, no sugar added
kretek: Indonesian clove cigarette
kway teow: flat rice noodles
lah: added to the end of a sentence for emphasis
leh: added to the end of a sentence for emphasis
LOL: acronym for 'Laughing Out Loud'
long time no see: not met each other in a long time

SINGLISH AND OTHER TERMS USED
(continued)

mee rebus: Malay for a spicy yellow noodle dish
mee siam: Malay for a spicy rice vermicelli dish
meesuah: Hokkien for thin noodles made of wheat flour
mee soto: Malay for spicy noodle soup dish
NSmen: National Service men
ORD: operationally ready date (completed NS)
ponteng: skip/play truant
roti prata: pan-fried flat bread
sambal belacan: a shrimp paste used in Malay cuisine
tahan: Malay for bear/stand
tong fang: consummation of marriage
three-tonner: a military truck (weighs three tonnes)
wah: expressing shock or surprise
wah piang: expressing shock
wah seh: expressing shock

The author lives with his wife in an HDB flat in Hougang, an idyllic backwater in the North-East of Singapore. They have no children.

ABOUT THE AUTHOR

Raymond Han is a late baby boomer in Singapore. He has worked as a banker, an editor, and a teacher. After he left the banking sector, he found a second career teaching English Language to upper and lower secondary students in Victoria School, Montfort Secondary School, Greendale Secondary School and Hougang Secondary School.

Raymond also taught English at 'O' Level and General Paper to students in a private school for several years. He has a Specialist Diploma in Psychology (Counselling Psychology).